Broken Beyond Repair

EMILY BANTING

Sapphfic Publishing
www.sapphficpublishing.co.uk

Broken Beyond Repair
Copyright © 2022 Emily Banting
Published by Sapphfic Publishing
ISBN: 978-1-915157-07-2
First edition: September 2022

CREDITS:
Editor: Hatch Editorial

1 3 4 5 6 7 8 9 10

ABOUT THE AUTHOR

As an author of LGBTQ+ romance featuring sapphic main characters, I'm passionate about increasing the representation of sapphic women over forty in literature and on-screen.

I write about women in their prime, experiencing everything life throws at them — missed opportunities: regret: lost loves: family problems: aching joints: and menopause.

With a passion for, and a degree in Archaeology and Heritage Management, I never miss an opportunity to sneak historic buildings into my books. The Nunswick Abbey Series features a Georgian country house, a quaint historic village setting and of course, oodles of ruined abbey.

When I'm not hiding behind my MacBook pretending to write whilst secretly consuming tea and biscuits, I bow to the unreasonable demands of my cat overlord and walk my starving velcro Labrador.

FIND ME HERE

I love to hear from my readers. If you would like to get in touch you can find me here…

www.emilybanting.co.uk

Or follow me here…

f facebook.com/emilybantingauthor

📷 instagram.com/emilybanting

🐦 twitter.com/emily_banting

BB bookbub.com/authors/emily-banting

g goodreads.com/emily_banting

a amazon.com/author/emilybanting

ACKNOWLEDGMENTS

I must admit I hate writing acknowledgements. I always write them at a time when I am utterly sick of words. I fear not only missing someone out but being unable to express my gratitude as well as I should like to all those that have given me so much.

They say it takes a village to raise a child and a book is no different. Even though it can feel like the loneliest job on the planet, I couldn't have brought it to fruition without a fantastic team behind me.

Laure, you are more than a beta and the greatest of friends. Thank you for kicking my butt every time I doubt myself, for holding me to account and always encouraging me to do better. I'm always grateful for your honesty and integrity, without which, this book wouldn't be what it is.

Connie your input, as always, is hugely appreciated. As are your words of wisdom, encouragement, and friendship.

Thanks go to my sensitivity readers, fellow authors Chloe Keto and Luc Dreamer, who answered a call for help without question — despite not knowing me. The love and support in our community is overwhelming.

Catherine, thank you for not only keeping me fit but also sane with our dog walks.

Jess, thank you once again for polishing my words with your editorial cloth. You are a magician.

Thank you to all my early readers for dropping everything and taking the time to read this book. Also to my ARC team for putting your hands up so eagerly.

And lastly, thank you to my readers for giving your time to read my words. I can only hope they were deserving of it.

For Laure
For your blood, sweat and tears.

CHAPTER 1

*B*eatrice scowled over her large sunglasses at the television in the corner of her hospital suite. The sound of a press helicopter hovering outside buzzed around her room like an irritating fly. Its footage was streaming straight onto the screen. When she got her hands on whoever leaked her location to the media, they'd wish they'd never been born.

"Production of Beatrice Russell's latest film has come to a halt following an unfortunate accident on set this morning," the entertainment correspondent on the television was saying. "The actress is rumoured to have sustained a broken leg during the rehearsal of a fight scene and has arrived at Ronald Reagan Medical Center where our live feed is coming from. Fans are rallying outside the hospital in support; some may ask if the actress is too old for action fil—"

Beatrice cut the journalist off at the touch of the mute button.

"I'm fifty-one for fuck's sake."

Pain tore through her left leg as she tried to adjust herself in the bed. With her leg elevated in a brace, there was little room for movement, and with the increasing irritability clawing at her body, she couldn't get comfortable.

The news of her accident having hit the headlines when she'd only been admitted an hour ago, wasn't helping. It was so indicative of Hollywood to embellish a story. The journalist was right in one regard, though: the accident had been unfortunate. Unfortunate that an incompetent props department failed to secure part of the set, causing her to fall in the first place.

If her ability to participate in action films came under question, it could derail her career — something she'd feared happening since she passed forty. It was testament to her professionalism, acting talent, and youthful appearance that she was still being cast as the lead in very sought-after roles. She knew it couldn't last forever, and although time was not on her side, she wasn't ready to give up more physically demanding roles — especially not at the behest of a damned rumour.

The door of her large suite opened. A tall man, sporting salt-and-pepper hair and a matching beard, entered. The back of his white coat trailed out behind him as he strode across the suite in a pair of brogues. Beatrice rolled her eyes at the walking cliché.

"Mrs Russell."

"Miss," Beatrice corrected him through a wince as she tried to position herself to see him better. Being on your back with a leg in the air wasn't a flattering look for anyone, let alone an internationally renowned actress.

"Miss Russell. I'm Dr Randall," he said, placing a hand on the brace. "Do try to keep as still as you can until we have set the leg."

"Set?" Beatrice barked, leaving a curl in her top lip.

The doctor recoiled and then blinked. "Yes. I'm sorry. The X-ray shows you've sustained a fracture to your fibula. You'll need a cast. It's only a minor fracture; you've been incredibly lucky considering. There's minimal damage to the surrounding blood vessels, soft tissue, or nerves. I expect the impact from the fall wasn't all that severe. It's possible that the break was a result of reduced bone mass due to your age and gender." His face softened with empathy as he finished his sentence.

Not normally lost for words, Beatrice opened her mouth in the hope something would come out. By the time she'd summoned a word, the doctor started up again. Her current irritable status upgraded itself to anger, which she tried her best to stifle.

"How long will I need a cast?"

"If all goes well, about six weeks."

"Six weeks!"

"If you're good, you could move into a walking boot in four weeks. That could bring about a swifter recovery."

'Good'. What did he mean by that? With a cast on one leg, she wouldn't be partaking in her usual extreme sport of wearing heels anytime soon. What the hell was she going to do in a hotel suite for six weeks?

"Can I fly?"

Dr Randall pulled his nose from his iPad and considered his answer. "You are otherwise low risk, but give it a few days at the very least, just to make sure everything is okay with the cast."

Beatrice's phone rang.

"I'll leave you to take that. If you have any questions, be sure to let me know." He took a card from his top pocket and placed it on her bedside table.

She flashed him the briefest of smiles and answered the phone as soon as the door closed behind him.

"Bea. Are you okay? I was heading to bed when I saw the ten o'clock news, only to find you all over it."

It was a relief to hear the voice of her agent Alison on the line.

"I fell on set," Beatrice explained. "My bloody fibula is broken. I want the production company to admit liability, Ali. We need to release a statement that it wasn't my fault before Hollywood pigeonholes me in the role of the neurotic mother in those tragic romcoms they seem so obsessed with."

"I'll get straight on it. Any ideas how long you'll be out of action?"

"Six weeks. The damn doctor implied I might have low bone mass due to my age. The cheek!"

Alison's laugh spilt out through the phone. "And he's still breathing?"

"Only thanks to the fact I'm on my back with the largest strap-on you can imagine attached to my leg."

"And sadly with no pleasure to be derived from it."

"Exactly," Beatrice replied, sniffing out a laugh.

She couldn't remember the last time she'd laughed. Though she'd spent the last two months on set, she hadn't bonded with any of the other cast members and kept largely to her trailer. Her exacting standards and high expectations in her working environment never made her popular, that much she knew. To everyone else, she was international star Beatrice Russell, aloof and challenging, but in reality, she was a lonely woman navigating her way around the wrong side of fifty.

She'd grown used to the solitude or so she told herself. In truth, most other people bored her; she was never one for small talk. She craved intelligent, dynamic conversation with individuals on her wavelength and refused to settle for anything less, even to quell her feeling of loneliness.

Alison, on the other hand, always made her feel at ease. Not only was she Beatrice's agent, but she was also her oldest — and only true — friend. Beatrice's position on the world's stage barely allowed friendships to form, let alone trusting relationships, yet Alison had been there from the beginning — well, what Beatrice had defined as her new beginning at age eighteen. With only her acting ability and reputation behind her, she'd been taken under Alison's wing, where she transitioned from child star to top-billed superstar.

"I think I might go home to Highwood to recuperate," she told Alison over the phone. "I can't be trapped in my hotel suite for the next however many weeks. I'll go crazy."

"That'd be good. You'd be able to see Xander... and me."

"Oh. Yes, of course."

A pang of guilt taunted her as she realised her son hadn't entered her thoughts for at least a week. If Alison was heading to bed in the UK, then it was possible Xander was already asleep. She would message him when she went to bed; he'd be up by then, being eight hours ahead.

"I think I'll go crazy anyway," Beatrice continued, fidgeting. "You know I can't be inactive."

"You could always—"

"No!" Beatrice put in before Alison could say the word.

"Come on, Bea. Now's a perfect time. Your body can't be active, so let's occupy your mind."

"Really?" Beatrice sighed, feeling the fight over this long-running argument draining from her. "You think it will sell?"

"I can guarantee it will sell millions, and we'll have publishers fighting for it."

Alison had been pushing her to publish her autobiography since she hit forty. Unbeknownst to her, Beatrice had attempted to document her past some years back. That was, until she decided her forties was not the age for any self-respecting woman to write an autobiography. She wasn't convinced publishing one in her fifties was either.

"I'll have to check with Xander. That's all I'm promising."

"I'll take that. And Peter?"

"He can go fu—"

The door to her room opened again, and a woman in uniform entered pushing a metal trolley.

"Sorry, Ali, I've got to go. It's a bit crazy here."

"No problem. I'll call the production company now and let you know the outcome. I'll get the feelers out on the autobiography too."

6

"Call me anytime. I doubt I'll be getting much sleep tonight."

"Me neither," Alison added before she hung up.

The nurse proceeded to extract her leg from the brace. Pain shot through Beatrice like a lightning bolt.

"Please," she begged, "be more careful!"

Fleur, her latest assistant, tottered in on high stilettos, trying to balance like a newborn giraffe. With the help of both, Beatrice was repositioned more comfortably.

Beatrice turned to Fleur as the nurse busied herself casting her leg. "I've decided I'm going home to Highwood for the summer. You'll need to find me a new PA in the UK instead of LA."

"I'll get right on it," Fleur replied.

"Not now, it's late in the UK. Call tomorrow… early, very early!" Beatrice rolled her eyes and waved the woman away with her hand. How could a PA, a French one at that, be so unaware of simple time zones?

Fleur gave a light bow as she always did when she left Beatrice's presence and backed her way out of the door.

Within an hour of her accident, Fleur had informed Beatrice that she'd found new employment and required a reference. Not that Beatrice would miss her; she was yet another in a long line of incompetent assistants. How did one write a reference for a PA of three months? It was enough time to discover everything she hated about the woman and realise how irritating she could be; it was hardly enough time to find one redeeming feature to recommend her.

She'd considered asking Fleur if she'd already lined up a new position before the accident or if the phone was in her hand as her current employer lay on the floor of the studio shouting for help. Either way, she feared the answer. There was no shortage of PA jobs in Hollywood, and she couldn't blame the woman if she'd been straight on the phone before she'd jumped in the ambulance beside her. There, she'd found a redeeming feature for Fleur — self-preservation.

Most of Beatrice's staff were supplied by the production company for the duration of her filming in the US. She knew they would be leaving like rats from a sinking ship once she announced she'd be heading to Highwood House for the summer. But it made sense to go back to England. She was exhausted from what had turned out to be a more physically demanding role than she'd expected, and she missed England. Her estate was always at its finest during the summer months, not that she would see much of it on her return.

Once back in the familiar territory of her hotel suite, her home for the last two months, Beatrice hiked herself onto the bed with assistance from Fleur. She'd made her escape in a wheelchair via the maintenance lift at the rear of the hospital, far from the prying eyes of her adoring fans and the press.

"Madame, we must elevate you," Fleur said.

Beatrice's leg was lifted with little grace as Fleur shoved two pillows underneath it.

A text flashed onto her phone.

Press release… check inbox. Prod Co will release own in due course, A x.

"My laptop." Beatrice clicked her fingers at Fleur, who

was already diving into her small bag to retrieve it yet somehow still couldn't find it.

Finally out of patience, Beatrice opened her mailbox on her phone instead and found the email amongst a lengthy list of others which would need attending to.

Actress Beatrice Russell sustained a broken leg on set earlier today as she rehearsed action scenes as part of her latest film. The actress is resting at her hotel in Los Angeles after receiving excellent medical care at the Ronald Reagan Medical Center. She thanks her fans for their messages of support.

Fleur had mentioned that social media was on fire with the news; Beatrice resisted the urge to check herself — that was a rabbit hole she didn't need to go down. Although most of her fans could be considered adoring, there were always the oddballs. It did no good for one's self-esteem to read about how she was a slag, a slapper, a whore, an ugly bitch, or even a MILF who was gagging for a good seeing-to… although the last item was cutting it close to the bone. Even so, she'd existed long enough in the world without social media, and she was more than content to continue her life without it.

Beatrice stared up at the ceiling of her hotel bedroom in the early hours of the morning. A streak of light was glaring back at her, coming from a crack in her curtains; Fleur couldn't even draw a pair of curtains correctly. Even out in Beverly Hills the light pollution was unavoidable. A mild panic sat with her as she'd lain awake. As a side sleeper, how on earth was she going to sleep for the next few nights with her leg elevated?

Her phone pinged, lighting the bedroom even further. It was a text from Xander.

Are you okay? What's happened?

It must have been morning in the UK, Beatrice surmised. She tapped out a reply.

I'm fine. I've broken my leg. Coming home for the summer. I would have texted you earlier but knew you'd be asleep. Mum x.

K.

It pleased her that her son had asked what happened rather than listening to hearsay; it was a practice she had instilled in him from an early age. Though why he insisted on showing his agreement with a *K*, she had no clue. What even was that? What happened to 'okay', or even 'ok'? Was this something all children did, or just hers?

She moved on to the question Alison had put in her brain: *How would you feel if I wrote an autobiography?*

Three little dots typed for a moment, then halted before *Meh* appeared on her screen.

Was the youthful reply of indifference also one of approval? He hadn't said no. Beatrice decided not to push the point; she would instead plough on with it. Alison was right — she would go crazy without something to occupy her mind.

Sinking back against her pillows, she wondered when she'd got so old and why she needed to pee again. Bloody Fleur with her, "Madame, you must drink."

Eyeing the door to her ensuite bathroom, Beatrice checked in with her bladder to see if it was a 'must' or 'can-wait'. It was a must. Although she was tempted to wake Fleur for assistance, she resisted. Getting to the toilet was hard enough; she didn't need the annoying French woman in her ear with, "A little further, Madame." The twenty-year-old made her feel like she was in her eighties. She'd be glad to see the back of her. Was this part of the problem with her PAs? They were all young; young and brainless.

Fleur at least had the foresight to leave the wheelchair by her bed. Beatrice pulled herself into it, lifting her leg onto the footrest. At least whilst she was up, she could take some more painkillers. She wedged an empty bottle of water between her legs and wheeled herself to the bathroom.

Her phone was illuminating the bed as she returned, another message. She heaved herself back onto the bed before checking it.

Are you awake? Ax.

Yes, she replied.

Alison's name flashed up on her phone as it vibrated in her hand.

"How are you doing?" Alison asked upon her answering it.

"Awful. I haven't been able to sleep with the pain," Beatrice replied, popping a couple of pills from their packet as she spoke.

"The production company are in touch with the hospital. They've covered all the costs of your treatment and sent their apologies. They have some other scenes to shoot without you, and then they'll shut down for the summer."

"If they have apologies, they can send them

themselves. Can you arrange a PA for when I return to the UK? I don't trust Fleur to set it up; her focus is elsewhere."

"I'll see what my assistant Tom can rustle up," Alison said. "I've spoken to Mrs Clarkson; she sends her best wishes. She's on holiday until the end of next week. She did offer to come back early to open the house for you, but as she's visiting her daughter, who gave birth to a baby this morning, I said you would cope."

"You did, did you? Then you better find me a PA that can cook and clean! And please ensure she's finished puberty."

A shrill laugh came back down the line, leaving Beatrice baffled as to what the joke was as she hung up.

CHAPTER 2

The echoes of a throaty exhaust bounced off the surrounding hedgerows of the narrow lane. The local wildlife dove for cover as the wheels of a pale blue VW camper van clipped the verges at its top speed of 50 mph.

Sydney glanced at her watch. "Shit. Come on, old girl. Nearly there."

They approached a blind corner, and Gertie choked as Sydney changed her down a gear. She knew Gertie, her camper van, well enough to rely on engine braking rather than her next-to-useless drum brakes to slow her.

"Don't go flaky on me again," she pleaded.

Arching her body to see around the corner, she tooted Gertie's comical horn that sounded like something from a Fisher Price toy.

Clear.

Just as she accelerated into the bend, a horse and rider appeared head-on.

Sydney's foot slammed onto the brake. She gripped the

skinny steering wheel, almost leaving her seat as she leveraged her weight onto the pedal. Gertie eventually caught up to her request and rolled to a stop.

How had she missed that?

The equestrian glared at her and shook her head. Sydney gave her a courteous flash of her hand as she passed and then swivelled it to give her the middle finger.

Fighting her way back to first gear, Sydney let out a long breath. Gertie spluttered into life and continued lolloping along the lane, blowing smoke from her arse as she trundled into the village.

Sydney spotted the church on top of a steep hill.

Seriously!

"Sorry, Gertie," Sydney apologised. "Up we go."

Gertie complained under the strain of the incline as she heaved herself and Sydney towards the church.

"Shit, nowhere to park…" Sydney said as she surveyed the small car park. "Ah, that will do. Let's squeeze you in there."

Jumping from the driver's seat, Sydney smoothed down her tan chinos and floral top, and slipped her navy blazer on. The creases she could do nothing about; that was camper life.

She reached back in and grabbed her phone from the seat, extracting her long, brown hair from beneath her collar. A message popped up on her phone as she ran up the path to the church.

You're late! J x

Blame Gertie! she texted James. *I'm outside.*

A turn of the metal handle on the old oak door produced a high-pitched creaking sound. She winced. Left with no option other than to continue, she pushed open the door and entered.

The church was heaving. Her stomach tightened as every pair of eyes turned to scrutinise the source of the disturbance — including those of the bride and groom.

Fuck.

"Sorry. Carry on. You'll find no objection from me," she said, reaching the aisle and blowing a kiss to the gorgeous bride.

She received an eye roll and a shake of the head, both of which were followed up with a smile. Her eye flicked to the best man. His face was familiar, though she couldn't put a finger on how she knew him.

Sydney slipped herself into a pew beside James and grinned at his neatly pressed, beige linen suit. He placed an affectionate kiss on her cheek and whispered, "I would never blame Gertie."

Sydney shot him a look and softened it with a smile as a man leaned around him and gave her a wave.

"Hi," he said. "I'm Will."

Sydney flashed him a smile. "Syd."

James took Will's waving hand and held it in his lap as all eyes returned to the matter at hand, the wedding of their best friend, Rosie Harris, to her long-term boyfriend, Greg.

With rings and vows exchanged, and even a tear wiped from Sydney's eye, they all followed the bride and groom outside. James was dabbing a handful of tissues at his own eyes as he went.

The happy couple couldn't have chosen a better day for

the ceremony as they stood outside the church in the scorching sunshine for their wedding photographs.

"Syd," Rosie called out. "Come on, you're up."

Sydney reluctantly joined Rosie and her new husband, Greg, on the step of the porch. She wasn't one for photographs.

"James, you too, if you've quite finished crying. Got to have one of the old gang."

As the two of them flanked the bride and groom, the photographer did his work.

Greg stepped out. "Now have one of the three of you," he said.

Sydney was pulled into Rosie's side, as was James. "Ah, look at us," Rosie said. "All grown up. I expect you two to reciprocate with a wedding invitation sometime soon. You can't call the gay card anymore."

Sydney peered around her at James. "You first," she told him. "You're the one with a boyfriend. I've heard that helps."

"Please don't give Will any ideas," James said. "I could *not* afford a wedding right now."

"If you could look this way, please, and smile," the photographer asked with a polite yet crabby tone.

Sydney and James placed a kiss on each of Rosie's cheeks to the delight of the cooing crowd.

"Cute, guys, cute! But, Syd," Rosie said, "that does not get you off the hook. Only you could drive the length of an entire country and not only turn up late but walk in at that exact moment."

"Sorry," Sydney said, and truly meant it. "Gertie conked out on me on the A34."

Rosie shook her head. "I knew I should have insisted you were a bridesmaid. Then you couldn't have been late!"

"I'm hardly bridesmaid material," Sydney scoffed. "Have you ever seen me in a dress? At least I made it for the important bit."

"Avoiding all the boring bits at the beginning. Masterful, Syd," James added, earning him a swipe on the arm from Rosie.

"Hey!" he griped. "Don't crease the linen."

"Too late for that," Rosie said, looking him up and down.

James inspected his suit in a panic.

"Made you look," Rosie teased, then turned to their friend. "How bad is Gertie, Syd?"

Sydney rolled her eyes.

"That bad?"

"It's typical. I have time off for a road trip and she starts getting flaky. She's starting to smell a bit musty, though that might be me."

A stern voice rose above the crowd. "Is anyone the owner of a VW camper? You're blocking the bridal car."

Sydney's eyes widened. "Oops, speak of the devil. Better move her — if she'll move."

"She better!" Rosie growled.

"See you at the reception." Sydney placed another kiss on Rosie's cheek. "Congrats by the way. You look sensational."

Greg appeared beside Rosie to resume the photographs.

"You too, Greg," Sydney added. "Congrats, I mean.

You don't look sensational." Taking a step back she gave him the once-over. "You scrub up all right, though."

He leaned forward and kissed her cheek. "Thanks. So do you, surprisingly." He lingered and whispered in her ear, "In case you hadn't noticed, Sam's here."

Sydney pulled back and found herself nodding. Forcing a smile out, she retreated into the crowd with her heart pounding. It was Sam's face that had been smiling back at her from the front of the church. She'd not recognised it in its current form.

"Hang on, Syd. Will and I need a lift," James said, scooping Will up from the sidelines and running after her. "I also need to talk to you about my overwhelming generosity as your employer and how that cuts both ways."

"No, James," Sydney called back as she made her way along the path.

Two men in top hats and tails shot her disapproving looks from beside a vintage Austin drowning in white ribbon.

She flashed them a smile. "Sorry."

Her apology was met with more disapproving looks.

God. Why was everyone so uptight around here?

Will stopped in his tracks, admiring Gertie. "Wow, she's a stunner."

"Do not be fooled by her attempts to woo you," Sydney replied, opening a side door for him. "She may be radiant on the outside, but underneath she's unreliable and she farts — a lot. If you don't drive her for long periods, she gets grumpy, like she is now, when I need her most."

Will jumped in the back, stroking the cream leather bench seat as he continued his assessment of Gertie's insides. "I love those curtains. Are they Laura Ashley?"

"Yes, my mum made them." Sydney smiled as she remembered picking out the material with her and feigning interest as she tried to explain how the sewing machine worked. Sydney was a hopeless case in that department; the only thing she could sew together was her fingertips.

James's pleading eyes were waiting for her as she clambered into Gertie.

"Syd, please," he begged, his tone turning so sickly it could make anyone vomit. "I need a favour."

"Not from me you don't. And not that," Sydney emphasised.

"What?"

She shook her head as she jammed the key in the ignition. "Don't act the innocent. That's the voice you use every time you need me to take on a difficult client. You may be my boss, James, but you're a boss who promised me some time off."

"But you're the best, Syd, and I need my best. It's Beatrice Russell. You know... *the* Beatrice Russell!"

Will shot forward and leaned over the front bench seat. "You didn't tell me it was her! Oh, I adore her."

James brushed him back. "You and the rest of the world, my love."

"She's so talented... and gorgeous," Will continued. "And, oh my, her dresses."

"I've never heard of her," Sydney muttered as she turned Gertie over and pulled away from the church.

"It's quaint that you avoid mainstream media, Syd, but you should acquaint yourself more with the people you work amongst."

"*You* need to know them," Sydney replied pointedly. "I prefer not to know them, not the mainstream media's image of them anyway. Then I won't be biased. I form my own opinions of people; it allows me to serve them better."

"God, you are good, aren't you?" James hissed cattily.

"As you said — I'm your best!"

James turned his attention to the view from his window, cracking open the smoker's flap. Sydney hoped that was an end to the pleading.

It wasn't.

"I've been trying to get her on to my books for ages," James said, "though it was an inevitability when you've worked your way through every other agency in the city."

That set off an alarm bell for Sydney. "What's wrong with her?" she asked.

"Oh, er… nothing. She has a bit of a reputation with PAs, that's all. I'm sure she's nothing you can't handle. Here, turn left."

Gertie bumbled her way along the winding, oak-lined road towards a grand Georgian house.

"Anyway, I'm busy," Sydney said.

"Doing what? She doesn't fly in until Tuesday, and she's only here for the summer. It's for six weeks max. You should see how much she's paying."

"Sorry. I have an important week this week."

"Who with?"

"No one you know."

James sighed. "Come on, Syd, no one can trump Beatrice Russell. She's the biggest profile I've had at the agency. If I can get her on my books, it will attract more of her ilk."

Sydney winced at his use of the word 'ilk'. James's appreciation for his clients only extended as far as the depth of their pockets.

"Will you fire me if I don't?" Sydney knew the answer to that question, but it was worth asking to bring an end to his pestering. She was the best PA on his books.

James folded his arms in defeat. "No."

"Then find someone else."

CHAPTER 3

*S*ydney pulled Gertie into a parking space outside the imposing hotel and drank it in.

"How did we spend three years living here and not know this was on the outskirts of the city?"

"We were students." James sighed. "We knew our way to the best pubs blindfolded. It was all we needed in life back then."

A much-needed glass of Pimm's was awaiting them as they entered the hotel for Rosie and Greg's wedding reception. They made their way through to a secluded garden on one side of the hotel to await the other guests.

"James said you've come down from Scotland, Sydney," Will said as they settled themselves at one of the more sheltered tables.

"Yep, from the top of the country to the bottom. Shame for Gertie it wasn't downhill all the way."

"Do you live up there then?"

"No, I was visiting my mum and taking some time out

between the jobs that your slave driver boyfriend has me doing."

James stuck his tongue out at Sydney, earning him a sly smirk from her in return.

"He's not that bad, surely?" Will asked, smiling around the straw in his mouth.

"Choose your next words very wisely, Miss MacKenzie," James said, adding a hint of a Scottish accent as he spoke her name.

"James… keeps me as busy as I wish to be," Sydney settled on. "This is my first break in a year." Glaring at James, she added, "Which is why I'm so keen to keep it."

"MacKenzie?" Will asked. "You don't sound Scottish."

"We're not far over the border. You don't cross Hadrian's Wall and suddenly develop a Scottish accent."

"But Scotland is home?"

Sydney considered his question for a moment before answering. *Home is where the heart is.* Where that was, she couldn't pinpoint. Thirty-six years on the planet and nowhere felt like home.

Although part of her heart was with her mum in Scotland, the small town an hour from Edinburgh wasn't home. After they moved there from Australia when she was seven, she'd never bonded with the polar opposite of her early childhood life. Gone were the sandy beaches, sunshine, and barbecues; in came the mountains, rocky shores, and waterproof clothing.

"Syd's a nomad," James answered for her. "She and Gertie travel the country wherever I give her a job. It works well, as she doesn't like to stay in one place for too long. She's popular amongst my clients that flit in and out of the country regularly."

"Don't you get stressed out jumping from one job to the next?" Will asked.

"No. I love it. I spent a lot of time on the sea with my dad when I was younger, so I've always had the urge to keep moving and explore new places. I've never been anywhere long enough to call home."

"But where do you keep your shit?"

Sydney twitched her head. "Sorry?"

"That's home," Will explained. "Where you keep all your shit from school — the pointless trophies, exercise books, cuddly toys."

"I threw it all out."

That was a lie. She'd kept Bertie, a bear her dad had given her when she was ten. She kept him in Gertie to this day. He'd initially come as a disappointment. By the age of ten, she was enamoured by camper vans, the idea of sleeping out and stargazing from the windows excited her like nothing else. Her dad had always promised her one, and each birthday she'd been met with, "Maybe next year."

She'd begun to give up on the idea when, on her seventeenth birthday, her dad handed her a present. She'd torn the poorly wrapped paper from the box and opened the lid to find a key with a keyring of a pale blue VW T1 camper. Her dreams had finally come true when she peered down from her bedroom window to see a full-sized version parked on the driveway. 'Gertie' was the first word from her mouth.

They had worked on restoring her bodywork together

during the holidays. It had taken until graduation to give her the finishing touches of a full respray and to fit her new interior. She was a stunner to look at but left much to be desired underneath her engine flap. Sydney returned to her life on the south coast with Gertie, on the promise her dad would upgrade the 45-horsepower engine the next time she returned to Scotland. Sydney felt glum as she recalled how her eventual return had been overshadowed, and Gertie remained underpowered, mechanically on her last legs.

"You threw it all out?" Will gawked. "Seriously?"

"I've never needed possessions," she said. "When we moved from Australia when I was little, we couldn't bring a lot with us, and then we moved around Scotland quite a bit. We never had a lot of money to buy anything, so I have no baggage and no bills to pay except for Gertie's and a mobile phone. All we need is a bit of fuel to keep us moving. I find it helps when I take on all that for my clients. I can focus on them."

James shook his head at her with faux disgust. "You really are dedicated to the cause. I guess I should be proud, but you'd only demand a pay rise."

"Are you Australian then?" Will asked, unrelenting with his questioning.

"I was born in Australia to Scottish parents. I'm not sure what that makes me."

"Confused?" James suggested.

"Your lifestyle sounds lush. I'm kind of jealous. I could see myself in a camper, living the dream," Will said, staring into the distance.

Raising his sunglasses over his receding hairline, James

glared at Will. "Don't you go getting any ideas. I need you at home by my side."

Will winked at him, scooped up James's hand, and kissed the back of it.

They were annoyingly cute, as most couples were when they were in their first year together.

Was home wherever the person you loved was? Sydney wouldn't know. She hadn't had a meaningful relationship since... *Sam*. She pushed the name aside and watched as James and Will shared a kiss.

It was a relief to see James so happy after being dumped by his ex, Matt, two years ago. Matt had set up the boutique London PA agency and asked James to manage the day-to-day operations. But James's life had changed overnight when he discovered a note on the pillow beside him instead of Matt. Matt had been having an affair with a Spanish waiter, a man James knew well from their favourite restaurant. Matt had gone off to Spain with him and said he was selling the agency. James decided he would buy it from Matt, after asking Sydney — who by that time was quite happy with her job, going wherever the wind blew her — if she would go in with him. It was too much commitment for her, but she encouraged him to go it alone since he'd effectively been running the business single-handedly for years.

Rosie emerged from the French windows of the hotel, pulling Sydney from her thoughts. Making a beeline for Sydney via a waiter, whom she relieved of a glass of Pimm's, Rosie embraced her childhood friend in a hug.

"I can't believe you missed me walking down the aisle!" she said.

"I can't believe it took you sixteen years to tie the knot."

"Why couldn't you fly from Edinburgh as any normal person would?" Rosie rebutted, ignoring Sydney's dig.

"What about Gertie?"

"Your attachment to her is unnerving," Rosie replied, turning to hug James and Will next.

"She's still the most reliable woman in my life," Sydney rebutted.

"Wow, that's saying something. Hasn't she been on her last legs for years?"

"I couldn't leave her. Can you imagine the look on her face if I told her I was coming to see you all and not bringing her? Anyway, I'm planning a little expedition with her."

"If she'll behave," James sniggered.

Sydney glared at him. "Thank you."

"So did you manage to pleasure yourself with Scotland's most unreachable, deepest parts?" Rosie asked, taking the seat beside Sydney.

"Sure did. I hit the Highlands, then went over to the Orkneys and Skara Brae. Then I zipped back to Mum's for a clean-up before coming here. I love Gertie to bits, but you can't beat a proper bed and bath. I'm thinking we'll head to Cornwall next; you never know, it may give me some inspiration to write."

A face caught her eye over Rosie's shoulder. She slouched in her chair and grabbed her Pimm's glass, hoping it would cover her face.

"What is it?" Rosie asked, turning to look over her shoulder. "Ah, Sam."

Of course Rosie would notice.

Sydney's heart quickened in her chest. Feeling hot suddenly, she gulped at her drink.

"Did you forget he'd be here? He is Greg's cousin and best man."

An age had passed since she'd thought about Sam. Or about the right amount of time for an ex-lover.

"No, of course not. I thought I saw him in the church. Wasn't he ostracised by his family?"

"He was." Rosie gave her an icy stare. "Not by us."

"Right, sorry."

"We didn't invite the rest of his family. They were quite put out."

"Good. They deserve to be put out."

Rosie spluttered her Pimm's back through the straw. "You're one to talk! You were hardly supportive of his transition."

"She's got you there, Syd." James piped up.

"I wasn't... unsupportive." Sydney choked on her words. Was that how her friends perceived it?

"You ran away," James laughed.

"To support my mum while she was going through *cancer*," Sydney added in her defence.

Rosie glared at her. "And that stopped you from keeping in touch?"

No, it hadn't. Sydney hardly needed reminding of how she'd handled things. They were young, and she hadn't been ready to commit to anyone, not even Sam. When she'd learned of Sam's gender dysphoria, it knocked her for six. She acted out in confusion, fear, even ignorance, shamefully. Had she run away just as an opportunity to escape presented itself?

Greg approached them then with Sam by his side.

"Hey, everyone." Sam nodded at Rosie, James, and Will, before his gaze finally met a blushing Sydney. "Sydy, good to see you."

That was a name she hadn't heard in a long time, and it hadn't been expressed in such a deep timbre before.

"Sam... wow, you look..." She stopped, knowing she was making a tit of herself. She tried to think back to the last time she'd seen him, then stopped herself and took him in as he stood before her. A thin face was covered with a stylish, short beard and complimented by a cute quiff. His upper body was challenging the seams of his shirt.

Sam offered her a rope. "Different?"

"Amazing," she corrected him as she clambered to her feet and embraced him.

The unfamiliar scent radiating from him confused her senses for a moment. Why was she expecting it to be the same as it once was?

"That feels a bit different." Sydney said, pulling back from the hug which felt so familiar yet unfamiliar. "So you finally did it."

"Yep." Sam beat his chest with a smile. "Sam became... Sam."

His smile was catching, and her lips stretched wide with genuine happiness for her ex-lover. "Well, I'm really happy for you. Are you happy?"

"I am," he replied, any awkwardness slipping from him as he nodded.

"Before I forget..." Greg passed Sydney a key.

Grateful for the interruption, Sydney took the key to

Greg and Rosie's cottage. "Are you sure?" she asked. "I can stay in Gertie and pop in to feed the cat."

"Yes. There's no point it being empty for a week whilst we're on honeymoon. No parties, all right? And Napoleon is in charge."

"Of course," Sydney agreed; the idea of being bossed around by a cat called Napoleon was certainly something to be entertained.

"If you're sticking around, it would be great to catch up," Sam said to her.

Sydney nodded. "Are you still down at the harbour?"

"Yes. I never left."

An awkward silence fell over the party of friends.

Never left, the silence implied. *Not like she had.*

"Come tomorrow... if you're free," he continued. "The weather looks great. I was going to take the boat out."

"Tomorrow?"

"Why not? Have a lazy Sunday. Come and recover from the hangover I'm sure you're heading towards."

Sydney briefly mulled it over. They had a lot of catching up to do, and she couldn't exactly say no. She owed Sam several apologies.

"Sure," she settled on.

"Good. It will be great to see Gertie again. We had some good times in her."

James laughed into his straw, causing his Pimm's to bubble noisily in the glass. Everyone turned to stare at him.

Sam continued. "Assuming you brought her."

"Of course," Sydney said, "though she's not in great shape."

James chuckled. "That's an understatement. She sounded like she's on twenty a day on the way here."

"I could take a look at her tomorrow if you like?" Sam said, plopping his glass on the table.

"Thanks," Sydney said. "That would be great."

Rosie crossed her arms and interrupted. "Erm, excuse me, day one of cat-sitting and you're already abandoning your post?"

James had put two and two together at this point. "Can I assume Napoleon is the someone you are ditching Beatrice Russell for?" he asked.

"Syd!" Rosie cried. "How could you agree to cat-sit when you've got an opportunity like that? Beatrice Russell is, like, one of the most famous actresses in the world."

"Even I'd choose her over Napoleon, Syd." Greg laughed, earning him a scowl from Rosie. "Not over you, though, obviously, my beautiful wife."

Sydney had to give him style points for his backtracking abilities.

"I should think so too! I loved her in that film with that woman. Oh, what was it called?" Rosie said, clicking her fingers.

"I've never heard of her and have no wish to," Sydney said, firmly in James's direction.

"I'd bet the last film you watched was *Jurassic Park*. The original one." James scrunched his face at her.

Sydney shrugged. "I prefer books. Shoot me."

"Didn't Beatrice Russell break her leg on set yesterday?" Sam asked.

Sydney scowled at James. "Didn't think to mention that? So you'd have me waiting on her hand and foot?"

"Yes," James conceded. "It's live-in on her estate in the South Downs. It's not exactly far. You could easily pop in on the bloody cat."

"Hey!"

"Sorry, Rosie," he apologized. "I'm sure Napoleon is adorable."

"I've been working non-stop for months," Sydney protested. "I promised myself some time off."

Rosie reached forward and placed her phone under Sydney's nose.

"This is her; you must know her face at least."

Sydney closed her mouth before she could embarrass herself with involuntary noises. Beatrice Russell was... exquisite. Her blonde, shoulder-length wavy hair encased an oval face, and her dazzling blue eyes were perched upon prominent, high cheekbones. An ethereal beauty.

In the picture on Rosie's screen, the actress was dressed in a red, off-the-shoulder silk dress with heels. Perched on a stool, Beatrice Russell's long dress was pulled up to her knees, showing off a pair of long, shapely legs. An attractive diamond necklace pulled the eye down to her ample cleavage. She resembled a predator about to devour its prey — after she'd fully intimidated it.

"Syd?"

Sydney glanced up at James, not wanting to take her eyes away from the photo.

"You've got a bit of drool, just there." He grinned as he rubbed the side of his mouth.

Her face flushed; she hoped no one would notice. "Shut it."

"I think we all have... and not only from the mouth."

"Eww!" Rosie slapped Greg playfully across the arm and popped her phone down the top of her wedding dress. "I'm sorry, Will. You've only just met us all, and some of us are already lowering the tone."

"Lower away," Will said with a wink.

"Hey, did you realise it's been fifteen years since we graduated?" Sydney said, changing the subject before they could get stuck further in the gutter.

"Did you all study business management with James?" Will asked.

"No, Syd did creative writing, and I did sports science," Rosie replied. "Greg wasn't a student. I met him in our final year. Sam was in tow — they're cousins. They eventually moved in with me and Syd."

Sydney eyed Sam. His top lip lifted a little at her as if he, too, was remembering their early days together, before things changed.

James leaned forward, swiping his drink from the table. "And I was left to feel like the spare wheel."

"Until you met Matt and abandoned us for London."

"Urgh, Matt," Greg moaned. "I never liked him."

"Neither did I," Sam added, trying to restrain a laugh.

James lifted a hand to his heart. "What! Thanks for keeping it to yourselves. You could have saved me the heartache."

"Oh, you wouldn't change a thing." Sydney laughed at him good-naturedly. "You love your job, and you wouldn't have that without Matt."

"I'd love it even more if Beatrice Russell was on my books!" he prodded her.

Sydney opened her mouth to say no at the same

moment a gong went off inside the hotel. James pulled his lips to one side as everyone got up. He'd got the message.

CHAPTER 4

A road trip in Gertie couldn't be beaten. With her many windows giving a panoramic view of the surrounding countryside, and a fresh breeze blowing through her sliding windows, her passengers could connect with all of nature's elements.

Camper life was great — unless it was raining. Then it was like being in a tin can being shot at by a water cannon. Even so, Sydney felt there was a certain level of satisfaction that came from having everything she needed on hand, not to mention the freedom to go anywhere a gust blew or a whim pulled her.

This morning it was to the harbour, somewhere Sydney had for a few years *called* home. She dropped James and Will off at the train station on her way out of the city. James pressed her not to abandon him for too long trying to fulfil her lifetime dreams of being a writer — unless she could fit it around her day job. The chances of that dream coming true were slim to nil. He'd shed a tear as he always did over their goodbyes and forced her to make yet another promise — to call if she changed her mind about Beatrice Russell. She'd told him to suck it, though she hoped she wouldn't live to regret it.

An hour's drive through the delightful countryside of the South Downs led her to the coast. As Gertie came to a stop in the dirt beside their old house, Sydney took in the familiar view of the harbour in the distance, where the tall masts of the sailboats were lined up in the marina. It was a strange feeling, being back in a place she'd thought she'd never return to. Now that she was parked in the same spot Gertie would reside in, she almost regretted coming back. Some endings shouldn't be revisited; time would tell if this was one of them.

Sydney left Gertie to bake in the sunshine and wandered down the path from the house to the boat workshop. It was a path she used to tread regularly with a cup of tea or beer in hand. Sam was working away in his usual spot on a boat engine hanging from a trolley, as if time hadn't moved.

"Hi, Sam," Sydney said, half lifting a hand to wave.

"Hey." Sam wiped his oily hands on a cloth. "You made it."

Their hug was longer than the awkward one they had shared the previous day. They both relaxed into it as old friends meeting after a long time rather than ex-lovers seeing each other for the first time in years.

"Lovely wedding," Sam continued.

"Wasn't it?" Sydney replied, relieved with the familiarity of the subject.

"You made quite an entrance."

"You know me."

"I know Gertie," Sam sniggered, taking a couple of bottles of water from a fridge under the counter.

Sydney smiled. He did know Gertie. It had been the three of them until they had split up, and Sydney had left with Gertie. It was the equivalent of one of them taking the dog.

"Here." Sam held out a bottle. "Let's sit outside."

"Thanks." Sydney pointed to the fridge. "How many times did I say you needed a fridge in here? Glad you finally listened to me."

"I only needed a fridge in here once you left and I had no one to bring me drinks."

Sydney folded her arms in mock frustration. "So you're saying you replaced me with a fridge?"

"Err, this sounds like a trap." Sam laughed nervously.

Sydney smiled, then spotted the old sofa in the corner of the workshop as they made their way outside. "I can't believe you've still got that old sofa," she commented.

"Yeah. It doesn't see as much action as it used to."

The comment tripped her as images of the times they'd spent on it were suddenly at the forefront of her mind.

"Sorry, too soon?" Sam asked.

"No, it" — Sydney's forehead furrowed — "just feels like a lifetime ago."

It wasn't a lifetime ago, nearer thirteen years since she left. It was bizarre seeing everything again, like a vivid dream where everything feels so real and yet at a distance.

She'd never really processed it all. Was there a right or wrong way to deal with being told by your partner of three years that they were struggling with their identity and would no longer identify as the woman you fell in love with? Where did it leave her identity as a lesbian? If Sam was living as the man he'd always been, they would be seen as a heterosexual couple.

In hindsight, she realised how ignorant she'd been. Sam was still Sam inside. He was possibly a truer form of the Sam that Sydney loved, now that he didn't have to hide behind a mask. Even though the world had changed in the last thirteen years, she should have spent less time back then worrying about what other people thought.

When Sam told her how unhappy he'd been feeling within himself, it had broken her. By then, cracks had started to appear in their relationship; whether that was to do with how Sam was feeling at the time, she didn't know.

Sydney shook off the ruminating thoughts and followed Sam around the workshop onto the deck where a light, salty wind blew across the shoreline. It was a refreshing change to the stifling heat inland.

"How's your mum doing?" Sam asked, taking a seat at the wooden table he'd built when they had moved in.

"Great, actually. It took her a few years to fight it, but she's been clear for ten now."

Sam nodded. "If anyone could kick cancer's butt, it was your mum."

"True," Sydney replied, choosing a shady seat beside Sam. "It hasn't been all plain sailing. She's never been able to return to work since... Dad."

"Rosie told me what happened," Sam said before pulling his lips tightly to one side. "I'm truly sorry. He was one of the best."

Sydney nodded. "After he... well, I couldn't get back on the boat and carry on without him. My uncle's doing a grand job now. Though the fishing industry isn't what it used to be. Have you seen your family since you…"

"Transitioned?" Sam supplied. "You know, it is okay to say the word."

She bit her lip. "Sorry."

"No, they barely accepted me before when I was *just a lesbian*. I have my workshop and plenty of boats for company. What more do I need?"

Sydney took a sip of her water. "A good woman to warm your bed?"

"I had one of those."

Their eyes met, and a sadness fell over Sam's. Sydney refused to feel sorry for herself. She had asked for that as much as a punch to the gut, and it winded her just as much.

"Sorry if I abandoned you in the middle of everything," she said.

"It's okay. Well, it's not, at all, but your mum needed you."

"So did you. I just couldn't see myself in a relationship with a man." Sydney closed her eyes briefly. "Even though I see now that I was already in one. It wouldn't have been fair to you, though, if we stayed together. You needed to find your way through it, not *our* way through it. Plus, we weren't in a good place. You were unhappy. I'd spent months believing it was me making you unhappy, so by the time you told me, I'd kind of already checked out." She stopped, realising she was rambling.

"Honestly, Syd, I'm good now," Sam reassured her. "I've even started a helpline. I help others just beginning to transition, and even though I've been through it myself,

I still find it hard to help others understand themselves. There is only so much you can do; the rest they must do themselves. We give them reassurance, kindness, and love as they go through it."

Sydney found she was unable to shake her guilt. "Which is what you deserved from me."

Sam sighed, and Sydney worried she may be asking too much reassurance from him. "What did you do except give me the space I needed to get myself together?" he asked with firmness. "You're right, any changes I was going to undertake with myself would have been done with you in the forefront of my mind, worrying about how it would affect you."

Sydney nodded. "Right. That wasn't the way to do it."

"No, it wasn't. It was something I needed to do for myself alone. I couldn't continue trying to make you comfortable at my own expense. We were great together, but I couldn't set myself on fire to keep you warm. I'm just sorry we didn't find a way to keep in touch."

"Yeah," Sydney said, feeling emotion well up as she met Sam's eyes. "That's on me."

"Hey now," he said. "We had a good few years together."

Sydney sniffed. "The best." She surveyed her ex's appearance before stating, "You really do look great. It suits you, not that you didn't look great before."

"Thanks. Sorry about these." Sam cupped his hands around his pecks. "I know you were a fan."

Sydney laughed. "The biggest."

"I didn't need surgery to survive, but I certainly needed it to thrive. I finally feel connected to myself now."

Sydney stilled, taking in the enormity of what Sam was telling her without saying it directly.

As if reading her mind, Sam added, "It takes time to get used to it all. Even I grieved in my own way."

Sydney nodded, appreciating his honesty and patience to make her feel better when he didn't have to.

Sam unscrewed his bottle of water and took a sip. "So, you've not settled down yet? You are getting on a bit. I'm sure the nomadic lifestyle was cute in your late twenties; it looks a bit sad in your thirties," he teased.

"Hey!" Sydney gave him a soft punch to his upper arm. "I've not met anyone to ground me anywhere. Who could compete with Gertie anyway? Even you struggled. And she likes to be on the road, though she's not suited to it at the moment."

"What's up with her this time? Honestly, I can't believe you've managed to keep her going on that old engine."

"I know her foibles well enough. Lately..." Sydney shook her head. "She's been running rough, rougher than normal, and flaked out on me a few times. She's just hit 120,000 miles."

"Bloody hell, Syd. I can tell you the poor girl's knackered without even looking. Those engines were never built to do that. I could try and find a second-hand Subaru engine for her, get her up and running again."

"Are you sure? That's a lot to ask."

"It might take a week or two to hunt one down, so you'll have to bring her back."

"I really don't want to impose, Sam."

"It's fine. It's the height of summer; every boat owner is out on the water. I only have a few jobs booked in. Plus, I don't want anyone else's hands inside her. You'll also need a flywheel and…"

"Yeah, I know the score. I also know how much it will cost." Sydney exhaled and played with the lid of her water bottle. "I could have done with a job to pay for it all."

"I thought you were taking the summer off."

"That was the plan. I just wanted a bit of me time. A chance to get a few words down."

Sydney stretched back in her chair and let the sun bake into her skin. Was she going to have to forgo some time off again? Gertie was what mattered, and if Sam was offering to fix her, then there was no one else better to do that. He'd spent enough time under her flap to sort her out.

"Still not a famous author then?" he asked.

"One day… maybe…?" She sighed. "Never. If I can just stop the relenting day job long enough and find the balls to publish something."

"Balls? I've got a good contact for those."

Sydney laughed. "You can keep it."

Sam fixed her with a sobering look. "You enjoy it, though, your job? I hope you do."

"Being a PA? Yeah, I do. Free food and accommodation, travel, perks, great pay — what's not to like? I never saw myself as one, that's for sure. But I'm damn good at it."

"You always were the organised one. I can't get over James being your boss."

"Yeah, it takes some getting used to. I only started as a favour. He had a client in Scotland. Low-key. Turned out it was just what I needed. Gave me something… someone else to focus on after…" She stared blankly at the sea. "Then I just took the next job, wherever it led me and Gertie. Ten years later and we've never looked back."

"There's you, sailing around the UK in Gertie, and I'm still here tinkering with engines."

Sydney scrunched her face. "Don't do that."

"What?"

"Put yourself down. You always did that, and it still pisses me off. You don't tinker with engines; you're a *marine engineer*, running a successful business repairing boats. My dad would have been proud of you, prouder than he is of me bowing to the whims of the rich and famous that he despised so much."

"He was always so kind to me," Sam said. "He was the one that encouraged us to come here and take the lease."

Sydney nodded; she remembered. "He wasn't too impressed that we broke up; he adored you. I think he would have preferred you to me; you were someone who could have worked on the boat with him. You could have been the son he never had."

"I could have done with a new family," Sam agreed, a flat smile pulling at his lips.

"I remember how impressed he was when I told him you were a mechanic who loved boats. Two and a half years into uni and they hadn't visited once; then I tell them about you, and they appear on my doorstep within the month."

Sam suppressed a chuckle. "Good old Mac. He always believed you'd make it one day as a writer. You know that, don't you?"

Sydney pushed her lips together and hummed in

agreement. "It's the main reason I keep going with it. Stopping would make him feel even further away."

"That's the spirit. Keep the dream alive for both of you." Sam leaned his forearms on the table. "You're welcome to stop here whilst I fix Gertie if you need to. Set yourself up on the deck and write away until she's back on her wheels and ready to whisk you off on your travels."

"That's kind of you, but fixing Gertie means I won't be able to afford to travel after, and if I don't fix her, she won't be taking me anywhere anyway."

"Why don't you take that job James was offering?" Sam asked. He sounded tentative, as though he had a feeling Sydney might have some grand objection to the idea. "It's not far from here, and he said it was just for the summer."

Sydney blew out a breath. "I know," she admitted begrudgingly. "I think it may be my only solution."

Yet again writing was going to have to take a back seat. It would need to be thought of as a delay, not a cancellation of her plans. She'd use her savings to fix Gertie and earn what she could whilst she was waiting for her, then be on her way again.

"Why don't you stay over tonight?" Sam suggested. "I can rustle us up something on the barbecue, and we can decide what we need for Gertie."

"That would be nice, thanks. And thanks for Gertie."

"Happy to help the old girl. Can I keep her old engine? It would be nice to have part of her," Sam asked as he stood. "Or is that weird and sentimental?"

"No, it's sweet." Lordy, was it sweet, so sweet Sydney could feel herself welling up. "I'd love you to have her old heart."

"Come on," he said, obviously pivoting the conversation away from Sydney's tear-filled expression. "Let's get you out on the ocean."

"I'll catch you up. I'm going to have to make a call to James first."

A smirk tore across Sam's face as he realised what she meant. "He's going to gloat."

"Don't I know it," Sydney replied, pulling her lips to one side.

And gloat he did.

"Why, hello, Sydney. Changed your mind already?" James asked as soon as he picked up the call. "That was quick."

"Only because Gertie needs work," she replied.

"Ha! I knew it. Well, it's gone."

Sydney's heart sank, lower than she'd like to admit. "What?"

She hadn't planned for this. She did really need the job now if she was going to get Gertie back in shape. Not to mention she was intrigued by Beatrice Russell — she liked a challenge.

"Sorry, bad joke," James confessed. "She's all yours."

"James, for fuck's sake." Sydney clutched her chest with her hand.

"So, Gertie, huh? Nothing at all then to do with how hot Miss Russell is?"

That was undeniable, Sydney thought as she recalled the images on Rosie's phone screen. Beatrice Russell was steaming.

"I'll take that as a yes then," he continued. "Anyway, I pay your wages, and you live out of a van when you're not living in a client's mansion. You can't seriously be rummaging around in your piggy bank to fix Gertie, can you? Not that I'm trying to persuade you against it; you've made a verbal contract, and I'll sue your arse if you go back on it."

"I keep enough to feed Gertie and myself, a small pot of savings, and then I send the rest to mum."

His voice lost its exuberance. "Yes, of course."

"If I use my savings, there's no road trip, and if I don't fix her — well, I doubt Gertie and I will be enjoying any road trip, let alone being able to make it to another job."

"Are you still at the harbour?" James asked knowingly.

"Staying over," she replied.

"Oh, yeah."

"Not like that," she said, putting the kibosh on his randy attitude. "Didn't you get the memo that I'm a lesbian?" She turned to look for Sam, only to spot him through the workshop window changing his dirty T-shirt. His ripped torso and bulging pecks made her suck in a breath. "And Sam is all man."

CHAPTER 5

*B*eatrice scooted back from the ensuite on her butt, dragging her lead weight of a broken leg across the floor of the hotel suite. She held a level of animosity towards it — it was seriously letting the side down. She was now going to spend the next six weeks dragging its incompetence around.

Why the casting nurse had used a blindingly pink fibreglass bandage was beyond Beatrice's understanding. She'd been too distracted with her phone when the woman had begun winding the atrocity around her leg.

Her phone vibrated on the bedside table; she scooted faster towards it before it could ring off.

"Hello?" she answered, out of breath from the effort.

"How are we?" Alison's welcome voice came back as Beatrice put it on speaker so she could clamber onto the bed.

"We are miserable. I feel like I've been clamped in irons. A physiotherapist has been in to tell me the rest of me is going to waste away in the meantime. She even had

47

the audacity to remove my wheelchair to force me to use these bloody crutches, which are going to drive me mad if they don't kill me first." Beatrice groaned and leaned back against the headboard. "I just want to be home, Ali."

"The production company — who reiterate again how sorry they are — have only extended their apologies as far as a first-class commercial flight. I assumed you wouldn't want to charter yourself. I saw the last settlement offer you made to Peter."

"Is this where you mention the prenup again?" Beatrice deadpanned.

Alison chuckled. "I've rubbed your face in that one enough."

"Book a charter and send them the bill, I'm not flying commercial with this leg. You can remind them I could remain in this lavish suite they're paying for; that should do the trick. I know how much they charge a night for this room, and frankly it's overpriced."

"It'll be Burbank, not LAX, as it's such short notice."

"That's fine; it's closer. Try and get something expensive and make sure it has a lift."

"I'll see what I can rustle up. In other news, we have a new PA."

"A competent one?" Beatrice asked, mindful not to get her hopes up.

"She comes highly recommended by her agency."

Beatrice pinched the top of her nose. "Urgh, don't they all?"

Alison chose not to comment on this. "I'll send you her phone number, and your flight details once I have them."

"I appreciate you sorting all this. Fleur's been AWOL

since she handed in her very short notice. I've been relying on room service and concierges to get by. I'll get her to pack my belongings and dispense with her — less a couple of days' pay."

"You outdid yourself with that one," Alison said with a light laugh. "Speaking of roles, I'm sending you a couple of potential jobs for next year. Let me know if any grab your attention, and I'll send the script samples over to you to peruse."

"Good. I'll need something to do on the flight home to keep me awake. I've been told to keep active."

"How's the book? Is it coming along or not?"

"Well, actually, I did start putting some thoughts down some years ago."

A lot of thoughts, in fact; she'd already covered most of the poignant events in her adult acting career. A particularly challenging role a few years before had affected her more than she would have liked, and writing was a good distraction from it.

"I didn't think we kept secrets," Alison snarked.

"*I* keep them when I find the alternative of you hounding me to the depths of hell too much," Beatrice rejoined.

"Speaking of secrets… there is something you should know."

The slowing of her agent's speech caused Beatrice's heart rate to pick up.

"Yes?"

"I know you said you didn't want to know when it happened." Alison exhaled. "Your father died a few weeks ago."

Beatrice stiffened. Her mother and father were dead to her when she turned eighteen.

Alison continued, "I went to the service. I hope you don't mind."

"Why?"

"I thought someone should pay their respects."

"That man deserved no respect," Beatrice bit out.

"Be that as it may, someone needed… to represent you. I know him being alive wouldn't have prevented you from being honest in your book." Alison paused. "I thought it was best that you knew."

"Were there many there?" Beatrice cursed her curiosity.

"A handful."

"Well, I have the first niggling of needing to pee," she lied, "and with the time it takes me to get to the bathroom I'll need to set off now."

"Sure thing, Bea." The tone of Alison's reply indicated she understood Beatrice wanted the matter closed. "Send me what you've done on the book, and I'll look over it."

Beatrice hung up and lifted her cast onto the mountain of pillows, covering herself back over with the Egyptian cotton sheet. A handful of mourners was five fingers more than her father deserved — she wouldn't waste her time sticking two up at him. Good riddance.

Turning her attention to her laptop, she retrieved her old file. There was no shortage of material to cover her fifty years on earth. She'd decided to go about it chronologically for ease and readability; it was simply a case of encapsulating that life in an engaging way whilst providing enough personal details to give insight into her character without being too intimate. She had no qualms over sharing most things, though some others needed to remain hidden — locked away and forgotten about at the cost of stardom.

How did one make noteworthy achievements, moments of adversity, and major turning points unfold like a story? A lot had happened to her, some good, a lot bad. It needed to sound genuine, not embellished for dramatical purposes. Remembering exact details was going to be difficult. Having already tried to recall her earlier childhood memories, she wondered if what she remembered was real, or just phantom memories placed in their stead, created off the backs of stories her parents had told her.

Her parents... there was another problem entirely. Alison was right: her father's passing made no difference to what she would say in the book; they deserved every bit of censure she would throw in their direction. She couldn't erase them; they were an important part of her history and part of the real story she needed to tell. What they had done had led her to be the success she was today — out of sheer determination.

Opening her emails to send the file to Alison, revealed an email from her with the contact details for Sydney MacKenzie. No doubt another airhead to test her patience and struggle with a simple coffee order. Milk was no substitute for cream in coffee; in fact, it ruined it entirely. It was the equivalent of asking for sugar and being met with salt. In the absence of cream, black was acceptable; milk was not. Beatrice didn't relish breaking in yet another new PA; it was hard enough when she had use of both legs.

A glance at her watch told her it was four o'clock in

LA, making it midnight UK time, a perfect time to call and introduce herself to her new PA.

Sydney roused to a vibrating sensation against her cheek. Disorientated in the pitch black of Gertie, she shot up. Her head collided with something.

Fuck.

Scrabbling around in the dark for what she could only assume was a stray vibrator, she spotted the light from her flashing phone. Squinting at it through one eye revealed a long overseas number, and that it was just after midnight. She must have only just dropped off. James told her to expect a call from her new employer who was currently in the States, and it seemed, incapable of understanding time zones.

She swiped the 'Accept' button quickly before she could lose the call.

A rich, effortless, articulate voice floated into her ear. "Miss Sydney MacKenzie?" The voice hung on to the *e* sound in Sydney a little longer than she'd heard it spoken before.

"Yes, hi." Sydney rubbed her head.

"This is Beatrice Russell. I hope I haven't caught you at an inconvenient time."

"Well, it's gone midnight in the UK."

"I'm glad to hear it."

Sydney cocked her head; was the woman being deliberately obtuse?

The warm, rounded voice continued. "You come highly recommended by your agency."

"I'm their bes..." Sydney squeezed her eyes shut, realising how pathetic she sounded.

"I would hope so. I expect the best. Sadly, I rarely receive it. Did your agency mention it was a live-in position? I find myself indisposed. As soon as my leg has healed, I'll be going back to the States to finish filming."

"Yes. I'm only available for a short time anyway."

"Perfect. I assume you drive?"

"Yes, of course."

"I'm flying out of LA tomorrow and will land on Wednesday. I'll need collecting from Biggin Hill; I'll text you the arrival time. Do you have a pen and paper?"

Biting down the urge to remind the woman of the time and inform her she didn't carry a notepad and pen in her ribbed tee and checked pyjama shorts, Sydney replied politely, "No, but I have a good memory."

She wondered if she'd set herself up for a fall as the woman reeled off a list of instructions.

"Go to my house, I'll text you the address. The gate code is 020728. Bring the Rolls — no, the Mercedes — I have a lot of luggage. The keys are in the box on the wall in the garage; the code is 260820. The code for the garage is 060218."

"Noted."

"Want the numbers again?"

"No, I got them," Sydney replied, loading them into her mind visually as dates and reciting them to herself.

"Very good."

The line went silent. Had the woman hung up on her?

Sydney opened a note on her phone and tapped out the numbers.

Within seconds her phone beeped with an address.

Highwood House, Bassington, West Sussex.

The woman's voice was still resounding in her head. It was the type of voice you could spend all day listening to and never tire of. It was as alluring as her photograph.

What was she thinking taking this job?

CHAPTER 6

S ydney punched a code into a small security unit attached to an old brick wall. Beside it stood two stone pillars holding a pair of intimidating, ornate wrought iron gates. A green light appeared on the unit, accompanied by a whirring noise as the gates slowly opened.

She leapt back into Gertie and drove through, ensuring the gate closed behind her with a glance in the rear-view mirror. The road wound through half a mile of romantic woodland, catapulting her out into a vast, rolling parkland with views extending for miles to more woodland on the horizon. It was so breathtaking she brought Gertie to a stop to take it all in.

"Bloody hell, Gertie! Do you see what I'm seeing? It's…" Sydney stopped, noticing a large, late Victorian house high up on the hill. "Magnificent. We've worked at some whoppers in our time, Gert. I reckon this one takes the biscuit. Oh, to be excessively wealthy." She lovingly patted the dashboard. "We'll keep dreaming."

Ascending the hill, the view only became more enchanting as she neared the sprawling three-storey mansion with its high-pitched roof, moulded gable barge boards, and terracotta hanging tiles. A pointed turret poked its head out over the roof. She would have to sneak a look in there; she was already imagining it would make a perfect writing den.

Gertie dragged her heels as the road transitioned into a gravel drive in front of the house. She was underpowered enough without gravel to battle against her rubber. Climbing from Gertie, Sydney admired the view down the hill to a lake, as a soft, warm, southwesterly breeze brushed against her. Although the house benefitted from being remotely situated within its own parkland, she would bet that the elements gave it a thorough battering during the winter months.

Turning, she took in the house again. The scale of it was off the charts. The windows were enormous with, she would guess, excessively large rooms beyond them. She couldn't wait to see inside.

Following the drive around the side of the house, she discovered it was twice the size she imagined it to be. At the far end, a modern ground-floor extension supported a large balcony, which disappeared around the other end of the house.

A large garden extended up the hill to the tree line, and a quick peek over a privet hedge revealed a swimming pool. A four-bay wooden garage with a terracotta-tiled roof stood to the right side of the house. Finding the side door with a security box next to it, Sydney punched in the number for the garage.

A fumble inside the door revealed a light switch, and with a click the darkened garage illuminated to reveal four vehicles. Sydney grinned as she drank them in. Moments like this would never tire in her mind. All her clients were wealthy, high-profile sorts, so she was used to seeing luxury cars — even driving some of them. It was one of the highlights of her job, along with living in multimillion-pound mansions.

All four vehicles were black. Either this woman thought she was the Queen, or she needed a serious injection of personality. She'd hazard a guess it was both. The first was a Rolls-Royce Dawn convertible, an excellent choice for gliding around the South Downs in the summer. She pressed her face to the window. A walnut trim, accompanied by light cream leather with black accents and the RR logo embroidered into the headrests. Gorgeous.

The second was another Rolls-Royce, a Ghost, just as elegant, with an identical design inside. She'd driven a Phantom, one of Rolls' sister models to the Ghost, before; it was like nothing else with its deafening silence and powerful serenity. Hard, tarmac roads became 13-tog-rated winter duvets. Jostling with traffic was a thing of the past as other drivers surrendered their position on the road. Speed bumps and potholes were flattened and filled as the Rolls drifted over them. Driving it was like floating on air.

The third was a Range Rover SV. Sydney ran her hand along the black satin finish, admiring the matching alloy wheels. A peek through the window revealed a similar finish in cream leather. This she anticipated to be her run-around — a £200,000 run-around.

Standing at the end of the garage was a Mercedes

Sprinter van, a rather unusual choice. Finding the box her new employer had described, Sydney punched the number in and extracted the key with a Mercedes fob. A click of a button opened a side door to reveal interiors straight from a private jet. Four cream leather reclining seats faced each other atop a soft, wool carpet. The passengers could also enjoy a mini bar and a TV on the rear bulkhead. A check of the rear revealed enough space for the luggage of the vainest of travellers. It put the likes of Gertie to shame.

Sydney could gain a good understanding of her clients by examining their cars. Beatrice Russell was a lady who was consistent in her style and knew what she liked — a selection of cars that would block out the morning sun. The lack of personalised number plates and privacy glass in all her vehicles said she liked to move around unnoticed. There was a great divide when it came to the rich and famous. There were the ones who liked to attract attention — usually those who didn't receive any — and the ones who shied away from it as attention was all they received. Beatrice Russell must have been the latter.

A check of her watch put the flight's arrival at two hours out. Allowing an hour and a half to get there, Sydney needed to make tracks. Another key on the fob opened the electric garage door. Taking position in the front seat, she pushed the start button only to be met with silence.

"Fuck."

She'd dealt with enough vehicles in her time as PA to know a dead battery when she heard one. It was common amongst the busy travellers who left their cars sitting idle for months on end. She was going to need to check all the other vehicles when she had time. For now, she needed a working 12-volt battery to jump it. She'd have to pray the electronic control unit didn't throw a hissy fit; she was down a vehicle anyway and the clock was ticking.

Gertie would fit the bill, thanks to her previous owners upgrading her underpowered 6-volt battery to a 12-volt. Sprinting across the drive to retrieve Gertie, she backed her up to the Mercedes and proceeded to hook them up with Gertie's well-used jump leads, remembering everything her dad had taught her: positive first, negative, earth. She turned Gertie over and let the two vehicles sit for a few minutes until she grew weary of waiting. If she was going to need a plan B, it would be better to know sooner rather than later.

"Come on, Gertie, this is your time to shine. Let's stick it to the moderns."

She hopped into the Mercedes and pushed the start button. The Mercedes sprang to life.

"Whoop whoop, Gert, you did it!"

Now time to get the hell out of here.

Leaving the engine running, she unhooked the cables and moved Gertie. She'd have to check her battery on her return.

Biggin Hill was already in the satnav of the Mercedes, and Sydney made it into the Signature VIP Arrival Lounge with five minutes to spare. A woman in sunglasses was being pushed into the lounge in a wheelchair just as she arrived, a bright pink cast poking out from under her dress. That was her, though her choice of colour for her cast was a little out of character for the profile Sydney had already established.

Even with the woman's diminished stature, her presence emanated from the chair; it was a presence that could not be ignored as she left those around her breathless.

Sydney sighed.

Beatrice Russell was magnificent.

She had a unique beauty about her rather than a classical beauty; her face on first impressions appeared quite plain. Her blonde, wavy hair dared you to stroke it to attest to its softness, and her prominent cheekbones enticed you to prod them to check they were real. Calling for a different touch entirely were her wide, rouge glossy lips.

Sydney gulped, bit her lips in, and plunged her hands into her pockets.

"Miss Mackenzie, I take it?" Beatrice said as she flicked the air stewardess away with her hand.

The warm voice that Sydney recalled from their phone call was replaced with a deeper, authoritative tone with a slight huskiness she hadn't noticed before. It would be clear even in a whisper. She braced herself, anticipating it to be the woman's disappointed voice.

"Yes. Please call me Sydney."

"You're late, Miss Mackenzie."

Okay, she was going for formal.

Though she knew she wasn't late, it was Beatrice who was in fact early, Sydney decided it wasn't her place to argue semantics. High-profile clients always needed to be right regardless of facts. Instead, she offered a valid excuse.

"Sorry, the Mercedes battery was flat. I had to—"

"So what you're saying is you failed to prepare for every eventuality."

Sydney remained silent; although she couldn't see the glare Beatrice was giving her from behind the sunglasses, she could certainly feel it.

"Doesn't sound like *the best* to me."

Changing the subject, Sydney asked, "Where is everyone else?"

"Were you expecting an entourage?" Beatrice covered a smirk with her forefinger. "Do I look like a woman who needs to keep an entourage?"

Sydney thought she didn't seem the type of woman who could keep an entourage.

"There's Jonathon, my bodyguard." Beatrice pointed to the reception desk, where a stout, middle-aged man stood. "He's taking a well-earned rest and flying on to..." Beatrice flicked her hand. "Oh, I can't remember. May we dispense with the questioning, or is there anything else you'd like to know? I've had a long flight and..." She flicked her hand again, this time towards her cast.

"Of course."

"Park me somewhere and summon me a coffee with cream, then load the luggage and return for me. Make sure my crutches are to hand or you'll be carrying me."

Sydney rolled her eyes as she went off in search of refreshments. She was used to demanding clients, though they were usually politer with their commands.

Returning minutes later with a coffee in hand she

braced herself. "They only had milk, so I assumed you'd prefer it black."

Beatrice slid her sunglasses down her nose and pouted at the cup of coffee before fixing a pensive stare upon Sydney. Her penetrative stare oozed power and confidence. Sydney could feel the weight of expectation burning from them. The woman lowered her gaze without so much as moving her head, taking all of Sydney in and leaving her feeling laid bare. As her eyes drifted back to meet Sydney's, she narrowed them, revealing attractive fine lines underneath. She finally pushed her sunglasses back up with her forefinger and exhaled a dismissive 'very good'.

Letting out a breath and telling her pulse to calm the fuck down, Sydney turned her attention to the suitcases.

Manoeuvring a broken-legged Beatrice Russell into a Mercedes Sprinter fifteen minutes later was no easy task. Allowing Beatrice to use her as a human crutch, Sydney managed to position the actress into the nearest luxury recliner. She reluctantly returned the airport's wheelchair and hopped into the driver's seat, where a pleasant aroma caught her nose. She sniffed her arm and inhaled a citrusy blend of jasmine and rose, followed by vetiver and patchouli. It was Beatrice's scent.

A stark voice boomed from behind her. "If you've quite finished sniffing yourself, may we depart?"

Sydney tried not to startle — at least not visibly. "Of course."

The divide between the front and back of the van slowly rose. She closed her eyes and tried not to wither inside from embarrassment.

Beatrice Russell was going to be a slippery customer that she was going to have to grin and bear until Gertie was repaired. Then she would be back on the open road — Gertie with a renewed energy; Sydney having had the life sucked out of her.

CHAPTER 7

"**W**hat is that monstrosity in my driveway?" Beatrice squawked as Sydney assisted her from the Mercedes.

Sydney contemplated letting the woman fall for calling Gertie a monstrosity. She refrained from pointing out that it was thanks to that monstrosity that Beatrice was home at all.

"That's Gertie."

"Gertie! You named that chicken coop? Keep it around the back of the garage, out of sight. I do hope it doesn't leak oil everywhere?"

Poor Gertie, she was a little on the incontinent side. Sydney was going to have to find a suitable time to mention that the chicken coop needed taking to the harbour. She'd leave it a while, at least until Sam confirmed that he'd managed to source the parts. Feeding Rosie's cat on Beatrice's time was going to be a separate challenge altogether.

Beatrice passed Sydney the key to open the imposing

oak front door. A light shone through its stained-glass inlays, casting multiple colours onto the geometric tiles beneath her feet. She'd never been so eager to see inside a house and prayed it was in its original condition, not stripped of its Victorian features. Rarely did she get to work in old houses; most of her wealthy clients owned drab, sprawling new builds with underground car parks, gyms, and swimming pools. They were not her cup of tea.

Stepping over the threshold, Sydney was not disappointed. An ornate oak staircase swept up to a galleried landing where an enormous window flooded the room in natural light. An elegant glass chandelier hung over a circular table in the centre of the room, and beside the bay window overlooking the drive sat a grand piano. A full-size grand piano.

"Are you going to stand there all day gawping?" Beatrice snapped from behind her.

"Sorry." Sydney moved to one side to allow Beatrice to crutch her way in. She took a closer look at the piano and nearly choked on her own saliva when she saw it was a Bechstein.

"Do you play?" Sydney asked, already imagining Beatrice's talents extending to those of a concert pianist.

"I can play," she allowed. "It doesn't mean I do."

"You seriously have a Bechstein and choose not to play it?"

"The point is I can choose to play it if I wish."

Sydney was unsure what she meant and decided it was best not to push the matter any further.

"Your house is…" Sydney was about to use the word 'exquisite' until a memory from the wedding reception stopped her. That word had been the one that came to mind when she'd first laid eyes on the woman across the room from her.

"...grand," she settled on.

That was better.

"I styled it myself," Beatrice said in lieu of accepting the compliment. "You'll have to find your own way around, I'm hardly able to give you a guided tour. There are plenty of bedrooms on the top floor, so take your pick. You'll find everything you need in the laundry room. My bed will need making up too. That's the suite at the back with the balcony."

"Of course."

"I'm going to have a lie-down in the drawing room before dinner; I don't have the energy to attempt the stairs. All my clothes will need washing or dry cleaning. I have an account with the dry cleaners in town. Use the Range Rover for day-to-day jobs. I ordered a food delivery; it should arrive shortly. I'm sure you can work out where everything goes, and I assume you can cook."

"Yes," Sydney said. James had failed to mention she'd be housekeeper and cook. But she was a PA, a role where lines were often blurred, usually to the advantage of the employer.

Beatrice made her way into a bright, spacious room to the right of the entrance hall. Her crutches tapped against the wooden floor as she went. At least Sydney would be able to hear the woman coming — slowly. Ensuring Beatrice was comfortably placed on one of the large sofas, Sydney closed the door behind herself so as not to disturb her employer. She had a lot of work to do and needed to familiarise herself with her surroundings.

A sweep of the ground floor revealed a cosy sitting room, a formal dining room, and a study with one wall made into an entire bookshelf. It was stacked with an impressive array of books.

The kitchen was across the entrance hall in a large, modern rear extension. It was a stylish space with the entire exterior wall being one large glass door that could be pushed aside, allowing a smooth transition from indoors to outdoors during the warmer months.

It was more of a family room with an L-shaped sofa and an enormous, wall-mounted TV in the far left corner. A less formal dining table was placed beside it with an outlook over the garden. The remaining half of the space was taken up with floor-to-ceiling white kitchen cabinets and a long kitchen island that ran parallel. It divided the two spaces perfectly. All was finished off with black granite worktops and grey slate floor tiles. The hob and sink were stylishly incorporated within the kitchen island.

An inspection of the rest of the house revealed numerous bedrooms on the first floor; Sydney lost count after the fourth. The larger bedroom at the back she assumed was Beatrice's, as its double doors led out onto a balcony where there was a table and two chairs. The room itself was divided into two zones. A huge bed sat against one wall with doors on either side, and the opposite wall held an enormous television, buttressed by two sofas.

Not wishing to intrude on the space, she turned her attention to the top floor, where the final room she discovered was the most anticipated. Squeezed between two bedrooms and accessed via a short staircase was the small, hexagonal turret room she'd spied from outside. It was adorable, with a wooden desk perfectly positioned under the window. It was enough to inspire any writer to greatness — or distract them from it. The remaining walls were bookcases, filled with books all the way up to where it transitioned into a hollow point.

A bedroom further along the top corridor called to her to take as her own. It was a large room with a glorious double-aspect view, yet it retained a cosy feel as it was tucked into the eaves. As she peered from the side window, she could make out Beatrice's balcony below.

Beatrice certainly had created a masterpiece with her design, despite it being a sympathetic modern interpretation rather than a fully authentic period restoration. The original fireplaces, intricate ceiling roses, decorative mouldings, and cornicing remained; long gone were the heavily patterned wallpaper and deep colours. Every room had a refinery and elegance about it, not just in its décor, but in the furniture too. Large armchairs, ottomans, and chaises longues were all perfectly placed and accessorised.

Between wash loads, she made up the beds and accepted delivery of an enormous number of groceries from a delivery man who was a little upset that he'd been pushing the gate button for ten minutes without a response. Her employer had thought of everything when she did the online shopping. There was enough fresh food to keep them going for a week.

Every job with a new client was initially frustrating and tedious until Sydney learnt her way around their home. It took ten minutes to hunt down some washing powder in the laundry room, and it wasn't until she was unpacking cold food into the empty fridge that she realised the thing wasn't even on. The hunt for the power switch took another five minutes.

The tangy aroma of the lemon-roasted potatoes must have made it as far as the drawing room as the taping sound of crutches came from the hall later that day. Beatrice's timing was perfect. The mussels were ready to go in the pot, and Sydney was just finishing the salad.

"You've only laid for one," Beatrice said as she took a seat at the head of the table.

"I assumed…"

"It's just the two of us for the time being; we may as well eat together. That way we can work. Not tonight, though. I'm too tired. Fetch me some painkillers, would you?"

Sydney placed a glass of water and paracetamol beside Beatrice as the actress tapped furiously at her phone.

"Actually, I'll have a glass of wine."

As Sydney reached for the box of paracetamol, Beatrice placed her hand on top of hers and without moving her gaze from her phone muttered, "I may still need those."

It wasn't Sydney's place to advise against mixing alcohol and painkillers. She withdrew her hand, the softness of Beatrice's hand against hers making the hairs on her arms shoot skyward.

They ate in silence. Sydney, taking her cue from Beatrice, absorbed herself in her phone.

"How was it?" Sydney asked as Beatrice finally placed her knife and fork onto her plate.

"Very good. You can indeed cook."

That was the second 'very good' she'd received on day one. Thanks to her upbringing by the sea, seafood was Sydney's speciality, and by the looks of Beatrice's food delivery, she, too, was a fan of it.

"I don't mind cooking for us — it makes sense — but would you clarify what else I'll be doing? I'm a PA, not a housekeeper."

"If you were any sort of PA, then you would have summoned a housekeeper," Beatrice replied dryly, glaring over the top of her black-rimmed glasses.

"I assumed you would have one."

Beatrice eyed her. "You assume a great deal." Returning her attention to her mobile phone, she added, "In this case, your assumption would be correct. There's Mrs Clarkson; she lives nearby and pops in most days. She's unable to join us for two weeks; until then you'll have to cope. Unless you feel such work is beneath you, of course?"

"No. I just like to be clear about what is expected of me."

Sydney found herself under Beatrice's scrutiny once again.

"Mrs Clarkson will do some cooking; you can discuss it between you once she arrives."

"Do you not cook?"

"God, no, I'm terrible at it. I'd kill us both."

Sydney made a mental note that should Beatrice ever offer to cook for her, it was a sign their relationship had reached the point of no return.

"She's only part-time. We adopted her with the house.

70

She's getting on a bit now, so she doesn't do as much. Xander will cook when he arrives. He has a passion for it. God knows where from."

"Xander?"

"My son," Beatrice replied, her tone questioning rather than informative.

"Oh, right. Sorry, I didn't know you had a son."

Beatrice removed her glasses and studied Sydney.

"What was the name of my last film?"

Sydney shrugged.

"My first film?"

Sydney shrugged again, unsure where Beatrice was going with this.

"Name any of them."

Would the woman sack her for not knowing her work?

"I've not seen any of them. I don't watch any films, TV, news."

"Surely, you're on social media? I thought all you youngsters were glued to it."

"I'm thirty-six," Sydney replied, her eyebrows stretching up. "And no I don't. I find it's all best avoided in my line of work."

Beatrice's forehead furrowed as she removed her glasses and rested the tip of one of its temples against her bottom lip. "Why do you not keep yourself abreast of the world and those in it?"

Sydney tried to stifle her laugh. "What makes you think I don't?"

"With what sources?"

"I move about in the world, and I interact with people. I read books."

"Books?" Beatrice gave a little twitch of her head before placing her glasses back on her nose. "You wouldn't consider them another source of 'propaganda'?"

"I wouldn't *trust* anything. I find them more reliable in that I know exactly what is being said, not implied, and by whom. The world is made up of groups of people trying to influence another group of people towards whatever agenda they have. News stations and newspapers are one-sided opinions directed at people with similar beliefs. Would you prefer that I came here having googled the hell out of you?"

"Well, no." Beatrice pondered further before continuing. "Most of it isn't true, and what is the truth is so often twisted it no longer resembles it at all."

"Exactly. I take people and situations as I find them."

"And how do you find me?" Beatrice asked, her expression finally softening.

How was she going to answer that? *My eyes think they've died and gone to heaven whilst the rest of me is stuck in hell dealing with yet another wealthy, self-centred egomaniac?*

"I…"

Beatrice intertwined her fingers, placing her elbows on the table. "Yes?"

"…don't know you well enough to make an assessment," Sydney finished.

Beatrice pulled her lips to the side and leaned back against her chair. "I think I'll go up now if you would be kind enough to lend me your shoulder."

With Beatrice's weight distributed between the stairs and Sydney, they had managed to manoeuvre her to the halfway landing when she stumbled. Sydney stepped in and caught her, holding her around her waist until she regained her balance.

"Damn this infernal leg!"

Sydney allowed Beatrice a moment to regain her composure, then urged her on. They repositioned Beatrice's arm around Sydney's shoulders and successfully made their way to the top.

"Crutches?" Beatrice demanded as soon as she was free of the stairs.

Sydney ran back down and returned with them, enabling Beatrice to hobble to her bedroom.

"I can manage from here. Wake me at nine o'clock," Beatrice barked, shutting the bedroom door firmly behind her.

It would be a few hours before she could fall into her own bed. There were countless suitcases that still needed going through. Two dollies in the laundry room were already straining under the weight of damp clothes. The rest would have to wait until tomorrow when she could hang it outside to dry.

Further investigation of the garage revealed that all the vehicles were off their battery tenders. Sydney pondered the incompetence of the person that forgot to put them on, knowing they would be left undriven for some time.

CHAPTER 8

*S*ydney woke exceedingly early the next morning. There was a lot to do before she roused Beatrice, starting with the laundry. Having sorted through the suitcases the previous night, she knew that there were two bags of clothing she would need to take to the dry cleaners.

Beatrice hadn't requested that she be woken with any refreshment, so Sydney took it upon herself to arrive with a cup of coffee with cream in one hand and a pile of freshly laundered clothes in the other. She knocked on the door and waited for an entry command, which followed immediately.

She entered to find the woman draped over one of the sofas watching television, dressed in only a long, red silk slip. Her mind flashed back to the photograph Rosie showed her of Beatrice in a red silk dress. The image before her was similar except for the bright pink cast sticking out the bottom.

Beatrice caught her eye.

74

"I know I look hideous — pink and red. We're going to have to rework my whole summer wardrobe."

'Hideous' was not the word Sydney would have used.

"It's a shame. Red suits you."

"I assume the coffee is for me?"

"Oh, sorry." Sydney shook her mind away from the thought of Beatrice's press photograph and placed the cup down on the table in front of her.

"Very good." Beatrice leaned over and picked it up, giving Sydney a full view of her ample cleavage.

Stop.

She turned away. A wave of heat flushed over every inch of her skin as the pulsing of her heart quickened.

No, no, no, this is not happening.

She made for the curtains, pulling them back and flinging open the balcony doors. She needed air. She couldn't keep thinking of her boss in that red, silky dress with her long legs and br... Sydney gulped the thought away and returned her attention to the laundry pile.

"Fetch me something to wear from the wardrobe." Beatrice pointed behind her, her eyes glued to the morning news. "A light maxi dress or something. The weather report says it's going to be hot again."

There was no wardrobe in the room.

As if Beatrice had sensed Sydney's confusion, an exasperated voice directed her: "The door to the left of the bed."

The other must be the ensuite.

The wardrobe, as Beatrice called it, was another room entirely, a dressing room with floor-to-ceiling fitted cupboards.

After opening the third cupboard door, Sydney found a rail full of summery maxi dresses. She naturally reached for a red one but stopped, giving the assortment of other dresses full consideration. Beatrice was tall and slender, yet womanly. Her figure would look stunning in any of them. Hesitating, Sydney finally decided on a blue one to match her eyes.

"Did you get lost?" Beatrice said through a yawn as Sydney re-entered the room. "Damn jet lag."

"Why don't you go back to bed?"

"I don't do staying in bed. I've spent the last few days on my back with my leg in the air. I have a lot of work to do. We'll set up in the kitchen; it's cooler in there. I assume you've found the laptops and my previous assistant's phone?"

"Yes."

In one of the hundreds of suitcases.

Sydney approached her with the dress. "This okay?"

"Very good. The grey laptop is mine. If you look in the top drawer of the desk in my study, you'll find my black book and everything else you need. The credit card PIN number is the gate code backwards. In the black book, you'll find the passwords for the phone and laptop. Emails from Monday this week will need attending to. Get set up and return for me in five." Beatrice reached for her crutches and struggled to pull herself up. "Make that ten."

Sydney left Beatrice to dress and busied herself with their laptops. She placed her own on the kitchen table and Beatrice's on a corner of the sofa, where she plumped the cushions so she could stretch out comfortably. On the table beside it, she popped a cold bottle of water and a box of painkillers.

Once Beatrice was settled onto the sofa with her leg elevated, Sydney occupied herself with emails until a clicking sound drew her attention. Was Beatrice seriously trying to get her attention by clicking her fingers? Oh God, she was.

"When you take the dry cleaning in," Beatrice said authoritatively, "I'll need you to pick up some more painkillers from the chemist and go to the delivery office and pick up my mail. You'll need the authority card."

Sydney waved the card at her that she'd found in the black book and picked up her mug.

"And pop into the florist and ask them to deliver my usual order tomorrow. Let them in and leave them to it; they know how I like things. Also, let the gardeners know I'm home for the summer." Her eyebrows jumped together. "What are you drinking?"

"Tea."

"I didn't even know we had any."

"I found some at the back of the cupboard."

Beatrice curled her lip. "I believe Mrs Clarkson drinks the insufferable beverage."

By mid-morning, the backing track of clicking keys and intermittent, frustrated huffs came to a stop. Beatrice had fallen asleep, her head flopped backwards with her hands still at her keyboard. It was a good opportunity to run some errands, and feed Napoleon. If Beatrice didn't know what time she left, she couldn't scrutinise her return time.

Sydney scribbled on a Post-it note, then placed it on the table beside Beatrice, allowing her gaze to fall on the sleeping celebrity. She was even more enchanting when she was asleep. People were always more attractive when they weren't barking orders or clicking their fingers. Which, in Beatrice's case, meant 'asleep'. Her face was relaxed, with little trace of the frown she'd been wearing since Sydney met her. Only a few lines on her forehead — the punishing war lines of a serial frowner — were visible.

Sydney shook herself; this wasn't appropriate. If Beatrice woke to find Sydney drooling over her, she'd sack her on the spot, and quite rightly. She needed to get a grip. The woman was hot, way out of her league, and with Sydney's luck, guaranteed to be straight.

Before heading into the garage to retrieve the Range Rover, she popped her head around the back to say hello to Gertie. Wedged between the back of the garage and an overgrown hedge she looked dejected.

The trip to Rosie's was a lot quicker than Sydney expected, helped by an extra 300 horsepower she wasn't used to. The cat greeted her on her arrival with a show of his rear end. "Careful, Napoleon," she cautioned, "or someone could think you're one of those funny towel hooks and stick a tea towel in that." He mewed at her and herded her towards the kitchen as she typed out a message to his mistress.

I've just popped in to feed Napoleon. He says, 'Meow.'

An immediate response from Rosie took her by surprise. Had she nothing better to do on her honeymoon?

Does this mean you took the job?

Yes, she replied. *Started yesterday.*

Would you rather I got the neighbour to look after him?

That would be great. Beatrice Russell is an organ grinder! It could be a struggle to get away again. Sorry!

No problem. How is the patient?

A few choice words came to mind, but she refrained from using them. Instead she went for one of Beatrice's.

Insufferable!

Feed her. Big meals, lots of protein. I'll send a list over of what to get.

Thanks, make it quick and I can grab some bits on my way back.

A picture of Rosie and Greg at the beach followed.

Looks lush. Enjoy! X

When she finally returned to Highwood, Beatrice was on the phone, speaking to someone in an unusually pleasant tone. Sydney was surprised she had one.

"You weren't to know I would break my leg. No, I'm absolutely sure. We'll cope until you return; Sydney is a fantastic cook. I'm going to have her send over a gift. Give me the address."

Noticing Sydney's sudden presence in the kitchen, Beatrice clicked her fingers in her direction and made a motion for pen and paper. Sydney passed her a pad of Post-it notes and a pen. The woman snatched them from her as if she had been waiting an eternity for them. She was probably pissed that Sydney had entered the room at the exact moment she'd been gushing over her cooking abilities.

Beatrice stuffed a note into her hand. It read *Harrods Baby Gift Hamper (approx. £500)* followed by an address.

It was a fun experience to shop for the rich and famous; instead of ordering the price from low to high, as she would for herself, she could play the 'high to low' game. She took the opportunity to order something else whilst she was online, something she hoped might make Beatrice slightly more pleasant in the coming days, and not just personality-wise.

Following Beatrice's call to whom Sydney could only guess was the housekeeper, she was back on the phone again. Unsure whether she should make herself scarce during her calls to afford Beatrice some privacy, she stayed put. The woman was frank enough to make it clear if she wanted her to disappear. No doubt at the sound of clicked fingers.

"I've gone through the scripts, and I'm happy to go with your suggestion. It's a perfect part for me." Beatrice paused, then pursed her lips. Sydney caught a glimpse of her as her face dropped. "Oh, Ali, tell me you're pulling my leg? She's five years younger than me." Beatrice ran her fingers through her hair and scratched at her head. "Yes, I know, and you know that doesn't always count for everything. Every wrinkle deducts a year of experience... Okay, well, set it up. Let's do lunch after. No... Sketch's décor makes me want to vomit, not eat."

Sydney listened as Beatrice continued her conversation with 'Ali' — whoever she was. The woman threw her head back as she howled with laughter, her large mouth projecting the sound like a megaphone. The relaxed and happy Beatrice was captivating to watch. Her smile lifted her cheeks even higher and created an attractive diamond shape of creases around the lower part of her face that pulled Sydney's eye to her wide lips.

A pang of jealousy reared its head as she continued to listen — jealousy for such casual conversation with the woman. Sydney had a habit of befriending everyone she worked with, even the most challenging of characters. This time, she knew that would not be the case. She already sensed that Beatrice's walls were impenetrable. Had she offended her in some way to cause her to treat her differently from everyone else? Why did she even care? She'd be gone in a matter of weeks.

Sydney blew out a breath, unintentionally making enough noise for Beatrice to glare at her from across the room. If that icy stare was supposed to chill her, it wasn't working. She fanned herself with a notebook to pretend she was suffering from the heat as Beatrice continued her conversation.

"Yes, on Saturday. He was due to spend the summer with Peter until the news broke of my coming back to the UK; then he was straight on the phone to ensure Xander would be coming here instead. He's not going to be happy about it. Hmm... you don't have to tell me."

Peter, Sydney assumed, was the husband or ex-husband.

Hanging up the phone, Beatrice made yet another call. A furious clicking from her direction caught Sydney's attention.

"Book the chap to come and check the swimming pool this week before Xander arrives; he'll want to use it." As quickly as Beatrice had turned her attention to Sydney, she turned it back to the person on the phone. "Darling, how are you? Oh, sorry I'll be brief, I didn't realise the time. Your father is terribly busy, so you'll be spending the summer at home... I don't know... yes, I know he doesn't have a job. Look, I'll be home, so you may as well base yourself here for the summer. It will be nice to spend some time together. I'll have my PA collect you from the station on Saturday; text me the time. Yes, he'll collect you the following Saturday for the week... You'll have to take that up with him."

Poor kid, Sydney thought. They were always the ones to suffer when a marriage broke down. Did he not realise his dad was clearly not interested? Not wishing to listen to the rest of the conversation and feeling the need to stretch her legs, she made her way outside to the patio area to check the state of the swimming pool. Her phone vibrated in her shorts pocket as she wound back the pool cover. It was James. He had a cheek.

"How's it going with the hottest actress on the planet?" he asked after she picked up.

"Don't."

"Are we still pretending not to notice?"

Sydney ignored his comment. "Did you know she'd have me doing the housework because the housekeeper is unavailable? Did I mention the laundry? And that I have to cook!"

"Ah, that's why they wanted someone who could cook."

"Seriously, James? You could have warned me."

"You're a great cook, Syd. Me talking to you now is only due to you keeping me fed at uni."

"Yeah, well, now I wish I hadn't," Sydney hissed, kicking at a clump of weeds between the patio joins.

James chuckled.

"You know, she clicks her fingers to get my attention; she's not said please or thank you once. Just *very good*. Four times."

"Look who's counting!"

"What?" Sydney didn't like what he was implying, although it wasn't far from the truth; she was counting. Technically it was five times if she included the 'very good' she had said on the phone the first time they'd spoken.

"Syd, you know these people; they are rarely the politest. Why are you letting her get under your skin?"

She knew why — she disliked rudeness. There was no place for it. Previous clients could be a little uptight, yet most of them had the nous to realise a PA was there to help, and the better you treated them the more helpful they became. A kicked dog only returned so many times with a wagging tail. She expected better from someone like Beatrice Russell; in truth, she was disappointed that someone so attractive on the outside could be so ugly on the inside.

That was another reason she kept her nose out of 'society' — it was true what they said about never meeting your heroes. Yes, Beatrice was an attractive woman who was beginning to make her a little hot under the collar, and yet she would benefit from a complete personality transplant.

"Can't you get someone else?" Sydney pleaded. "She doesn't need or deserve the best."

James didn't reply.

"You *did* have others lined up, didn't you?"

The realisation hit her when he continued to be unresponsive.

"You asked everyone else, and they said no, didn't they?"

"You insist on not knowing about who you're working for. Everyone else informs themselves. Which is why you're the sucker that got stuck with her."

"Jam—"

"Which is why you're the best, Syd. You treat everyone as if you don't know their sordid secrets because you don't. And everyone has them, trust me."

Did Beatrice have sordid secrets? She'd like to know them.

"Come on, think of Gertie," he urged. "How would she feel if you gave up on the job that'll get her fixed? Grin and bear it for her, eh?"

"I'm going to make you pay for this, James," Sydney muttered.

"I know, and it will be so worth it."

CHAPTER 9

*B*eatrice fanned herself with her notebook; the summer heat was unbearable. It was hard enough trying to sum up one's life in an autobiography let alone doing it whilst baking in an oven, with one leg suffocating in a fiery blaze under a cast. It felt like acid was melting her skin.

A quick search on the internet reassured her that the jolts that shook her awake the previous night, along with the never-ending, thundering aches, the twinges that erupted randomly during the days, and the zings of electricity that zap her nerves repeatedly, were all normal healing signs.

It was a week since she'd sustained the injury, and her patience was already beginning to wear thin. It was going to be non-existent in the coming weeks, especially if the heat didn't let up. Her LA hotel would have at least had the benefit of air conditioning; her home did not. With the amount of sweat her cast was producing, she was seriously concerned her leg would have rotted away by the time the cast was due to come off. The itching was something else.

She eyed her new assistant beavering away at the kitchen table. Sydney was a good-looking woman, even with her unusually large ears clinging for dear life to the sides of her head. Her brown hair pulled back in a high ponytail was doing nothing to disguise them.

She had to admit, Sydney wasn't quite what she'd envisaged. A woman in her mid-thirties was a definite improvement on her previous PAs, and she held the energy of someone in their twenties. She had also proven herself to be competent; more than competent. In fact, Sydney was like no other assistant; she'd survived everything thrown at her in the last twenty-four hours.

Sydney was… quite remarkable.

It was strange that she wasn't married, though, of course, going around in that ridiculous vehicle was hardly going to attract any normal companion, and with a job as a PA it was unlikely she would have time for one anyway.

Even so, Sydney had appealing qualities, especially of the domestic sort. Not only had she got her coffee right, but she'd also cooked the most amazing mussels Beatrice had ever tasted. Her first impressions of the woman were set when she logged in from the plane to her garage CCTV system to ensure the Mercedes left on time, only to find her new assistant lusting over her cars on the playback. The way Sydney touched them was the way Beatrice touched them herself, with an appreciation for the design, the contours, and the finish. She took it as quite the compliment. All the cars were built to her own specifications to suit her taste. It pleased her to see someone understand them as she did.

Her impressions were further elevated when she'd forwarded through the footage and found the woman using her own vehicle to start the Mercedes. It reminded her that she had told Mrs Clarkson not to worry about putting the vehicles on to their battery tenders and that she would do it before she left for the States. The woman wasn't so steady on her feet anymore, and the last thing she wanted was for her to fall in the garage.

This new PA had initiative, and yes, she was remarkable, yet she had still to prove herself as reliable, trustworthy, and loyal. Traits that her predecessor was not blessed with. As soon as the news had spread that Beatrice and Peter were divorcing, the media declared that she was dating a male co-star. She believed that rumour came from Fleur herself, though she couldn't prove it. She would have sacked her immediately had she been able to. Fleur had happened to walk into her dressing room, though, at the exact moment he brazenly propositioned her — with his tongue.

She envied people who built long-term relationships with a PA, ones that went on so well they became best friends. It was impossible to find an assistant to do their job properly, let alone move one into the friendship zone, and Beatrice could never be friends with someone who wasn't competent. To have that connection with someone would make life a little less lonely, but seeing as her PAs only lasted on average six months, she'd given up trying to get to know them long ago. It was simpler to bark orders and bark louder when they weren't carried out to her exacting standard.

With so many PAs in her rear-view mirror, Alison's PA had suggested a change of agency to find some fresh blood. It was a drawback in her industry that everyone knew everyone. She knew she held a reputation for being unable to hold down a PA and hoped it was because she didn't tolerate incompetence as opposed to being difficult to work for. Really, though, she didn't care if it was the latter — she was past hoping she could make a friend. She was destined for a life of solitude whilst working in an industry that surrounded her with people.

If what Sydney said was true, that she never read any rumours in the press, Beatrice thought she might be able to have clean start with her. The woman clearly had good taste; they'd barely known each other for twenty-four hours when Sydney observed that red suited her. This she already knew, of course. Her iconic look was a red dress; it complemented her blonde, wavy hair and piercing blue eyes and highlighted her wide lips, which she always ensured were adorned in red lipstick when she was out in public.

That reminded her. She clicked her fingers at Sydney, then again louder when she didn't respond.

"I need to stock up on some cosmetics whilst I'm home," she said when the woman finally looked up. "I could be in the States for a few months when I return. You can find everything under my account with Harvey Nicks."

She watched as Sydney riffled through the black book. That was a difference between her and other PAs. She always used her initiative first rather than disturbing her. She was *very good*.

Beatrice woke with a start to find her phone vibrating on her chest. Falling asleep on the sofa was becoming an afternoon habit since she'd broken her leg. Noticing Sydney was absent from her post, she swiped the phone to answer. It was Alison. Beatrice was hoping she would call to discuss the more recent additions to her autobiography. It was now pretty much up to date.

"How was what I sent you so far?" she immediately questioned, forgoing any greeting.

"It certainly covered the last thirty years of your career," Alison said noncommittally.

"I admit I started with the easiest part. Is it informative?"

Alison hesitated. "Informative? Yes."

"I sense a but. Be honest."

"It's just… there's some disconnect. It's monotonal, rigid, disjointed."

"Okay," Beatrice replied, bracing herself for more.

"The emotion is not coming across on the page. It feels soulless. Bring your barriers down, Bea, or this book is going to be worse than a wet weekend in Brighton. Pour your heart and soul into it and allow the emotion to tell the story. Tell the reader how things made you feel, how it affected your life, your relationships."

She meant Peter. The jury was out on how she would include him. She knew exactly what she wanted to say where he was concerned, but there was Xander to think of. She couldn't trash his father to the world as much as she desired to.

Alison continued. "You need to focus on getting those early years down; they're what made you who you are today."

"It's hard going back there," Beatrice replied, drawing her bottom lip in and biting at it.

"I know, Bea. How does Xander feel?"

"He seems indifferent. He already knows about most things, of course, from the absence of grandparents on my side. I'm undecided what to include about the status quo."

"Not to add pressure… I've got a publisher interested, the best. I started at the top, and that's where I ended. They want to release it in time for Christmas."

"Next Christmas?"

"No."

"What?" Beatrice replied, almost choking on her own saliva as her throat tightened.

"Someone on the schedule died and the family have pulled his autobiography for the time being, so the publishers have a spot they are eager to fill. They're offering a lot, Bea, *a lot*. I'll send the contract with the deadlines. This is the time to do it, and you *can* do it. We both know you'll struggle to find the time when you return to work. You need to get this done now."

Her schedule *was* looking hectic for the foreseeable future. Now that they were going to be six to eight weeks behind on the production of her current film, she would need to work the promotion of her latest film that was premiering before Christmas around it. It would be

Alison's problem to schedule a book launch into the mix too.

"I've begun the descent into the hell that was my childhood," Beatrice admitted, "and it's a mess of very scattered thoughts, anger, resentment, and tangents wild enough to lead you to Mount Doom. I'm an actress, not a writer, and it's bloody impossible balancing a laptop with your leg elevated."

"You're the control freak who insisted on writing this yourself. You'll have to find a way to make it work. Can't Sydney help you? She's a writer. Couldn't you talk and she type?"

"Is she?" Beatrice said, trying to keep the level of sarcasm in her voice to a minimum. "Why is she my PA then?"

"She has a degree in creative writing," Alison clarified. "It's on her CV. It says she writes in her spare time. Though I doubt she gets much of that working as a—"

"Send me a copy," Beatrice demanded, cutting her off.

"Of her CV? You've never asked to see one before. Why now?" Intrigue filled Alison's voice.

That was true. Her previous PAs certainly held no interest for her. Most of them were nothing but a hindrance.

"I'd like to see what it says, that's all," she replied as casually as she could. She was intrigued to discover more about this *competent* PA.

"I'll email it over. Why don't you send her what you've sent me? See what she makes of it. You never know, she could inject some creativity into it. Someone will have to, or it will be left in the hands of the publishers, and who knows what they will do to it. I've got to dash; I have a meeting with my most important client."

Beatrice was about to object, but Alison cut in with, "Only joking, you are all my most important client."

Beatrice hung up with a "Hmm."

A noise from the kitchen drew her attention. What on earth was Sydney doing? Her question was promptly answered when Sydney presented her with a glass of liquid pink.

"What is this? I didn't ask for anything."

"It's a nutrition shake. You need it to aid your recovery."

Beatrice eyed it. "What's in it?"

"The usual. Protein, vitamin D, calcium, zinc."

"Go easy on the protein; I don't need to be packing the pounds on."

"Your body will use it, not store it. Ten to twenty grams of protein a day can speed up the healing of a fracture."

So that was Sydney's plan — aid a swifter recovery so she could get away from her sooner. Forty-eight hours in and she was already planning her escape. When they first spoke, she'd mentioned she was only available for a short time. Did she have somewhere more important to be? Or someone more important to be with? The thought caught her unawares and left her with that familiar feeling that etched away at her soul. Loneliness.

Sydney took a step to return to her desk at the kitchen table.

"Wait. Sit," Beatrice ordered, placing her good leg on the floor to make room for Sydney, sucking in a breath as she did from the pain. She wasn't sure which leg hurt more, the broken one or the one working so much overtime she expected it to resign soon.

Sydney perched on the sofa. "Is your leg okay?"

"Nothing a rest — like the other leg is getting — won't fix."

"Here." Sydney beckoned her leg back onto the sofa.

Beatrice obeyed, then immediately retracted it when she realised Sydney was going to touch it. She hadn't washed properly in a week, and she shuddered to think of the forest-like growth on her leg.

Sydney put her hand out and stopped her, her eyes meeting her own with reassuring encouragement. "It's fine. Let me help."

Beatrice's leg was already being lifted onto the lap of her assistant; she was going to have to go with the flow on this. Sydney placed the bottom of the draping maxi dress over her leg. It must have been hideous if she couldn't bear to look at it. A pair of hands disappeared underneath it and she braced herself. Sydney's hands were soft and warm, bringing about immediate relief as her fingers worked Beatrice's aching muscles.

The feeling of being touched by another person after a lengthy period without contact was an immensely pleasurable experience. Though she wasn't one to instigate physical interaction, Beatrice found her body still craved it. She would occasionally receive a hug from Alison when she saw her, which was a rare occurrence of late.

"God, that feels very good."

Sydney smiled at her.

She groaned internally; she hadn't meant to say that aloud.

"Alison, my agent, tells me you're an" — she refrained from using the word 'aspiring' — "a writer."

"I guess I am an aspiring writer, yes."

Ha, her words, not mine.

"I'd like to see some of your work."

Sydney's hands paused on her leg, and her forehead twitched as they made eye contact. "Sure. May I ask why?"

She didn't want Sydney to stop. The massage hurt like hell yet felt so good at the same time. It was a much-needed release of the tension in muscles that had been asked to take extra weight and were twisted and pulled into awkward positions.

"I need help with a project I'm working on. You may be able to provide some assistance. First—"

Beatrice flinched and tensed as Sydney dug her thumb into a sore muscle.

"You'd like to judge—" Sydney began.

"Assess your capabilities." Beatrice's voice strained as she quickly finished her sentence, hopeful her answer would result in the clamped thumb retracting.

Sydney ruminated for a moment before finally releasing her thumb. "I'll email something over."

"I'll read it tonight. I could send you something too. I'd like your opinion on it."

"Okay."

"Very good. We can exchange thoughts tomorrow."

Sydney slipped herself from under Beatrice's leg, placing it back down onto the sofa. She tapped the toes that poked from the cast. "You need to wiggle these toes, and often."

Beatrice would pay Sydney to sit all day and massage her like that again. If only she didn't smell, that was; she must have repulsed the woman.

Initial impressions indicated there was no end to Sydney MacKenzie's talents. Beatrice prayed they reached as far as reworking thousands of soulless words.

CHAPTER 10

*S*ydney rummaged in a drawer full of swimwear. Surfacing some swimsuits she delved further, a hint of red caught her eye. She grabbed at it, relieved to have found a bikini top and bottom.

She exhaled, deflated; she would now have to see Beatrice wearing it. There was sure to be a different-coloured bikini somewhere in there. Her hand hesitated, finally deciding to shut the drawer. She was being ridiculous; she could assist her employer into a bath in a red bikini without having a lady crisis, couldn't she?

Pulling her thoughts from the gutter, she focused instead on the irritating personality and unrelenting demands of said employer. Like the three a.m. wake-up calls she'd received the last two nights when Beatrice clearly couldn't sleep. She'd given Sydney a task for the next day and then texted until she received an acknowledgement. It was easier to relent than to turn her phone off, which she expected would result in Beatrice dragging herself up a flight of stairs to her room to demand a response.

Sydney roused herself from her thoughts and made her way back through to the bedroom, where Beatrice was sipping at her cup of coffee in bed. She placed the bikini beside her.

"I do hope you don't expect me to wear that today," Beatrice said with a raised brow.

"I've bought you a waterproof cast protector. It's bath time."

Sydney watched with delight as Beatrice's face battled against the sheer joy of the thought. Constraint finally won out.

"I'm assuming you will need some help getting in and out of the tub, in which case a bikini is better than... nothing." Sydney gulped as she waited for a response.

Beatrice turned her attention back to her phone, and only once her eyes were fixed upon it did she reply.

"Very good."

Sydney nodded in satisfaction. "I'll run the bath whilst you change," she said before making a quick exit. She was relieved Beatrice was amenable to her suggestion. She had appeared uncomfortable when she massaged her leg the day before. Sydney had used her dress to cover the leg and save Beatrice from embarrassment — she feared she may be paranoid about the hair growth on her leg. Hairy legs were nothing to her, though; Sam had always kept a healthy growth.

The bathroom was yet another excessively sized space. A roll-top bath sat in front of the window overlooking the parkland. Sydney kept the bath shallow and with few bubbles so as not to risk getting the cast wet; she was unsure how well the waterproof cast protector would do its job. As she tested the temperature of the water, Beatrice made her entrance wrapped in a black silk robe, pushing the door open with a crutch.

"Where would you like me?"

Sydney stumbled over her answer until she realised Beatrice was referring to her placement for the cast protector to be put on.

"Can you perch on the toilet?"

As Beatrice placed herself on the toilet lid, her robe slipped to the sides, revealing her long, ivory legs. Sydney unwrapped the protector, placing it over the casted foot and up over her knee. Her hands smoothed out the tight neoprene seal against Beatrice's thigh, a little too efficiently as she begged her eyes not to wander.

"Are you done?" Beatrice asked.

"Yes," Sydney said, blushing as she stood. She must have stood up too fast.

Beatrice extended her hand. Sydney was about to take it when the woman barked, "Crutches."

Retrieving them from the floor, she returned to find the silk dressing gown dropping off Beatrice's shoulders, revealing her form in her red bikini.

Wow!

Trying not to look, yet realising she needed to pick the robe up off the floor as the woman stood, she well and truly got her eyeful. The woman was perfection, with smooth curves in all the right places.

Needing her mind back on business, Sydney opened her mouth to speak, then failed miserably to find words. "I suggest... don't submerge... drape your leg... over..." She stopped before she embarrassed herself completely, thankful Beatrice was too absorbed in the logistics of movement to notice her assistant's wandering eye.

With a crutch and Sydney's shoulder for assistance, Beatrice perched on the side of the bath and swung her good leg in, lowering herself into the water whilst keeping the cast elevated on the side of the tub. It was a challenge, one she hoped Beatrice wasn't going to insist on becoming a daily occurrence.

"I'll pop back in fifteen minutes?" Sydney suggested.

"No, stay. Sit," Beatrice demanded. "We have much to discuss."

The only options for sitting were the toilet seat or the floor; she opted for the toilet seat.

"Did you read what I sent you last night?"

"Most of it."

Beatrice eyeballed her. "And?"

As soon as she had begun reading Beatrice's work, she knew it would be best to get the woman's thoughts on her own offering first. Once she'd given her honest opinion to Beatrice on her work, she feared reprisal may come in the form of a dishonest attack on her own writing. Her novel was something she'd been working on for years and never shown to anyone else, so an unbiased opinion was important to her. No doubt Beatrice would pick holes in it anyway, even though Sydney considered it to be her finest work to date.

"You first. What did you think of what I sent?" Sydney asked.

What did she think?

How did she tell her assistant that she thought it was one of the most remarkable books she'd ever read — without giving her a big head? How did she admit it made her cry and feel emotions she thought were lost to her?

Her heart was torn from her chest when Sydney's character Skye lost her father overboard whilst working on his fishing vessel. Her description of how he was swept over the side during a storm, haunted not only by the image of it but the fear in his eyes in those final seconds, had truly overwhelmed Beatrice.

The way she had described her character's grief when no body was recovered and how she was left with nothing to bury and no closure, was mortifying. Skye lived in the hope of never finding his body yet knew she would live in limbo until it was found. She never gave up looking for her father; she'd search a crowd for his face in the hope of one day finding him. How anyone could move past an experience like that was beyond Beatrice. It was a wound unable to heal.

She was so drawn into the story it took her a while to realise it hadn't happened to her. It wasn't her story despite Sydney's skill to make the reader feel it was. It left Beatrice with unexpected envy for the love the character held for her father — something she'd been unable to feel herself. Skye was unable to grieve, and she had no father worthy of her grief.

"Well?" Sydney prompted.

"It was... quite remarkable? You're exceptionally

talented. I stayed up late reading it in fact and finished it this morning. Have you tried to find a publisher?"

"I'm not sure I'm ready for that. Writing exposes our fears and weaknesses to us; publishing exposes them to the rest of the world. Plus, I don't exactly have the time to scout around and beg for a random stranger's approval of me so I can give them a share of my royalties." Sydney shrugged. "Maybe I'll self-publish one day. I don't see why I should do all the work and have someone else reap the benefits."

"May I now ask what you thought of mine?" Beatrice said.

Sydney's pause would have given her cause for concern if Alison hadn't already been brutally honest.

"I thought it was cold, stagnant, and unengaging. The writing," Sydney was quick to clarify, "not your life. That's exciting, amazing... scary at times. I think we just need to inject some life into it; put some meat on the bones."

"*We?*"

"I assume that's why you asked me to read it."

"Indeed it was," Beatrice replied, a little annoyed and impressed that Sydney was always one step ahead of her.

"I've already made a start on the first few chapters. We'll need to sit down and go through parts I've marked — a lot of parts in fact."

Beatrice lifted her eyebrows at her diligent assistant before brushing a soapy sponge along her arms. A bath had never been so welcome.

"Just areas I think need improvement," Sydney continued. "I assume I would be free to embellish as necessary."

"You can embellish the writing, not the story. I don't wish to discover I once stripped for *GQ* Magazine."

A glare from Sydney reminded her that she was the least likely of anyone to furnish a story with lies.

"Do what you feel necessary. I can always choose to ignore it," Beatrice replied with a sharp lift of her cheeks. "Would you mind?" She gestured with the sponge to her back.

Sydney's hesitation reminded her of the previous day's leg massage. She'd offered to do it. Had it been done out of pity and ultimately repulsed her? Was she asking too much by requesting a back scrub?

Her assistant approached and took the sponge from her. Beatrice clung to the sides of the bath and leaned forward to clamp her leg down and allow Sydney access to her back. As her hair was swept to one side and the warm sponge lightly scratched her back, her whole body tingled; it was ecstasy. She hadn't had someone wash her back since Peter, and although they had separated well over a year ago, there had been no intimacy between them for a long time before that, let alone a back scrub. Just thinking about him now made her skin crawl.

"Would I get a writing credit?" Sydney asked, all business.

"I'm sure we can come to some arrangement."

"Great. Let me know where to sign."

"I'll get Alison to draft something up. I want you to start right away. In the meantime, I will continue my attempts to recall my childhood. I cannot emphasise enough the importance of speedy work on this. It's top priority; we're working against a tight deadline. It's going to squeeze the life out of us in the coming weeks if it's going to hit the shelves in time for Christmas."

"Christmas!"

The sponge stopped in the centre of her back, leaving Beatrice aching for more.

"*This* Christmas?" Sydney clarified.

"Indeed." Had she sounded this absurd when she had the same conversation with Alison?

"But isn't that impossible?"

"You would think. I have a contract that says otherwise. The publishers have a team on standby waiting for it. We just have to hit our deadline. We're not looking for a polished product, but it needs to be ninety-five percent there. I'm not leaving room for editors to mess with it. Leave me now but fetch me a razor from the cupboard."

There was battle to be done.

CHAPTER 11

*S*ydney let the two ladies from the florist's into the house as she left to collect Xander from the train station. Shooting back into the kitchen to let Beatrice know they'd arrived, she was met with —

"Chop chop or you'll be late."

Chop chop. Did that mean she had been downgraded from a click or upgraded?

She rolled her eyes as she crossed the entrance hall.

Why did I take this job again? I could be anywhere now, but no. I'm waiting on Beatrice fricking *Russell and her infernal clicking fingers.*

A check of Gertie before she entered the garage reminded her why she was doing it. She'd need to call Sam soon and check in with how his part sourcing was coming along. She sensed she'd need to give some notice to slip away with Gertie to the harbour. At least with Xander being around, there would be someone else to meet Beatrice's demands.

Unsure of how much luggage Xander would have and

with dry cleaning and groceries to pick up beforehand, she decided on the Mercedes. Driving it into town, she yawned continuously. Having spent most of the night reading more about Beatrice's lavish lifestyle, she believed she understood the woman a little better. Parts of her life weren't so lavish after all.

Early on there were wild parties, recreational drug and alcohol use. Alison, it seemed, had been her turning point. She brought her back from the brink; why she was on the brink, she didn't say. Even under the watchful eye of Alison, Beatrice wrote about being groped and propositioned by those higher up in the industry. Knowing it happened in Hollywood was one thing; knowing it had happened to Beatrice was shocking. Were experiences like that what made her so hard now?

Although the actress had been honest and frank in some places, Sydney sensed she was holding back in others. There was little said about recent events, and her family barely got a mention. What had led her to the wild parties, the drug and alcohol abuse? She'd need to find out what Beatrice wasn't saying if she was going to make this book compelling.

She had to pinch herself that she was helping write and edit a book that was anticipated to hit the top of the bestseller charts. All those years of work during a small amount of downtime, teaching herself and honing her craft, were finally paying off. Definitely another reason to stick around.

As she pulled into the station's car park, it struck her that she didn't have a clue what Xander looked like or how old he was. He was at school, she knew that much, and owned a phone, so she supposed somewhere between eight and sixteen. From the snippets of conversation she'd overheard with his mum, she would hazard a guess at early teens. He'd been old enough to interrogate her over the absence of his dad and Beatrice spoke to him like she would a young adult.

A train pulled into the station five minutes later. Sydney watched as a handful of people made their exit through the small Victorian station house into the car park. A young man in skinny black jeans and a white T-shirt emerged. He carried himself in the typical teenager way, with rounded shoulder and a hunch, looking down, distracted by something in his hands or ears; in this case, both.

He must have known the car as he sloped towards her. It was him all right. The resemblance to Beatrice was uncanny, although his hair was darker. He put his bag in the back and then, much to her astonishment, climbed in the front beside her.

"Xander, I take it?" she asked.

"Alex."

Alex? Beatrice's son was called Xander. She twigged the name connection of Alexander as he clarified.

"I go by Alex now. I prefer it."

"Ah, right. Fair enough."

"So, you must be this week's PA."

Sydney spat out a laugh; the kid was funny and smart.

A confused smile twitched at his lips as she laughed. She guessed it wasn't the reaction he was expecting.

"Yeah, I'm Syd. I'm here until your mum's leg heals and she can get back to the States."

"That will be a first; Mum leaving before the PA legs it. I bet you run first."

"I bet I don't."

"You're on." He held out his hand over the centre console. "Fifty quid?"

Sydney liked him already, though part of her couldn't help feeling a little sorry for Beatrice.

"I'm not sure either of us should be placing bets over how long I can tolerate your mum."

"I won't tell if you don't."

She shook his hand if only to satisfy him — which it did. What he hadn't accounted for was her love for a giant heap of metal. Or, in his mum's view, scrap metal.

Alex grappled with his belt as Sydney drove off.

"Why the name change then? Do you not like Xander?"

Alex slumped in his seat, his previous confidence melting away.

Sydney hesitated a guess. "Or do the other kids not like it?"

His silence spoke volumes.

"I was bullied at school, you know," Sydney recalled.

"Really?" He turned to face her. "Why?"

"Not sure. I wasn't different; I just wasn't like them."

Alex scrunched his face. "That is different."

"Well, yes. I wasn't *actually* any different. We were all kids finding our way in the world, dealing with insecurities; some of us were just dressed differently with different hairstyles. All kids are the same at the end of the day. It's natural for some to believe they are better than others. It doesn't stop when you grow up either; by then, though, you'll find you can get away from them more easily. Bullies are the most insecure of the lot and are often bullied themselves by someone at home or school."

"Really?" Alex ruminated on it and then changed the subject. "Is my dad still coming to get me on Saturday?"

"I believe so. I've not heard any different."

"I was supposed to be with him for the whole summer. Now Mum's home, I'm going to be stuck at Highwood." He exhaled a huff. "She ruins everything."

If Sydney was going to be stuck anywhere in the world, she could think of worse places to be. The thought occurred to her that it was being stuck with his mum that was more the issue.

Alex disappeared into his headphones until Sydney pulled the Mercedes up outside the front door of Highwood House. Beatrice was hobbling into the entrance hall to greet them as they entered.

"Xander, darling!" Beatrice said, her warm, kind voice back in place. "Come and give me a hug. I can't believe how much you've grown."

He put down his bag and approached Beatrice, then gave her the swiftest hug possible. With her hands on her crutches, Beatrice was unable to reciprocate. Her expression fell flat at the briefness and coldness of the hug.

"It's Alex now, Mum. Yeah. Even the dinner lady can remember."

"Sorry, darling. Habit. What's going on with your hair? Shall I get my hairdresser to cut it?"

"No," he said, self-consciously running a hand over the shaggy style. "I like it like this."

"Really, it looks like you picked a fight with a cat and lost. Are you hungry? Sydney can fix you something."

"I'm fine."

Beatrice shook her head and clicked her fingers. "Sydney—"

"Mum, I'm not hungry," Alex said, voice raised. "Stop fussing!"

The entrance hall fell into silence.

Beatrice's face twitched a little with what Sydney could only assume was embarrassment.

"Settle in, darling. We'll catch up over dinner." Beatrice turned her eyes to Sydney and deepened her voice. "Sydney, I believe we have much work to do."

How could she forget?

"Of course. Give me a minute to unpack the car and I'll be right with you."

Sydney had made a plan and was perfectly ready to execute it as she sat beside Beatrice, moving the coffee she'd made her to within reaching distance. She'd written a list of areas that needed attending to over the coming weeks, and she intended on starting with what she thought might be the rawest emotionally for Beatrice. If she was going to inject some emotional highs and lows into the book, she needed to make sure the actress was capable of emotion. First impressions suggested she wasn't, which would be why her writing lacked it.

"So, where would you like to start?" Beatrice asked once Sydney had touched the 'Record' button on her phone's app.

"#MeToo," Sydney said casually, looking up from her notepad to gauge the reaction to her request.

Beatrice remained silent for a moment before answering. "As you wish."

"You describe what happened to you… on several occasions. Too many occasions."

Their eyes met. Sydney's were sympathetic as she searched for some emotional response, but Beatrice withheld anything she could have shared behind an impenetrable stare.

Beatrice shrugged. "It happens."

"And it shouldn't. Not once do you acknowledge that. Did you not feel angry?"

"Beauty comes at a price. Everyone wants a piece of you."

Sydney gulped back her own guilt; it's not like she hadn't admired the woman's physical appearance in ways she shouldn't have. When she was asked to scrub her back in the bath, her mind and body battled. Before she knew it, she was running a warm, soapy sponge over Beatrice Russell's back.

"Why mention it at all if it didn't affect you? Which I don't believe for a second it didn't," she amended. "Isn't the point of an autobiography to capture all those notable events in your life, your career, and lay them bare?"

What was wrong with the woman? Did she feel nothing? Or was she so numb she just accepted it, blamed herself, and moved on?

With no response from Beatrice, she tried another angle, one that could seriously backfire.

"Was it a high point or a low point? Because you're not telling me in your writing."

"How dare you suggest—" The words were out, but then Beatrice clammed up again.

Her walls were coming down and her face knew it.

"How did you feel the first time it happened?" Sydney pushed, her patience growing thin. "For God's sake, give me something to work with!"

Beatrice's face twisted. It was such a terrifying sight that Sydney sucked in a breath.

"You want to know what I was feeling the first time someone cornered me in my dressing room and shoved his tongue down my throat whilst he copped a feel of my tits?" Beatrice bellowed. "I was scared, terrified, shaken to my fucking core. I feel guilt and shame to this day that I did nothing back then. I didn't stand up and call those men out or prevent others from experiencing what I did. Have you ever thought why all those women never said anything? We didn't think anyone would have listened, and you know what? They wouldn't have."

Beatrice stopped for a breath and immediately started up again, though a little calmer.

"It's easy to question other people's behaviour in the past if you've not experienced what they have. Not had a director slip his hand up your skirt for a grope when you've never had anyone touch you like that before. You freeze, Sydney. You blame yourself. Ask yourself if you did something, said something to encourage him to do it. Back then I had nothing; I was desperate for work. Yes, I'd been a child star..."

What?

The look of surprise that washed over her face wasn't missed by Beatrice.

"I take it you didn't know that about me either. I suppose I should be pleased. At least you are looking at this from a clean angle; it does you credit. I had a part in a long-running series from the mid-seventies to early eighties, followed by several successful movies throughout my teen years. I worked under my real name back then. When I reached eighteen, I needed a fresh start."

"A new beginning," Sydney said, recalling the name of the first chapter she'd read.

Beatrice looked across to Sydney, the smallest hint of a smile flexed her lip. "Yes."

Sydney paused the recording on her phone. "That's more like it. I think we're in business."

"I can't believe I let a woman I've known hardly a week record all that," Beatrice muttered, her jaw clenching a little.

"Yes, is that okay?" Sydney fussed with the edges of her phone case. "It's going to prove useful — in a responsible way, I promise."

Beatrice nodded, her expression jaded. She'd given her everything — the disgust, the fear, the guilt, and some of the weight.

All Sydney wanted to do was give her a hug and tell her how sorry she was that she had gone through that.

Fuck it.

Although a hug wouldn't be welcome, the least she could do was show the woman some kindness.

"I'm sorry that happened to you," she offered up.

Beatrice responded with another shrug. "As I said, it

happens. It will always happen. Men are like fires; you hose one down and another pops up."

"A nightmarish game of Whack-A-Mole," Sydney suggested.

"Indeed," Beatrice replied with a roll of her eyes.

The question remained: What happened to Beatrice Russell as a child to have the need for a new beginning when she became an adult?

Temptation gnawed at her to google Beatrice; her integrity ignored it. She would know soon enough, when Beatrice finished vomiting her childhood into her laptop for Sydney to make legible. The strangest thing was, she didn't even know the woman's real name.

When Sydney reappeared late that afternoon to start dinner, she descended the stairs to the mouthwatering aroma of roast chicken. Alex was busily preparing something as she entered the kitchen; a peek over his shoulder revealed a potato salad in the making.

"I was coming down to make something," she said. "You've beaten me to it."

The teenager flinched. "Sorry."

"Don't be. It's nice to have someone else cook, and this looks and smells amazing."

"I can do it every night... until I go to Dad's, I mean."

"If you're sure."

Alex nodded, seemingly eager to help. "I'll need a few things, though."

"Write me a list and I'll make sure they get added when I do the next order."

Alex volunteering to make dinner for the next week was very welcome news to Sydney. It would free her up to get more work done or may even allow for a brief afternoon nap like the one she'd just enjoyed. It increased her productivity late into the evening.

A glance over at the sofa brought a smile to her face. Beatrice glared at her laptop through her glasses; it was nice to see her death stare wasn't reserved solely for humans.

With Alex's dinner served, Sydney intended to skulk off to devour her delicious plateful of food and afford the mother and son some privacy, but Beatrice called out in a smoky voice, "Sydney… aren't you joining us?"

Her eyebrows sprang up. "Sure." She took her usual seat with a smile.

"This is really good, Alex," she added after her first mouthful.

"Thanks. I want to be a chef one day."

"Oh, are you still on that?" Beatrice groaned. "You could be anything you want to be."

"And I will be. A chef."

Beatrice pulled a face like she'd sucked a lemon. Sydney knew better than to get involved in a disagreement between mother and son. She struggled to contain a smile at Beatrice's disgust at his ambition.

"Are you seeing any of your friends over the holidays?" Beatrice asked, changing the subject.

"No, they are all off to their holiday homes with their *families*."

Ouch, the kid really knew how to kick his mum metaphorically.

Beatrice remained quiet for the rest of the meal, leaving Sydney and Alex to discuss his favourite subjects at school and his passion for hockey and cooking. He revealed — much to Beatrice's further disgust — that when he finished school, he intended on going to culinary school in Paris. He was twitching with excitement as he announced he'd set up a cooking club at school, which was now catering some of the school events.

Sydney made sure to encourage and congratulate him enough to cover for the lack of enthusiasm from his mum. She could see why Beatrice had asked her to join them — so she could hold the conversation with Alex and not her. Did the woman not know how to talk to her own son?

Once their plates were empty, Sydney cleared them and began packing the dishwasher as Beatrice and Alex attempted to converse.

"Don't mention the autobiography to your father when he comes, please," Beatrice said. "I'll tell him when I'm ready."

"Okay."

"Oh, and... you should know that George died. Some weeks ago apparently."

Alex nodded.

Who was George? From their faces, the person didn't seem to be anyone important. If it was weeks ago and Beatrice was casually mentioning it after dinner, how could they be?

"Ali went to the funeral."

Alex nodded again.

So they were important enough that Beatrice's agent went to the funeral instead of Beatrice and Alex.

Mother and son fell into silence as they each dove into their phone. Not ready to return to work, Sydney suggested they play a board game.

"We've got Monopoly," Alex suggested. "Dad and I used to play it."

"Great! One of my all-time favourites. Prepare to be thrashed. Beatrice, will you join us?"

"Mum doesn't play board games," Alex replied, resting his chin on his fist.

"What? Not ever?" Sydney chuckled. "Come on, Beatrice. Play with us."

"No!" Beatrice snapped before emphasising, "I don't play board games."

Sydney flinched as Alex shot her a look that said loud and clear, *I told you so.*

CHAPTER 12

*a*n early start the next day resulted in Sydney yawning by eleven thirty. An early lunch break was in order. She'd relocated herself to the hexagonal turret room for the last few days. It afforded a cool breeze and a haven away from Beatrice and her infernal clicking fingers.

It was Beatrice's suggestion that Sydney should work on the autobiography where she could concentrate. She hadn't realised at the time that the clicking-finger demands would come via an endless series of text messages instead. She politely told Beatrice that to help her focus she would keep her phone off and, as Alex was around, perhaps her son could assist her instead.

The household had fallen into a rhythm since his arrival. Sydney would wake early and work for a few hours, checking through the previous day's work before sending it to Beatrice. Then she would begin on the next section until she woke Beatrice and spent some time with her either in the kitchen or in her bedroom, talking through areas of the book for which she required more information. They would then discuss what she had already worked on, and Beatrice would either approve it or make further changes.

Sydney would take an hour off at lunchtime and either go for a walk around the grounds or swim. Beatrice would often fall asleep in the afternoons, the urge coming from the high-calorie lunch Sydney was feeding her under Rosie's guiding text messages. She took Beatrice's afternoon naps as an opportunity to have another break, either to spend time with Alex, who was usually lounging around the pool, or to have a snooze herself. She would then work for another few hours before dinner. Working intense twelve-hour days it was a relief not to cook, and Alex was proving to be a talented chef.

As she arrived on the first floor and passed Beatrice's bedroom, she heard a voice.

"Sydney."

She popped her head around Beatrice's open door.

"I need you to drive us into town. Xander — sorry, Alex — needs a new wardrobe."

Alex dropped his shoulders and rolled his eyes.

"Why can't I go on my own? You can't even walk."

"Do you want me to take him?" Sydney suggested.

Alex pressed his palms together. "Please, Mum."

Beatrice answered after some consideration. "Very well."

"Yesss!" Alex hissed as he headed for the door, flashing a smile of gratitude at Sydney as he passed her on the way out.

"Is there a budget?" Sydney asked.

"No."

That sounded about right. It was typical in her experience that the only restraint rich people forced on their children was the amount of time they spent with them.

"Do keep in mind, though, how many clothes a teen requires when he spends most of his time in school uniform."

"I'll take Gertie if that's okay?" Sydney said. "I need to keep her ticking over."

"If you'd prefer to be seen in that rabbit hutch than in one of the luxury vehicles at your disposal, so be it. Whilst you're out, get his hair attended to."

"I'll try."

"Do more than try, Sydney. Succeed!"

Sydney wasn't convinced forcing a teenager to get his hair cut was within her skillset — or anyone's skillset for that matter.

Alex exited through the front door of the house in what Sydney assumed was his signature skinny black jeans and a tight, white T-shirt. He stopped and stared at Gertie. A smile crossed his lips as he took her all in.

"Is this yours?" he asked, approaching the driver's window.

"Yep, this is Gertie. She needs a run, and I thought you might like to meet her."

"She's sick." Alex jogged around to the passenger side

and jumped in. "This is so cool! Can I look in the back later?"

"Sure," Sydney replied as she coaxed Gertie over the gravel and down the drive.

"Thanks for taking me. I couldn't face Mum coming."

"It would be difficult with a broken leg."

"It's not the leg as much as her getting spotted. Then she gets swamped. Unless Jonathon's around; no one dares mess with him."

"It must be difficult not being able to do normal things with your mum, like go to the cinema, eat out."

Alex shrugged. "It's something I've got used to."

She'd hear the same story from her client's children wherever she went. It was the price of stardom that wasn't quite appreciated by the parents. Sadly, the children of celebrities would never lead a normal life. They couldn't go down the road and play with friends at the park, run out to the ice cream van in the summer, or pop to the sweetshop around the corner, working out the greatest number of sweets they could buy with a pound coin.

"Mum would never let me buy the clothes I want," Alex added, still on his 'celebrating my afternoon of freedom' kick. "She always prefers that I wear a certain style."

"She's not here," Sydney observed. "If she wants to see what you've bought, you can always separate out what she won't approve of."

Alex grinned at the potential deceit.

"When I was a little girl, my mum always put me in dresses," she commiserated as the shade from the wood they entered offered relief from the sun, "and I hated it.

120

You won't catch me in a dress now. I prefer the plain image of men's clothes; it's a shame it's all too big for me or I'd wear it myself. I don't understand why they think we women want something put onto everything. I'm not a sequin girl, and I don't want a cat or a bee on my jumper."

Alex laughed. "Agreed. You must admit that women get much nicer-fitting clothes, though. It's all so well styled. I buy a size down in men's now."

"I say wear what makes you feel comfortable. Life is too short to be a follower of fashion."

"Don't let Mum hear you say that!"

Sydney curled her top lip. "Good point."

Alex turned to her. "You're not like the other PAs, always brown-nosing Mum. Why do you do so much for her, no matter what she does or how she treats you?"

"It's my job."

"No one else could put up with her."

"Then it doesn't sound like they were particularly good at their job. Or perhaps I have a little more patience and understanding than others." She didn't believe the latter, but she could hardly say, *Your mum is pushing me to the very edge of my limits, and I'm sticking around because she's hot and it turns out she could potentially break open my career.*

Alex peered over his shoulder as they waited for the electric gate to open. "Do you sleep in here?"

"When I'm on the road, yes, which is rare at the moment."

Alex's eyes sparkled at the thought. "I'd love to have something like this I could drive off in and go anywhere."

"The freedom is exhilarating, I must admit, though I

think I would have enjoyed boarding school. You must get a real sense of belonging there."

"Only if you fit in, and you wouldn't enjoy it if you'd been there since you were seven because your mum was too busy with her job to look after you. Mum's career always came first. As soon as I was old enough, she put me in boarding school. Then she drove Dad away, and now I have three homes I'm passed between."

Her heart went out to him; Alex had a lot of deep-rooted issues with his mum. What kid wanted to spend his childhood being passed between parents? Especially when neither party showed much interest in him.

"Are you helping her with her book?" he asked when Sydney remained silent.

"I am. Mainly editing," she replied. "How do you feel about it?"

Alex stared out the passenger window and sighed. "It's going to make everything worse."

Everything. She remembered when everything was *everything*. It was tough growing up.

"I'm sure if you ask her not to publish it, she won't."

Alex turned to Sydney with his eyebrows raised. "You haven't tried saying no to my mum yet then."

That was a true statement.

"Do you know what it will contain?" she asked diplomatically.

"She's told me everything."

Sydney didn't believe that for a second. There was a lot Beatrice wasn't even saying in the book, and it was unlikely she'd told Alex anything beyond the basics. It wasn't what happened to someone that made a story; the story came from how it affected those involved, how they dealt with it or ultimately didn't. The latter she knew too well from her own experience.

She'd read the odd celebrity autobiography of people she'd worked for, once she'd left their employment, and knew they rarely laid everything bare. They gave enough to make it feel believable, a selection of perfectly curated stories from their lives, while keeping the dirty laundry well behind closed doors. She would do what she could to ensure Beatrice's was as authentic as possible without crossing boundaries that couldn't be un-crossed.

"Alex, can I ask who George was?" she asked as she found a parking spot. "I heard your mum say he'd died."

"My grandfather," he explained.

"Oh. I'm sorry." She questioned her surprise at his answer. Had they not displayed enough grief in front of her for her to have thought it was someone close? What was enough grief? What was too much? She pushed the last thought away.

Alex shrugged. "I never met him or my grandmother. Mum hadn't seen them since she was eighteen."

Intrigued, yet aware she'd already been nosey enough, she refrained from asking more. The last thing she wanted was for him to mention to Beatrice that she'd been asking about their family.

As she cut the ignition, she said, "So, this haircut."

"Not happening," Alex answered, folding his arms.

"Fair enough."

She'd tried.

CHAPTER 13

*B*eatrice adjusted the cushion under her leg and re-seated her cast against it more comfortably. She was beyond sick of the irritating, itchy cast, though it wasn't the only thing causing irritability. Constant waking in the night was leading to afternoon naps, which led to sleepless nights; a vicious cycle she couldn't seem to pull herself out of. Her whole body was irritable; some muscles hurt from overuse whilst others ached from lack of use.

The hopping, scooting, pulling, hoisting, and need for excessive amounts of patience were all getting old. Incredibly old. After three weeks it was weighing on her, the burden getting heavier that she could feel her mind becoming vulnerable. The pain itself was easing and controllable. The hindrance of the cast was neither.

Mrs Clarkson had rung earlier to say her daughter has been admitted to hospital and that she would be unable to work. With Alex taking on the cooking that week, they had coped without her. Sydney had kept up with the laundry and managed light housework between writing stints. It was now Saturday, though, and with Alex due to be picked up by his father, Beatrice dreaded telling Sydney that she'd soon be back to cooking for the two of them.

Sydney had spent the last few days in the turret, ploughing through her work. Her absence at the kitchen table was noticeable; the woman was good company and Beatrice missed every moment of it. She relocated herself to her bedroom, where she would feel it less and where it was cooler. There she worked from either the bed or her sofa, or occasionally ventured outside into the sun.

If Sydney's absence made afternoons and evenings miserable, mornings were something to look forward to. Sydney would appear, and they would spend an hour or so discussing sections of Beatrice's adult life that her PA would be editing or even rewriting entirely that day. With Alex leaving later that afternoon, it was going to be a miserable, lonely week. Could she demand Sydney's return to the kitchen table? For the company, of course.

The whiteness of her laptop screen mocked her inability to continue summarising the first eighteen years of her life. Maybe she had a mental block from the trauma; she'd never considered that before. Self-preservation at work. Her lack of focus for the last hour, however, was due to the noise coming from Sydney and Alex in the pool. The last time she'd poked her head out onto the balcony, she'd heard them arguing about who was the better swimmer.

Alison's name flashed up on her mobile, reminding her she hadn't taken it off silent following her nap. The distraction from her distractions was welcome.

"I've just finished reading the latest draft. I'm

impressed, Bea. Bloody impressed. She's worked miracles."

"Indeed she has," Beatrice replied. It was undeniable that Sydney had injected life into her life. "I hope she'll finish by the end of next week so we can move on to my childhood."

"How's Xander?"

"It's Alex now, apparently. I'm not sure what was wrong with Xander."

"Oh! Okay. I'll have to remember that when I write his birthday card."

"Peter will be here later to collect him, and he'll spend the week with him."

"Where's he living now?"

"Some flat on the outskirts of London," Beatrice replied, wiping a speck of something off her laptop screen.

"Don't let the arsehole get to you."

"I'll try not to."

"And if he tries to discuss the divorce settlement, tell him to contact your solicitor."

"Mm-hmm." Whether Peter would listen was another thing.

"Okay, I'll see you on Monday at the audition."

A laugh alerted her that Sydney was still outside, no doubt enjoying herself when there was work to be done. What on earth did her PA and her son have in common that they could spend so much time discussing? It was time to find out.

She hung up the phone and made her way through the balcony doors, ensuring the crutches didn't make any noise that would expose her. Sydney was directly below her, wearing a black bikini, her legs dangling in the water. Alex sat partially submerged on the steps beside her.

"I've told you my school nickname. Now you tell me yours," Sydney said, pushing a wave of water toward him with her foot.

Damn, a minute earlier and she would have heard Sydney's nickname. *That* she would have liked to know.

"Nancy," Alex uttered.

The name ripped through Beatrice. It was a name she knew well.

Sydney frowned. "Why is Nancy your nickname?"

"My mum was in a lesbian film. Nancy was the name of her character."

"Oh," Sydney replied, scrunching her face.

"All the boys have watched it at school, for obvious reasons, and my mum was topless in it. It's been described to me so many times that I feel like I've watched it."

That answered a question Beatrice had long been harbouring as to whether Alex had watched the film. Although hardly sexually explicit, there were scenes in it that would have made anyone uncomfortable watching their mum perform. A bit like Sydney's face was now. If she thought a lesbian film was disgusting, she'd be horrified if she knew the truth about her employer.

Alex stood and made his way up the steps. "I'm getting a drink, Syd. Want one?"

Syd. How could two people who'd only known each other for a week be so familiar?

"No. I'm good, thanks," Sydney replied as Alex disappeared into the kitchen below, still sporting his unkempt hairstyle.

For someone who appeared competent in many respects, Sydney failed in the basic task of ushering a child into a barber. Beatrice didn't even want to know what clothes he'd bought, they would no doubt be unfit for purpose.

She couldn't prevent her eyes from wandering as Sydney leaned backwards and closed her eyes, soaking in the sun. Her body was well toned with a flat stomach, shapely hips, and long legs lightly tanned. By the time her gaze worked its way back up as far as Sydney's perfectly proportioned breasts, she realised Sydney was staring back at her. She sucked in a breath.

"You are neglecting your duties, Sydney," she said once she regained her train of thought.

"I'm on a break."

"Well, your break is over," Beatrice replied firmly.

"A break from writing. Ever heard of burnout?"

"Then you can assist me with a bath. If it's not too much trouble."

It was time for her assistant to refocus her attentions where they were needed.

Emerging five minutes later from her dressing room in a bikini, she could hear the bath already running. Her obedient assistant was leaning over it, testing the temperature with her hand. Although she'd thought to cover her bikini with a T-shirt, she hadn't thought about how far it would cover — or wouldn't in this case. She averted her eyes as Sydney pulled herself upright.

"Sit." Sydney pointed at the toilet as she fetched the cast cover from where it was resting on the radiator.

Beatrice complied. "You are taking a keen interest in my son."

"Someone needs to."

Beatrice could see the regret in Sydney's eyes as soon as she spoke the words.

"What does that mean? Are you suggesting I'm neglecting him?"

"I'm suggesting it can get quite lonely up here, and you are indisposed," Sydney quickly added, looking up from her crouching position in front of the cast.

"I am only too aware of both of those facts, Sydney," Beatrice said, more sharply than she'd intended.

Out of all her PAs, she needed this one, and she was growing fond of her, even though it was too late now to be trying to form a friendship.

"Mrs Clarkson called," she said. "She won't be coming to assist us after all."

"Oh."

She tried to gauge the meaning behind that *Oh*, but Sydney was frustratingly sphinx-like.

"Yes. Her daughter was admitted to hospital last night with a pulmonary embolism, so she's needed to help take care of the baby. It is very inconvenient yet... necessary. We'll have to find a way to soldier on without her. With Alex away this week, I'll be relying on you to cook until he returns. Will that be acceptable?"

Sydney remained silent for a moment as she smoothed out the cover around Beatrice's thigh.

"I would rather not bring a stranger into the house," she added.

"Okay," Sydney finally said.

She searched Sydney's face for any sign of anger; there was none. Did the woman not mind resuming her cooking responsibilities?

"My agent is impressed with your work, by the way. Extremely impressed. You'll meet her Monday when I go for an audition in London; she'll be joining me for lunch afterwards, so book the Ritz. Oh, that reminds me; the Rolls will need a clean."

CHAPTER 14

$\mathcal{T}$he hose pipe vibrated in Sydney's hand as the line of soapy water neared the top of the bucket. She turned it off and stuffed her hand into the woollen wash mitten before plunging it into the bucket of lukewarm water. With the blistering sun on her bare back, the car would have to forgo a hot wash. She held no objection to washing cars; it was therapeutic, and she did love Beatrice's vehicles.

When Beatrice informed her that the housekeeper wouldn't be coming, Sydney had expected to find herself objecting to taking on more tasks. Yet she hadn't; she'd simply agreed. Was she enjoying caring for Beatrice more than she realised?

Although the woman displayed an inability to express her thanks verbally, she could feel some sense of gratitude from her, whether Beatrice knew she was exuding it or not. This didn't mean she wouldn't appreciate the occasional thank-you from her — if only to make the point that the woman could show some verbal appreciation. The extra housekeeping chores were manageable so far. Alex wasn't a typical teenager. He cleaned up after himself, particularly in the kitchen, and did his own laundry. She would be counting the days to his return.

The Rolls was far from dirty, but she'd still feel a sense of satisfaction that within the hour she would have achieved something tangible, something she could look at and know she'd completed. It was so unlike the long work in progress that was editing. Her brain was desperate for a break from writing — or rewriting in this case. It was fuzzy and foggy and rarely performed well under those conditions.

She'd extracted about ten career-turning moments that led Beatrice to her current position on the world acting stage. This then led Sydney down a rabbit hole of restructuring entire chapters to create more of a story arc, including some emotional response to those moments and the setbacks Beatrice had experienced along the way.

She was looking forward to more downtime that evening, when she planned to escape for a drink with Rosie, who was back from her honeymoon. She was due a night off, but whether Beatrice would agree or not was another matter. The woman could surely cope for a few hours without her — even a puppy could manage that.

She rubbed the wash mitten over the bonnet of the Rolls, covering it in a thick soap. Her mind drifted to the thought of Beatrice in a lesbian film — she'd have to avoid that. She was struggling enough as it was. Her body was very much pointing at Beatrice and waving at her, wondering if the communication system between them was broken and why her brain was ignoring its signals. It was totally unaware of who Beatrice was and every reason that nothing could ever happen. She wasn't sure how many more baths — let alone topless lesbian scenes — she could handle.

It filled her with pride, though, that Alex was comfortable telling her about his nickname. Her blood boiled to think his peers were bullying him about it. So what if his actress mother played a lesbian role? It didn't make her a lesbian, and it wouldn't matter if she was. Kids were cruel; cruel and stupid.

Her mind wandered as she reached further up the bonnet, imagining that Beatrice liked women, one woman in particular — her. She imagined Beatrice using her slow, low-pitched voice to call her into her bedroom as she passed, *Sydney. Come here.* She'd turn to see Beatrice in her red silk slip, beckoning her with a demanding finger, a finger that couldn't and wouldn't be disobeyed. As she entered, the finger turned its attentions to the straps on her red slip, teasing them from her own shoulders and dropping it to the floor to reveal…

"Oh, God." Sydney groaned.

A wolf whistle from beside her yanked her from finishing her train of thought. *Damn it.* She pulled herself upright to find her denim shorts and bikini top covered in foam.

A man stood in the driveway behind her watching, a grin slapped across his face. "Sorry, didn't mean to interrupt… whatever it was you were doing there. Carry on, don't mind me."

Sydney brushed the foam off herself and paused the music on her phone. What did he think she'd been doing?

She'd only been reaching up the bonnet whilst gyrating a little to the music and avoiding catching her groin on the gold Spirit of Ecstasy. This was one sick man if he'd put all that together and come up with what she thought he'd come up with.

The skinny, dark-haired man in his fifties, sporting a five o'clock shadow, was without a doubt, Peter. A dark blue BMW sat further down the drive. She must have been so distracted she hadn't heard it pull up or even the footsteps across the gravel as he approached. Not that she'd put it past Beatrice's ex to creep his way across the driveway to enjoy whatever it was he found so enjoyable.

Alex opened the side garden gate that led along to the pool, full of enthusiasm.

"Hey, Dad! I've just had a swim. Give me ten minutes and I'll be ready to go."

"No worries, dude."

Alex retraced his steps, his head down. Something had suddenly rattled him; Sydney had noticed the same thing when he'd greeted his mum the first time.

The smell of rank smoke wafted under her nose. She turned to find Peter sucking on a cigarette a few feet from where she stood.

"Do you mind?" she asked. "It's hard enough cleaning this barge-size car without suffocating on your second-hand smoke."

Peter stepped back. "The view's better from here anyway."

Seriously?

Once she'd rinsed the car off, she noticed Peter, whom she'd made a point of completely ignoring, had disappeared. Raised voices from Beatrice's bedroom balcony told her where he'd relocated.

Alex came down the path then, carrying his bag. Sydney watched him as he put it down and held his phone in front of him. His eyes were elsewhere, his concentration fixed on the screaming match between his parents. Why adults argued within earshot of their kids, she'd never know; it was so damaging. Every relationship within this family was toxic. It was hard for Sydney to swallow, coming as she did from a loving family that would have done anything to be together now.

Alex took out some AirPods and inserted them into his ears, glancing up at her as he sought to drown out the voices with more pleasant ones. She offered him a sympathetic smile, which fell flat in mid-air. There was no sugar-coating this kind of behaviour.

Sydney turned her attentions back to the Rolls and towelled down its paintwork with one eye on Alex. Peter materialised a few moments later with a smirk slapped on his face. He ruffled Alex's hair as he passed and picked up his bag. Alex ducked and pulled out his AirPods.

"Mum says we're to get your hair cut."

"I'm not getting my hair cut." Alex smoothed his hair back down and tucked it behind his ears.

"Okay, dude. No skin off my nose," Peter replied, placing the bag in the boot.

"Stop calling me that," Alex grunted as he opened the passenger door. He looked back at Sydney, dejected.

He was a troubled soul. A soul she was going to miss. She watched as they drove off, completely bewildered by what Beatrice had ever seen in Peter.

CHAPTER 15

*G*lass knocked together as Beatrice fumbled in her bedroom drinks cabinet for a bottle of... anything alcoholic. Her heart was pumping so fast from fury that her head was spinning.

"That fucking arsehole of a man."

She ripped at the cork of a bottle of whisky with her teeth, desperate for the taste of it to touch her lips and burn down her throat to soothe her. Burn it did, as much as the regret she held for telling Peter all those years ago how she really felt, how she'd felt for a long time. It was a careless slip when she'd wanted to hurt him. Now he was holding it over her, using it to squeeze everything out of her in their divorce.

Nancy hadn't exactly been an awakening, more a point of no return. Following the events of two years ago, when she'd played a character falling in love with another woman, she could no longer deny it to herself: she was as attracted to women as she was men — maybe more so.

She'd never jelled with any other character as much as Nancy.

In the film, Nancy had lost her husband in the Vietnam War and befriended the wife of her husband's fellow fallen soldier. As the two characters fell in love, Beatrice had been consumed by envy — in a strange way. Peter was like a chain around her neck at that point, and she would have done anything to have stayed in character and carried on living in the sixties with Sarah, the co-star playing her love interest, Alice. Sarah was someone she let her guard down around and was even beginning to consider a friend, even if she was secretly feeling something much deeper for her. Beatrice knew she would need to be careful not to make that mistake again.

Each day she returned to her trailer to find Peter there, doing whatever it was Peter did. She didn't see him as her husband any longer, he was a reminder of her unhappy existence and a marriage she held together for the sake of her son. She hadn't wished for Alex to grow up in a broken household like some of his friends at boarding school. That was, until the day she returned to her trailer to find Peter five and a half inches inside Sarah. That was finally enough to call time. She'd found the betrayal from Sarah harder to take than from Peter. She knew what he was like.

Now he'd heard about the autobiography, he believed he was due more in his settlement. He was refusing to sign the latest documents, wanting to hold off until after the book was published to gauge its success and how much extra he might be due.

Another mouthful of whisky hit the back of her throat,

burning her senses and relaxing her muscles as it took hold. Re-corking the bottle, she manoeuvred her way over to the sofa with one crutch, dropping the bottle onto it and returning for a glass. Frustration was biting at her. She would never take such simple tasks for granted once she could walk again.

Sydney marched through the partially open door without knocking, her expression riddled with disgust. "You do realise Alex was listening to you two arguing."

"Is this where you accuse me of neglecting him again?" Beatrice bit back as she lowered herself onto the sofa.

A loud sigh came from her assistant as she stepped into the room. "I'm not your enemy, Beatrice; you don't need to be confrontational. You may be rich and famous, but that doesn't give you the right to treat other people badly. It places more responsibility on you to set a good example. You should know that. You've experienced first-hand other people's bad behaviour; I'm surprised you accept it from yourself."

"Are you seriously comparing my behaviour to that of my abusers?"

The colour drained from Sydney's face as she stumbled for an answer. "Not the nature of the behaviour obviously; the intent behind it to put people down."

"You believe me to be on a power trip, is that it? You've read about my life, and now you think you know me?"

"No, clearly I don't. Your dad died and you tell your son like he was some passing acquaintance. Who does that?"

"Don't you dare bring my father into this," Beatrice growled through her teeth. "You have no idea."

"No, because you won't tell me! I'm supposed to be writing about your *privileged* life, yet half of it remains a mystery."

"Are you quite done?" Beatrice snapped to shut Sydney down.

"No, whilst I'm at it, would it hurt you to say please or thank you occasionally? Oh, and you can stop clicking your damn fingers. I'm not a dog. You already have *all* my attention."

Sydney turned and left the room, leaving Beatrice to regain her breath and ponder the meaning of *You already have all* my *attention*. Was Sydney suggesting she was sucking the life out of her?

Within half an hour, Sydney reappeared in the doorway. Beatrice assumed she'd come to apologise until a second glance revealed Sydney to be wearing a pair of tight, dark blue jeans, a crisp white shirt, and a light blue blazer. Her hair held an attractive loose curl to it. She was Sydney quite transformed. It took her a moment to peel her eyes away and remember she was mad at the woman.

"I'm going out," Sydney said.

"What? You can't," Beatrice snapped.

"I can. You buy some of my time, not all. I've been working tirelessly for you and your deadline. I'm owed at least one evening off."

"We need to work."

"You're in no position to work. You shouldn't even be drinking in your condition. Your body needs to heal, not drown in a…" Sydney picked the bottle up from the table, her eyebrows shooting up as she read the label. "…four-hundred-pound bottle of Talisker 25?"

"I've earned the right to drown myself in anything I wish to, thank you! Without question from anyone," Beatrice replied curtly, grasping the bottle from Sydney. "And you can't go. What if I need something?"

Sydney picked up the crutches from the floor and placed them beside her, a little too firmly. "Try these! Because I'm sure as hell not going to sit here all night and watch you wallow in self-pity. There's leftover lasagne in the fridge; I'm sure even you can manage to reheat it without killing yourself."

"Go on then, leave me, like they all do!" Beatrice could feel her voice breaking and hoped it wasn't noticeable over the sound of the rain pounding against the windows.

Sydney turned, her face washed a deep pink. "Don't be so dramatic, I'll be back. And have you ever considered that they don't leave, you drive them away?"

The parting remark cut so deep she bit back, yelling after her, "You might as well not come back. I thought you were different, but I was wrong. You're just like all the others."

Within a second Sydney reappeared in the doorway, making Beatrice jump, fearful of reprisal. What if the woman took her up on it?

"Don't use the crutches on the stairs, will you? It's not safe."

Her softened tone took Beatrice by surprise.

She was gone again in a flash, taking the last word with her. In a moment of fury, Beatrice pushed the crutches across the floor, only to realise she was going to have to get them.

"Bloody leg." A tickle on her cheek alerted her to a tear

running down it. She wiped it with the back of her hand, hopeful Sydney hadn't noticed her moistened eyes.

A thunderclap outside made her reach for the blanket on the back of the sofa despite the humidity in the room.

What was it with assistants? Was Sydney not in fact worse than the others? She'd failed to bond with any of them, but at least they had had the decency to leave quietly. Sydney well and truly aired her issues to her face. Was Sydney right? Did she really drive them away with her direct manner and endless demands? What did she do differently from her peers? Did they make friends at the risk of leaving themselves vulnerable to people who wanted to take advantage?

As for Sydney's charges regarding gratitude, had she not said thank you on many occasions? She could recall several times she'd said *very good*. Was that not gratitude? Did the words have to be spoken for them to be understood? The bottle of Talisker found its way to her mouth again, despite the fact Beatrice knew no answers lay at the bottom of it.

CHAPTER 16

*M*ore anger than rainwater was dripping from Sydney as she entered the pub. She was going to need a drink herself following her heated conversation with Beatrice. Everything she said had needed saying, but it didn't feel good to get it out. Beatrice's glistening eyes were at least a good sign that she had taken something from her words. Beatrice's last comment, that she had thought Sydney was better than the others, sat with her on her journey. The disappointment in her employer's voice played over in her mind.

Rosie welcomed her at their table with a warm hug and a source of distraction.

"Sorry about the cat," Sydney said as she pulled away and took her seat.

"It's fine, plans change. Some people get a better offer." Rosie winked, earning her a scowl from across the table. "Next door was fine. She usually looks after him when we go away."

"Before I forget, here's your key back." Sydney pushed it across the table. "So, how was the honeymoon?"

"Amazing. Not long enough, but I can't put my patients off for too long. How did it go with Sam?"

"Great actually. I hadn't realised how much I missed him. I hope we can keep in touch."

"I'm pleased and relieved."

"He's fixing Gertie for me. I just need to find time to get her down to him. Following tonight's performance by Beatrice Russell when I dared to leave her company, it may be a challenge I've underestimated."

Sydney gulped at the shandy as soon as the waitress placed it in front of her. When she'd drained it of a third of its contents, she let out a long breath and relaxed back into her chair.

"Is it common for an employer to get you this wound up? Surely all your clients are high maintenance. What's got you so hot under the collar about this one? Or is that the issue?"

"What?" Sydney's eyebrows sprang together.

"She has got you hot under the collar, hasn't she?" Rosie's lips tightened. "And you're disappointed that she's not everything you dreamed she might be."

"She's way out of my league, and anyway, she likes men," Sydney replied as she scanned the rest of the pub's clientele.

"No denial there then," Rosie muttered under her breath, loud enough for Sydney to scowl at her.

"I met her husband today," she offered up. "What a sleazy arsehole he was. He came to pick up her son, who is a delight and surprisingly not as damaged as he probably should be. He and Beatrice started arguing — loudly enough that we could hear them outside. I think she took it out on me... and a bottle of Talisker 25."

"Ooh nice! The whisky, not her being mean to my best friend. Won't she sack you for leaving?"

Sydney laughed. "No, she can't do without me. I'm rewriting her autobiography for her. I best not be out too long, though; she was in quite a state when I left. I expect she'll be in a worse state when I return."

"That's amazing. Congratulations." Rosie, ever one to find the silver lining, reached across the table and squeezed Sydney's arm.

"Thanks. I hope it means I'm irreplaceable, especially with her deadline. I imagine that's what gets to her the most; I'm her first competent PA, and she doesn't know how to handle it. She needs me and she knows it. When I first met her son, he made a bet with me that I'd quit before she went back to the States."

"Ouch. Maybe if she was a little politer to her PAs, they'd stick around longer."

Sydney pursed her lips. "Mmm. Something is a bit off with her. I don't know, she seems paranoid. When she boiled over this evening about me leaving, she was vicious; she told me not to come back."

"Is she controlling?"

"No, she doesn't micromanage me as some do. It was like she didn't want me to have a break, go out and enjoy myself."

"If she can't, maybe she's jealous you could." Rosie shrugged. "Maybe she's just lonely."

"Hmm. There's been no sign of any friends. She has her

agent, whom she seems close to. Other than that there's the housekeeper she speaks to with the sweetest of tones. It's just me she has a problem with."

"And the ex."

Sydney nodded.

"No one should treat anyone else poorly; she must have a reason."

"Yeah, she's wealthy and famous."

Rosie frowned. "You're better than that, Syd. Find her reasons."

Rosie was right. She was going to have to prise Beatrice open and knock down her defences if she was going to find out what made her heart so icy. The chances of that happening after pointing out a few home truths were about as probable as Beatrice saying thank you. Sydney would be amazed if she still had a job in the morning. Although Beatrice needed her, she wouldn't put it past the woman to cut her nose off to spite her face.

"How's she getting on with the cast?" Rosie asked, sipping her wine. "Is she itchy?"

"Yep." Sydney's eyes widened. "The only bit of pleasure I get is watching her try and scratch at it."

Rosie smirked. "You're mean."

"I know."

"Don't let her stick anything down the cast to scratch it. You *can* use a hairdryer on the cool setting to ease it," Rosie said, calling on her wealth of medical experience to make the suggestion.

"Great idea. Though I'll make her suffer a bit longer."

"Is she keeping up with physio on her other leg?"

"No, she complains it's restless. I think she doesn't

want anyone near her. She's probably paranoid she smells, which in all honesty the cast is beginning to."

"Understandable. This heat isn't helping. She must exercise her other leg or it will waste, and she'll end up with twice the amount of work to recover. Does she not have a physiotherapist?"

Sydney shook her head. "Not that I know of. The only thing she has coming up is an appointment with a private hospital in a couple of weeks. That's for an X-ray and cast removal if everything is okay."

Rosie hummed. "She should be undergoing some form of physio or at least doing some exercises. I'm happy to see her if you like."

"I didn't know you did house calls."

"I do for the infamous Beatrice Russell."

"I'll mention it, though she tends to get funny about strangers in the house."

"The offer is there. I also have something in the car that might help her and allow you a little respite."

"Excellent, I'm all for a little respite from Beatrice Russell," Sydney replied with a sigh, knowing that was a complete and utter lie.

It was late when she finally put the key in the lock of Highwood House; much later than she'd intended on returning. Time ran away from her as she and her dear friend chewed over old times. Relieved to see the lights were on and the doors were locked as she'd left them, she ran up the stairs to check on Beatrice. She discovered her asleep on the sofa in her bedroom.

In the low light of the room, the actress lay peacefully in contrast to earlier that evening when she'd been full of rage. Sydney had chuckled to herself as she'd heard what must have been the crutches flying across the room. Beatrice was going to have to crawl across the floor on her butt to retrieve them.

Her hand reached out to the woman's bare arm and stroked it. "Beatrice, can you get up? I need to get you into bed."

"Sydney? I thought you'd left me," she replied softly as her eyelids fluttered open.

"No. I said I was coming back. Despite your opposition."

Leaning over, Sydney placed her hands around the back of Beatrice's shoulder. The actress's scent wafted pleasantly under her nose as she prised the woman up.

Beatrice wrapped her arms around Sydney's neck and stared intently into her eyes. "You're very beautiful."

The urge to lean in and place what would be an inappropriate kiss on the woman's lips soon dissipated as the stench of whisky breath hit her nostrils. Beatrice's words were only an observation, nothing to get excited about. She was drunk and didn't know what she was saying, and even if she did, it wasn't necessarily meant in the way Sydney hoped.

Heaving Beatrice up, she placed herself under one shoulder, put a crutch optimistically into Beatrice's other arm, and manoeuvred her to the bed. She was still fully dressed, and Sydney realised she was going to need to get her dress off. Would that be inappropriate? Rational thought decided that doing anything beyond what she would do for anyone else was inappropriate, but undressing a drunk employer was something she'd done many times before.

Lowering Beatrice onto the bed, she unzipped her dress at the back and slipped it down to her waist, keeping her gaze well above shoulder height. As Beatrice flopped back into bed, Sydney teased the dress down over her hips and quickly covered her with the duvet. Easy.

Hair had fallen across Beatrice's face. Sydney swept it to the side and tucked it behind her ear.

"Don't leave me," Beatrice said, her eyes firmly closed.

"I won't. I promise."

I can't.

Despite her antics last night, Beatrice Russell was having a major effect on her, one her brain was struggling to control. Her body's desires were beginning to win it over. How long she had left in charge was anyone's guess. She hoped it would be long enough that she could do her job and get off the Highwood House estate in a few weeks without embarrassing herself.

CHAPTER 17

*W*hen Beatrice woke in the early hours of the morning with a dry throat and a pounding head, she discovered that not only was she in her bed in her underwear, but a bottle of water and a packet of painkillers were on her bedside table. What was she going to do without Sydney pre-empting her every need? Even after they'd had a falling-out.

A light snoring sound came from the other end of the room. The low sunrise gave her enough light to make out a figure tucked under a blanket on one of the sofas. A tingling sensation in her stomach made her clutch it. Sydney had spent the night with her to make sure she was okay. Did Sydney care? Or did she not want her death on her conscience when she woke to find her in a pile of her own vomit in the morning? Which, considering how she was feeling, was still a possibility.

After taking a couple of painkillers and consuming half a bottle of water she'd later regret when she had to try and get to the toilet, she fell back to sleep, pushing away any thoughts of the previous night's heated discussions. That would wait until later that morning.

When she did wake again, the first thing on her mind was Sydney. She sat up and eyed the sofa, regretting her swift action as the pain of her brain catching up to her skull reminded her that a hangover was very much in residence. The sofa was vacant. Had she imagined it, dreamt it... desired her presence?

She tapped out a message on her phone — *I'll be staying in my room today. I'll text you if I need anything* — and headed to the bathroom. Emerging ten minutes later, she spotted a tray on her coffee table holding a cafetière of coffee, a jug of cream, a couple of pastries, and a bowl of fruit.

Her phone pinged from her bed.

Eat.

Her fingers hovered over the phone.

Thank you.

Sydney's reply was immediate.

You're welcome.

She had thought her assistant's attitude might be cumbersome this morning; instead, she was acting like nothing had happened the previous night. Beatrice didn't feel like she was able to do the same. Inside she was dying of embarrassment and would be avoiding Sydney as much as possible.

As she poured her coffee, she recalled how childish she'd been, telling Sydney she couldn't go out. Why had she reacted like that? Why had she blown up at Sydney when she'd done nothing except care for her and ask for a night off? Fucking Peter. He was why she'd been in a bad mood, and she'd taken her anger out on Sydney and her own liver.

By midday she was starting to feel human again and capable of work rather than staring blankly at the television. The warm sunshine coming through her balcony doors called her outside with the script for the following day's audition. She'd read it a hundred times that week already, being a believer that failing to prepare was preparing to fail. She still didn't feel she'd fully grasped the character's persona.

A splash from the pool pulled her towards the railing to check it was her assistant and not a gang of roving youths trespassing. Sydney was lapping the pool in her black bikini, swimming like a fish, with perfect form, style, and grace. It was hypnotic to watch. Sydney stopped and rose up the steps, her bikini bottom snapping as she rearranged it. The woman was phenomenal. Her slender body was perfectly proportioned except for her large feet, which no doubt helped her swim like an otter, and complemented her enormous ears.

Beatrice tore her eyes away; she shouldn't be ogling her assistant.

You're only appreciating the female form, a voice told her.

You know that's not what I was doing, she snapped back at it. She closed her eyes as she recalled telling Sydney she was beautiful as she helped her to bed. How could she have been so careless?

Biting her lip, Beatrice quietly hobbled over to her sun lounger, fearful of being spotted once again. Her upper arms strained as they took the weight when she lowered herself onto it. Her upper body was certainly getting a workout.

She folded back the first few pages of the script, trying different voices and expressions only for her concentration to wander. Her thoughts constantly pulled her back to Sydney, the first assistant she'd ever desired to know more about. Where did she come from? Who were her family?

The sound of Sydney's voice drifted up to the balcony.

"Hey, Sam, it's me... Yeah good, thanks, it was great to catch up."

Sydney fell silent for a moment before starting up again with greater enthusiasm.

"That's fantastic! Thanks again for doing this. Yes, I'll see if I can get away this week."

Where was her assistant hoping to go now?

"It won't be tomorrow, though; I've got to take her to London."

The use of the word *her* pained Beatrice more than she thought it could.

"Okay, I'll let you know. Bye."

A deafening silence hung in the air when all Beatrice wanted was to hear more of Sydney's voice; to know she was close by.

Realising she wasn't about to look at it any time soon, she placed her script on her lap. She had to admit it pleased her that the two of them were alone again at Highwood. She had missed Sydney being around the last week; most of all, she missed her energy. The few times they'd spent together over the last few days they'd been discussing work, eating dinner with Alex, or more recently at cross words.

Beatrice was beginning to feel the truth of it. She didn't want Sydney to be anywhere else or with anyone else; she liked to have the woman by her side. She was jealous of the attention she gave to her son, the person on the phone, and whomever she'd been out with. Had she been out on a date? Spent the night with a man before returning to deal with her drunk employer? Beatrice's eyes closed with embarrassment, and then her heart sank at the thought of Sydney being intimate with someone else.

Could she really be developing those types of feelings for her assistant? The type of feelings that left you a jealous ball of queasiness. The woman's efficiency and competency would be massive turn-ons for anyone, wouldn't they?

She shook her head in disbelief. It must be admiration for a job well done, something she didn't recognise because she hadn't seen it before. She was still angry with Sydney after everything she had said the night before. An apology for which she felt should be forthcoming. To drag her father into it with no idea what he'd put her through was despicable. Her conflicting thoughts about her assistant were becoming too much, and Beatrice decided to give into the siren song of a much-needed nap.

CHAPTER 18

*F*or all its grace and glory, a Rolls-Royce was not an enjoyable ride from West Sussex into London. The relentless traffic, buses, and width restrictions, combined with the vague, light steering and barge-like dimensions of the car, made for a stressful drive. There was also the matter of the distraction that sat in the back seat. Sydney had adjusted her rear-view mirror so she couldn't see Beatrice.

She'd lost her breath when she'd stepped into Beatrice's bedroom that morning to find her dressed in a black pencil skirt and white silk blouse. She'd not seen her in business attire before; it was a look that suited her. Her prominent cheekbones were enhanced by expertly applied make-up, and her eyes accentuated with a black liner. With her hair drawn up into a messy yet perfectly styled bun, it was a look that took ten years off her.

Beatrice had barely spoken to her since they'd had words. Food requests came by text message, and each time they were delivered, Sydney found she had retreated to the bathroom. She was unsure if the woman was deliberately hiding. With the delivery of her evening meal, though, Beatrice sat on the sofa in her bedroom. The only acknowledgement Sydney received was a reminder that they would be going to London for the audition, followed by lunch with her agent, and that she wished to be woken at seven thirty. A light thank-you was issued as Sydney left the room. As light as it was, it still brought a smile to her face.

She wasn't sure if the actress was embarrassed at being called out over her behaviour or if she was furious at her for what she'd said — perhaps a mixture of both. Whatever it was, she was sulking about it. If Beatrice was waiting for some form of apology, she'd be waiting forever. Sydney hadn't said anything that was untrue.

Her only slight regret was the way she had gone about airing her issues. It was done now, though; there was no do-over. It was up to Beatrice to decide whether to ignore her or punish her, and it appeared she'd chosen to do a bit of both. On the bright side, with fewer demands from Beatrice, she'd been able to catch up on a lot of work and speak to Sam, who was ready for Gertie. Now that she and Beatrice were at odds, it was going to prove even more difficult to ask for time off, considering her last request to leave the property had landed them in this mess.

The silent treatment of the previous day continued during their journey into London. Beatrice wasn't the type for excessive conversation, yet Sydney found herself missing the little they had shared all the same. Their conversations covering the adult years of the autobiography had dried up over the last few days what with her making the final changes. Once they were complete, unless Beatrice needed help with her childhood, she would be back to occupying her time with housework and cooking.

She'd come to enjoy spending hours upon hours a day playing with words on her laptop. Over the last few years, the urge to write had increased, and the more she wrote, the more it called to her. It was beginning to act like a drug, all culminating in her need to take time off to get a much-needed hit. If only she could make writing pay as well as being a PA.

"Here. Pull over," Beatrice hawked from the rear.

Sydney pulled the car into a lay-by outside a new office block as instructed. A young man and an older woman were standing by the kerbside, their eyes fixed on their mobile phones. The woman spotted them and approached the car, opening Beatrice's door.

"Well, look at the state of you."

"Thank you, Ali," Beatrice replied dryly, passing out her crutches to her agent.

"Bright pink, nice choice," she snarked as she assisted Beatrice from the car.

"Find somewhere to park. I'll call you when I'm done," Beatrice instructed Sydney, the door immediately slamming shut behind her.

Sydney watched as Alison and Beatrice made their way inside the office building, Alison with both their handbags over her shoulder. The woman wasn't quite what she had been expecting. She put Alison in her mid-sixties; her short, grey pixie cut hardened what otherwise would have been a kindly face. The young man was no longer with them. She glanced around to see where he had gone, only to find him getting into the passenger seat beside her with a large boutique bag.

"Ah, the new PA. I'm Tom, Alison's assistant."

"How do you know I'm new?" Sydney asked as she pulled the car out of the lay-by.

"Because all her PAs are new," he sniggered. "We have a bet running in the office on how long you'll last. We're amazed you've lasted this long, actually. I guess you're not Peter's type."

"What?"

"Have you not met him yet?" Tom nodded. "That explains why you're still here."

"I've met him."

"Then you're definitely not his type." Giving her the once-over, he added, "Strange, 'cos you're pretty. I thought any PA with a pulse and a pussy was his type. Maybe he hasn't had the opportunity yet. I'd watch your back."

The realisation of what Tom was saying hit her. "Does she know?"

Tom scrunched his lips. "Doubt it. Would you wanna tell her?"

Was this why Beatrice couldn't hold down a PA? Her creepy ex would show up and proposition her PAs, or worse, assault them? He'd only made inappropriate comments towards her, and she believed him capable of going further given the chance.

"I met him once," she admitted. "He made my skin crawl."

"You and every other PA."

"Does Alison know?"

"If Alison knew, Miss Russell would know."

"Every PA?" Sydney asked, able to believe it, yet not wishing to.

Tom nodded. "Pretty much. It's why we expanded the search to find you. We don't normally use your agency for our clients. Your boss was super keen to make a deal."

Sydney rolled her eyes at the thought of James salivating down the phone when he received the call.

"Word spreads in the PA world, you know," Tom said, pointing out the window. "Take a right down here; you can usually get away with parking there."

"I keep myself to myself," Sydney replied, cursing her work ethic. The thought that Alison's employees were throwing young women into Peter's path rather than addressing the problem made her sick to her stomach. "Surely Alison must know?"

Tom shrugged. "She knows more than anyone that Miss Russell is a bit of a ball breaker. She probably thinks they run a mile when they realise they aren't up to the job — as I would guess Miss Russell does too."

"Something should be done," Sydney said, bringing the car to a stop alongside the kerb.

"Indeed. It won't until someone stands up, though. People are fearful for their jobs. It's their word against his; not one of them will have a queue of women behind them to back them up. They're more likely to call you a liar. Who wants to employ a PA involved in a case of sexual harassment? It's easier to move on. I have a few calls to make," Tom said, stepping out of the car and leaving Sydney to churn over her thoughts.

She could see how it would be easier to move on and

leave Beatrice believing there was something wrong with her rather than dealing with the issue, but it didn't make it right. Yes, her employer was difficult, yet she was nothing a good PA couldn't handle. Her own words to Beatrice, suggesting she drove her PAs away, taunted her. This was wrong, all wrong. She could feel her body vibrating at the injustice of it. Poor Beatrice. She couldn't be the one to stand by and do nothing. Beatrice deserved more than that.

CHAPTER 19

"This bloody cast. It makes me feel old and pathetic." Beatrice exhaled, relaxing back into her chair as she marvelled at the sparkling chandeliers and marble columns in one of the most stylish dining rooms in the world. The Ritz was her top choice when it came to eating out.

"I suggested a wheelchair," Alison said with a *told you so* tilt of the head.

"That would have been a winner at the audition; a woman over fifty in a wheelchair. It was bad enough on crutches. You know what these directors are like — one whiff of a lame duck and they might as well have you taken out and shot. I think it went well; they made the right noises anyway."

"Well, I think you're looking fabulous, even with the cast," Alison said, taking a sip of champagne the instant the waiter finished pouring it into her glass.

Beatrice flashed her a smile of thinly veiled gratitude.

It took a lot of effort to make herself 'audience ready',

and this morning was no different. She'd lowered herself to the floor in front of the bath and kneeled on a cushion to use the shower attachment to wash her hair. With a blow dry and hairspray, she'd whipped it into shape. It took well over an hour sitting at her dressing table to achieve it and then to apply her makeup. From the glimpse of Sydney's mouth opening when she'd walked into her bedroom that morning, she approved too.

Beatrice wasn't going to let her leg hold her back from pulling out all the stops for the audition, an audition that frankly shouldn't have been necessary for an actress of her calibre. There was a time when parts were written for her, and no one would have dared ask her to audition. Now it was a case of seeing if they could get away with using her for roles younger than she was.

"How are you and Sydney rubbing along?" Alison asked. "She seems nice."

"You only said hello on the ride over; it's hardly enough to judge fairly."

"Is she not nice then?"

Beatrice pondered her agent's question as she sipped her drink. *Nice.* The worst word in the dictionary. Was that a word to describe Sydney? No. It was way off. Sydney was honest, caring, reliable, and hardworking. Her empathy and compassion could use some work, considering how she'd thrown accusations at Beatrice about her lifestyle. As for Sydney's insinuations regarding her behaviour, yes, she was demanding. Could Beatrice go about voicing her demands differently? Perhaps. Did she find her PAs that little more efficient when she was barking orders? Also yes. If the only thing she could rely upon from a PA was that they would up and leave, wasn't it better to make them as efficient as possible in the time she had? This nonsense about her driving them away, did Sydney not think she'd tried to be pleasant? They left anyway. Niceties proved to be fruitless.

"Bea?" Alison shot her a quizzical look, still waiting for an answer. "If her PA skills match her writing skills, I think you're onto a winner. She doesn't strike me as the usual airhead."

Beatrice sighed, tilting her head as she rolled her eyes. "I've come to realise that."

"What's happened?"

"We've had a falling-out of sorts."

"I thought I sensed some tension on the way here," Alison said, her lips tightened in amusement. "Is it normal PA tension or something else?"

She wasn't about to reveal Sydney's thoughts on her behaviour; Alison would laugh and agree with the younger woman.

"Nothing I can't sort. It happened shortly after Peter left."

"I told you not to let him wind you up!" Alison chided. "He does it on purpose, you know."

"I'm well aware. It doesn't make it any easier to prevent. He's heard about the book. The publishers announced it, which I would have known if my PA dared to follow social media. You know he has an alert on his phone to tell him whenever my name is mentioned. Now he's demanding royalties."

"The bastard. The amount of money he's wasted of yours. He should have cut and run ages ago."

Beatrice sighed and took a sip from her glass. "He's like a noose around my neck, Ali, and he's not going to stop until he's squeezed everything from me, including my last breath."

"You don't need the money, do you?"

"No," Beatrice said with a shake of the head.

"So give the royalties away. Give them to someone he wouldn't dare take it from — put them in trust for Alex."

With a glint in her eye, Beatrice grinned. "Checkmate. I doubt it will move me any closer to a signed divorce paper, though. He'll find another reason to delay."

As their food arrived, discussions of Peter ended; she didn't want to waste another breath on him.

"I arranged for a clearance company to deal with your father's house," Alison said, stuffing a forkful of sea bass into her mouth.

"That was good of you... thank you," Beatrice said, squeezing the last two words from herself. Alison would do anything for her, she knew that, yet she could see that a little more verbal gratitude was appropriate here, for her oldest friend.

"You're... welcome," Alison stuttered, clearly unfamiliar with those words coming from Beatrice. "There's the slight issue of the ashes. Your mother's ashes were in a cardboard box in a wardrobe, and there are your fathers, too, along with a few photo albums. I had Tom put them in your car."

Beatrice flashed her a smile of appreciation, not wishing to appear ungrateful for all the work Alison carried out on her behalf with closing her father's estate, though the unwelcome mementoes were something she could have done without.

"That reminds me… photoshoot. As soon as the cast is off, we need something for the book cover. I thought we could do it at your house."

"Great idea." She couldn't face coming into London again so soon. "I have an appointment booked at the end of next week, so I should have a better idea by then of how it's healing."

"How are the dreaded early years coming along?"

"Slow. I feel like I'm writing more tripe that Sydney will have to rewrite."

"Then stop. She's nearly finished the work on your adult years from the look of what you sent me last. Sit down with her, talk to her about your childhood, and describe how you felt about what happened. Let her listen and write; then you only need think about your flow of thoughts. Allow her to hear your voice; it's your voice the audience wants to hear."

Beatrice toyed with her butter knife. "That's a lot of trust to put in someone I hardly know."

"Then get to know her. It's always easier to talk to a friend, and the two of you have a few weeks ahead of you yet."

Beatrice wasn't convinced she could sit down and pour her childhood out to a stranger; she could barely pour it into a laptop. Was Sydney a stranger? The woman had witnessed her at her worst. The fact she was still at Highwood was a wonder, and probably had more to do with the credit she would receive for helping with the book. Would she still be hanging around if there was no book? Beatrice gulped and pushed the thought away; she didn't want to think about the answer.

"If she's earned your respect, give it to her, I say," Alison said as she flagged the waiter for more drinks. "She's certainly earned mine. Why is she even working as a PA, I'd like to know. What a waste."

Beatrice mused on that. Sydney certainly earned more of her respect than any of her other PAs, but that was hardly a gold star achievement. There was so much she didn't know about the woman. How on earth was she going to get to know her when they were barely on speaking terms?

CHAPTER 20

"*W*here would you like this bag to be put?" Sydney asked as Beatrice collapsed onto the sofa in the kitchen.

Beatrice peered over the back of it and scrutinised the bag.

"Throw it anywhere?" she offered.

"The bin?" Sydney asked with a hint of sarcasm.

"Yes, for all I care."

Sydney frowned. "What is it?"

"My parents' ashes."

"Seriously?" Sydney grimaced, understanding now why it was so heavy. Just as she had begun to understand Beatrice a little, here she was, perplexing her again. Whatever her problem with her dad was, it extended to her mum. Not everyone was lucky enough to have the ashes of a loved one when they were gone.

She would need to hold her tongue. Beatrice had been correct the other night: she did have no idea about that part of her past. Her parents hadn't made an appearance in the parts of the book Sydney had seen so far. Beatrice was all alone at eighteen, that much she did know.

With no further communication from her employer, she decided it would be best to place the ashes in the under-stair cupboard for the moment.

"I'll make us some dinner," Sydney said as she re-entered the kitchen.

"Thank you."

There it was again — a word of gratitude. Beatrice had listened; she was trying to do better.

Sydney took a deep breath and perched on the coffee table in front of her.

"I'd like to apologise for the way I spoke to you the other evening. It wasn't very professional, which doesn't sit right with me. I would like to make it clear that I'm not apologising for what I said about your behaviour towards me. That I meant."

Beatrice turned her head away whilst her eyes swept up to bore into Sydney for a moment before she lowered them to the floor.

"My PAs are usually incompetent," she stated.

"Is that a compliment?" Sydney asked, trying to break the awkwardness.

Beatrice ignored her.

"I don't even know why I do it; people expect you to be tough."

"No, they don't."

"Well, when you're around others in the industry you put on an act. It's the only thing I can do. You end up becoming an image of what you think you should be. It becomes a habit and... you eventually lose yourself."

Beatrice sighed and ruffled a hand through her hair. "I, too, am sorry about the other night. I try not to drink, especially when I'm already emotional — it's not pretty."

"I think you're pretty." *How did that slip out?* "So does most of the world, no doubt," she quickly added.

A smile twitched at the corner of Beatrice's mouth and then disappeared.

"Peter... has an effect on me. Not a nice one, I'm afraid."

Sydney bit her lip at Beatrice's despondent tone. "I should have noticed you were vulnerable after Peter came. I'm sorry I didn't."

"I should have admitted I needed you a little more eloquently." Beatrice paused. "Thank you for sleeping over. I appreciated your... diligence."

Sydney blushed. She'd slipped from the room early in the hope her presence would go unnoticed. "It was necessary. I didn't want you to choke to death on your own vomit."

Beatrice's shoulders dropped at her comment.

"I also wanted to make sure you were okay," Sydney added, making the sides of Beatrice's mouth twitch again.

"I also want to make something clear," Beatrice said, her eyes firmly back on Sydney. "My wealth and fame may appear *privileged* to you... my life, however, is not. In fact, your comments were judgemental. I have problems too. Even though I'm successful and wealthy, it doesn't remove my problems; it brings you more than you can imagine. It can't have escaped your notice that I have few friends, and even with hundreds of acquaintances, the only person I can rely on is Alison. It's easier to push people away and live a lonely existence than to be let down by people you thought you could trust. Can you imagine that?"

Sydney shook her head. She knew she could rely on all her friends.

"This job, this lifestyle, it comes at a price. Trust me, it's cost me more than you can imagine. I never used to be like this. When you've been through as many PAs as I have, you find your guard goes up a little further each time one of them leaves. It's a special relationship, and yet they would always leave eventually — with crappy excuses."

Crappy excuses that were nowhere near close to the truth of a handsy husband.

Beatrice continued. "What's the point in getting to know someone if you know they are going to leave soon anyway? You'll be gone soon, but I know that's not a reason to treat you the way I have been."

It wasn't like Sydney hadn't thought about leaving. The sadness that consumed Beatrice was the reason she knew she couldn't leave her. It surpassed Gertie, her writing, any of her other reasons. If so many had left her in the past, it wouldn't be fair to abandon her to loneliness again.

"I'm not going anywhere." Sydney reached forward and placed her hand on Beatrice's arm. "I'm here for you; to help you."

Beatrice glanced down at her arm. Sydney withdrew her hand, realising she'd overstepped.

"I'm not Gertie. I may be glam on the outside and broken on the inside, that doesn't mean you can fix me."

"You're right." Sydney nodded. "Only you can fix yourself."

"I must appear very self-absorbed to you."

"You're not my first highly strung client." Sydney closed her eyes as soon as she said it. "Sorry, that came out wrong."

"I'm not sure how a statement like that comes out right, Sydney. I must focus on my career, and my career is this — me. I have nothing else. I'm about to be a divorced woman in her fifties, and my son hates me."

"He doesn't hate you."

"He seems to like you better," Beatrice observed.

"I listen to him, give him the time of day. He's a good kid."

"He blames me for his father leaving when actually..." She paused before admitting the truth. "...when actually he had an affair with one of my co-stars."

It took a moment for Sydney to summon the power of speech. "What an epic arsehole!"

So Peter did have affairs with other women, some that Beatrice knew about too. Sydney was more determined now than ever to deal with her employer's toxic ex in some way.

Beatrice let out a smooth, intoxicating laugh at Sydney's statement, the type that swept around you and pulled you into her, or at least that was the desire it was conjuring in Sydney.

"Indeed. It was whilst we were filming. I'm probably responsible; he certainly claimed his cold, heartless wife drove him to it."

Sydney noticed her hand was back on Beatrice's arm again, and as the woman didn't flinch, she left it there.

"Beatrice, you're not responsible for that, and I don't

believe you're heartless. A little cold…" Sydney flattened her lips and tilted her head. "But I'm sure we can warm you up."

For a fraction of a second, their eyes met. Sydney pulled hers away almost immediately, unable to hold contact with eyes that could bore into her core and devour her soul.

"You should set Alex straight. He *needs* to know the truth."

"No," Beatrice snapped. Her face was instantly full of regret. She continued more softly. "I don't want him to know. He *needs* to have a relationship with one of us, and he's always adored his father. It has to stay that way."

"At the expense of your own relationship?"

"Yes," Beatrice replied firmly. "He has little stability, and I know it affects him. It's not easy being the son of a famous actress. Every relationship becomes dispensable when you're someone like me."

Sydney's heart was breaking for her. "Even with your own child?"

"Even with your own parents," Beatrice replied, taking a deep breath. "I never went to school, not one day. I was educated, of course, but a normal childhood and upbringing escaped me, and not once did my parents ask me if it was what I wanted. I was simply moved from one acting job to the next. I can't claim any childhood friends, as there was no childhood in which to form any."

"Did you not make friends with other children on set?"

"Child stars are pitted against each other from the off, and remember we spent our days in an adult workplace."

Sydney nodded and stroked Beatrice's arm.

Beatrice yawned and moved the arm to cover her mouth. "Enough about that for today. I will require some assistance with the remainder of the book. Or the beginning, if you will. Where it all started."

"Of course. You know I'm at your disposal, in any way you choose." Sydney chewed her bottom lip. She hadn't intended for it to sound so suggestive.

Beatrice pulled her lips in and moistened them.

"I enjoyed getting out today," she ventured, "even if it was work-related. Do you think you could take me somewhere tomorrow, anywhere... your choice?"

"What about work?"

"I think we both deserve some time off, don't you?"

Sydney wasn't going to argue with that, even though she couldn't afford to take the time off from the book, especially now she was going to be helping Beatrice with her formative years. She'd have to make up the time later that evening, once Beatrice was in bed.

"I've felt like a bird trapped in a cage these past weeks. I'm not used to being inactive. This cast is not helping."

"There's nothing I can do about the cast. I can get you out of here, though, and as you can't move, I'll move you. I know just the place."

This was a chance to kill two birds with one stone.

It was a good feeling to be lying on her bed after a long day. It would be more enjoyable if one leg didn't itch and the other didn't ache. Despite the discomfort, a load had been lifted from Beatrice's shoulders since Sydney offered some form of apology and she'd managed to air her own grievances in return. Opening up a little about her past felt better than she thought it would. She hoped clearing the air would be a turning point for them.

A light tap came from the bedroom door.

"Come in."

Sydney's head peered around it as it opened. "I'm heading to bed; do you need anything before I go up?"

"A double amputation?" Beatrice replied as she scratched at the top of her cast, knowing full well the itch was coming from underneath it yet hoping psychologically it would have some effect lower down.

Sydney entered the room. "That I can't do. There is something I could try to distract you."

A breath caught in Beatrice's throat, making her cough. Part of her was relieved to see Sydney unplug her hairdryer from beside the dressing table and plug it in beside the bed. The other part was disappointed she hadn't meant something else.

"You okay?" Sydney asked, passing her a bottle of water from beside the bed.

Beatrice nodded as she cleared her throat and took a sip.

Sitting beside her on the bed, Sydney directed cool air from the dryer down her cast. Her hands pushed the skin down around the rim to allow greater access to the covered skin beneath the fibreglass.

Her touch sent the same ripple through Beatrice as it had when Sydney touched her arm earlier. The cool air filled her cast and brought such relief she accidentally let out a groan, bringing a smile to Sydney's face.

"Thank you. That's done the trick."

"How's this one doing?" Sydney asked, nodding at her unbroken leg as she placed the hairdryer on the floor.

"Sore."

Sydney climbed onto the bottom of the bed and sat with her legs parted on either side of Beatrice's good leg. Her hands reached out and massaged her foot and ankle, her touch melting away the ache. Beatrice refrained from groaning this time, instead allowing her head to fall back against the headboard. The lids of her eyes dropped as Sydney worked her way up her calf, then above her knee. She felt her foot pressed between Sydney's breasts as the woman reached further... as far as her thigh. Her eyes opened, eager to see Sydney touch her, wondering how high she would go; knowing it wouldn't be high enough to satisfy her.

"That's enough. Thank you," Beatrice said, almost snapping as she realised where her thoughts were leading.

"Of course." Sydney leapt from the bed. "Have you considered physical therapy? It would help you to stick to a schedule with assigned exercises."

"I don't think so. I don't want to deal with strangers."

"My best friend is a physiotherapist. The one I went out with the other night."

So it wasn't a date.

"And you discussed me?" Beatrice asked.

"We discussed the recovery of a broken fibula, amongst other things. She could see you. The hairdryer was her trick."

"I'll think about it."

She noticed Sydney's gaze lower to the ground at her reply, so she added, "Thank you for the suggestion."

Sydney left the room with a smile on her face, a smile that Beatrice realised was surprisingly easy and satisfying to have put there. Her own face had a smile etched on it too. She couldn't remember the last time she'd had that much physical contact with someone in one day, let alone someone who made her feel like it would never be enough.

CHAPTER 21

"Sydney, would you help me with this zip please?" Beatrice's voice drifted through from the dressing room.

A shiver rushed over Sydney as every hair on her body stood to attention at the sight of Beatrice in front of a full-length mirror in a red, strapless A-line satin dress. The material glistened in the sun as it shone through the large Victorian window.

The woman was simply divine.

"I can't reach it," Beatrice continued, sweeping her shimmering curls to one side.

Sydney stood behind her, her eyes wandering over her bare shoulders and neck. She paused as she reached out to the zip. Instead of grasping it, she lifted her hand higher to the base of Beatrice's neck, where she allowed her fingertips to lightly brush the soft skin.

Beatrice's torso lifted as she inhaled, and then held her breath. Her shoulders twitched and her head tilted as Sydney's fingers zigzagged slowly down to the top of the dress. Beatrice's shoulders dropped as she let out her breath.

Finding the zip, Sydney pulled it down to reveal Beatrice's bare back. She gasped as she realised there was no bra hiding behind it. The front of the dress gave way as it finally lost its hold on Beatrice's breasts.

Her middle finger traced around the woman's side, causing her skin to goose-pimple in reaction. She reached for a bare breast and cupped it. A light squeeze prized a moan from Beatrice.

Sydney pressed her body into her back, closing the gap between them. Her other hand reached around for the other breast. She lightly caressed them, their warmth penetrating her palms and her heart. Teasing Beatrice's nipples between her thumb and forefinger, elicited a cry of pleasure from the bewitching beauty.

Drawing her lips in, she moistened them before pressing them hard against the nape of Beatrice's neck, causing the breathless woman to arc her head back and moan again. Sydney's lips teased her skin.

Releasing one breast, she slowly slid her hand down to Beatrice's belly and pulled her into her. With Beatrice's butt firmly pressed against her groin, the pulsing the woman was already causing in that area quickened.

Her hand slipped lower, under the waistline of the dress down to where she expected to find the material of an undergarment, instead finding soft hair. A gasp escaped her own lips as she realised Beatrice was completely naked under the dress. Her fingers desired more, reaching lower until they became moistened, and Beatrice let out a soft whimper.

"Not yet," she gasped, turning around. She pulled Sydney into her, whispering into her ear as she lightly nibbled her earlobe. "I want you first, Sydney. I want every inch of you."

Beatrice pushed Sydney back. The backs of her knees collided with the diamond-tufted brown leather ottoman that hogged the centre of the dressing room. Sydney dropped down onto it, finding herself face to face with Beatrice's belly. She pulled it toward her, kissing it as she reached around for the zip, eager to see every inch of Beatrice.

Her fingers pinched the metal zip again and pulled, causing the dress to slip down over the remainder of her elegant frame. With all of Beatrice in her sight, she swallowed, her mouth watering in desperation for a taste of her. As the dress hit the ground, Beatrice stepped out of it and pushed it aside.

"Beatrice, where's your cast?"

"What cast?" Beatrice replied.

Sydney opened her eyes to the familiar sight of her ceiling and sucked in a breath.

Fuck!

She gulped, feeling almost teary as she ached for the reality of the dream.

It was hardly surprising she dreamed about Beatrice; she was all she'd thought about for days. The nature of the dream was a little unexpected, yet welcome. After their closeness yesterday, when Beatrice finally opened up a little more, Sydney hadn't been able to help reaching out to her physically to give her some relief. Of course, she was unsure if she was soothing Beatrice or herself at that point.

She was grateful Beatrice snapped her out of her enjoyment of the massage before she went too far. She'd reached the stage where real life was starting to blend with her desires. The dream was not going to help with that problem.

She could still feel herself throbbing, and a glance at her watch told her there were ten minutes before she needed to get Beatrice up for their trip to the harbour. Five minutes was all she needed. She closed her eyes, if she couldn't subconsciously finish that dream, she was damn well going to finish it consciously.

CHAPTER 22

*B*eatrice lifted her sunglasses onto the top of her head and glared at Sydney as she pulled up beside the front door.

"Not the horse box!"

"Yes, we're taking her to a friend who's going to put a new engine in her."

Beatrice was about to object when Sydney put in first.

"You said it was my choice where we went, and you didn't stipulate the method of transport, so shush. I need to pop this into the house first."

Sydney extracted a strange object with wheels from the back of Gertie.

"What on earth is that contraption for?"

"You. It's a scooter. You'll be able to fly around downstairs now."

Beatrice's face contorted as she tried to suppress an element of delight. "And if one does not wish to fly around one's house?"

"Then one can continue to move very, very slowly instead."

With a bit of heave-ho, mostly on Sydney's part, Beatrice dropped onto the passenger seat. She was astonished by the cosiness of the camper. She'd keep that to herself; she was enjoying teasing Sydney about the state of her mobile shed far too much to compliment it.

Unsure of what she was expecting from a journey in a sardine can, she was relieved to find it smooth, though that may have had more to do with the speed at which they were driving.

"I know you said you could move me," she began. "Do you think you could move me over thirty miles per hour? I feel like the pope. I'll have the urge to start waving soon if we don't pick up speed."

"Keep your waving to other campers only."

"Oh!" Beatrice chuckled. "Is that a thing you have between you all? Like a club?"

"And what if it is?"

"Nothing." Beatrice looked out of the window to hide her smirk, not wishing to offend Sydney too much.

"Come on, old girl."

Beatrice turned to her, dropping her sunglasses down her nose. "I thought we were beyond insults, Sydney."

Sydney shot a look of horror at Beatrice. "Oh, I was talking to Gertie."

Another smirk edged its way onto Beatrice's lips. "It's a ridiculous notion, naming a car."

"Says the woman who has a car named Dawn."

"I have a Rolls-Royce Dawn; she is not named Dawn." Beatrice sniffed out a light laugh and changed the subject.

"So, will this new engine sound like it's fuelled by petrol rather than gravel?"

"I hope so, or we'll have to send her to the knacker's yard."

"Or the local poultry farm," Beatrice whispered.

"I heard that."

"You were meant to."

Beatrice admired the photogenic view of the harbour as they pulled up beside a house an hour later. The late morning sun was glistening on the sea, and the seagulls screeched overhead.

"This is us," Sydney said, switching off the engine.

"Wow, this is… something."

Sydney jumped out. "I'll come around and help you down."

A man appeared from a workshop and approached Sydney. Beatrice eyed them as they embraced each other. Was this a love interest? A pang of jealousy hit her square in the stomach. She needed to stop these feelings before they ran out of control.

As if finally remembering her existence, Sydney opened her door and assisted her to the ground.

The man approached them. "Hi, I'm Sam."

"Beatrice. It's nice to meet a friend of Sydney's. You can tell a lot about someone by the company they keep."

"Or don't keep," Sydney snarked back.

"Touché."

"So here she is, Sam. Ready for surgery," Sydney said, giving Gertie a light tap. "Be gentle with her."

"Of course, there is no other way to treat her."

Beatrice sniggered behind her hand. "Not you as well."

"Sorry, Sam. Beatrice thinks it's funny that we call her Gertie and refer to her as she."

"Oh, yes, I suppose it is a bit strange," Sam said, running his hand over Gertie's paintwork. "Gertie's like a member of the family, aren't you, girl?"

"Why don't you reach down and give her a tickle under the chin?" Beatrice scoffed, unable to contain herself any longer as she burst into a fit of giggles, only to be met with two pairs of raised eyebrows.

"Please excuse my childish employer," Sydney uttered. "I'm sure she'll get over it… eventually. In the meantime, can we borrow a boat, Sam?"

"A boat?" Beatrice asked, regaining her composure. "Where do you intend on taking me?"

"Up the harbour. I thought we might get lunch."

"I'll do one better," Sam said. "I'll run you up there myself. You're going to need some help embarking and disembarking." His gaze fell to the bright pink cast poking out from under Beatrice's floral dress.

"That's a great idea. Thanks."

"I'll get a boat prepped. Meet me down there," Sam said as he trundled off towards the jetty.

They followed behind, sticking to the flattest path possible until they reached the wooden jetty.

"Is Sam an ex-boyfriend?" Beatrice asked as they approached the boat.

"Er, we used to be a couple, yes."

Sam surfaced from below decks. "It's okay, you can tell her. I don't hide it," he said as he jumped from the boat. "Two minutes. I need to fetch something from the workshop."

"He used to be my girlfriend," Sydney clarified.

"Oh... erm... oh," Beatrice garbled as she processed what that meant.

"Is that a problem?" Sydney asked, eyebrows raised.

Beatrice met her gaze. "Of course not."

"He runs a helpline now for people struggling with gender dysphoria."

"That's great. Good for him."

Her thoughts caught up to her as she realised what that meant about Sydney. Had she already suspected? Or was it wishful thinking that Sydney was inclined that way? The way Sydney glanced at her sometimes could be considered unusual. Beatrice was used to people looking at her, but Sydney gave her sideways glances as if she wasn't looking. Initially, she had thought it was done with an element of contempt, yet with this new information it could be read entirely differently.

The look of disgust she'd given at the mention of a lesbian film Beatrice now realised must have been disgust for those bullying Alex. Was the way she covered her leg the first time she'd massaged it been to spare her embarrassment rather than Sydney feeling repulsion at her hairy legs? The woman's reluctance to scrub her back in the bath, was that hesitancy simply restraint? Could her assistant even be feeling the same draw she was?

A smile tore across her face at the ridiculousness of her thought. Someone as young and sexy as Sydney was going to be way out of her league. Just because she was a lesbian didn't mean she would have any interest in her.

"Something funny?"

"Like you wouldn't believe," Beatrice replied.

Sydney gave a questioning frown.

"Never mind."

The boat trip up the harbour was exhilarating. Beatrice removed her hat for fear of losing it, and the wind blew through her hair, leaving her with a sense of freedom she hadn't felt in a long time. With Sydney sitting beside her, her body and mind were at ease.

Sydney pointed to where they were going; the noise of the engine would have drowned her out had she spoken. They were heading for a small jetty which led up to a modernised medieval barn with a large balcony overlooking the harbour. It was idyllic, and as they approached on foot — literally, in her case — Beatrice realised it was a Michelin-starred seafood restaurant.

They chose to eat inside where it was quieter, though most customers opted for the balcony to enjoy the sun and warm sea breeze. Beatrice sipped her gin and tonic as she observed Sydney scanning the other occupied tables in the restaurant. Was she being protective? Watching her back in case someone recognised her employer under her enormous sunglasses?

With lunch served, Beatrice decided it was time to find out a little more about her assistant.

"So, tell me about yourself, Sydney. I know nothing about you. I do have to know one thing… what was your nickname at school?"

"Weren't eavesdropping at that point then?" Sydney pulled her lips to one side and glared at her.

Beatrice smirked as she filled her mouth with salad.

"Fish Fingers, if you must know."

Beatrice covered her mouth with her hand as she choked back a laugh. "Sorry."

"No, you go ahead. Bask in my childhood trauma."

"Because you're a…"

"Lesbian," Sydney answered for her, eyebrows raised.

"Well, I wouldn't like to assume… you did introduce me to someone who was once your ex-girlfriend."

Sydney paused for a moment before speaking. "Because I came from the fishing community."

"Oh. Right," Beatrice replied, feeling foolish. Was she not a lesbian then?

"And yes, because I'm a lesbian," Sydney teased.

Beatrice rolled her eyes at her. It was good to have it confirmed, not that it meant anything to her anyway.

"Why the name Sydney? It's a little… unusual."

"My parents were both Scottish; they met in Australia at a party on Scotland Island in Sydney Bay. Turned out they only lived a few miles from each other when they were growing up. It took them a trip to Australia to find each other. They married and had me, then returned when my grandfather became terminally ill when I was seven."

"Do you have Australian citizenship?" Beatrice asked.

"Yes. I was born shortly before they changed the rules. I never returned, though."

"Would you like to?"

Sydney shrugged. "I don't know really. I suppose. It's not like I have any family there. Isn't Australia on everyone's bucket list?"

"I've been many times for filming. It's certainly a diverse and vast country. I recall spending days travelling to various locations. I find I prefer England; everything is in easy reach. What family do you have here?"

"Only my mum and uncle in Scotland."

"Oh, so few," Beatrice remarked, draining her glass. It was still more family than she had.

"And my friends, they're like family. My boss, James, and Rosie, the physiotherapist I mentioned, we all met at uni. I was only down here for Rosie's wedding — to Sam's cousin Greg."

"So you all go way back," Beatrice replied, setting down her knife and fork.

"In some ways, yes... not too far," Sydney said, mirroring Beatrice and placing her cutlery down onto her empty plate.

"Scotland then," Beatrice said to change the subject. "You're a long way from home."

"Gertie is about the closest thing I have to a home. I feel no affinity for Scotland. The weather is enough to make any sun lover run for the border. I think moving there from Australia may have traumatised me as a child."

"I can imagine it would."

"I suppose we better get back," Sydney said as she caught the attention of the waiter and signalled for the check. "I'll message Sam to collect us."

Beatrice retrieved her handbag from the floor and rummaged for her purse.

"Put it away. This is on me," Sydney said.

"Are you sure?"

"Call it a small gesture of thanks for the opportunity you've given me."

Beatrice tilted her head as she raised her eyebrows. "Even though it wasn't part of the job description?"

She had her there, and Sydney's pursed lips said she knew it too.

"Even so."

"Thank you," Beatrice said as Sam lowered her onto the jetty where Sydney was waiting with her crutches.

"The pleasure is all mine, believe me."

She did believe him. It was unlikely he'd lift an international film star on and off a boat again.

"How long do you think it will take to fix her, Sam?" Sydney asked as they made their way up the jetty.

"I've got everything I need, so give me a couple of weeks."

"I should be out of my cast by then," Beatrice said. "I can bring you back."

"Thanks," Sydney replied with a smile. "I'm going to pop to the loo, and then we better head off. Are you still okay to give us a ride back, Sam?"

"No need. I have a car," Beatrice put in.

"How?" Sydney asked, her hands slipping to her hips.

"Jonathon. He's been tracking us all day."

"Don't you trust me to get you home?"

"I don't trust anyone," Beatrice replied, trying not to notice the look of disappointment on Sydney's face.

Sydney tilted her head. "You should work on that."

"Perhaps I already am. Albeit slowly."

Sydney turned on her heel and headed along the jetty up to the house.

"This is an idyllic spot, Sam," Beatrice said, looking out over the harbour. "I'm sure I could sit here all day and listen to the waves washing up the beach."

"Thanks. It certainly brought much inspiration to Syd when she lived here."

"You lived here together?" Beatrice asked, trying to quell her surprise. Knowing she was on Sydney's old turf helped her feel that little bit closer to her assistant.

"Yeah, for a few years. We ran the business together, and she'd write when she could. It was her dad that encouraged me to follow my dream and set this place up. I wouldn't be here if it wasn't for her. We had our problems, but I spent some of the best years of my life with that woman. It's a shame they ended the way they did. She's a special person."

Beatrice followed Sam's gaze to Sydney as she entered the house. "I'm beginning to see that."

Was he still harbouring feelings, or was it more a passing feeling of nostalgia?

"So you can fix *Gertie* then?"

"She's all glamour on the outside, but underneath she's hiding a lot of problems," Sam replied. "She's broken—"

"But not beyond repair?" Beatrice finished hopefully.

"No. At least I hope not. Who knows what I'll find when I strip her down to her bare bones?"

"It seems to have quite the hold over Sydney," Beatrice said, flatly refusing to use a personal pronoun for the camper van like everyone else did.

"Gertie's all she has left of her dad; he bought her for

her seventeenth birthday. They worked on her bodywork together, and now it's time to fix the heart of her. She only stayed down here to get the money together to fix her. By rights, she and Gertie should be roaming the countryside now. I'm glad she did, though; it gave us a chance to reconnect."

"You'd lost touch then?"

"We broke up about ten years ago. It was my cousin's wedding that put us back in touch. I hadn't realised how much I missed her. She's a good laugh."

Beatrice smiled. It was another thing she was beginning to discover for herself.

"How much does it cost to do whatever it is you're doing?"

Sam sucked in a breath. "Parts alone are into the low thousands. It all depends on how much needs doing once I open her up."

"You do what needs doing, and when the time comes, give me a call for payment." Beatrice rifled in her handbag and presented him with a card. She waved it at him to gain his attention, which had glazed over at Beatrice's request.

"Are you... sure? That's incredibly generous."

"Let's keep it between us for the meantime, yes?" Beatrice asked, noticing Sydney emerging from the house.

Sam nodded and took the card.

CHAPTER 23

"*S*ydney, these aren't mine."

Sydney glanced up from the washing basket to see a pair of her blandest black Marks and Spencer knickers hanging from Beatrice's finger. She begged the ground to swallow her whole.

"Erm, sorry," Sydney replied, retrieving them from a smirking Beatrice, dying a little more as she realised they weren't even black, more like a thousand-wash grey.

"Would you assist me with a bath?" Beatrice said, blessedly moving the conversation along. "I need to wash my hair after that boat ride."

"Of course, I'll run one now."

Thoughts of their visit to the harbour filled her head as fast as the bath filled with water. It was like two worlds colliding showing Beatrice her old territory and introducing her to Sam. Not to mention the small moment of declaring herself a lesbian to her employer. It was an unexpectedly enjoyable day, considering how the weekend panned out. The food was delightful, the company more so. Beatrice poked her head out of her shell a little more and showed a humorous side to her personality that Sydney hadn't noticed before — a side that suited the woman. It was a much-needed win for peace and harmony at Highwood House.

The woman arrived in the bathroom in her bikini, forgoing her dressing gown, and made her way over to the toilet seat, ready for Sydney. They were like a well-oiled machine with Beatrice strapped into her waterproof cover and in the bath within two minutes.

"Would you assist me with washing my hair, please? I find I need to keep one hand on the side of the bath to stop myself slipping about."

Sydney was more than happy to oblige and worked the shampoo into Beatrice's hair with her fingernails, rubbing at her scalp. Beatrice's fingers clenched the top of the roll-top bath in sync with her touch, her body writhing a little in the warm water. She was working her like a puppet master.

Her mind unhelpfully recalled the dream of the previous morning, a dream she'd fought to keep far back in her mind and was now struggling to. It made her realise she'd do anything for the woman who was now at her fingertips. She longed for the next time she might hear Beatrice say, "Very good." The tone in which she said it left you unsure if you had satisfied her or dissatisfied her. Even if she was saying it to get rid of you, you didn't care — all you wanted was to hear it again.

After the bath, they hobbled downstairs, where it was time for Beatrice to try out Rosie's scooter. It brought much delight to her when Beatrice first saw it. Watching her face contort with a mixture of pleasure and disgust as if she were laying an egg was something Sydney wouldn't forget in a hurry. After five minutes of practice and another five minutes of fretting over whether the device had left marks on the floor, Beatrice was a pro. She was like a kid wheeling around on an office chair.

"You'll be able to fetch things for me now," Sydney joked.

"Let's not get too far ahead of ourselves," Beatrice proposed. "And nothing hot! Okay? You'd have to come down for it anyway. I may be mobile again but only one floor at a time."

"Well, I thought I might work from the dining table again whilst Alex was gone. Unless you'd prefer to be alone?"

"No," Beatrice replied quickly with a smile. "I'd like that very much."

Sydney thought she noticed a little blushing on her sharp cheekbones as the woman manoeuvred herself onto the sofa from the scooter.

"Have you thought any more about physiotherapy?" she asked.

"I suppose I need to be fighting fit for when I return to set. Put something in the diary for next week, if your friend is available," Beatrice said as she clawed her fingers around the top of her cast.

Sydney quickly tapped out a message before she could change her mind, knowing Rosie would make room in her busy schedule if it meant meeting Beatrice.

Carrying her laptop to the sofa, she took a seat beside the actress. "Come on, focus on something other than the itch. It's time we tackled these formative years. What did you mean by your 'new beginning'? I know you reinvented yourself, but I don't know why. Has it something to do with your parents and the lack of childhood you spoke of?"

She was determined to get to the epicentre of Beatrice's trauma, something she was sure followed her to this day. Her reaction to her parents' ashes had been bizarre.

"I was three when I was first thrown into acting," Beatrice said. "I was in a cereal advert."

Sydney set her phone to record and also began tapping on her laptop.

"I'd spent my childhood acting, missing out on a normal upbringing, only to find out that all my work barely earned me a penny." Beatrice paused, her eyes falling to the floor. "My parents spent the bulk of it, chalking it up to expenses."

"Shit." Sydney's forehead creased as quickly as her eyes shot from the laptop to Beatrice. "Couldn't you have sued them or something?"

Beatrice shook her head. "What would have been the point? At the end of the day it wasn't about the money but the exploitation. I punished them by removing them from my life. I cut myself off from them on my eighteenth birthday and followed the only route I knew — acting. This time on my terms. Though not before I blew what they did leave me on drugs and alcohol. The few people I did know were going through much the same thing; we shared a flat in London — well, more of a squat. One of them, Naomi, whom I'd... grown close to, was severely sexually abused as a child. She later overdosed. I discovered her body. Are you getting this all down?"

Sydney stared at her, not realising her fingers had stopped typing. "I... I'm going to need a moment to process everything you just said."

"If you wish," Beatrice replied blankly, taking a sip of water from her glass.

Sydney rubbed her stomach, hoping it would alleviate her nausea. How did someone move past being taken advantage of as a child? What sort of person, or persons, in this case, would even do that? To then go on to discover the body of someone close to her felt unfathomable.

"I'm so sorry. No one should have gone through that. Any of it."

Beatrice acknowledged her comment with a flick of the head and continued. "I knew I couldn't let that be my story, so I picked myself up and promised her at her graveside that things would be different for me. I knew I owed it to her to create a success story for the both of us."

If this was the moment Beatrice was choosing to get it all off her chest, Sydney wasn't about to stop her. She couldn't type, not that she needed to; nothing Beatrice was saying was going to be forgotten.

"Shortly after, I went for an audition and Alison recognised me. She was starting out as an agent at the time. She bought me lunch and I told her everything. I didn't know her from Adam, yet there was something about her I trusted. She took me back to my flat, saw the hell I was living in, and told me to pack my bags. She rescued me. I owe everything to her. She took me under her wing, nurtured me as my mother failed to do."

Beatrice paused for a moment, regaining her breath. "From then on Alison created Beatrice Russell. My real name is Victoria Harper. Alison wasn't married and didn't have any children; she was happy to let me stay with her in her flat for a few months until I got back on my feet. The months turned into years."

A ball of regret weighed in her stomach at her words to Beatrice when they had fought. This was no privileged life; it was a living nightmare.

"It was brave of you to walk away from your parents," she said.

"Was it? I ran from my problem. It would have been braver to stay and have it out with my them. I was so angry. They'd robbed me of my childhood making me work like a slave for them. It wasn't even the worst of it. As I grew older, I received a lot of unwanted attention. My parents knew and turned a blind eye to it; they said learning to deal with men was part of growing up. I couldn't take it anymore. If my parents wouldn't keep me safe, what use were they to me?"

Closing the lid of the laptop, Sydney placed it beside her and turned to face Beatrice. She wasn't sure she could take anymore, and she was only listening. Beatrice had lived through it.

"Do you not have any happy memories from your early childhood? You didn't discover what your parents did until quite late on, and I'm assuming the unwanted attention you received wasn't until you were in your teens — I hope at least."

"Any happy memories are now bad memories, all tied in with what they were doing at the time without me knowing. Yes, my early years were enjoyable at the time. Who wants to go to school? I was no different. Hitting my teens and realising my parent's attitude to the abuse was to suck it up should have been a warning sign. If they weren't on my side about that, what else weren't they on my side about?"

Sydney shook her head, still struggling to take it all in. "No one expects those dearest to them to be working against them."

Beatrice twisted her lips and continued. "There were tutors that I recall with fondness. I remember one of them asking me once if I enjoyed what I did and if I wouldn't rather be in school with the other children."

"What did you say?" Sydney asked, intrigued to know.

"I have no idea," Beatrice said with a shake of the head. "I also remember playing board games and chess with my father in trailers to pass the time between takes. I enjoyed that... at the time."

Sydney caught her eye at the mention of board games. Was this why she refused to play them now? A fun pastime of playing them with her child had been ruined by her parents.

"My father taught me how to play the piano, too, more forced me than encouraged me to learn. It must have been their backup plan for me if acting didn't work out. My skills on the piano, however, are limited. When I bought this house, the first thing I bought was that piano." Beatrice nodded to the entrance hall. "It was my choice to buy it and play it, no one else's. I bought it for a house I earned. It serves as a reminder that I *can* play it and it's my choice *to* play it."

"Can I play it?"

"You play?" Beatrice asked with astonishment.

"A little, yes." Her dad had taught her too.

"Feel free."

"Thank you. Now tell me more about this unwanted attention."

"For a time I avoided settling down. I didn't exactly have the lifestyle for it. Then I naively believed the best way to avoid unwanted male attention was by marrying. Peter was on the very short list of men I could tolerate — at the time. It turned out it didn't stop unwanted male attention and Peter became jealous and controlling." Beatrice smiled and then let out a light laugh. "You know, he even tried to sack Alison once and told her he was taking over as my agent. She told him to fuck off of course. I do wish we could hurry this divorce along; first it was my parents and now it's Peter. Dead weights trying to drown me."

"Do you mind telling me what the delay is?"

"Let's just say he's using everything he has over me to wring my neck for more money."

"Like what?" Sydney asked, knowing it was unlikely she would tell her but figuring it was worth a try.

"A potential career-destroyer."

The thought that the odious man held power over Beatrice incensed her. The desire to know what the career-destroying secret could be was going to drive her to distraction.

"Give him more."

Beatrice laughed, tilting her head back a little.

Sydney's lips twitched upwards as she watched her. Desired her.

"I do adore your naivety. When he asks for more again, do I continue to give it to him?" Beatrice shook her head. "It's never-ending. It's just a game to him, to play for as long as he can. We've been like this for months. With the autobiography coming up, it would be nice to draw a line under it. He sees it as another money spinner and more to which he is owed. He'll want to see how the sales are going so he can take his percentage. It's just another attempt to control me."

"I don't believe anyone could control you."

"As I said before, what you see is a façade; it's all an act. I'm like this for a reason. So people don't trample on me again."

"I don't think it's a façade. I think it's you. The stronger part of you protecting the more vulnerable Beatrice. That part seems slightly resentful, angry, sometimes a little vicious... for good reason."

Beatrice fell silent for a moment before she said, "Alison advised me to take out a prenup, but I regrettably ignored her. She was never a huge fan of Peter, but I was getting on a bit by then and thought myself in love. It's difficult meeting people when you're famous... people you can trust. She respected my decision. It was a turning point for me to even put my trust in someone, and that was something she encouraged. I fell pregnant, and rather than give up work, we agreed that Peter would instead — he was a failing musician, so it was no hardship. All he wanted was fame, and he could get that by marrying me without lifting a finger." Beatrice sighed. "The two of them came with me wherever I went, and it was bliss for those first few years until Alex hit school age. We bought this house, and I'd hoped Peter would stay at home with him, give him some stability; the normal upbringing that I never experienced."

She reached for her glass of water and took a sip.

"Peter had different plans. He persuaded me that Alex should go to prep school at age seven. What Peter wanted was to continue following me round so he could drink and visit brothels and casinos on my money without our son cramping his style."

"Shit."

Beatrice had been betrayed by everyone she was supposed to be able to trust. No wonder she was defensive and spent most of her time in attack mode, Sydney thought. She was like a kicked dog.

"I should have put my foot down at the time, yet in hindsight, it was best he was away from his father full time. By then I think I was starting to realise who Peter really was — a leech like the rest. I don't relish the fact I put my career before my child, and I know Alex resents me for it."

Sydney nodded. "He thinks it's your fault he was put in a boarding school. That you wanted Peter by your side and sent him away."

"I guessed as much." Beatrice picked at her fingers. "As I said before, I'm not going to be the one to tell him what his father's really like. He needs a relationship with one of us."

"And that should be you, Beatrice," Sydney replied, her voice spilling over with frustration.

"I'm hardly a role model."

"You work hard to provide for him. For this house. To give him one of the best educations in the world. You're a better role model than his lame-arsed dad could ever be."

Beatrice levelled her with a stare. "Nothing about Peter is to go in the book. Understand me."

Sydney gave a reluctant nod. It was more than the creep deserved, and Beatrice was far more generous than she'd ever given her credit for. She'd let her son believe she was the evil queen just so he could have a relationship with that sack-of-shit. She was admirably insane.

"You're happy for him to see you drag your parents over the coals and not his dad?" Sydney couldn't help asking.

"He never met his grandparents; never idolised them."

Sydney wasn't so sure that Alex did idolise Peter as much as Beatrice believed him to, though it wasn't her place to question it.

"So you find me a broken woman, Sydney," Beatrice summarised.

"Broken women can be fixed. Look at Gertie."

"Are you comparing me to that..." Beatrice pushed her lips together as she thought. "Okay. I've run out of insults."

"Finally! You know, you two are about the same age."

Beatrice's eyebrows shot up.

"You are looking much better for it, though. I think Gertie's well past her pulling time."

"As am I." Beatrice chuckled.

"What? You're an intelligent and beautiful woman in the prime of her life."

"Kind of you to fuzz over the fact I'm self-centred, menopausal, overbear—"

"Stop. You're remarkable. You're strong; you're a survivor. Any man should be proud to have you on his arm."

"Whether I would wish to be on *any* man's arm is up for debate. Anyway, I've already proven myself to be unlovable."

"You are not unlovable," Sydney said, as she nervously turned her gaze towards Beatrice. "Believe me."

The corners of Beatrice's lips tightened making Sydney's heart beat a little faster.

"No one is," Sydney added. She stood, feeling the need for a bit of space between them. "I'll make a start on dinner."

CHAPTER 24

"*I*t's Alex's birthday a week on Tuesday. Can you buy him something, please?" Beatrice said from her usual spot on the sofa.

"What does he like?"

"Get him a watch or something."

Sydney knew Beatrice's tones well enough to know she held no interest for the question and expected her to deal with it.

Beatrice's eyes shot to her phone as the buzz of the gate bell came from it.

"Is that Alex?" Sydney asked.

"And Peter." Beatrice sighed. "I don't want to see him, not after last time."

"I'll go meet Alex," Sydney said, "and make sure Peter doesn't step foot inside the house."

Beatrice sighed again, this time with relief. "Thank you."

"He really pushes your buttons, doesn't he?"

The silence from the sofa said everything.

Sydney made her way out along the back path and around the side of the house as Peter and Alex were getting out of the car.

"Bye, Dad."

"Bye, dude."

Alex huffed and rolled his eyes as he came towards Sydney.

"It's nice to have you home, Alex."

He gathered a smile together for her as he passed.

"Sydney! Not washing cars today?" Peter asked, looking her up and down as he approached her. "Shame, you put on quite the show last time. Can I persuade you to put on a repeat performance for me now?"

"Would you like that?" She prised out her best smile, hoping it would entice him towards her.

Peter edged uncomfortably close. His stinking breath made her hold her own.

She placed her hands on his upper arms, bringing a smile to his face. She clamped hold and lifted her knee firmly into his groin. He grunted in both pain and surprise. This hadn't exactly been part of the plan, but if the plan didn't work, Sydney at least wanted some satisfaction from their encounter.

"There is literally nothing you or any man has to offer that I could possibly want," Sydney spat into his ear as he bent over double.

"Fucking bitch." Peter coughed and spat on the ground. His strained voice was filled with venom. "You're well matched then. Is that why she hired you?"

"What?"

The confusion on her face encouraged him to clarify after regaining his breath.

"Bea's into the ladies. Didn't you know?"

What the actual...?

"It's hardly surprising when she's married to you," Sydney replied quickly before she got caught up in her thoughts. "You're enough to turn any woman's stomach, let alone her sexuality."

"You know she did a lesbian film," Peter said, lifting himself up, still nursing his balls with his hands. "We split shortly after; she enjoyed her role a little too much." He laughed, then winced. "I saw the way she eyeballed her co-star. Bea was hungry — so I ate for her."

Bastard.

She clenched her teeth and would have kneed him again if he wasn't still cradling his package.

"I did wonder about leaking it to the press, but you know" — Peter shrugged — "the kid."

"Alex. Your son," Sydney reminded him, although she was astonished he gave a shit about Alex. "The one you insisted on abandoning to a boarding school, despite his mum's objections, in exchange for casinos and prostitutes."

He straightened gingerly, pulled a packet of cigarettes from his trouser pocket, and shrugged again. "Maybe one day I will leak it. In the meantime, it keeps her in check."

Sydney nodded, trying to keep her cool whilst her insides burned with rage. "So this is why you aren't signing the divorce papers — you think you have a hold over her? I don't think you have any intention of leaking Beatrice's sexuality to the press. What man would want the world to know your wife would rather be with a woman than you? You'd be the man that turned the most successful actress of her generation off men. Not a good look when you need to find the next woman to sponge off. You think you could ruin her reputation? She can ruin yours too. Beatrice is no longer part of your life, and it will be difficult to start a new one with the shit she'll expose in her autobiography. Prolific sexual predators don't do so well now, you may have noticed."

"Predator?" Peter blew smoke in her face as he spoke.

Refusing to rise to his taunt, she added, "Yes, predator. I assume you gained some pleasure from your actions or were you just driving her PAs away to hurt her?"

A smile rippled across his mouth; the awkwardness behind it was enough to tell her that he was annoyed that he'd been found out.

"That was your intention, wasn't it? To have her believe there was something wrong with her as she watched them walk out on her one by one."

"Of course. *One* of the intentions at least." He gave her a sleazy wink.

"She trusted you," Sydney hissed through her teeth. "You knew her history, yet you still decided to betray her, over and over. Men like you make me sick. What is it? Can't stand a woman being more successful than you so you knock her down? Sign those divorce papers, take the no doubt far too generous settlement, and stay the fuck away from her."

"Why would I do that?" Peter smirked as he took a drag on his cigarette.

"Because it would take me five minutes to round up

every assistant you assaulted. They are all very willing to discuss it now they realise how many there are of them," she bluffed.

"Assaulted!" Peter dropped the cigarette and stamped on it. "I didn't assault them. I admit I may have got hands-on, but those girls were asking for anything I gave them. It wasn't my fault they all turned out to be frigid."

"Asking for it? 'Didn't assault them'?" Sydney barked in disgust. "The moment you lay your hands on a woman who doesn't want them on her, it's assault. And for the record, no woman is asking for it. That's something filthy bastards like you tell themselves to justify their behaviour. What will those women say when I tell them they were asking for it?" Sydney picked a number. "All fifteen of them."

Peter recoiled. "Fifteen? There was only ten."

"You only assaulted ten?"

"Yes."

Sydney took her phone from her pocket, unsurprised the bastard kept count. "Thanks for confirming — for the record."

Peter's face reddened as he realised he'd been tricked into incriminating himself. "What the fuck! You've been recording this the whole time?"

"Shortly after I kneed you in your tiny bollocks. I wouldn't want to incriminate myself, would I? Even though technically it was self-defence. What would Alex make of his dad being a dirty letch? I wonder if any woman would touch you in the future if they knew what you were like."

Peter lunged at her, trying to snatch the phone. She was

too quick for him and slipped it down the front of her shorts as she stepped back.

"Come and get it if you dare." She egged him on with a twitch of her hip.

"You bitch!" Peter hissed.

"I won't be here forever..." She paused. Saying it aloud kicked her in the gut, reminding her she would have to leave in a few weeks. "So I'm going to make sure every PA that follows knows about you. I suggest that you don't come around here anymore. You clearly upset Beatrice. Unless she approaches you, stay away in future. Alex will soon be old enough that you'll never need to speak to one another again." Sydney turned towards the house, calling over her shoulder, "You have until Alex's birthday to sign those divorce papers."

"I'll sue if you use that recording."

"Use it? I don't need to use it; this is for my own entertainment. I have a line of women ready to tell all at the press of a button. It would be easier for everyone if you signed the papers and moved on with your life, you sleazy prick."

As a parting remark, Peter kicked gravel at her back. She was tempted to kick some back at his car but couldn't bring herself to damage the paintwork — Peter's taste in cars was as fine as his taste in women.

As she shut the front door, she allowed her thoughts to finally settle on what she'd learned. Her heart drummed even harder than it had when she confronted Peter. Beatrice was into women. Not one to listen to idle gossip, she'd never hoped more for something to be true — not that Beatrice would ever give her the time of day in that department. She would still consider it a win for womankind.

Beatrice had said herself Peter held something over her, so it must have been true. It would explain why he had such an effect on her, and why she was so upset the first afternoon that Peter showed up. When the woman was at a low point, Sydney had waltzed in and given her another kicking. She was as bad as the rest of them.

To hear Peter confirm he'd driven away anyone that Beatrice relied on, just to undermine her confidence. It was tantamount to cruelty. Of course, the question could be asked: Was Beatrice particularly 'challenging' for her PAs because she knew they would leave her anyway, as she claimed, or did Peter simply make it easier for already disgruntled PAs to leave? From the woman's behaviour over the last few days, she already knew the answer. There was nothing wrong with Beatrice Russell and everything right about her.

She knew she was going to have to tell her about what transpired. She toyed with how much to allow Beatrice to hear of the recording, only to realise she must play it all. She wanted her to know that she knew everything, that she didn't have to hide herself from her. That she wasn't alone.

CHAPTER 25

*B*eatrice opened her eyes, immediately sensing something was different to other mornings. A smile forced its way onto her lips at the familiar sound of light snoring, this time coming from beside her. Her assistant was lying on top of the duvet, fast asleep in pyjamas shorts and a vest top, looking perfectly dishevelled.

She'd come to her room last night to clarify some things surrounding Naomi's death. Beatrice recalled inviting her onto the bed to talk through it only for sleep to take them both.

Beatrice couldn't recall waking that night, the first time in a long while, even before the annoyance of the cast. Whether that was a result of Sydney spending the night beside her she couldn't answer, even though Sydney made her feel safe — more than anyone else ever had.

She also made her feel cared for, something all her other PAs failed to achieve — if that was even part of a

PA's role. They were there to assist, make life easier, but to make someone feel cared for, wasn't that above and beyond? The role of looking after someone with a broken leg required a level of personal care not required of her other PAs. In a short space of time Sydney had seen her physically and mentally exposed. She'd told her everything — well, almost everything. There was one secret she kept to herself, and with the woman lying beside her on the bed, that was becoming increasingly difficult to hide.

Sydney's morning face was soft, not yet hardened against the day's demands. The urge to reach out to it and stroke it was so overwhelming that before she realised what she was doing, her hand was brushing the hair from Sydney's face. Her eyes opened, locking onto Beatrice's and creasing a little at the side as she smiled. A second later panic washed over her face.

"Sorry."

"It's fine." Beatrice placed a hand on Sydney's upper arm to prevent her from bouncing up.

"It's not. I shouldn't be here."

"Sydney, it's fine. We were working late; we fell asleep and… overslept, it seems."

Sydney sat up, scrabbling for her phone. "Rosie will be here soon."

Finding her laptop further down the bed, she was gone from the room in a flash, leaving Beatrice to hold on to that initial hint of pleasure on Sydney's face at waking up beside her.

The only sight Beatrice had of Sydney before Rosie's

arrival was when she brought a coffee back up to her room. Again she was gone in a flash. Beatrice found her own way down the stairs on her backside.

As she popped her knee onto the scooter awaiting her at the bottom, the gate bell rang on her phone. "Sydney, your friend is here."

Sydney darted across the entrance hall from the kitchen and out through the front door to receive her. Her assistant was a little on edge this morning.

With introductions out of the way, they crossed through to the kitchen where Rosie unfolded her treatment bed.

"Have you a towel we can use?" Rosie asked.

"I'll fetch one from the laundry cupboard," Sydney said, dashing from the room.

"Beatrice, let's have you up here so I can examine you." Rosie said, patting the bed. "Then we'll have you up and working."

Beatrice scooted her way over to Rosie, where the woman assisted her onto to the bed.

"You and Sydney have been friends for some time, I understand," she said as she got as comfortable as possible.

"Yes, since university. She's one of the best, our Syd."

"Are you a fully paid-up member of the Gertie fan club too?"

Rosie let out a light chuckle of amusement. "I am one of the biggest fans. Gertie's one of the family."

Family. A word Sam used too. She intended to press Rosie a little on Sydney's father, in the hope she would expand on Sam's comment about Gertie being all she had left of him, but the physiotherapist spoke before she could.

"Sydney said you were getting on well with the scooter."

"Yes, thank you for that. It's helped my sanity enormously."

"And mine," Sydney said as she entered with a towel and passed it to Rosie, drawing a smile from them both. "I'll leave you two to it."

"Stay," Beatrice found herself saying a little too eagerly.

"If Beatrice is fine with it, it might be a good idea for you to take note of the exercises I show her," Rosie said, checking over Beatrice's good leg. "I'll go through some exercises that you can do once the cast comes off. Is that later this week?"

"Yes, and I can't wait for a proper bath."

"Don't go scrubbing at it, will you? The best way to remove the dead skin is to soak it in warm water for twenty minutes twice a day and avoid shaving until the skin is healed. Gently rub or pat the skin with a soft towel. Don't scrub the scales off as it could cause irritation and lead to infection."

Beatrice shuddered at the word 'scales'. Would she be part reptile at the end of this frustrating process?

"Apply an alcohol-free moisturising lotion, and over time the dryness will resolve, and the scales will fall off."

"I'm sure we can manage that," Sydney said, making a note on her laptop at the table.

The thought of Sydney seeing her scaly leg made her shudder again.

"This leg doesn't seem too bad," Rosie said as she manipulated Beatrice's calf. "It's obviously been taking up a lot of slack."

"It's sore a lot of the time. It seems to switch between being painful, and achy."

"Sydney, come. I'll show you how to massage it. Assuming that's okay, Beatrice?"

"Of course, Sydney has already been helping in that department." Her eyes flicked to gauge Sydney's reaction, only to find Rosie winking at her friend, who then scowled back at her.

What was that about?

Beatrice relaxed back as Rosie placed the towel under her leg and began massaging it. She wasn't relaxing for long. Rosie knew all the places to touch that would hurt, digging her fingers in, stretching, and holding the sore muscles until she was breathless from the pain. This was a serious pummelling compared to Sydney's sensual massage — Beatrice knew which one she preferred. Her hope that Sydney wouldn't be taking too many notes was dashed as Rosie directed Sydney in hunting for areas of tension in her leg, encouraging her to knead them as Beatrice's face twisted in pain. She wasn't going to be enjoying Sydney's massages quite as much as before — that could only be a good thing.

"Try not to enjoy yourself too much, Sydney," Beatrice said dryly when she caught her breath.

"I'll try. I doubt I'll succeed." Sydney grinned as she held down a tight muscle, causing Beatrice to flinch and suck in another breath.

"Now, ladies, play nice," Rosie smirked as she observed Sydney's handiwork. "That's spot-on, Syd. We're trying to encourage blood flow to the area to help heal it. You broke your leg four weeks ago this Friday, is that right?"

"Yes," Beatrice replied, amazed at how well informed Rosie was. What else had they discussed about her on their night out?

"All being well, they should move you into a walking boot for a couple of weeks, which will protect the bone whilst allowing movement of the surrounding muscle tissue. The walking motion will reduce muscle wasting and make physical therapy more effective as you can start strengthening exercises sooner."

After fifteen minutes of further torture at Rosie's hands, her leg was beginning to feel better. They then went over ankle stretches, ankle rotation, and ankle flexibility exercises that she would need to do daily once her cast was off. Rosie had her writing out the alphabet with her good leg, drawing a snigger from across the room.

"I can hear you sniggering, Miss MacKenzie. If you can't be professional, I suggest you leave the room." She allowed a hint of flirting to enter her voice, pleased her assistant had lightened up a little since the arrival of her friend.

A stifled giggle came from behind her laptop. "Sorry."

~

With Rosie seen back to her car half an hour later, Sydney reappeared in the kitchen and headed straight to the kettle, flicking it on.

"Thank you for encouraging me to have physio," Beatrice said. "That really helped. I'll be out of your hair in no time with her hardcore regime." With no response forthcoming, she looked over to find Sydney staring at the kettle. "Sydney, are you okay? You seem a little distracted since… we woke."

"I'm fine, it's…" Sydney turned to her, agitation etched on her face. "Look. I've been thinking about the book; are you absolutely decided that Peter should be left out of it?"

"He'd sue me if I wrote anything about him."

"But it's all true." Sydney joined her on the sofa and took a deep breath. "And there's more."

Beatrice's eyebrows twitched. "More?"

Sydney nodded and then opened her mouth to speak only to close it again.

"It's okay. I can take it," Beatrice reassured her, desperate to know what was so bad it could silence Sydney. Was this what was playing on her mind?

"It wasn't only your co-star and prostitutes…"

Beatrice's stomach tightened in anticipation.

"He got hands-on with… most of your assistants."

Beatrice's gaze fell to the floor. After a moment of silence, she found her tongue.

"How did I not see that?"

"There's a lot you miss when you're looking at yourself."

It was the truth, but it stung like hell.

Sydney placed a hand on her arm and gave it a light squeeze. She was growing fond of that hand reaching out to her, reassuring her in moments of need.

"It was never you, Beatrice. Always him. There's never been anything wrong with you. You're perfect. I'm sorry I suggested you were driving them away."

"I'm sure Peter can't have a claim to all of it. I know I can be... challenging."

"Are you? Or are you a result of a lifetime of manipulations by those who were supposed to love you?"

She examined the anxious expression on Sydney's face, confused as to why it held so much concern.

"It's kind of you to even suggest that. Thank you for telling me. However... I cannot prove it."

"I can," Sydney said, pulling up a recording on her phone. Her finger hovered above the play button. "Are you sure you want to hear this?"

Beatrice would have no idea if she wanted to hear it until she'd heard it, so she encouraged Sydney with a nod.

Once a coughing sound subsided, she could hear Peter and Sydney talking. Her face twitched as Peter told Sydney that she was 'into the ladies'. Her eyes shot to Sydney's, which were already waiting for hers. Her lips offered a faint smile in what she hoped she was reading correctly as empathy at being exposed.

Her eyes closed altogether at the crassness of 'Bea was hungry'. She had been and remained so.

As Sydney attacked back, she glanced over at her, only to find the woman grinning to herself.

A smile came to her own lips as Peter rebutted the use

of the word 'predator'; that was exactly what he was, and he went on to openly admit to assaulting ten women. One was too many, but ten! That Peter had done that under her nose to women she owed a duty of care to was sickening. She hoped they didn't think she knew or condoned it. Sydney was clever with her exaggeration of the numbers to garner a reaction. It was unlikely a man had ever admitted to assault as swiftly as he had.

Beatrice shot a questioning look to Sydney as she could be heard spurring Peter on to retrieve the phone. Sydney pointed down the top of her trousers, causing Beatrice to laugh out loud.

"Why was he coughing at the beginning?" Beatrice asked as the recording ended.

Sydney's eyes glistened. "I kneed him in the balls."

"Oh, thank you!" Beatrice chuckled. "I've wanted to do that for a long time. I didn't think it was the done thing these days."

"I think it needs to be done more."

"Did he try it on with you?" Beatrice held her breath as she feared Sydney's response.

"Verbally, not physically, and I admit I encouraged him towards kneeing distance."

Sydney had put herself in harm's way for her. Beatrice clutched her stomach to settle a tingle of delight, even though it was more pleasant than the feeling of sickness it replaced.

"I am grateful for this, Sydney." She tapped the phone. "If he doesn't sign those papers, though, then you've left me in a difficult position. Can I assume you don't have a string of my previous assistants lined up to point the finger for assault?" Just the thought of it again was enough to re-establish the nausea.

Those poor women.

Sydney shook her head sheepishly. "I've been told by Alison's PA — he was the one who told me — that none of them would either."

Beatrice exhaled. "Then we best hope that you did enough to convince him that we have."

A hot tear rolled from her eyes.

"Hey," Sydney uttered sympathetically, "it's over now."

"Over. Your optimism is misplaced. Until he signs, it's not over."

Beatrice realised then, that the tear was from relief that someone else knew her secret. She'd spent so long terrified that Peter would tell someone — or that she might inadvertently give it away herself. It might have been different if it was anyone else, but Sydney understood how she felt; she understood her. There was nothing that Sydney didn't know about her, and that made her feel seen. For the first time in her life, someone knew *her*, and she trusted that person with all of it.

She'd never told Alison about her sexuality. Being her closest friend and agent was a difficult role to navigate, and she'd never wanted to put Alison in a position where she might have been conflicted as to what might be best for her client and friend personally and professionally.

Now that Beatrice considered the information divulged about her on the tape, Sydney's behaviour that morning came to mind. If Sydney had known yesterday that she wasn't the only one of them interested in women, had waking up in bed together made her uncomfortable? Her behaviour was a clear overreaction to something. Adrenaline coursed through Beatrice's veins at a thought — had Sydney developed feelings for her? As much as the thought excited her, it also petrified her.

CHAPTER 26

"It suits you," Sydney said as they left the consultant's office. "I'm not sure the bright pink did much for your image."

"Now you tell me!" Beatrice laughed. "It's so nice to be able to walk again unaided."

"Not totally unaided," Sydney said, her voice strained as Beatrice took a step and she took on a disproportional amount of her weight.

"Sorry." Beatrice adjusted herself slightly, only to stumble.

Sydney tightened her grip around her waist to stabilise her only to find her hand on the side of Beatrice's breast.

"I've got you."

She slipped her offending hand back down to Beatrice's waist with lightning speed, hopeful the flub went unnoticed.

"Thank you."

She refrained from saying that she'd always got her. Things were awkward enough since that morning when she'd woken up beside Beatrice. She'd stared into those seductive blue eyes and smiled, believing herself to be in a dream, only to realise it wasn't.

"Are you okay? You seem a little unsettled since we arrived," Beatrice asked as Sydney assisted her through the hospital reception.

Scanning the room, Sydney answered, "I hate hospitals. I spent a lot of time in them when my mum was ill. I can't stand the smell of them... even the posh ones."

"I'm sorry to hear that; you should have said something. You didn't have to walk me in."

"I did," Sydney said with a smile. She dropped her sunglasses onto her nose as they stepped out into the sunshine.

"I appreciate that. I hope it wasn't too traumatic for you."

Sydney shook her head. "Just one of the many things I need to get over."

"May I ask the nature of your mother's medical condition?"

"Breast cancer. It's why I left the harbour. She needed me; I went."

"Is that why you and Sam broke up? Was it too much to have a relationship at opposite ends of the country?"

"Sam is a man. I'm a lesbian. I loved him, but it wouldn't have worked."

"Yes, of course, sorry. So, was your father not able to cope with looking after your mother?"

Two women approached them as they reached the car.

"Beatrice Russell?" The women's faces lit up as they

realised they were correct. "Can we get a photograph please?"

"Of course you can," Beatrice replied, slapping on a smile.

It was a smile Sydney didn't recognise. Almost fake. She sensed it was the one Beatrice reserved for fans, the type pulled out of the bag at a moment's notice to cover how you were really feeling.

One of the women passed a phone to Sydney. "Would you mind?"

Sydney watched on the phone's screen as the two women flanked Beatrice, who graciously placed an arm around each of them and smiled. This time she knew it to be her genuine smile.

"Thank you," the other woman said. "We love your work."

"No trouble. I appreciate that."

Sydney passed them the phone and smirked as they weaved their way across the car park whilst admiring the photos like a pair of giggling schoolgirls. She hadn't quite appreciated Beatrice's stardom. They'd barely left the estate in four weeks, and they'd managed to avoid all attention when they dined at the harbour.

"Nancy fans," Beatrice said as she hobbled towards the Range Rover and reached out for Sydney's assistance.

Sydney gave a questioning tilt of the head as she helped her in.

"They were lesbians. They all seem obsessed with the film. They think they're fans of Beatrice Russell when, really, it's Nancy they love."

223

"How do you know they were lesbians? They could have been friends."

"Trust me, you get to know your fan base... and they were holding hands as they approached."

How had she missed that?

Avoiding watching *Nancy* was becoming increasingly challenging.

Back at Highwood House, Sydney steadied Beatrice as she climbed the stairs. She was beginning to get the hang of the boot and hobbled across her room to the bed unaided.

"First thing I need is a bath," Beatrice said, collapsing onto it.

"I'll run one now."

"I can manage... thank you, Sydney." Beatrice directed her gaze towards the door. "I don't intend to continue bathing in my bikini."

"Sorry." Sydney closed the bedroom door behind her, realising that now Beatrice was able-bodied, she wasn't going to need her as much.

The image of Beatrice without a bikini filled her mind as she wandered back down to the kitchen to work. She opened the patio door and leaned against it, admiring the view over the garden and pool, and the small coppice on the brow of the hill. It was a view she would shortly never see again; the very thought made her feel sick.

Beatrice's cast removal was the signal of the beginning of the end, and it hurt like hell. Moving on had always been part of the job; in the past, it had been easy. New adventures always followed. Moving on from Highwood House was going to be a wrench. It was the first time Sydney had felt grounded anywhere; she'd even go as far as to admit to being blissfully happy.

It wasn't just Highwood House she was going to miss; it was its mistress. She was so ensconced in Beatrice's life, and with it, Alex's, and she liked it. In fact, she loved it. She would be quite content for the summer to never end.

A vibration in her pocket pulled her away from her depressing thoughts.

"How's the patient?" Rosie asked as soon as Sydney picked up.

"We have a boot!"

"Hurrah."

"Now she's in the bath, without me. Oh, I didn't mean it to sound like that."

"Feeling unloved so soon?"

Sydney exhaled at the truth of it. "Don't."

"I'm glad to have met her. She's an impressive woman. You two are getting along a little better than when we last spoke — a lot better, in fact. I'm sure there was some drooling on your part..."

"Shut up," Sydney cut her off as she stepped onto the patio to angle the chairs correctly against the table.

"...maybe even hers," Rosie continued with a giggle. "I can see the headlines now: *Camper cutie captures the heart of Beatrice Russell.*"

"Meanwhile, back on planet Earth... we chatted and worked through some issues. So yeah, things are much better, as you saw."

"You don't sound too pleased about that."

"In all honesty, I'm not. It was easier when she was unlikeable."

"Oh, dear. You've got it bad, haven't you?"

Sydney couldn't find the words to describe her feelings.

"I'll take that as a yes. Come on, Syd, you of all people can be professional. Box it and get on with the job. Remember why you hated her a few weeks ago."

Sydney wasn't sure she had ever hated Beatrice in the time she'd known her. She'd been frustrated, annoyed, and disappointed by her for sure. But hated?

"I can't. She's changed since then."

"You've taken the ice queen from hard scoop to soft serve, and now you want a taste, is that it? Would Madam like chocolate sauce with that?"

"Okay, this conversation needs to end," Sydney demanded as she stepped back into the kitchen.

"If you insist," Rosie giggled. "Don't forget to do the exercises I gave you a couple of times a day. Don't let her push through the pain; she needs to back off when it hurts. Take her out for short walks... you could enjoy an ice cream together."

"I'm hanging up now."

"Where's Mum?"

Alex's voice made her jump as she hit the 'End Call' button. She turned, relieved to find him a good distance away. She'd been careless with her conversation. Not that she said much; Rosie was the one implying things.

"She went up for a bath as soon as we got home from the hospital."

Alex pushed a glass against a lever in the fridge door. Ice dropped in, followed by water. "Want one?"

"No, thanks."

Alex approached her, sipping his iced water, his eyes twitching as the brain freeze hit. "How did it go?"

"She's in a boot, so she'll be able to bear weight on her leg."

"She can walk?" he translated.

"Yep."

Alex laughed. "What a relief, for both of us."

"Indeed! I hear it's your birthday next week."

"Yep, and no doubt there will be another watch from Mum."

"Not into watches then?"

"I have a phone. What do I need a watch for? Plus I have tons of them. I started selling them at school."

Sydney smirked at the thought. "What would you like?"

Alex grew solemn at the question. "It would just be nice to spend the day with her," he admitted, almost under his breath. "When I was younger we'd always do something together on my birthday – as a family."

That was one hell of a random statement from a teenager. Sydney had a mind to check his temperature. That the kid was so disconnected from his own mum wasn't good; that he craved her attention was even sadder. She was going to need to pull something out of the bag for both of them on his birthday next week.

CHAPTER 27

"*J* thought we'd go for the iconic red dress; it makes you look sexy. Don't you agree, Sydney?" Alison asked, placing a hangered dress against Beatrice as she stood in front of the full-length mirror.

"Yes," was about all Sydney could say aloud as Beatrice's eyes pierced her own as they met in the mirror. There was so much more she wanted to say.

The whole situation was beginning to feel uncomfortably close to her dream, albeit with the welcome presence of Alison.

"It will stand out on the bookshelves, too, and blend perfectly with Christmas colours," Alison said. "I'll leave you to dress. I'm sure Sydney can assist you."

Seriously!?

Sydney took the dress from her and watched as the woman closed the dressing room door behind her. Her eyes returned to Beatrice, who had since slipped off her silk dressing gown and was now in a matching set of red lace underwear. A red that matched the colour of her lipstick.

Sydney sucked in a silent breath and exhaled slowly. Beatrice was enchanting, even with the addition of the walking boot.

"Dress?" Beatrice asked, raising her eyebrows as their gaze met again in the mirror. "Please."

"Sorry."

Sydney snapped herself out of it and pulled the dress from the hanger. She took the weight of Beatrice with her shoulder as she stepped into the gown, pulling it up over her legs. The red underwear screamed at her like a warning button — "Don't touch!" — when all she wanted to do was touch. Passing the dress to Beatrice to position across her chest, Sydney diverted her attention around to the back, where the actress's pale skin presented itself to her. She knew she had to do everything she could to resist touching it with her fingers — or her lips.

"Sydney, zip?"

Her fingers brushed the top of her lace knickers as she fumbled for the zip. Finally grasping it, she lifted it until it fought back, resisting her request as if it understood her reluctance to lose sight of Beatrice's back. Moving closer, she took both sides of the material and then blew softly across her shoulders. Beatrice inhaled and her body lifted, allowing Sydney to pull the material together and zip her up.

"Thank you," Beatrice said, turning. "How do I look?"

"Stunning." Sydney gulped, only able to see the afterimage of Beatrice in her underwear.

"Then let's get this over and done with," Beatrice said, hobbling from the room.

The entrance hall was buzzing with people and photographic equipment. As Beatrice made her way down the stairs, assisted by Sydney, everyone turned to look up at her.

Gasps filled the air.

"Annabel. What a delight to be working with you again," Beatrice called out.

The photographer met her on the stairs, and they shared a tight embrace. "Beatrice," Annabel crooned. "It's been a while, but you've barely aged. How on earth do you do it?"

Beatrice scoffed. "Nonsense."

"Right! Let's have that boot off. Makeup! If we can have a final check, please."

Several people swooped around them, brushing Beatrice's face, clicking light meters at her, and teasing her curled hair into position. Once they'd dispersed, Sydney removed the boot from Beatrice's leg and saw it for the first time. The skin was discoloured in places, agitated and dry. Ensuring Beatrice was steady on the stair and secured onto the handrail, she backed away and joined everyone else in admiring the beauty from the entrance hall.

The shutter of the camera clicked away as Annabel played with several angles. After discussions with her technician and much gesticulating at a laptop, Annabel said, "Come down a step please. That glorious window of yours is working against us."

A woman shot forward and rearranged the bottom of the dress.

"Let's try not looking at the camera this time. We're going for demure. Tilt your head down and to the right a little."

Beatrice did as instructed, only for her eyes to drift back up and settle on Sydney. Both sets of eyes locked onto each other.

"Hold that." The camera clicked furiously. "Perfect, Beatrice. Perfect."

The intensity of her stare bored into the very heart of Sydney. Blood rushed through her, leaving her light-headed. Beatrice's face relaxed and her lips curled up as the intensity increased, exciting the photographer further as another set of clicks resounded through the room. Sydney knew she couldn't look away; breaking the hold could cause Beatrice to lose her pose. She wasn't even sure if it was possible to look away. Would her eyes move even if she forced them?

"Beautiful," Annabel shouted. After another round of clicking, she turned to the technician behind her and checked their laptop. "That's the one. Thank you, everyone." She turned to her model and bowed. "Beatrice, you are art itself."

The photographer was spot-on.

The entrance hall transformed into a flurry of activity with lights coming down and black cases coming from nowhere. It was free and clear of people within fifteen minutes, when Sydney closed the door on everyone but Alison, who assisted Beatrice back to her room to undress. Sydney was grateful that someone else would have to deal with that zip, yet also a little disappointed it wasn't her. It was difficult enough zipping her up. Unzipping would have broken her, or at least the friendship they'd begun to build.

She returned to her position at the kitchen table, choosing not to relocate to the secluded turret despite Alex's return last week. With the days edging away from her, she wanted to be in Beatrice's company as much as possible. Now that she'd laid down the bulk of the words for Beatrice's childhood, it was merely a case of editing, which required a certain level of concentration to rearrange words, just not as much as actually finding some.

Time rolled on, and neither Alison nor Beatrice made an appearance. Was there anything more to their friendship? They'd been in her room for some time now, *undressing*. Alison was unmarried, according to Beatrice; all her life, one would assume. Was there more to Alison's kindness over the years? Was it driven by something deeper?

Sydney dropped her head into her hands. She was unsure if Alison even knew about Beatrice's inclinations. It was churlish of her to assume that something was going on above her, much less to give into jealousy.

"I'm off, Sydney," Alison said, suddenly appearing in the kitchen. "It was nice to see you again."

Sydney got to her feet. "I'll see you out," She crossed the entrance hall and opened the door.

Alison turned on the doorstep and placed a hand on Sydney's arm.

"Whatever it is you're doing, Sydney, keep at it, won't you?"

With that she was gone, leaving Sydney to ponder her

meaning. What was she doing, and with what? The book? Beatrice? Both? Keeping at anything she was doing was going to be an impossibility when it was taken from her shortly.

Back at her desk, Sydney tapped at the side of her keyboard, partly in time to the music filling her headphones, partly with frustration at not being able to structure a sentence.

The difficulty was writing it in the first-person perspective. She was a third-person writer, and first-person was a completely different kettle of fish. Not only that, the voice she was writing wasn't of her own creation; it was a real person. Putting herself in Beatrice's shoes day after day was challenging, but she had to allow her tone, diction, and syntax to flow through her to create an authentic piece, something that was often missing from ghostwritten autobiographies.

Rereading all her earlier work, she'd realised she'd used the voice of the harder, stonier Beatrice that she'd first met. Beatrice had changed in her eyes. She wasn't the same person she'd met at Biggin Hill or made assumptions about early on and chastised for her rudeness. She'd discovered the real Beatrice, one that could be humorous, caring, and forgiving. Yes, she could be cold, demanding, impatient, and at times abrasive. Weren't those terms really caution, perfectionism, determination, and defensiveness in a clever disguise? Beatrice was a product of those around her, of her experiences — as was Sydney. As were Alex's bullies.

From what she understood of Beatrice, she'd not loved or felt loved in so long — if at all. She'd never experienced parental love, true love, or even loved as a mother, yet to Sydney, she was a loveable woman. She knew she could love her for everything she was, not the image Beatrice built of herself.

She jumped as a weight touched her shoulder. Whipping her headphones off, she turned to find Beatrice right behind her.

"How are you getting on?" Beatrice asked, leaning over her to look at her screen.

It took her by surprise. It was the first time Beatrice had entered her personal space; it was always she who entered Beatrice's. She could feel her breath on her skin; smell that soothing scent of hers. The hair on her arms stood on end. She pulled her sleeves down to cover them.

"Getting there. I can't believe how much we've covered."

"You've done a great job reworking my ramblings."

"They weren't ramblings. They were confused thoughts from a confused life."

"Well, thank you for helping me file everything correctly."

"It's what a good PA does."

She could still feel Beatrice's hand on her shoulder. She wanted to reach up to it, hold it, kiss it, and never let it go.

"I need some fresh air." Beatrice tapped her shoulder and then removed it. "Would you walk with me? Just down the drive a little."

"Yes. I need a break." Sydney stood, arching her back and stretching her arms up. As she turned to face Beatrice, the woman turned her head away sharply. *Had she just been checked out by Beatrice Russell?* Every part of her pulsed at the possibility of it until she convinced herself there was no chance of that ever happening.

Beatrice hooked an arm into Sydney's for extra support as they made their way slowly across the loose gravel drive. As they reached the harder, more compact part of the road that led down to the wood, Beatrice remained attached. She wasn't going to complain; she was grateful to have her there.

She listened as Beatrice pointed out all the areas of the estate she'd restored over the years and filled her in on the history of Highwood House. It was built by an architect whose wife was a writer. He'd built the turret so she could appreciate the beauty of the estate whilst being shut away for hours, working. Sydney knew that room had called to her for a reason.

"Did you hear back about the audition you went for?"

"Yes. Alison told me this morning that they gave it to someone younger."

Sydney wrinkled her nose. "Sorry."

"It's for the best. It would have taken me to Africa for three months next year with a punishing schedule. I'd like to do more in this country. I'd gladly swap Hollywood for Highwood. Anyway, there's already talk that the male co-star will be earning more than her."

"Really? That's horrific. You're best out of it then."

Beatrice sighed. "It's not great for the self-esteem if I can't even get the roles where they intended to pay less. I would have fought it, of course, had they given me the part."

"If it happens at the top, it must happen all the way down."

"You bet it does. For one film I did years ago, the male co-star was paid twice as much as me for less screen time. That was the only time I might add. Alison demands to see male co-stars' contracts before allowing me to sign, to ensure I'm paid equally. Luckily, I can pick and choose my parts. At least I could; the tide looks to be turning away from me. Maybe I should take it as a sign to slow down and reduce my workload."

"Why? So you can bow out before you're dumped?"

Sydney's supporting arm jerked as Beatrice shrugged.

With no verbal answer forthcoming, Sydney continued. "You need to fight back; you've got your best years to come. The most difficult years juggling motherhood and a career are almost behind you. What was all that for if you give it up when the going gets tough? Ageing hasn't diminished your talent; it's increased it. Show them. It's time to reinvent yourself, write your own narrative, take control. Don't run from it."

"Perhaps," Beatrice sighed wistfully.

"What makes you choose a part?"

"The character. I need to feel a connection. If I don't feel a passion for their story inside me, I turn it down."

"Even if it's a great part with a great team?"

"If there's a great team, there's a great script, so it's rare that I turn something down like that unless there's a scheduling conflict. There's just something magical about being with a group of people who are all at the top of their game. It's like an enthralling conversation at a dinner party."

Sydney nodded; she understood what she meant.

"Do you struggle to move on from a character? Do you bring them home with you?"

"I try not to, but I find with every character I play I take a little bit of them away with me, their perspective of the world, how they deal with things. It develops your own character in a way." Beatrice came to a stop. "Let's turn back."

Sydney's thoughts turned to the character in *Nancy*. What had Beatrice taken away of her?

"Can I ask you something?" Sydney said as they began to tackle the slight incline of the driveway.

"You've done nothing but ask questions for the last four weeks. Why ask for permission now?"

Sydney fell silent. This was a personal question but with an intent behind it; she needed to know the answer for herself this time, not for the book. They hadn't even discussed the subject since Sydney became aware of such a personal piece of information about her employer.

"Go on," Beatrice encouraged her.

"Does Alison know?"

"About what?"

"Your..." Sydney struggled to find the right word. She didn't want to say 'sexuality', unsure of what that was.

"No, she doesn't. Just you and Peter."

A wave of relief came over her to know there was nothing between the two women other than friendship.

"Do you think he'll sign before his time is up tomorrow?"

Beatrice paused for a moment before answering. "I'm not holding my breath."

CHAPTER 28

*B*eatrice woke on the morning of Alex's birthday to the news she'd feared would never come. An email from her solicitor confirmed Peter has relented on the divorce and signed with a few minor additions she could live with. Desperate to share the news with Sydney, and to thank her, she made her way downstairs after a quick text to Alison.

Before she reached the bottom of the stairs, Alison's name was already flashing up on her phone. She swiped at it with her thumb.

"Alison... I can't tell you what a relief it is," Beatrice said as she hobbled across the entrance hall, her morning legs struggling to walk with the heavy boot.

"Well, I have Sydney to thank for that... yes... it was all her," Beatrice continued as she entered the kitchen to find her clever assistant making coffee.

"I must go. I'll catch you up on it tomorrow. It's Alex's birthday today... yes, I'll pass that on, and your card."

Beatrice hung up and placed her phone on the worktop as Sydney twitched her head at her.

"He's signed, Sydney. He's blooming well signed." Beatrice clenched her fists and shook them.

Sydney jumped with joy and shot towards her, stopping awkwardly short of embracing her. Beatrice couldn't resist wrapping her arms around her and squeezing her. There was so much to thank her for.

"I can't believe it! Thank you."

Sydney's arms squeezed her back. She didn't want to let go; to lose this moment. As Sydney's body loosened, she realised it would be awkward to hang on any longer. Without thinking, Beatrice kissed her cheek as she pulled away. It was innocent, yet it took her assistant by surprise.

"What a relief. I'm so pleased for you." Sydney smiled as she regained her composure. "Coffee?"

"Please," Beatrice said, noticing Sydney's cheeks redden.

She perched herself on a stool at the kitchen island, making sure to tuck her walking boot onto the crossbar for support. As she sipped her coffee, she noticed how clean the kitchen was.

"Have you been cleaning the kitchen all morning? It looks cleaner than when it was installed."

Sydney smiled at the compliment. "*You* have something special planned for Alex today."

"I do?"

"Yes, and it requires a spotless kitchen."

"Can I ask what it involves?"

"That's the best bit. You get to sit there most of the day."

Beatrice's forehead twitched. She was all up for that, but what sort of special birthday involved sitting in one's kitchen?

Her frown drew further comment from Sydney. "You'll find out in due course. Just don't act too surprised. You arranged it, remember."

"I can't believe he's fifteen already. Where does the time go?" Beatrice pondered rhetorically. "For one of his birthdays, I took a day off from filming, and we flew him over the Grand Canyon in a helicopter. Those were the days when he adored me." She sighed to herself; she missed those days.

"I'm sure he still does in his own way..." Sydney paused and cocked an ear towards the ceiling. "I think I hear movement upstairs. Follow me."

Beatrice followed her into the entrance hall where she watched the woman take a seat at the piano. The sound of 'Happy Birthday' filled the hall as Alex reached the galleried landing halfway down the stairs. Sydney broke out into song, so she joined in, only for Alex to blush and run back upstairs.

"I'm only coming down if you stop," his voice called down the stairs.

"Oh dear, Sydney. We already have a request and it's not for an encore," Beatrice chuckled.

As Sydney stopped playing, it struck Beatrice that she had no present to give him. Was Sydney's special plan the present? Alex reappeared at the top of the stairs as Sydney joined her, shoving a heavy present into her hands. The woman was like clockwork.

"Happy birthday," she said, handing the gift to Alex.

Alex took the present to the central table and tore into it.

"Wow! Henckels knives. These are what some of the top chefs use. Thanks, Mum, they're brilliant. So much better than a watch." Alex shot a smile in Sydney's direction.

"I'm pleased you approve."

"This is from me." Sydney passed him a smaller, flat present, which he peeled open immediately, extracting a white chef's jacket embroidered with his name.

"Thank you, these are amazing! Best presents ever," Alex said as he collected them and headed for the kitchen.

"More coffee?" Sydney asked Beatrice as she followed.

"I thought you'd never ask."

Beatrice couldn't stop smiling as she watched Alex fawn over his presents on the sofa. He laid out his knives and inspected each one until eventually he boxed them and placed them on his lap and watched television whilst scrolling on his phone. It reminded her of birthdays when he was little. He'd sit with his new toys and examine them for hours before he'd play with them. It was as if he was figuring out what to do with them.

She turned to find Sydney watching her.

"Thank you," she said again.

"You're very welcome." Sydney smiled and blew on her coffee to cool it.

"I would never have thought of..." She trailed off, realising that was her problem. Thoughtlessness, at least when it came to others. "I'm grateful that you took the time to consider Alex. Though giving a set of knives to a child?"

"A chef, Beatrice. A chef."

Beatrice pulled her lips to one side and nodded.

"Encourage him to be the best of what he wants to be, not what you want him to be." Sydney tapped the work surface with her finger. "Oh, and no more watches, okay?"

The woman was infuriatingly perfect in everything she did. Perfection was something Beatrice always strived for herself, yet only achieved in her career, not personally. Sydney, on the other hand, appeared to have it in all aspects of her life. How did she do that? At least with the divorce papers signed she could finally breathe. Perhaps she could start again, another new beginning — until she got it wrong again no doubt.

The gate app flashed onto her phone.

"You'll want to open that," Sydney said knowingly.

"Why?"

"Just do it."

She pushed the open button despite her assistant's refusal to inform her who she was letting on to her estate. Within a few minutes, the doorbell rang.

"Alex. There's someone at the door."

"Can't you get it?" Alex cried lazily from the sofa.

"No. It's for you."

A puzzled Alex sloped off the sofa and into the hall as Sydney flicked her head at Beatrice, encouraging her to follow. Intrigue pulled her up on to her boot in seconds.

"What are you up to, Sydney?"

Alex was opening the door as they reached the hall. He partially collapsed in disbelief at the figure at the door.

"Hi. You must be Alex."

Beatrice recognised that voice.

"Your mum asked me to come and spend some time teaching you some cooking skills."

"Oh my God, Chef Anthony! I can't believe it's you. I've watched all your shows."

"I should think so too. Where else would anyone learn to cook? Am I coming in, or are we barbecuing?"

Alex opened the door wide. "Sorry."

"I didn't know you knew Anthony," Beatrice whispered to Sydney.

"I used to work for him until he moved his TV show to the States. I happened to notice he was in your black book, and he happens to owe me a favour."

"Anthony owes you a favour?"

"Yes." Sydney pretended to zip her lips together.

Despite her desperation to know what Sydney had done to be owed a favour by one of the biggest celebrity chefs on the planet, Beatrice knew that was a sign not to dig further... for now.

Anthony sidled up to Beatrice and slipped a kiss onto her cheek. "Beatrice. As soon as Syd called me and said who she was working for, I knew she'd need help."

Beatrice pursed her lips at his comment. "Thank you, Anthony. Always nice to see you."

He turned to Sydney and scooped her up so her legs were off the ground before dropping her back down with a kiss on the cheek. "Syd! The car is full of shopping, would you mind?" Anthony dangled his car key off his finger.

"Just like old times," Sydney smirked as she took them. "Still got the Lambo?"

"Of course. I wouldn't sell my baby, would I? Now come on, Alex, show me to the kitchen and we can get started. We've got a lot to get through. I hope everyone is ready for a gourmet lunch. I have a flight home this evening, so I can't stick around any longer. But we'll pull an afternoon tea together for the ladies, eh, Alex?"

Beatrice's stomach rumbled at the thought as she followed Alex and Anthony through to the kitchen with a smile.

"Look what my mum bought me." Alex grabbed his knives from the sofa and displayed them on the kitchen island.

"Impressive. Now let's see how you use them."

Alex was in his element in his chef's jacket, making macarons and scones. The only time he took his eyes off Anthony's hands was to pay attention to his own hands. As the morning rolled on, Alex pulled together a lunch of Thai prawn curry under close instruction, serving it to them all at the table. Anthony and Sydney reminisced about their time together as they ate. It was clear the chef respected Sydney — everyone respected her.

After lunch, her assistant continued her work from the table whilst Beatrice positioned herself back at the kitchen island where she could continue to watch everyone, including Sydney. Anthony taught him new skills and showed him how to build on his current skills, particularly where the knives were concerned.

She'd never seen Alex as happy as he was now. A tear pooled in her eye at his enthusiasm for his passion. A quick wipe and it was gone before anyone could notice. Her smile widened further as she gazed over at her diligent assistant typing away on her laptop; the first, and likely only, assistant she was going to miss.

By the time they'd said goodbye to Anthony, Alex was a different chef altogether.

"What would you like to do now?" Beatrice asked.

"How does anything beat Chef Anthony? Seriously, Mum, that was amazing. I can't wait to tell my friends."

It wasn't as if Alex hadn't met swathes of celebrities over the years, yet this one had made an impact on him.

"Well, how about a board game whilst we enjoy that delicious-looking afternoon tea you made?" Beatrice suggested, eager to dive into a scone.

"You'll play?" he cheered, his eyes widening. "Which one?"

"Your choice. Sydney, you in?"

"You bet I am," Sydney replied with a grin.

Beatrice had never seen a laptop close so fast.

"How about some champagne to go with it? We are celebrating after all. Sydney, would you do the honours?"

"Can I have some?" Alex pleaded.

"One glass."

Alex's eyes shone. "Thanks, Mum. You're the best."

It warmed her heart to hear such praise from him.

Beatrice drained her glass as she stared at the rain lashing against the patio door. Alex was in the final throes of thrashing Sydney at Monopoly, having bankrupted Beatrice early on.

"This weather was going to break at some point." Beatrice yawned. "At least it will give the grass a much-needed drink."

"Typical of it to rain on my birthday," Alex groaned.

Sydney reluctantly placed her dog counter on Mayfair, where a hotel was parked.

"Ha!" Alex shouted, his mood suddenly swinging.

Sydney raised her hands. "Okay, you win."

"Yet again!" he said, getting up and scowling through the patio doors. "I wanted to go in the pool today."

"And why can't you?" Sydney said. "I'm going to. Right now, in fact."

"Cool. Can you pack up, Mum? I'll grab my shorts." Alex ran out of the kitchen without waiting for an answer.

After packing up, Beatrice headed to her room with the intention to have a nap. As she drew the curtain, she noticed the shower had passed. The dark grey cloud had moved beyond the hill. On opening her balcony door, a cool, much-needed breeze of fresh air hit her. She could hear Alex and Sydney lapping the pool, racing each other again.

She changed into a bikini instead, her red one and checked herself out in the mirror. It was a similar image to the one from yesterday, when she'd been standing in her red lace underwear in front of Sydney. Although they covered the same amount of flesh, there was something more exposing, being in one's underwear as opposed to a bikini. Bikinis were worn to be seen; underwear was intended to be hidden, except around special people.

She'd enjoyed Sydney seeing her like that and believed the feeling may have been mutual. The woman had certainly taken her time in dressing her and zipping her up. Her breath on her skin had made Beatrice inhale deeply, though it was likely a polite way of asking her to breathe in.

Returning to the kitchen, she sat by the open patio door to remove her walking boot. She could hear Alex and Sydney chatting in the pool.

"Have you considered moving schools? A fresh start as whoever you want to be?"

"What if I don't know what that is?"

"It takes us all time to figure that out. Sometimes we never figure it out; we must go with the flow and see where it takes us. Sometimes we think we've figured it out, and it turns out we were wrong, and we choose another route. There's no rushing these things."

Beatrice frowned as she released the last strap on her boot. Earlier today he had wanted to be a chef, and now he didn't know. Children were so fickle.

"What did your dad get you for your birthday?"

Beatrice shuddered at the reminder of Peter's existence.

"A PlayStation 5. I'm glad he isn't here today; he would have only upset Mum. I don't want him around anymore if he's going to do that. It's best they are far apart from each other."

Beatrice was awash with pride at his words. How had he turned into such a considerate young man? She wasn't sure she could take any credit for it, and he certainly wouldn't have learned that behaviour from Peter.

Slipping her leg out of the boot, she made her way outside with the help of her crutches. Her leg was beginning to feel normal again. Although the boot was just as heavy, if not heavier than the cast, it weighed less on her mind. Knowing she could remove it at any time no doubt helped, and it certainly made a difference to her mood when it wasn't on.

She'd given up wearing it at night, which not only improved her sleep but also accessibility to the bathroom. The skin was already beginning to heal in the few days since the cast removal. Regular soakings in the bath, followed by a light dab with a towel and a moisturiser, as instructed by Rosie, was doing wonders.

She lowered herself on the first step of the pool and let her legs float in the cool water.

"Are you not coming in, Beatrice?" Sydney asked.

"I don't want to get my hair wet."

"Come on, Mum. Come in," Alex said, splashing her with water.

Her jaw dropped as she wiped her face. She retaliated, sweeping the back of her hand across the surface of the pool, only to completely miss Alex and hit Sydney with a face full of spray.

"Sorry, Sydney! I was aiming for Alex," Beatrice said, failing to keep a smirk from her lips.

"Oh yeah?" Sydney spluttered, reaching her arm back, her hand scooped.

Beatrice's hands shot to defensive mode in front of her face. "Sydney, no. I forbid it."

"You forbid it." Sydney's eyebrows rocketed. "Really?"

Realising her error in her attempt to dissuade Sydney, she tried again. "Okay. I beg you, please don't."

"Do it, Sydney!" Alex shouted from the sidelines.

Sydney scooped some water in her hand and threw it at Beatrice, making her scream. Alex let out a howl of laughter.

"Sydney! I even asked nicely."

"Yes, you did, but you need to learn that sometimes asking nicely won't get you what you want either."

"Hmm," Beatrice muttered, unconvinced by Sydney's tactics to make her see things differently. "Well, I'm wet now, so I may as well get in."

Pushing herself from the step with her good leg, she let herself glide into the water.

"I'm going to shower and then choose a movie?" Alex said, climbing the steps.

"Great idea," Sydney replied.

"I'm sure we have some popcorn somewhere," Beatrice called after him.

Alex disappeared into the house as Beatrice swam slowly towards the deep end to join Sydney.

"I'm not sure this was a good idea," Beatrice said, beginning to flounder. "I can feel my leg beginning to tire already."

"I'll rescue you if you drown."

"Very reassuring, Sydney."

Sydney smirked and turned her back to her. "Hold on to my shoulders. I'll take you back to the steps."

"Then you will drown, and no one will rescue me."

"Don't be so dramatic. You're not that heavy."

"Huh." Beatrice clung to Sydney's shoulders, only for her to immediately sink into the water. Beatrice gasped. "Sydney!"

Her assistant emerged from the water, laughing. "Sorry. Couldn't resist."

It earned her a slap on the arm. "Don't do that."

"Sorry. I'll behave this time. I have lifeguard

qualifications, you know. I've saved grown men from the water before."

"Impressive. Were any of them worth saving?" Beatrice asked. She hung off Sydney's shoulders as she paddled them back to the shallow end.

"I couldn't possibly comment." Sydney chuckled, turning as she reached the corner of the pool so Beatrice could sink onto a step. She took a seat beside her and tucked her elbows back onto the step above. Arching back, she surveyed the house as the automatic lights flicked on and illuminated it.

Beatrice mirrored her.

"Your home is…" Sydney trailed off, unable to find the appropriate word for Highwood House.

"I know," Beatrice answered.

"Are you two coming or what?" Alex hollered from the kitchen fifteen minutes later.

Sydney stood and held her hands out to Beatrice. She'd been enjoying the silent company of Sydney beside her so much she was reluctant to take them, not wanting the moment to end. She couldn't bear to think about a time when she would no longer be there. Finally taking her hands, she stood, bearing the weight on her good leg.

Finding herself face to face with Sydney, she said "I've had a fantastic day, not even counting my divorce." She flicked the end of Sydney's nose with her finger. "You are quite extraordinary, Sydney McKenzie. Thank you."

"It's not over yet. I smell popcorn."

Having towelled herself dry, she followed Sydney back inside.

"Here's a little trick for you, Alex. Next time you smell

a fart at school, tell everyone you can smell popcorn and then watch their faces as they take a deep breath."

"Oh, Sydney, that's awful!" Beatrice howled with a mix of disgust and delight as she lowered herself from her crutches to a chair.

Alex grinned. "Epic."

CHAPTER 29

*T*he cool water of the swimming pool soothed Sydney's burning feet as she rested them on the first step; they hated this hot, sticky weather. She touched the water, gliding her hand through it as she recalled Beatrice in the pool earlier. How much fun they'd enjoyed messing about as a… she caught herself thinking of the word 'family'. Beatrice and Alex were a family. She'd been given the immense honour of joining it for a brief time, and soon that time would be over. She would move on with Gertie and be gone forever.

She arched back and gazed at the stars. Her eyes descended to Beatrice's balcony, where beyond the woman she desired was alone and would remain so. Now hardened against the world, she couldn't see her opening up to anyone again, but there was always a chance. A hope. And if you asked Sydney, Beatrice deserved true happiness.

Part of falling in love was allowing someone to see you for what you were and them still being there after learning all the good and bad in you. Beatrice was going to need someone to read her autobiography before she went on a first date… or to have written it even. Sydney sighed at the thought. What she'd do for one night with her. It would be enough to ensure Beatrice would never let her leave her side.

The urge to be with her was so strong she imagined herself storming up to her room to declare herself so Beatrice could throw her out and put her out of her misery. It was the only way she was going to be able to move past the feelings eating her alive and the frustration gnawing at her from not knowing what Beatrice was thinking. Rejection was the only option, and for that, she would need to declare her feelings.

She laughed at the stupid thought. She knew already rejection would be swift; she didn't need the performance of it. Ruining her last week with Beatrice was not going on the agenda.

She'd achieved what she set out to and more. Watching mother and son enjoy a day together, a movie, a laugh — a day she had choreographed. Sharing in that was part of the reward she would take from her time at Highwood. It was a place she never wanted to leave, a place she felt she could call home if Beatrice and Alex were with her.

She would bet the two of them hadn't shared a more enjoyable day together in recent years. As Beatrice watched the chefs at work, Sydney had seen her smile, laugh, grin, chew her lip, and even squint as Alex used his knives. She smiled as she recalled how Beatrice rested her hand on her chin and glanced over at her as she worked.

Twice she'd made a point of catching her eye to let her know she'd noticed her.

What was going through the woman's mind?

"Hey. Has Mum gone to bed?" Alex asked, poking his head out the patio door.

"Yes, she went up a little while ago."

"Thanks for today. I know it was from Mum, but I guess it was your idea."

"You're welcome… on behalf of your mum… and me. She'll come around about you becoming a chef, you know, and the best bit is, you get to spend every day proving her wrong. Show her you can make it to the top by getting there."

Alex nodded. "I will." He hesitated for a moment before adding "The best present was seeing Mum so happy. I have you to thank for that, too, don't I?"

"I couldn't possibly comment."

Alex smiled at her. "Night."

She couldn't comment. Was she the reason Beatrice was brighter, lighter? She hoped so. It was more likely the weight of the divorce coming off her shoulders. Something like that hanging over you was enough to change you. Yes, she had something to do with it, but only incidentally. She had held a mirror up to Peter, that was all; held him accountable and then threatened and physically attacked him. She smiled as she recalled the moment. On behalf of all abused women, she'd served justice with a swift jab of the knee. It was a risky move to trick him, their only move. One that could have backfired yet hadn't, and she had received her reward from Beatrice.

That hug.

That kiss.

Both were etched in her mind and her heart — on replay mode.

She didn't feel ready for bed; her mind was still racing. With everyone else safely in their rooms, it was time to watch *Nancy*. She couldn't resist any longer. She needed more of Beatrice despite only saying goodnight to her half an hour ago. She settled herself on the sofa with the remainder of the second bottle of wine they'd opened that day.

Beatrice's performance was as elegant and tasteful as her interior design. She was beyond perfection, inhabiting the body and soul of her character and a husky Southern accent.

The story was just as perfect. Two women in the grip of despair after losing their husbands in the Vietnam War found themselves crossing the boundary from friendship to something deeper. Both question their feelings as their grief, community, and Christian beliefs challenge them, all the while unable to restrain themselves physically from their overpowering attraction to each other.

Sydney watched as she reached the part she'd been waiting for — when the two women finally gave in to their desires. They laid themselves bare to each other, realising that the holds over them weren't as powerful as their feelings for each other. She couldn't take her eyes from Beatrice as her co-star undressed her.

She fanned herself with her hand, unable to cool the parts of herself that really needed cooling down at this moment. Her heart was pounding in her chest at the sight of Beatrice's flesh, her breasts, her passion, the desire she was showing for her co-star. Every inch of her own body craved that passion, her touch. Parts of her burned at the very thought.

The kitchen light flicked on, making her jump from her skin. She grabbed the remote, hitting 'Pause' instead of 'Stop', and leaving Beatrice's right breast on the screen.

Fuck!

Beatrice appeared behind her in nothing but a short, black slip.

"Sorry, I didn't realise you were still up. I came down for some hot milk to help me sleep."

Beatrice looked from Sydney to the screen. Sydney's heart pounded even faster, poised for a reaction.

"Is that my breast, Sydney?" Beatrice asked, her tone unexpectedly jovial.

Finding herself unable to speak, she was grateful that Beatrice continued.

"Put it back on — assuming you were enjoying it."

"Of course!" Sydney cursed the level of enthusiasm with which she'd replied.

"The ending is lovely. Would you like some tea?"

"Please," Sydney replied, noticing the bottle of wine and her glass were now empty.

Beatrice busied herself in the kitchen, leaving Sydney to continue watching her very employer groan in pleasure in front of her on the television. She blinked, wondering if she was in one of those dreams again.

Beatrice appeared beside her minutes later and placed two mugs on the table.

"Don't mind if I join you, do you?" Beatrice asked, sitting down beside her without waiting for a reply.

"Err… no." Sydney's words failed her about as much as the silk slip was failing to cover Beatrice's skin. "I've been admiring the fashion of the time." She blew out a quiet breath to slow her heartbeat.

"They went for authentic, so pointy bras and everything. It was a relief to take them off."

Sydney choked out a laugh as an elbow nudged her arm.

"I mean after filming, not during."

Their arms remained touching.

"Oh yeah. I don't believe that for a minute."

A shot of Beatrice's breast came on to the screen again, followed by her co-star's mouth as it covered it and then a close-up of her tongue on Beatrice's nipple. Sydney hoped to see Beatrice naked at some point, but she hadn't expected to watch it on the screen next to the woman herself. She wanted to disappear into the sofa.

"Is this when one of us points out how awkward this is?" she asked, fidgeting in her seat.

"Don't be embarrassed. It's some of my finest work. Nancy was my favourite… and most challenging role. It made me finally admit to myself who I was. Art imitates life and all that, or should it be the other way around?"

"I assume this was the co-star that Peter…"

Beatrice flattened her lips and nodded before Sydney could finish her sentence. She needed more than a nod to distract her from what was happening on the screen, where Beatrice was lying topless on a bed. A weight fell over her body as blood pumped around her, every part of her pulsing.

"How did Peter find out about you to use it against

you?" Sydney asked, pretending not to pay too much attention to the television.

"I told him to hurt him in the heat of an argument. I'm sure he already suspected. When I confirmed it, he it took as permission to use it against me. Peter always had a wandering eye, and I admit I developed one too. All the times he thought I'd caught him looking at other women, I'd been looking too. Our taste in women was the only thing we ever had in common."

Beatrice's naked back came on to the screen, all of it, head to toe, as she lay face down on a bed. Sydney's heart quickened again.

"Then everything changed after *Nancy*. He thinks it was my moment of awakening. It was bullshit of course; I'd known long before then, but I'd been good at keeping it buried. In his eyes, it confirmed everything, and in mine, it proved what a sleaze he was for thinking that when I was only doing my job. I was nothing but professional during filming; that's not to say I hadn't developed some feelings for my co-star. He said I was way too into it. It made me realise he didn't think I had any acting talent. Then he…" Beatrice pointed to her co-star on the screen, her tongue teasing a nipple again.

Sydney leaned forward and retrieved her mug; it was something to hide behind at least. It was strange that Beatrice was so comfortable watching herself. Then again it was part of her job. She would have exposed her body like that knowing it would be seen.

"By that point," Beatrice continued, "I was so exhausted pretending our marriage was something it wasn't. I admitted it — with relief. *Nancy* opened my eyes to how powerful two people's love can and should be. It made me realise that I never loved him." Beatrice twitched her shoulders. "I was fond of him, but as he grew harder to live with, when Alex went to school, fondness turned to hatred. Deep down I don't think I ever trusted men after Dad... and those other men."

There were no words Sydney could offer that she hadn't already, and Beatrice would just bat them away as she had before. She didn't want sympathy, just someone to listen.

"Peter attacked me after that. Not physically, but verbally. Although he was the one caught cheating, he acted like I'd bashed his masculinity when it was nothing to do with him and everything to do with me. That's what he's like, you see, egotistical. Everything is about him and how he's affected. I was great for his ego to begin with. He'd captured the heart of Beatrice Russell. Then I overshadowed him, and everyone soon forgot who he was. But hey. It's done now, thanks to you." Beatrice gave her a light tap on the leg. "I have my divorce. I can move on with my life — again."

"Where to this time? "Sydney asked, pulling her legs up onto the sofa and turning to face Beatrice.

"I have no idea."

"Come on, you must have some idea what you want. What do you desire most? Why not do that? You're a free woman now."

"What I desire most?" Beatrice inhaled and then let out a deep sigh as her hand reached for the side of Sydney's head where her thumb caressed her cheek.

Sydney, quite unable to believe what was happening,

kissed her thumb as it brushed over her lips. She held her breath as Beatrice edged closer to her until her soft, eager lips were against her own. Beatrice's mouth opened, inviting Sydney in, where she found her warm tongue as it came searching for hers.

Sydney couldn't remember if she'd ever been kissed so passionately or as earnestly as Beatrice was kissing her, the woman she was beginning to fall in love with. Finally, her body was getting what it desired, and this time it wasn't a dream. Beatrice Russell was all over her.

Knowing Beatrice was unable to move easily with her boot strapped to her leg, Sydney lifted her knee to straddle her. Beatrice's hands were immediately on her, pulling her T-shirt up. Sydney pulled it over her head and discarded it, only to find Beatrice's hands undoing her bra. It joined the T-shirt on the floor seconds later.

Beatrice pulled Sydney towards her, taking a breast into her mouth as they met halfway. She sucked her nipple and teased it with her tongue as Sydney moaned and ran her fingers through her blonde waves. As Beatrice came up for air, Sydney dived back into her mouth, forcing her back against the sofa.

Beatrice arched back, turning her head, encouraging Sydney down to her bare neck. She was more than happy to oblige and kissed her way down, letting her lips explore every inch as her fingers slid the straps down on Beatrice's slip. Sydney's hands reached for the bare breasts that revealed themselves from behind it.

Her mouth was eager to be where her hands were and continued kissing its way down Beatrice's chest. Her eyes widened as they finally saw her breasts; they were even more amazing in the flesh. She didn't stop kissing until she felt a nipple against her lips. She teased it, claiming it for herself. Beatrice moaned as she gently applied pressure and then released it.

"You smell so good, Beatrice," Sydney mumbled softly. "Always so good."

Sydney's hand slid lower, brushing over her soft belly, desperate to feel every part of her. Her fingers made their way to a pair of lace knickers, then under them, the warmth of Beatrice's desire enticing her further down.

Beatrice grasped her hand. She hoped it was a sign of encouragement, but mutterings from Beatrice made her pause.

"I'm sorry, I can't."

"What?"

"I can't. Please get off."

Sydney slid off her as Beatrice pulled her straps back onto her shoulders.

"I'm sorry, I really am. I can't do this. You deserve better than what I can offer."

"Beatrice," Sydney pleaded as the woman stood and smoothed down her slip.

She would have bet on her running out if the boot hadn't hampered her. Instead, she hobbled across the kitchen in a slow retreat of regret. It left Sydney wondering if she overstepped, gone too far before Beatrice was ready. Now she was left with a desire for more and the pain of knowing Beatrice wanted more yet felt unable to give it.

CHAPTER 30

*A*fter a night of broken sleep, Sydney was tired and miserable. She made her way downstairs, noticing Beatrice's bedroom door was open. She must be up already. It was going to be awkward running into her.

"Morning. The kettle's just boiled," Beatrice said as soon as she entered the kitchen.

So that's how they were playing it. Casual. She could go along with that. It was the easiest option under the circumstances.

"Morning. Sam texted last night." She gulped, realising she'd referenced the night before. "Gertie is ready. Would you mind if we went down today?"

"Missing her, are we?"

"As a matter of fact, yes, I am," Sydney replied, matching her tone to the level of sarcasm Beatrice had injected into her question.

"I don't see why not. You can drive us down in the Range Rover. I'm sure I'll manage the drive back. It's automatic, so I won't need to use my left leg."

"Thanks. I'll let him know to expect us."

Alex lolloped into the kitchen, yawning.

"Do you fancy a trip to the coast to collect Gertie, Alex?"

"That's a great idea," Beatrice agreed, rather too quickly.

Sydney suspected her agreement was much for the same reason as she'd suggested it: it would be less awkward with Alex there. She also wanted him to meet Sam. If she was correct in her observations over the last few weeks, Sam might be able to offer the kid some help.

"Sure," Alex replied with a shrug.

"Great. Shall we leave after breakfast?"

The journey to the harbour was quiet, deathly quiet. Alex was plugged into his headphones in the back seat and Beatrice stared out of the window, not engaging at all. As they pulled up at the harbour, Alex gave much the same reaction as his mum had when she'd first seen it. He gawped at the view as he jumped out. Sydney made her way around to Beatrice's side and opened the door, offering a helping hand.

"I can manage. Thank you, Sydney."

Was she not able to offer help now if it involved touching Beatrice?

Sydney stepped back, leaving her to negotiate the grab handle, side-step, and walking boot. Manage it she did, much to Sydney's annoyance. She didn't want to see Beatrice fall flat on her butt, but a little difficulty and a call for help would have made her day.

"Gertie!" Alex exclaimed, running to her and stroking her bonnet. "Do you feel better now?"

"Oh, wonderful. Now you've infected my child with your—"

"My...?" Sydney raised her eyebrows at Beatrice, daring her to finish her sentence.

Beatrice's lips contorted, restraining a smile. Instead of replying she limped towards the workshop.

"Good to see you, girl," Sydney said, giving Gertie a light pat as she passed her.

She left Alex and Beatrice outside the workshop and wandered in to find Sam inside a small boat in the dry dock.

"Hey."

"Sorry, I didn't hear you arrive," Sam said as he jumped off the boat.

"Gertie looks to be in one piece."

"As good as new."

"Thank you. What's the damage? I'll transfer it now."

Sam pulled a folded-up piece of paper from his back pocket. "Here's your invoice, though it's already been settled."

"What? By whom?"

Sam's eyes drifted to Beatrice outside. Sydney's followed.

"When?"

"When you dropped Gertie off. She insisted she was covering all costs."

What on earth had Beatrice been thinking to do that? And at a time when they'd only just made up after their falling-out.

"And you let her? Sam!"

"She's pretty scary. I can't imagine anyone saying no to her."

"I can. I can't accept that. It's thousands of pounds."

Sam shrugged. "I'd take it; it's not like she'll miss it. She obviously thinks you deserve it. Who's the kid?"

"Alex. Come, I'll introduce you." Sydney slipped the invoice into her pocket. That would be a conversation for when they were alone.

"Alex, this is Sam. An old friend of mine."

"Hi, great place you have here," Alex said. "Can we go out on a boat?"

Beatrice scowled at Alex. "I'm sure Sam is very busy and needs to get back to work."

"It's fine, Beatrice. I finished some repairs on that yacht this morning," Sam replied, pointing to a yacht moored along the jetty. "Fancy taking her out for a test run?"

Alex's face lit up. "Yes, please. Can I, Mum?"

"Sure."

"You two coming?" Sam asked.

Sydney waited for Beatrice to answer first.

"I won't, thanks. I'll sit a while and watch the world go by."

"Syd?"

"I'm going to keep her company as she watches. Make sure she doesn't pick a fight with it as it goes."

Beatrice's face twisted as Alex and Sam laughed.

As much as she'd like to be out on the sea, it was an opportunity for some privacy she wasn't going to pass up.

"Make yourself at home, Beatrice." Sam pointed to the deck area. "There's cold drinks in the fridge."

"Thank you."

"You head on up to the boat, Alex. I'll grab the keys."

Sydney followed him back into the workshop as Beatrice and Alex wandered off in opposite directions.

"Do me a favour, Sam. Talk to Alex about your work with the helpline."

"Okay. Are you going to give me any more than that?"

"From what I see, he isn't entirely happy in his skin. I wonder if you might be able to help him. I might be wrong, but if I'm right, he might benefit from a little help." Sydney shrugged. "If not, then no harm done."

Sam nodded and placed his hand on her shoulder. "Of course. Leave it with me."

"Thank you. He's important to me."

"Then he's important to me too."

Sydney flashed him a warm smile of gratitude, aware that Sam's kindness towards her was more than she deserved.

She joined Beatrice on the deck, where she was leaning on the wooden fence that overlooked the water.

"We need to talk," Sydney said firmly as soon as they had waved Alex and Sam off.

"About?"

Sydney took the invoice from her back pocket.

"Gertie and the invoice I've just tried to pay."

"Oh."

"Thank you for the gesture, but I need to repay you."

"You only took the job so you could fix Gertie, but you've helped fix me too. I owe you a debt of gratitude I can never repay, Sydney. So, please, consider this a bonus for services rendered. I'll be offended if you discuss it any further." Beatrice turned her attention back to the view.

"I…"

"No," Beatrice snapped.

Realising there was no hope of winning, Sydney said, "Can I at least thank you?"

"You may."

Following the previous night's escapades, Sydney hadn't intended on physically thanking her, yet her arms were around Beatrice before she realised what she was doing. Her body's attempts to overrule her head were infuriating.

"Thank you."

As she pulled back, she placed a kiss on Beatrice's cheek. It was more to see her reaction than anything else. She lingered a moment, wanting to stay there forever.

Beatrice was the one to break the embrace, leaving Sydney feeling guilty for pushing.

"You're welcome. Look, I'm sorry about last night," Beatrice said, taking a seat at the table.

So was she. Sorry that Beatrice had stopped her when she did. Sydney took a seat beside her, turning it towards her. If it was going to be one of those talks, she wanted to look the woman right in the eye as she rejected her.

"I should never have kissed you," Beatrice said. "It was a mistake. Any relationship beyond the professional is inappropriate."

"It didn't feel like that last night. You don't trust me to keep it low-key, is that it?"

Beatrice met her gaze briefly and then stared out to sea.

"I don't trust myself to treat you the way you deserve to be treated, Sydney," she replied firmly.

"Do you think you don't deserve me? Is that what you were saying last night? Because that's not true."

Beatrice's eyes returned to hers. "I can't hide you, Sydney. You're not someone to be hidden. You deserve so much more than I could ever give you. Don't you see that I couldn't be with you and not show you off to the world? And that's not an option for me. I put a stop to it because I'm not one for a one-night stand and I can't offer you anything more than that. I didn't want you to feel used."

She'd be happy for Beatrice to make her feel anything, even used.

"If we'd gone further, we would never have stopped. I would have lost control of a situation I barely have a grip on as it is."

A situation. Was that what she was to Beatrice? She didn't want to dispute the point with her when she had clearly made up her mind. The last thing she wanted was to fight with her when they were finally in a good place, despite everything that had happened.

"So I really can't persuade you to do it again?" Sydney asked in a final attempt.

"Please, Sydney, don't be like all the others. Please respect me when I say no."

That was an end to it. Beatrice shut the conversation down, something she was highly skilled at. There was no way Sydney was going to be disrespectful towards her and no way to approach it without being so. She was going to have to let it go... for the time being.

"So, are you going to tell me why Anthony owes you a favour, or are you going to keep me guessing?" Beatrice asked, changing the subject.

"Antony's eldest daughter was a little on the wayward side. She used to drink heavily, take drugs, and party until all hours. I know because I was the one picking her up, quite literally sometimes, often in a pile of her own vomit. I put her on the straight and narrow whilst I was working for him. She's at Oxford now."

Beatrice's lips tightened. "You never cease to amaze me. You certainly have a way with children. Look at Alex since you arrived; he's so much happier. You've changed him."

"I don't think he's changed. It's you that has, and that's changed his attitude towards you."

Beatrice thought for a moment. "Perhaps you are right."

"I am."

CHAPTER 31

The bubbles were all but disappearing in Beatrice's bath, leaving the view of her bare breasts wallowing in the water. Her nipples poked through the surface. It was a view that she'd become accustomed to, yet it was an ever-changing landscape like the rest of her body. It was beginning to shed its autumn leaves as it prepared for the transition into winter in the coming years. She cupped some water in her hands and threw it over her cold, exposed shoulders and then her face, washing away the fatigue from a poor night's sleep.

It was strange to think a woman fifteen years her junior thought her body was attractive, enjoyed it — for a moment at least. Visions of Sydney enjoying her breasts had consumed her mind since. The thought of it made her body yearn for more, for Sydney's mouth to press against her own again, her roaming fingers to have finished what they tried to start before she'd put a stop to it. She'd never felt that depth of desire inside herself for someone before.

She'd allowed Sydney to see her in a natural state, in

body and mind. Her audiences had seen her body. Not that she'd wanted them to, but sometimes it was part of the role. Being seen by someone she did want to see her naked, though, was empowering. To have shared such an intimate moment with her, however short, exposing herself and leaving herself vulnerable, felt liberating. Wasn't the need to be seen human nature? To be seen was to exist.

She was old enough to believe that every human body was beautiful in its own way. Beauty was very much in the eye of the beholder in her book, and her body had received rave reviews from onlookers. The few times she'd ventured to look online, it was all people spoke about. Anywhere there was space for a comment, she would find most people admiring it. As for the rest, she'd often wondered what sort of people took time out of their day to leave rude remarks about other people's bodies online. Did they have nothing better to do?

Even with all the positive comments, there were still parts she wished she could change. Didn't everyone have a list? Her thighs could be slenderer, her tummy tighter, her breasts perter. The constant battle against time was not to be won, and so not one to be fought. Everyone was a loser when pitted against it the moment they were born. The only way to outsmart it was by leaving the world too early — and that was no win.

As much as she had enjoyed that brief moment with Sydney, it was a careless slip. Allowing herself to be carried away in the heat of the moment was unlike her. It had taken every ounce of self-restraint to stop it and even more not to do it again. The passion with which Sydney responded suggested it would have been more than welcome. Beatrice's attraction to her was undeniable, but she could see no future for them, not whilst she needed to hide herself for her career. It was something she despised doing, yet was a necessity.

Sympathy would be overflowing for the abuse she had suffered over the years; abuse that was out of her control. To reveal to the world she wanted to be with a woman, something else out of her control, she would be judged, ridiculed, and ostracised. The world was so full of bigoted people who thought their opinion mattered when it came to how others wished to live their lives. Two women loving each other was no different to any other relationship. If the world could rid itself of compulsory heterosexuality, it would be a better place for it.

There was a reason so many actors were closeted. It was their only line of defence. One actor she worked with on a film brought his gentleman friend to set every day under the guise of being his PA. When she'd accidentally walked in on them holding hands, the actor revealed to her that they'd been living together as a couple for twenty years. The media were still speculating about which of the women he dined with regularly might be a love interest.

She could never hide Sydney, and would never ask her to hide, even if it meant being without her. She knew from experience how exhausting it was to live a lie. Some lies were easy to live with whilst others ate you up inside. Hiding was part of her life; it hadn't been easy to suppress that part of her, yet she'd dealt with it, learned how to manage it. Being around Sydney certainly tested everything she'd put into practice over the years.

As Alison helped her undress after the photo shoot, she had interrogated her about why she wasn't taking Sydney to the States. She fobbed her off with the excuse that Sydney had much-needed downtime owed to her. It wasn't a lie. Anyway, she was destined for greater things than being a PA, and with the book release, her career as an author might finally gain some traction.

What she hadn't disclosed was the need for distance between them; 5,456 miles should about do it. She wasn't sure Sydney felt anything more than a crush for her, an infatuation even, and she wasn't about to turn her life upside down for that. She wasn't even sure of the extent of her own feelings. She was smitten with Sydney; that was undeniable. It was a great feeling to find that connection with someone, for them to know everything about you and see you, like you even, for exactly what you were. But that didn't mean it ran deeper. What she was sure of was that hitting her fifties was a pivotal point in her career; it had never been so fragile.

She didn't relish telling Sydney that their time together was ending sooner than planned. Stepping from the bath, she dried herself, relieved to see the skin on her leg improving after a week with no cast. Entering the bedroom, she secured her towel around her only to find Sydney placing a pile of laundered clothes on the bed.

"Sorry. I was hoping to be in and out in a flash." Sydney blushed as her eyes darted in every direction other than towards Beatrice.

"It's fine," she sighed as she sat on the bed. It was far from it. Sydney was a couple of feet away, and she had nothing covering her except a towel. She wanted to throw it off and give Sydney everything she wanted. The voice of restraint helped her keep her nerve. *You'll regret it. One time won't be enough.*

Her head twitched as she tried to shake off the voice.

"You okay?"

It was a question best left unanswered.

"Alex has been invited to spend the last few weeks of the holidays at a friend's house in Cornwall. Can you make travel arrangements for him by train, please? I'm… also returning to the States a little earlier than planned." Her eyes drifted to Sydney, hoping to gauge a reaction, though she regretted it as soon as she saw her assistant's pained expression. Was she about to be sick? "I need a period of adjustment before I begin filming again, and as I can walk now, there's nothing holding me here." Her eyelids dropped with regret at her phrasing. "I mean…" She paused again.

"It's okay," Sydney reassured her as she took some more clothing from the bed to a drawer.

"You don't have to put my clothes away for me. It was kind of you to do it whilst I was incapacitated, but I didn't expect you to keep doing it once I was weight-bearing. I'm aware I've asked more than expected of you. More than anyone can ask of an assistant."

"I don't mind. I like looking after you."

"It's not your job," Beatrice said, ensuring there was enough firmness in her voice to carry the message yet not too much to sound ungrateful. "You're not a carer, and I no longer need one anyway."

"What do you need?"

Beatrice gulped at the question.

"I need you to book a flight. Commercial, first class to LA. Send the flight schedule to Jonathon; he'll be returning with me."

Sydney's face dropped with disappointment, dragging her own down with it. The last thing she wanted was for their last few days together to be full of sadness, regret, and disappointment.

"Why don't we go out somewhere?" she questioned. "We could go for a drive and stop somewhere for a picnic. Celebrate our success in getting the book towards a close."

The suggestion did the trick; the light was back in Sydney's eyes.

"I know just the place. There is something I've always wanted to do that Gertie could never manage. Assuming you don't mind going in Gertie."

"Oh, what the hell! Why not?" She'd give her assistant all the small wins she could now.

"I'm hoping she won't let me down."

Sydney spoke so flatly that Beatrice wondered if it was a genuine wish about her vehicle or if there was something deeper aimed at her behind it.

An hour later they were encamped in Gertie, heading towards London and what Sydney assured her was a very steep hill where they could test her limits.

"Other camper enthusiasts have tried it with the original engine and recommended avoiding it."

Beatrice's lips quivered; she rubbed at them before they could expose the mischief they held.

"Out with it!" Sydney demanded from the driver's seat.

Too late.

"What?"

"Don't act the innocent. That smirk you're failing miserably to hide. What's it for this time?"

"You said 'enthusiasts' when I assume you meant to say 'nerds'."

"Ha," Sydney replied. "Don't cut yourself on that wit of yours, will you? It would be terrible if you were to bleed out."

"I'm sure an enthusiast could recommend a good camper cleaner if I were to."

"I'm sure several could help me dispose of a body too."

Beatrice winced. "Oof."

"Too far?"

"A little."

Returning her attention to the delightful countryside with a smile on her face, Beatrice realised this was what she was going to miss most about Sydney, well, apart from her walking around in a bikini. The intelligent, dynamic conversation she craved had been in abundance over the last few weeks. Sydney was on her wavelength, whether they were sharing this jokey banter, talking in depth about the book or passing the time over dinner.

The woman was intelligent first and foremost, and that was the most attractive part of her, that and her passion and determination to do the right thing and do it correctly. She could have chosen to leave at any point; she'd been given plenty of opportunities to admit defeat and declare her employer unbearable to be around. Even in their darkest moments, when Beatrice had yelled at her not to come back, there she was sleeping nearby, making sure she was okay.

She inhaled and then sighed, not realising how loudly until it was too late. From the corner of her eye, she could see Sydney glance at her. Grabbing her phone from her handbag she typed out a message to let Alex know they would be back in a few hours, assuming he was now up after yet another late-night PlayStation session with friends. A simple 'K' came back. Was there any hope for the future of the English language? She'd been quietly pleased when he'd declined the invitation to join them and rolled over and gone back to sleep. She wanted Sydney all to herself for one final outing.

They sat in silence for the remainder of the journey, a comfortable silence. They often sat working in the kitchen for hours at a time, neither speaking. After five weeks living together they knew each other well enough not to have to fill every quiet moment.

The hill on the horizon finally grew larger in her view. As they began their ascent, Sydney became a little excitable. So excitable, Beatrice thought she should have worn a fancier hat and placed a bet; it was like a day at the races.

"Come on, girl, you can do it!" Sydney coaxed.

A drop of gear and rev of the engine propelled Gertie up. Her engine strained but still pulled, working her way onwards at a steady pace. As they reached an even steeper incline and the momentum they'd built dissipated, Sydney dropped to first gear. It was all or nothing now. Get up or go home.

"Come on, we're nearly there. Keep going," Sydney pleaded as she began jumping forward in her seat, giving Gertie every bit of help she could to make it to the top.

Even Beatrice found herself egging Gertie on in her head.

As they finally reached the crest, Sydney cheered and punched the air. "Attagirl! I knew you could do it."

Beatrice surprised herself by clapping and cheering.

They parked up in the viewing area of a large, busy car park. She was going to need to arm herself with her usual disguise of sunglasses and a hat.

"The ground doesn't look very flat. We better have the picnic near the van; we don't want you falling and breaking another leg."

Another six weeks at Highwood with Sydney and she'd be wearing a T-shirt that said, 'I'm not a lesbian, but my wife is.' She rolled her eyes at her silly thought; she wasn't in love with Sydney — was she? She could see herself being so if she was around her for much longer. It was best to be gone and forget the summer ever happened. Restore some normality to her life.

Once Sydney laid out the blanket and picnic, she held Beatrice's hands and lowered her to the ground, pulling a couple of cushions from Gertie to add a little comfort. The view was outstanding, the clear air allowing them to see all the way to London. The Shard stood out like a beacon on the horizon.

"Where will you go once you leave Highwood?" Beatrice asked, twiddling the stem of her wine glass.

"I don't know, I haven't really decided. My plan for the summer was to go to Cornwall and get some words down, but I'll be happy not to see another word for some time. I might head east to the coast; take in the Garden of England." Sydney yawned and leaned back on her elbows, closing her eyes as she let the sun warm her face. "Life is a journey, not a destination. It's why I've always been happy doing my job. I'm not aiming for anything; I'm enjoying what I have and making a difference in people's lives as I come and go. I'm there for people when they need it most, and I'm good at what I do. Wherever that may be."

Was Sydney's choice of words a dig at her?

"Whereas I am aiming for something?" Beatrice bit back. "Is that so bad?"

"I didn't mean it to sound like I was questioning your life choices."

Beatrice sighed, sorry to have snapped.

"Sorry. I'm a little sensitive when it comes to my decisions. I may have spent close to fifty years journeying around the world to create entertainment for people, yet personally, I don't appear to have evolved. I'm still exactly where Victoria Harper was, pretending to be someone else for other people, in my career and personal life. The only difference is now I do it with wrinkles and a different name."

What had it all been for?

Her ambition had always been to do what she could do to the best of her abilities, yet had she ever stopped to question what that resembled? What was her end goal, the destination she'd been aiming for all those years ago — to be rich and famous? Where had that got her? She had one friend; two if you counted Sydney. She had a broken marriage that she should never have gone into and a child that resented her for her achievements because ultimately it had cost him the most.

Beatrice reached across for a sausage roll at the same time as Sydney. As soon as their hands touched, their eyes locked.

"Your wrinkles only add to your beauty, Beatrice."

A warming in her cheeks made her withdraw her hand.

"Wow, do you find touching me that difficult?" Sydney asked, her forehead creasing.

Beatrice stuttered. It was instinctive; she hadn't even thought about how Sydney would take it.

"Has our time together been that regrettable?" Sydney continued.

She knew what Sydney was getting at. She wasn't talking about their whole time together, just that brief, intimate moment they'd shared.

"I don't regret it. That doesn't mean I can embrace it either. My image... my brand, they are everything, and I don't believe either can withstand me coming out." She gulped at her wine, which was beginning to warm in the sun. "Plus..." Beatrice's customary hard-eyed expression softened. "I can't be anything to you because I don't even know who I am. I know what I've become, and I'm sure that's not me."

"I'm sure too. Be yourself, not a fake version of it to make everyone else comfortable."

"Easier said than done. Anyway, you have Gertie. I'm not sure there is room for any other woman." Seeing an opportunity to change the subject, Beatrice added, "Speaking of which, I'm giving you credit as a writer on my book. I'll retain one hundred percent copyright, and you'll have a share of the royalties. The rest is going in trust to Alex, to make sure Peter doesn't get his hands on any of it. I discussed it with Alison after the photoshoot, and she sent through a new contract for me to approve this morning. It's only fair. The book wouldn't be what it is had it not been for you. It will be enough to keep Gertie well lubricated for you, whatever the two of you choose to do next."

"Seriously? Thank you," Sydney said, wrapping her arms around Beatrice and squeezing her. "It will all go to my mum," Sydney replied, releasing her. "She doesn't have much."

Did this woman's generosity know no bounds? She could build long-lasting friendships with people she worked for, befriend their children, and have a group of friends singing her praises. More importantly, she was genuinely happy. How did one even begin to achieve that? Yet something was off.

She watched as Sydney scanned the groups of people coming and going from the footpaths to their cars. She'd been doing it since they'd arrived.

"Tell me something. That story I read about the young woman losing her father overboard. It was you, wasn't it?"

Sydney nodded. "Skye is my middle name. When did you realise?"

"Only recently, embarrassingly." Beatrice bit in her bottom lip before continuing. "You speak about your mother whereas your father barely gets a mention. I got the impression your father had died when you went a little crazy at my lack of interest in my father's death. When we're out, you're always scanning for something, like you are now. I thought you were watching my back when actually you were looking for someone — your dad." When Sydney didn't contradict her, Beatrice softened a bit. "You'll surely drive yourself crazy if you don't stop looking. He's gone. He doesn't have to be dead to be gone. Mine was gone a long time before he died."

"I know… I do know. I just don't want to believe he has. I've always kept moving, always searching in the hope one day I might see him, and I could bring him home to Mum. The police assumed he was dead." Sydney picked at her fingernails. "We couldn't accept that, not without a body. We waited the time that they said it would take for a body to wash up in various places with the current — he never did. So, I promised Mum I'd find him, and began searching. James and Rosie saw I was becoming obsessive and held an intervention. James gave me work to distract me; I kept searching. As the years passed, Rosie suggested I channel it into writing, so I wrote that book."

"And wrote the ending into something nicer."

Sydney nodded. "A happy ending I'll never have. Although, even if he was to turn up one day with amnesia, it would be bittersweet." She let out an unexpected laugh. "It's funny. You've been hiding from something that can't be hidden, and I've been searching for something that can't be found."

"We're a proper game of hide-and-seek." Beatrice laughed.

"Except you're not a fan of games."

"I don't like games that remind me of my father. You'll have noticed I'm working on that."

Beatrice appreciated the flash of a smile from Sydney that acknowledged her effort.

"I have an odd request," Sydney said then. "Say no if you like. I don't have a photo of us together, and I'd like one. If you're okay with that?"

"Do you intend to sell it to the newspaper and tell the tale of your quick fumble with a closeted actress?" Beatrice asked with a smile twitching at her lips.

Sydney clearly regarded her comment with scorn as her own lips twisted.

"I was thinking more along the lines of remembering our time together."

Beatrice took out her phone by way of assent and held it in front of them as she tucked her face against Sydney's. With a quick turn of her head, she planted a kiss on Sydney's cheek. A parting kiss. Something for them both to remember.

"There, you can have that to remember me by. Use me gently... or don't."

Sydney's phone beeped as the photo message arrived.

"Thank you. I will use you with respect."

As they were about to leave, a middle-aged couple approached Sydney. She could make out enough of the conversation to know they were discussing Gertie. The pair were fawning over her so much that Sydney showed them the new engine. Was Gertie really that captivating? At this moment she was more impressive than the famous actress who was cooking in the heat in the front seat, admittedly hiding behind her enormous sunglasses.

CHAPTER 32

S ydney and Alex stepped from the Range Rover, meeting in front of the bonnet where he dropped his bag by his feet. He was different to the kid she'd picked up all those weeks ago. Something had changed that she couldn't put her finger on. Deciding it was her view of him that had changed, she held out a flat palm to him.

He cocked his head.

"You owe me fifty pounds. Your mum ran first."

She waited for the inevitable look of horror as he realised he'd not only lost the bet, but she remembered he'd placed one.

It came.

"I'm kidding. You keep it. This win is enough for me."

"Ha!" He laughed in relief. "Thanks for sticking it out with her. She's chilled a lot since you've been around."

"I wish I could have stuck around for a lot longer."

"Me too. Forever even."

Sydney gave him a flat smile. "You have my number.

I'm always at the end of it. And go easy on your mum. She's had — and still has — a lot to deal with. It's not easy being her, as it's not easy being her child. You'll both do better if you're on the same side."

"I know." Alex nodded. "I wasn't going to say anything... I overheard you and my dad talking."

What the...

"No! Oh, Alex." Sydney sighed. "You shouldn't have heard any of that."

He gave a despondent shrug. "It's okay. I needed to hear it. Kids are always told lies by their parents to protect them when the truth is what protects us."

Sydney exhaled nasally in amusement. "Wise words, Alex. How old are you again? Your mum was always trying to protect you. She got a bit mixed up on the best way to go about it."

Alex nodded. "Thanks for introducing me to Sam. He's amazing."

"Don't I know it," Sydney agreed. "Look what he's done with Gertie. A full lung and heart transplant."

She opened her arms. Was a hug too much to ask from a teenager? It wasn't. He stepped towards her and embraced her.

"I'm going to miss thrashing you in the pool on a regular basis," Sydney said with a grin.

"I'm going to miss thrashing you at Monopoly on a regular basis."

"You'll be able to thrash your mum now instead." As they pulled apart, Sydney added, "You can only be one thing in life, Alex, and that's you." Pretending to hook her hair behind her ear, she brushed a tear away.

He nodded and picked up his bag. "Bye."

She'd dropped off plenty of employers' kids at train stations before, but this time something was different. It was like watching a friend or a favourite nephew walk away. She'd grown fonder of him than she realised.

If this was hard, it was going to be even harder to drop his mum at Heathrow in a couple of hours. She couldn't have been less ready to say goodbye to someone. They'd spent the last few days packing Beatrice's suitcases and enjoying the odd joke as friends, the type of friends who would promise to keep in touch but wouldn't. That would be best all round anyway. A clean break was best in situations like these — for everyone.

The divide between the front and rear of the Mercedes was down, yet neither spoke on the way to the airport. They'd grown so much closer since the last time they were in the vehicle together, yet from the moment they re-entered it, that distance had returned.

All those weeks ago Sydney had looked forward to this moment when she could escape Beatrice; now all the time in the world with her still wouldn't be enough. Why couldn't she have broken her tibia instead? Sydney was mildly embarrassed by the *Misery*-like thought. She would have been laid up for much longer, allowing Beatrice the time she needed to realise they could have a future together.

Waking up in Gertie tomorrow with Beatrice across the Atlantic was going to be unbearable. She always loved getting back on the road with Gertie, but it wouldn't feel the same anymore. The bewitching Beatrice Russell and her picturesque estate had ruined it for her. Life was going to suck until she could erase the past weeks from her mind and clear her body of the drug it was addicted to. It was going to be a rough couple of weeks on the biggest withdrawal of her life.

Maybe Scotland was the place to go; she could wallow in the familiarity of her mum's house. If all she was going to feel for the next weeks or months was grief-stricken, the last thing she wanted was to feel like that living in Gertie. She didn't want to end up resenting her by wishing she was somewhere else the whole time.

She could check herself into a clinic... ask to be locked in a room for a month so she could cry her eyes out. Rosie would have her, but even she was marred by memories of Beatrice. No, a clean break was what Sydney needed.

Her heart quickened as she pulled up outside the entrance to the VIP lounge. This was it. If she wanted to see Beatrice again, she was going to have to turn on her television.

Jonathon was tracking their arrival on his phone and was waiting outside. He pointed the concierge towards the boot and then assisted Beatrice from the Mercedes. As Sydney joined her, she politely shooed him away.

"Well, Sydney," Beatrice said, fiddling with an earring. "Thank you for all your hard work. You were indeed the best."

Sydney nodded and pulled her lips to one side. "I did tell you."

"You did." Beatrice smiled. "I'm going to miss you."

"Likewise. Don't forget to play nicely with your new assistants."

Beatrice narrowed her eyes a little and raised her cheeks. "Very good."

The words melted into Sydney's brain, shooting endorphins to every inch of her. This woman was literally a drug. She racked her brain for all the things she wanted to say to her, only to find silence. She couldn't think straight.

"Well, goodbye, Sydney." And with that, Beatrice turned and shuffled through the automatic doors. She'd ripped herself away as quickly as a plaster, leaving a burn etched into Sydney's skin.

What was she expecting? A protracted goodbye filled with confessions of love. A little more than a brief thank-you would have been nice, as would a hug. She'd counted on one of those — one last touch. Perhaps it was too much to ask of the woman when she'd made herself clear on where she stood and why. It didn't make it hurt any less.

It took a moment before Sydney could move. She stared at the silhouette of Beatrice through the closed doors as she passed the security guard and disappeared from view with Jonathon.

Her hand reached for her phone in her back pocket. She prayed Rosie wasn't with a client and would pick up.

"Rosie," she said after her friend answered. "She's gone."

"Are you crying?"

Fuck!

"No," Sydney replied, wiping tears from her eyes.

"This wasn't unexpected. You knew she'd be going back to the States eventually."

"Oh God, Rosie." Sydney put her hand to her mouth, feeling she was about to be sick. "It hurts… like I've been punched in the stomach."

"You really fell for her, didn't you? Look, if she doesn't feel the same way, then there's not much you can do about it. You've got to pick yourself up and move on."

"That's the thing, she does—"

"No!"

"Yes. Though she won't act on it. Well, she did once for about five minutes, but she's still gone."

"Whoa. Rewind. Five minutes. You mean, you and she…?"

"Yep," Sydney confirmed, wiping another tear from her cheek with the back of her hand. "The briefest and most memorable kiss I'll ever have."

"Bloody hell, Syd."

Her body was already aching for her, and she'd only been gone a few minutes.

"We're right for each other, Rosie — in so many ways. I hoped she'd be brave."

"Brave? She's an international star. She doesn't get to be who she wants to be; she gets to be who she has to be. Have you been brave and told her how you feel? How you really feel? You can't expect her to when she's the one that has everything to lose."

Sydney stuttered. "No."

Rosie was right, she'd shown intention, she'd implied her feelings, yet not told Beatrice the depth of them. Would that make the difference? Was it time to say those words that we keep under the surface, the things we're too afraid to say?

"I'll call you back."

Hanging up the phone, she ran towards the lounge, only to find a security guard blocking her.

"I'm with Beatrice Russell," she explained. "I need to speak to her. I forgot to tell her something."

"Then call her. You can't come through here without a valid ticket or VIP pass. Do you know how many loonies we get here, pretending they're with some star or other? Ha, you must think I was born yesterday."

"I was here, saying goodbye, like five minutes ago," Sydney said, her body twitching with agitation.

"I didn't see you."

Realising she was getting nowhere, and she didn't fancy her chances at running past him, she retreated outside and tapped out a message on her phone, hoping she wasn't too late.

Beatrice took a seat on a leather sofa and took a gulp of the coffee she was presented with by the attendant.

Ouch!

The heat burned as much as walking away from Sydney had. She couldn't stand long goodbyes, especially those she didn't want to be making anyway. It was best to get this one over with before she became unravelled.

Her phone vibrated on the glass table.

You've left something behind.

What could she possibly have left behind? Unless the concierge left one of her bags in the car.

She retraced her limping steps to the entrance, passing a grumpy security guard. Jonathon was two paces behind to deal with him.

There she was again. Sydney. She lifted her sunglasses onto the top of her head and made her way outside.

"What did I leave?"

"Me."

Beatrice's eyelids dropped as she came to stop in front of her. "Sydn—"

"Hear me out, okay? I don't think I told you how I really feel, and I need to tell you in case it changes how you feel." Sydney paused for a breath. "I told you once that you had all my attention. I meant it. You have all of it. You have all of me, Beatrice; my head, my heart, my body. I have nothing left."

"Sydney," Beatrice replied with compassion. Although it was everything she wanted to hear, this wasn't helping an already tricky situation. Sydney's honesty wasn't going to change the position she was in.

"I'm sorry," Sydney continued, beginning to ramble nervously. "I know you don't want to hear this, but I can't live with the regret of not saying it. You once asked me how I found you."

"I did."

"I have my answer."

Beatrice braced herself.

"You have a strong sense of self, but you let everything that's happened to you in the past control you. You believe keeping people at a distance will protect you. Your parents hurt you; you picked yourself up and you carried on, only for the next person you let get close to you to hurt you too. Are you really concerned about what coming out will mean for your career, or are you afraid to let someone in again?"

In truth, it was both.

"I know you feel the same way. I can see it in your eyes."

Beatrice turned away from Sydney's gaze. "I don't get to feel that, Sydney. My life is not my own."

"Who's saying that? This Beatrice..." Sydney stepped forward, placing her hand on Beatrice's heart.

She inhaled sharply at her touch.

"Or this Beatrice?" Sydney stepped back and gesticulated towards her with her hand.

She wanted to call Sydney back to her, but the words wouldn't come out; weren't allowed to be spoken.

"Which one are you... really?"

Beatrice had no answer. All she wanted was to end her pain; In reality, it hadn't even begun.

"It's your life, Beatrice. Only you get to choose. Don't hide behind an imaginary wall because you're scared of what might happen. You'll get stuck there, on the wrong side. The opposite side to where I am. We've not been in each other's company for long, and already I don't know how to exist without you."

"And I don't know how to exist with you."

Jonathon stepped forward. "The car's ready to take you to the plane, ma'am."

Beatrice took a step forward and pulled Sydney into her. A parting hug was all she could give her. "I'm sorry I can't be what you want me to be," she whispered into her ear.

"I want you to be you, Beatrice," Sydney exhaled in desperation.

Beatrice wrenched herself back even though her body ached to stay pressed to her.

"My career is all I have; it's the only thing that hasn't let me down. I can't be the one to let it down."

"I won't let you down either," Sydney pleaded.

"Everyone lets me down eventually," Beatrice said, wiping a tear from Sydney's eye with her thumb. "Especially those I trust most."

Not waiting for a response, fearful she may be unable to maintain her own composure, she turned and headed back through the door to catch her flight.

Only once ensconced in her pod in the first-class cabin did she look back to the terminal.

The attendant twitched her head as she placed a glass of pre-take-off champagne on her table. "Are you okay, madam? You look very pale."

"I have the feeling I may have left something important behind."

"I always have that feeling. It usually passes somewhere over the Atlantic." The attendant flashed a warm smile and moved along to the next seat.

Flying commercial was the right choice. The low-level chatter from her fellow passengers was enough to bring some distraction. She didn't need to be alone on a charter flight now, in the quiet where she could hear her heart breaking.

CHAPTER 33

*B*eatrice sat in the waiting room of what she was assured was the best clinic in Beverly Hills. She resented waiting, but the doctor came so well recommended by her newest PA, Connie, who so far had shown competence beyond all her previous assistants — bar one — that she sucked it up.

Her hands wrestled with each other in her lap. If she let them go, they would shake, and she didn't need to attract the attention of anyone in the waiting area. So far, her sunglasses and baseball cap were doing a superb job of disguising her. She crossed her legs and wiggled her foot. What was taking so long? With filming completed on her current film a month ago, she was on a punishing schedule in the States and the UK to promote her book alongside her current film release. There was no time for waiting.

"Miss Russell, you can go in now."

About time!

"Good afternoon, Miss Russell. Please sit."

The doctor gestured to the chair opposite him as if she

hadn't been to a doctor's office before and had no idea where to sit. It earned him a roll of the eyes, which he missed anyway since he didn't even bother to look at her.

Beatrice took the seat opposite him, resting her handbag on her lap. She didn't intend to be in the seat any longer than was necessary.

"Have there been any further attacks since I saw you last?"

"No." Thankfully, although the mere thought of what had happened to her on that aeroplane two weeks ago was enough to induce another one. Fighting for air, a simple breath, was the scariest moment of her life.

"And the list of symptoms you gave me last time, you're still experiencing them, yes?"

Beatrice nodded. The list — sudden onset of sweating, a racing heart, the feeling of panic, nausea, loss of appetite, brain fog, insomnia, headaches — was similar to the symptoms she reeled off to a doctor about seven years ago when she was informed she was perimenopausal.

As if reading her mind, the doctor asked, "When was your last period?"

"Over a year ago."

The doctor nodded. "Hmm, so you're post-menopausal now. Well your blood work and MRI show there is nothing physically wrong with you. You're in perfect shape." He dropped his glasses down his nose and poked his lips with his finger. "Your schedule, I understand, is somewhat frantic. You've cancelled two appointments with me already."

Beatrice responded with a flat smile. She'd been

avoiding the results, unnecessarily apparently, if there was nothing physically wrong with her.

"I'd say you have anxiety, Miss Russell."

"Anxiety?" Beatrice laughed. "Nonsense."

She'd been through hell in her life and not once suffered from anxiety. The doctor's stern face told her he was serious about his diagnosis.

Her head shook in disbelief. "How? Why now?"

"That I can't tell you. A common cause is overworking."

"I've always managed my schedule perfectly, thank you."

If this was another doctor referencing her age again, she was going to scream.

"It could have been triggered by something. You said previously the attack happened shortly after take-off. Do you have a fear of flying?"

Beatrice shook her head. That day had been particularly busy. She'd been in England for a couple of days staying with Alison whilst she carried out promo work for the film release. The day she was due to fly out to LA, she spent in the board room of Alison's office, signing the first batch of books. Alison travelled with her afterwards to the VIP lounge, stopping for coffee and going over her work schedule for the next few weeks. The last thing she'd done was scribble a note to Sydney for Alison to send on to her with a signed book. She'd struggled with what to write, finally deciding on a short message, refraining from adding, *I miss you*, at the bottom. Before she put it in the envelope, she'd rubbed her wrist on it.

A low, drumming sensation began in her chest.

"Have you experienced trauma recently, a big, life-changing event? I understand you broke your leg some months ago. Sometimes physical problems can cause mental anguish that we don't realise until it later manifests with physical symptoms."

Beatrice stared at him, mystified as to how a broken leg would cause her body to behave in that way.

"No, the symptoms started after my leg healed. After I left England."

An image of Sydney standing outside the VIP lounge at Heathrow lodged itself unhelpfully in her mind. She could see herself hug her, remember how her body felt against her own. Then she'd walked away with nothing other than a simple yet heartfelt apology.

The drumming in her chest intensified. She dragged her fingers down either side of her warm, tingling face, pushing and pinching at the skin in the hope of relieving the tightening. Blowing out a slow breath made her head feel even lighter, like it wasn't attached to the rest of her. The doctor's mouth was moving, but she couldn't hear him; her ears were muffled as if full of cotton wool. She closed her eyes, hoping that would stop everything, but it only made her more aware.

She opened them again slowly and took what breath she could get as her chest resisted her.

A glass hovered in front of her.

"Here, drink this."

She reached for the glass with two hands and gulped at the water. Her mouth was so dry. The doctor took the glass from her and placed it on the desk. He grasped her wrist, searching for her pulse, stopping as he found it.

"What were you thinking about?" he asked.

"Someone."

"Someone close to you?"

"They were, not now," she answered, licking her dry lips.

She took a deep breath, her lungs finally giving in to her desperate need for air.

"These symptoms you've been experiencing can manifest with grief," the doctor continued cautiously. "If you've recently lost someone—"

"They're not dead. They're just not part of my life anymore."

"And that... pains you."

Beatrice gave the smallest of nods, reaching for the glass and taking another gulp of water.

"And may I ask if this person was a love interest?"

"You're not suggesting I'm lovesick, are you?" Her hand went to her mouth, partly to choke down a laugh but also because the contents of her stomach were threatening to make an appearance at any minute.

The doctor casually returned to his seat. "There is a root cause to most ailments, Miss Russell. I can give you some beta blockers to take daily; that will help keep the physical symptoms at bay while you..." He waved his hand. He never finished the sentence, and she exited his office a minute later with a prescription for a condition she definitely didn't have.

She pulled her phone from her handbag, texting Connie to bring the car around. It was waiting for her as she stepped from the elevator and crossed the lobby. Her elderly driver was standing beside the open car door as she pounded down the steps and across the sidewalk.

Connie was waiting for her inside, working away on her laptop.

How could she, Beatrice Russell, be lovesick? What a ridiculous notion. She was going to need to get a second opinion, a proper opinion. There had been little time to think about Sydney. Admittedly she'd called Connie by Sydney's name for the first month she'd worked for her, but it was difficult to remember everyone's name. It wasn't like every time she spoke to Connie, she hoped Sydney would answer. That was only about 90 percent of the time. In the few moments between the crazy, her thoughts may have drifted to Sydney as they did when she went to sleep and when she woke. When she thought she was dying during her first panic attack, of course Sydney was there in her mind. She certainly wasn't sitting in the car now with her eyes closed, imagining it was Sydney driving.

Shit!

She was lovesick.

It would pass. It had to. If it didn't, she was unlikely to have a career left. Then everything would have been in vain. Filming had run over by a day due to her forgetting her lines and experiencing brain fog. The crew weren't pleased, and the production company was furious as it hit them in their pockets every day they ran over.

She'd take the beta blockers and find more things to distract her.

"I'll need these before my flight to New York tonight," she said, passing the prescription slip to Connie.

CHAPTER 34

*B*eatrice studied herself in the mirror as the final curl dropped down from a curler and bounced against her cheek. The stylist made a few further adjustments to the hair that framed her face and then left the room. She was alone at last with her thoughts — as she preferred to be before she went onstage. Tonight was a big night. She was in the first slot with the most popular late-night talk show host in America to promote her latest film release and autobiography.

Her flight back to the UK — where she would finally have a few weeks off over Christmas — was early the next morning. Time off to do what, though? Her busy schedule was the only thing keeping her close to sane. She covered a yawn with her hand. Sleep would be the first thing on the agenda. She could have done without this stopover in New York for the talk show.

It would be the first time she returned to Highwood House since she'd left it in the summer. She hadn't been ready to deal with any feelings being alone at Highwood would bring during her short returns to the UK. It wouldn't feel the same without Sydney there. She didn't feel ready now either, yet it wasn't practical to stay in a hotel or at Alison's over Christmas. She knew one day she was going to have to go back there, and armed with the beta blockers the doctor gave her, it was time. She could see herself wandering around Highwood House in her red dress, Miss Havisham style, pining for her lost love.

She sucked in a breath, feeling her face flush at the mere thought of Sydney. Something she'd come to realise was the first sign of an anxiety attack. She reached for the packet in her handbag and pushed a pill out of its silver housing. She'd feel better in ten minutes, just in time to go on air. First her leg, now this. It was ridiculous for her body to be behaving like this over anyone. It was tantamount to a tantrum — over an ex-assistant! At least she was in 'perfect shape'; that she liked to hear.

A copy of her autobiography on her dressing table caught her eye. A crew member had asked her to sign it for her so she could give it to her sister for Christmas — another *Nancy* fan. Taking the pen that had been left on top of it, she opened the cover and scribbled her signature onto the title page. As she closed it, her eyelids shut as she let out a sigh. She'd spent the summer being truthful and honest in her autobiography — at least truthful about the parts she was able to share — and now she felt she would be promoting it to the world dishonestly. That didn't sit well. Nothing about any of it sat well, particularly the way she'd felt over the last three months since she'd parted with Sydney. After the panic attack, the nausea was the worst.

A knock at the door made her jump. A production assistant popped her head around the door.

"Miss Russell, I have someone asking to see you."

Beatrice stood, smoothing down her asymmetrical, scarlet dress that hung off one shoulder. She wasn't expecting anyone, and they certainly didn't let just anyone wander around the studio.

The door reopened and a grinning Alex entered the room.

"Hi, Mum."

"Alex! What on earth are you doing here? I thought you were staying at your father's for Christmas."

"I was, but I wanted to see you." He eyed her. "Are you okay?"

"I'm fine, a little tired. So you flew halfway around the world to see me. That's extremely sweet, but I have a flight booked tomorrow. I was coming home for Christmas. Though it will be nice not to fly alone for a change."

It would be good to have the company over the holidays too; it might even prevent a full-blown Dickensian Christmas.

"Yeah, about that. I'm not coming home for Christmas."

"Where else are you going to be?"

"I'm staying here if you'll let me. Chef Anthony has a house here, and he's invited me to stay with him and his family for a few weeks. His youngest son, Freddie, is my age. I played against his school in hockey. We swapped numbers and we've become friends."

"That's very generous of him. I'll need to call him and check everything's okay."

"It is, Mum, honest. I flew out here with them. They're watching the show. You can talk to him after. He's going to help me develop my skills whilst I'm here, too, and he said I could do some shadowing in the kitchens of a couple of his New York restaurants." Alex stopped to take a breath. "I couldn't say no, Mum. Dad spoke to him, too, and said it was okay for me to come out here with him but to see you first."

"He did, did he? And how does he feel about you not spending Christmas with him?"

"He has a new girlfriend; she's horrible. I could tell they didn't want me there." Alex hesitated. "I don't want to go to his place anymore. I don't feel comfortable. Is that going to be a problem for you during the holidays?"

Beatrice frowned and slowly shook her head. "No. I'm sure we can sort something out. Why don't you want to stay with him? Did something happen when you were there?"

Alex shook his head. "I know about him, Mum. I know everything."

Beatrice blinked. *Everything?*

"I overheard Syd and him talking the day he dropped me home."

Everything!

"I'm sorry he put you through all that," Alex said wiping his moistening eyes. "And I'm sorry that I thought it was you that forced me to go to boarding school."

Beatrice reached out and stroked his hair. "Hey. It's okay." As he didn't brush her off, she put her arm around him and pulled him into her. He came easily. "I would have had you by my side every day if I could have. It's this damn job."

"Even so. I know you weren't responsible for Dad leaving us. Dad's the dick."

Beatrice laughed, making Alex laugh. He pulled out of the hug.

"I understand why you didn't tell me, but you should have."

"He was your hero as a little boy. I didn't want to destroy that."

"I get it. You were doing what mums should do, protecting me. Like Syd said, you got it the wrong way around."

"You spoke to Sydney about this?"

"Yes. She's been a good friend to me, Mum."

Why didn't that surprise her? Sydney was a good friend to everybody.

"She's also been helping me... with something else. Well, Sam has."

"Sam?" When the marine engineer returned to her mind, Beatrice immediately knew what that meant. How could she have been so blind? "Is this why you've been so sad all the time? You're struggling with your identity?"

"I'm not sad because I'm questioning my gender, Mum. I'm sad because people will hate me and attack me for it. I'm sorry I didn't come to you about it, but..." Alex shrugged. "You know."

"I do know, and I'm sorry I've not been there for you. I promise I'll do better from now on and I'll support you with whatever decision you make about how you want to live your life. I'm glad you were able to talk to Syd and Sam."

It explained why Sydney was keen for Alex to join them when they collected Gertie; she wanted him to meet Sam. Beatrice had thought the woman didn't want to be alone with her. She'd agreed for what she thought was the same reason. Yet again she owed more to Sydney than she'd given her credit for, and she'd already given the woman a lot of credit.

She'd felt something wasn't right in Alex's world for a while. She foolishly put it down to the standard teenage angst. Didn't all teenagers struggle to find their place in the world? She hadn't recognised that Alex's struggle went beyond that. A good mother would have asked what was wrong. Even if Alex hadn't wanted to talk to her, it would have shown she cared. Instead, she'd buried her head in the sand like she did with a lot of other important things.

"It seems I never got the owner's manual on being a man," Alex said.

"There isn't one, darling. Everyone is muddling their way through something and desperately trying to look as if they are in control. Are you changing your pronouns?"

"No, Mum. I'm just figuring things out at the moment. Sam made me realise that we don't decide our gender; we discover it and then decide how to apply it. That's what I'm going to do. I'm writing my story, no one else is. It's time you wrote your own story, too, Mum. To those who matter, it won't matter, and everyone else can fuck off."

She thought to chastise the bad language but couldn't bring herself to. It was the truth.

"Perhaps it's time we all faced ourselves."

Alex nodded. "You know… you and Syd made a good team — the best team. It's a shame you can't become a permanent team."

"What?" Beatrice asked, her eyes widening.

"I saw how you were with each other!" Alex insisted. "You're not the only one that goes downstairs for a drink at night."

Beatrice's hand shot to her mouth. "Oh, God! Please tell me you didn't see us." She couldn't handle the thought of Alex witnessing that. It was enough to scar him for life.

"I saw you kissing, that's all. Trust me, no kid wants to watch their mum kissing for a second longer than they must." He shuddered. "It's sad that you're scared to be with her."

"I'm not scared," Beatrice protested.

"You are. Otherwise, she'd be here with you. It's okay to be scared. Fear is what makes us question something, so we don't make a mistake, but this isn't a mistake, Mum — it's you."

She composed herself, reality biting. "Okay, so maybe I am a little bit scared."

"A lot."

Beatrice beamed at him. "When did you get so smart, eh?"

"When you weren't paying attention."

"Sorry." Her eyes fell to the floor. "It's not simple for someone like me… to be me."

"Life is as simple or as complicated as you make it. I was scared to tell you how I was feeling because of how you might react, but we can't live our lives worried about what others think. Especially when they might not even think that way. I liked who you were when you were around her."

Beatrice had to agree with him. Sydney brought light into her life, she made everything easy, and she made life enjoyable.

Alex looked up at her, his eyes subdued. "I miss her, Mum."

"Me too, kid. Me too. So you don't mind, then, if I like women?"

"I only care that you're you and you're happy, and I know you're not. And I can't be happy with that. You be you and I'll be me, promise?"

"Promise." The word fell out of her mouth so easily. Could she promise that?

"And Dad can fuck off."

This time it was a little far. "Alex!"

"Sorry," he replied, though he seemed self-satisfied with the swear. "Syd suggested I move schools, have a fresh start, reinvent myself somewhere new."

She recalled the conversation she'd overheard between them, when she'd thought they were talking about what he wanted to be when he grew up. How stupid she'd been not to realise. Yet Sydney had. She had made sure someone was there for Alex when no one else was. When no one else was paying attention — even though it was their job to pay attention as a parent — she'd been listening.

"Do you want to move schools? It is an option."

"No. I'm going to stand my ground and be who I am, no matter what anyone else thinks. It's them with the problem, not me. It's what you should do too. Choose happiness and we'll sort out the rest... together."

She'd received a severe talking to from a fifteen-year-old, and he was right. It was time to write her narrative. The truth this time. Lying and hiding were exhausting, and they had cost her the best thing to ever happen to her after Alex. Here he was, encouraging her to be herself when he was the one she'd been protecting from herself. If a fifteen-year-old could stand up to the world, couldn't she? She had enough money saved if it turned sour. She could happily live the rest of her life as a recluse at Highwood if Sydney was beside her. Was it time for her to finally face who she was, to put the important things first and sod the rest?

There was a knock at the door and another young woman popped her head around the door. "Miss Russell? It's time." The woman turned to Alex. "I'll show you back to your seat."

"Thank you." Alex turned before he left the room. "Mum, Syd said something to me when I last saw her. You can only be one thing in life, and that's you. Now, I'm saying it to you."

Beatrice kissed her child's forehead. "I'll see you back here after the show."

CHAPTER 35

Sydney leant against the railing overlooking the harbour as a salty, wet wind hurled itself at her. A morning walk in weather like this couldn't be beaten; it was guaranteed to wake you up. Pulling her hood up over her head, she zipped up her coat against the freezing mist surrounding her. The hottest of summers often led to the harshest of winters.

The waves crashed below against the harbour wall as the hum of the ocean deafened her ears. It was the exact spot she'd stood in as she watched the coastguard and lifeboat crew coming and going during the days and nights following her dad's accident. Sometimes she'd spent hours there, waiting, hoping — for any sign, any change.

As the days went on, she even hoped for a body to give her some closure to the gut-wrenching pain she was experiencing from not knowing. It would be a signal for her own body to move on to the next stage, grief. But it would never come. She was forever wedged in this limbo of hope that one day he might return, all the while knowing the chances were now zero.

Her eyes ran along the harbour wall where her dad would chase her younger self to his fishing vessel. Her mum would walk a few paces behind them, worried that she'd trip on the cobblestone path. It was a well-trodden path for them as they waved him off to sea, never quite sure when he would return.

When she was at school, her mum would see him off alone. At noon, she would come to the school to help with the children's lunches and give Sydney a nod that he'd gone. It was a job she'd only taken on to help Sydney adjust to her new school after they moved back to Scotland. She'd loved it so much that she ended up staying until she received the devastating cancer diagnosis many years later.

Following her mum's diagnosis, Sydney had done everything she could to help, taking on all her household work and becoming her carer whilst her dad was out for days at a time fishing. It was a distraction from having to make decisions about what she wanted to do with her life now that she'd left her old one behind.

Although she'd enjoyed university and garnered useful skills within her creative writing degree, she'd also enjoyed the following years with Sam, building up the business and assisting him with fixing the boats. When she returned to Scotland, fleeing the dark cloud over their relationship only to immerse herself in yet another problematic situation, one shining light remained within her — the desire to be on the ocean again.

Once her mum received the all-clear from cancer,

Sydney was desperate to get back out there and work. With nowhere else to be, and with jobs scarce in the small fishing town, Sydney badgered her dad into letting her resume her old summer job and work alongside him.

As a teenager, he'd allowed her to accompany him on some of his trips during the summer holidays. She had worked belowdecks, where it was safer. With a team of six men to feed and clean up after, it was a full-time job. He'd eventually relented to her pressure, though, and taught her to steer and navigate the boat. It turned out she was a natural.

Her mum put up a fight against her returning; she couldn't bear to have them both risking their lives in the wild, unpredictable North Sea. It was only since surviving cancer that she'd objected; life became that little bit more precious to her after that. But with more skills learned from her time living with Sam, piloting boats around the harbour, Sydney was finally allowed to be in the captain's chair.

They'd worked together on the boat for over a year when the worst moment of her life occurred. The storm that hit them was stronger than expected. They'd hoped to be on their way back to the harbour before the worst of it hit. A caught net delayed them, and fierce winds fought against them. The men tried to persuade her dad to come inside; the deck was a death trap with twenty-foot waves crashing over it. There was one last net to pull in, though, and he wasn't going to leave it behind. That's where she got her discipline from, the need to complete things, to tick the box. It was the last tick he'd try to make.

The sea was a volatile workplace. The wind would

change and with it your luck — or in this case, her life. She'd gone outside herself to plead with him to come in, only for him to shout back, "Last one." She could still hear his voice in her head and see the smile on his face. He didn't see the freak wave that crashed over him a second later.

Sydney did.

She watched it hover above him, suspended in time. At least that was her memory of it. The wall of water crashed down over him, throwing him off his feet just as the boat listed into the depression the wave left. She'd clamped herself to a handle on the wheelhouse, only able to watch as he fell backwards overboard, his smile replaced by panic and fear as he took a last look at his daughter.

He was gone. Absorbed into a body of water he so loved.

She'd never told her mum that it was she who witnessed him fall overboard, that she was the last one he'd looked at with that panic in his eyes. It would haunt her for the rest of her life; she didn't want it to haunt her mum too.

The wind was picking up, and she'd have her mum worried if she didn't head back. Sydney turned her back on the sea just like she'd done that day. She couldn't step back on the boat without her dad there, so she'd left the job of carrying on to her uncle.

As she approached the road, she stopped on the spot where the police car had pulled up. She'd opened the door to help her mum out, only for the fragile woman to fall to her knees, overwhelmed by what was happening. The news she lived in fear of had finally come for her like the Grim Reaper.

Sydney put aside her own fears and feelings to pick her mum up off the ground and guide her to the harbour; to hug her, wipe the tears from her face, and reassure her that they would find him, knowing she needed to cling on to that hope herself as long as she could. They both knew well enough from similar incidents that there was no hope in these situations, yet all they could do was cling to it. The alternative was too horrific to consider.

In the following days they would sit in silence, their faces sullen, exhausted from crying, jumping every time the phone rang or the doorbell chimed. Each time they allowed themselves a little hope of good news, only to have to shoo away a well-wisher or journalist. People from the community would bring them food, though neither of them had an appetite. As the search wound up and everyone else lost interest, Sydney and her mum were still sitting there, waiting.

Sydney grew so angry that no one was doing more that she decided she couldn't sit back and wait any longer; she was going to look for him herself. She got up, hugged her mum, and promised she was going to bring him home. It was a promise she could never fulfil, but without making it, she might have given up searching a long time ago, and then she might have missed his face in a crowd. She needed to keep herself accountable.

She wiped a tear from her eye as she made her way down the road. She hadn't shed a tear for a few years over her dad. The pain didn't live on the surface anymore; she kept it somewhere deeper. This tear she knew was for someone else she'd lost, a pain that did sit on the surface.

Beatrice.

At least she was still alive, merrily living her closeted existence without her. Not that Sydney had been stalking her, but she had created a social media account and made a point of checking it regularly to catch any news of her. It had been reported that Beatrice had been spotted heading into a medical clinic. Although it was likely to be a check-up on her leg, it didn't stop her worrying.

Taking a lungful of salty air, she pushed it back out as hard as she could, and then climbed the hill to her mum's house. Beatrice was out of her life forever; her medical status was none of her business.

CHAPTER 36

Sydney closed the door of the small cottage and hung her thick coat up on the hook. "Mum, I'm back."

"I'm making us some cheese and pickle sandwiches for lunch," her mum called from the kitchen.

"Great!" It was one of her favourite combos.

Rhona, a slim, pale woman with the complexion of someone ten years her senior, moseyed into the hallway. "Where did you walk?"

"Down to the harbour."

"Oh. Right," she replied softly, her gaze falling to the floor.

Why had Sydney let that slip? She hadn't intended on mentioning it. She didn't even know why she had gone or what she expected to find there. All it did was bring back painful memories.

"This came in the post this morning," her mum said, taking an A4 card envelope from a small table and handing it to her.

It was already open, so Sydney reached inside and extracted a green piece of paper. Her dad's death certificate. She looked at her mum.

"We left enough time, didn't we?"

Rhona gave a gentle nod. "More than enough time. We should have done it sooner."

Sydney reached for her, as she noticed a glistening in her mum's eyes, and pulled her into a hug. "It all seems so final now, doesn't it?"

"It needs to. We should move on. It's what he would have wanted." Rhona pulled back and wiped her eye. "You should stop searching too."

Sydney opened her mouth to speak.

"Don't deny it. I saw you in the supermarket yesterday, scanning everything except the groceries. It's time to stop."

Sydney gave an obedient nod. It was her mum she'd made the promise to, and if she said to stop, she would. She thought she had; she'd certainly been trying since Beatrice said the same thing. Her insides fizzed at the thought of Beatrice, causing her to let out a little sigh. Luckily her mum hadn't noticed.

"A parcel came for you," she added. "I put it in your room."

A parcel? Sydney wasn't expecting anything.

"I thought we'd eat early, and then we could go to the cinema — catch the matinee. That woman you worked for has one out. Do you want to see it?"

"I don't know, Mum. Can we see how we feel after lunch?"

Seeing someone you were trying to forget at ten times

their true size a few meters from your face was not going to help with Sydney's fizzy feelings. On the other hand, her mum was suggesting they go out, and as she rarely left the house, except to buy groceries, Sydney wasn't sure it was wise to refuse.

"Go on up, open your parcel while I finish these sandwiches."

Running up the stairs, two steps at a time, Sydney discovered a flat parcel on her bed, postmarked London. She ripped it open to find a copy of Beatrice's autobiography. She sucked in a breath at the words 'Co-Author Sydney MacKenzie' gracing the cover.

The excitement she should have felt at seeing her name on the front cover of what was to be one of the hottest books of the year was masked by the pain of her distance from the woman on it — the breathtaking woman in a red dress, whose eyes were once again penetrating her own as they had when the photograph was taken.

The chosen photograph was a pose with a sullen look on Beatrice's face rather than one taken seconds after, when she'd been unable to withhold her smile. It was the right choice; it fitted the tone of the book. As she opened the book to its title page, Sydney noticed a signature — *With love, Beatrice x.* No doubt generic. She tore at the envelope that accompanied it, sitting on the bed to read it. A small card with 'Heathrow VIP Lounge' stamped at the top held Beatrice's handwriting. So she'd been in England recently.

Not bad for an aspiring writer, who was never an aspiring writer!

The moment you do is the moment you are.
Don't forget to sign it, too, partner.
B x

A hint of perfume hit her senses. She ran the card under her nose, taking her back to that night when they'd kissed, when she'd told Beatrice how good she'd smelt. *Oh God.* Sydney's body ached for her. She longed to be in her presence and hear a click of her fingers; that would be enough to keep her going for a week. But then what? She'd just want more of her.

The sound of her mum coming up the stairs startled her from her daydreaming.

"What was it? Anything interesting?"

Sydney passed the book to her mum as she entered the room.

"Bloody hell. Is that you?"

"Do you know any other Sydney MacKenzie?"

She watched as her mum opened the book and read the inscription. It was funny to think how she'd fought for her precious time off to write, only for another book entirely to fall into her lap. A book that she hoped was going to be the making of her.

"I know you said you'd helped her with it, but co-author — wow. Your dad would have been so proud." Rhona looked at her daughter and gave her a rueful smile.

"Yeah, I know, Mum."

"That was well worth giving up a bit of travelling time, don't you think?"

"Every bit."

Catching another glimpse of Beatrice as her mum

closed the book, Sydney blurted out, "I've changed my mind. Let's catch that matinee!"

Beatrice was sensational, just as she had been in *Nancy*. Those smouldering eyes, sideways glances, the way she could slowly look up at you whilst tilting her head away… How did she do that? It was enough for you to rip your own heart out and throw it at her. The thought that she had kissed those lips, tasted her, was like a dream now. Had she imagined the entire summer?

The light, vibrating sensation of her phone rippled through her backside. Extracting it from beneath her, she shielded the brightness with her jacket and opened a text message.

B has set the world alight — for you! Watch this right NOW!!!

Without even knowing what the hell Rosie was talking about, Sydney's heart was fluttering, dancing in anticipation. What had Beatrice Russell done… for her?

She clambered to her feet. "I'll be back in a sec, Mum."

Once in the cinema's foyer, she clicked the link Rosie had sent. On the screen flashed a video of Beatrice sitting beside a talk show host. Sydney's whole body groaned as she took the woman, and her fine red dress, in. She was dazzling, just like the first image Rosie had shown her all those months back.

"You spent the summer in England convalescing, I believe," the talk show host was saying, "and in a heat wave too."

Beatrice nodded. "Despite the broken leg, I had a fantastic summer at home. There was time to reflect and grow closer with Alex, my teenager."

Sydney smiled. That was one of the better outcomes of the summer.

"I'm actually heading back to the UK tomorrow for a quiet Christmas," she added.

"And no doubt deserved. You've been keeping busy for someone with a broken leg!" the host joked. "You've just released your autobiography, *Broken Beyond Repair*, just in time for Christmas." The host held up a copy of her book to the camera.

"I have."

"Is the title a question or a statement?"

Beatrice grinned slyly. "I'll leave that for the readers to decide."

"I hear it's hit number one on the *New York Times* Best Seller List."

Fuck. Had it?

Was that what Rosie meant? She'd happily take it, but she'd be lying if she wasn't disappointed if this was Beatrice's way of *setting the world on fire for her*. She wasn't sure she could watch anymore, not without vomiting anyway.

"You have the awards season coming up too. You've been nominated for Best Actress, I understand."

"I have."

The audience clapped as Beatrice gave her most humble smile.

"And they've asked you to present an award?"

"They have indeed."

"Will you be bringing a plus one? I know you recently went public with finalising your divorce." The host surveyed the crowd and gave a smarmy eyebrow waggle. "Beatrice Russell is back on the market, everyone!"

The crowd cheered and clapped with even more enthusiasm than they had about her Academy Award nomination.

Beatrice blushed and took a deep breath. "Well, I did meet the most amazing person over the summer."

Sydney's heart rate picked up so quickly she placed a hand over it to stop it from beating its way out of her.

The talk show host edged closer to Beatrice over the desk. "A summer romance? Tell me more."

"*Ooooh.*" The audience continued their participation.

"I wouldn't go that far. But, you know, summer romances are what they are — over in the autumn."

"Well, I'm sorry to hear that. He doesn't know what he's missing."

"She," Beatrice corrected him. Then she seemed to freeze, poised for the inevitable reaction.

The audience drew in a collective breath whilst the host held his hands to his chest.

"What the fuck!" slipped from Sydney's mouth as she backed herself against the wall, sliding down it to the floor before her legs gave way.

"So if my career makes a nosedive now, you'll know why," Beatrice said through a nervous laugh.

"So you are well and truly back on the market, and open to everyone?" the host asked.

"Perhaps just one."

What did she mean by that? Did she mean her?

"But I felt I needed to bring this up," Beatrice said. "We don't talk enough about our differences, not in a positive way anyway. Hollywood has always been so toxic and will continue to be so if we don't challenge it."

Sydney watched in awe as Beatrice took control of the situation.

The host withdrew his phone from inside his suit jacket and mock-answered it.

"Hello? Oh, it's for you. The awards administrators say they are withdrawing their offer."

Beatrice howled with laughter. "You joke, but I am now anticipating that call. You know, so many excellent television shows and films are completely ignored when it comes to awards, just because they have LGBTQ+ characters and cast. Actresses expertly portray notable historical lesbian characters and are completely overlooked. Hundreds of actors are hiding their identity, their own existence, for fear of reprisals from people who own their careers. Well, I say: fuck off!" As the censor bleeped out the curse, Beatrice stood and threw her hands into the air. "It's time to stand up and be counted — hashtag #OutAndProud. The more there are of us, the louder we can tell them to fuck off. We exist, and if you don't like it, then tough. We have a population in fear of a population we couldn't like less, who bully us into hiding."

Sydney wiped a tear from her cheek; she didn't even realise she was crying at Beatrice's words.

"So are you going to boycott awards season?"

"No, but I'm sure as hell going to make as much noise as possible," Beatrice replied, laughing as she scooped her dress around her legs and reclaimed her seat.

Sydney had never felt so proud of someone. All she wanted to do was kiss the woman. Beatrice had indeed just started a media shitstorm. She was so different, so confident. It was a side Sydney had not seen before. It was Beatrice the celebrity and actress, but this time, she wasn't pretending. She was being herself, and she was heading home. With a quick time zone calculation she realised she needed to get her skates on.

Making her way back inside the theatre, Sydney gave her mum a kiss on the cheek.

"I'm sorry, Mum. I've got to go. For the first time in my life, I know where I want to be."

She'd expected her mum to be confused by the statement, but instead, Rhona said, "You go get your girl."

"What?" Sydney asked, baffled.

"Her." She nodded at the screen, which was currently displaying a close-up of Beatrice. "You couldn't take your eyes off her, and you smiled every time she came on the screen."

There was no hiding anything from her mum.

"Right. I'll call you, okay? Look after Gertie for me." Sydney passed the key to her. "Tell her I'll be back for her soon."

"Good luck."

Sydney hot-footed it out of the cinema. She needed to get to Beatrice as fast as she could, and even with Gertie sporting her new engine, she wasn't going to be fast enough for her.

As she hit the chilly air of the Scottish winter, her

phone lit up. It was a text message from Alison that read *BA1710*. She must have seen the interview, too, and guessed who Beatrice was talking about. A check of the flight number gave Sydney an arrival time of 7:45 p.m. If the next flight to Heathrow from Edinburgh had available seats, she'd arrive in time to surprise Beatrice at the airport.

Another text message flashed up on her phone, this time from James.

Please tell me she wasn't talking about you! he messaged.

Okay. She wasn't talking about me.

She so was, though, wasn't she?

Yes! Sydney replied even as she ran across town to grab some belongings from her mum's house. *I'm heading to Edinburgh airport.*

What have I told you about mixing business with pleasure?

Take every opportunity??

Very good!

Those two words, even from her good friend, sent a thrill up Sydney's spine.

She replayed the video repeatedly once safely in the back of the taxi and heading for the airport. She was beginning to wonder what the hell she was doing jumping on a plane to London and needed the video for reassurance that she wasn't going mad.

Perhaps just one.

Had Beatrice meant one specific person or just not everyone? Had she read everything wrong? Inhaling a deep breath, Sydney stowed her phone in her pocket and sat on her hands to control her twitching mess of a body. There was only one way to know — find Beatrice.

CHAPTER 37

*B*eatrice fidgeted in her seat and checked her watch for the tenth time that hour. Was there a strong crosswind making the plane particularly slow across the Atlantic today? They were due to land in an hour, and it was going to be the longest hour of her life. She wanted her feet on the ground so she could begin her hunt for Sydney.

She woke her phone up for the first time during the flight; she couldn't ignore it forever. Alison had begun calling as soon as her eggs Benedict was placed in front of her, which, thanks to her 7:45 a.m. flight time to London, she'd eaten at JFK airport at 6:30 a.m. The talk show would have aired at 3:00 a.m. UK time, so Alison would have woken to find Beatrice all over the news.

There were ten missed calls from her leading up to the time of her flight; she'd ignored them all. She needed time to get used to being an out actress before she faced the world. Strangely it didn't feel any different. Was it supposed to? In the end, all it took was one simple

325

correction, *he* to *she*, and it was done. A weight lifted. Yet another in an extensive line of shackles she'd needed to cut away.

A quick check of WhatsApp revealed Alison immediately started messaging once the flight took off. It was the only way they could communicate whilst Beatrice was in the air.

Why didn't you tell me, Bea? I would have supported you.

That one hit hard. It was going to be the hardest one to answer.

I'm guessing you didn't trust me.

That one made her eyes water.

You not trusting me is on me. I'm sorry.

That one made her reach for a tissue.

Alison blaming herself was not what Beatrice had expected. When you keep a secret like that about yourself, there's the time before you reveal it and the time after. The time between them amounts to a fraction of a second, and you can't take it back. All views of you change from that point, and not one view will ever be the same as another.

When and how you decide that point is never easy. What difference did her finding women and men attractive make to anyone else anyway? Alison would have told her to keep it hidden, so what was the point in her knowing? Apart from that fraction of a second when it finally happened and those closest to you examined the time before, the time when they didn't know; when they asked, *Why didn't I know? Was I not worthy to know that about you?*; apart from that, it was really nothing to do with them — any of them — and everything to do with you.

I understand you might not want to talk about it, Alison

had messaged next, *but for what it's worth the phone hasn't stopped ringing. Everyone wants you.*

There it was, the blur between the personal and the professional. Alison was upset she wasn't told as her friend, yet in another breath, she was back on the professional level. This was what Beatrice had been trying to avoid — a conflict of interest.

She smiled as she reread the words *Everyone wants you.* That made two unexpected reactions: Alison blaming herself and everyone wanting her.

Hadn't Alex said as much? We can't live our lives worried about what others think, especially when they might not even think that way. He'd grown up so much over the summer, matured, even become wise. There was so much to thank Sydney for — if she ever saw her again. Her stomach wrenched at the alternative.

Beatrice reached for the flight information card to fan herself, taking short breaths to steady her tingling nerves. Had Sydney seen or heard what was happening — that Beatrice Russell had come out on television? She would have been in bed when it aired, like Alison. Assuming she was in the UK. Another wash of panic tried to take over her. With a deep breath and self-reassurance that Sydney would be in the UK, it subsided. The beta blockers were taking the edge off.

A brief glance at social media over breakfast at the hotel was enough to tell her it was all people were talking about today. The LGBTQ+ community were particularly pleased with her. That gave Beatrice a warm glow of accomplishment. The hashtag #OutAndProud was trending, with four other celebrities following her lead. It was hardly a substantial number, but it was a start.

It was unlikely that Sydney was checking social media for signs of her ex-employer coming to her senses. There hadn't been a message from her. What would it even say? *Congrats on finally coming out, thanks for ruining my life anyway?*

Two weeks had passed since she'd given the note to Alison to post with her book. She may not have posted it yet. Beatrice hadn't sent it in the hope of hearing something back from Sydney, though an acknowledgement would have been nice.

She gulped at the thought that she may have just made the biggest mistake of her life. Yes, there were cheers now, but what about later? She'd done it with Sydney in mind. What if Sydney had moved on? What if she'd realised that she made a mistake and no longer held an interest in a washed-up, wrinkling actress who was fifteen years her senior?

God, it's going to be a long, lonely, depressing Christmas.

The flight landed five minutes behind schedule, enough time for Beatrice to feel vindicated in her assumptions about the crosswinds. In need of some fresh air, she made her way through the VIP lounge to the security desk, where they confirmed her bags were being unloaded from the plane and her vehicle would be with her shortly.

The biting winter air hit her as the automatic door opened. Tightening her scarf around her neck, she dropped her sunglasses to her nose and ventured outside.

She detested wearing sunglasses in winter, much less at night, but needs must.

A snapping sound came from behind her as she stepped onto the pavement. It sounded like clicking fingers.

Her face dropped as quickly as her head turned and her stomach jumped into her throat.

"Sydney."

Beatrice removed her sunglasses as they strode towards each other. She needed to see her properly, without the dark filter — to check she was real. Finding Sydney to be very real indeed, she finally allowed a slow smile to creep onto her lips, and the words "You're here" to slip from her mouth.

They stopped a meter apart. Their bodies could only take them so far; there was still a chasm between them that their words would need to fill before they could cross further.

"Of course I'm here," Sydney said. "Where else would I be other than hanging around outside the Heathrow VIP arrival lounge? In the very spot you left me."

"Anywhere, knowing you. How did you know what flight I'd be on?"

"Alison sent me your flight number; I can't imagine why." Sydney smirked. "I assume it was she who sent me your book."

"Our book," Beatrice corrected.

Sydney gave a light nod to accompany the smile that formed on her lips. "It feels a little out of date already."

"There's always part two," Beatrice proffered.

"In which we tell the world about Peter?"

"Tempting. Unfortunately, he put a clause in the divorce agreement."

Sydney's shoulders slumped. "Of course he did."

They fell into silence, unable to take their eyes off each other.

"I heard you were unwell," Sydney said. "I hope it's nothing serious."

"I thought you didn't follow the media."

Sydney's lips contorted. "I didn't. There was no one worthwhile following until recently."

"It is serious." Beatrice couldn't hold herself back anymore. She took a step toward her. "The doctor insinuated I was lovesick, and there's only one cure for my lovesickness — you. You seem to have penetrated my walls and brought me to my knees, Sydney." She pushed aside a mental image of Sydney on her knees to focus on what she needed to say. "Walking away from you was the hardest thing I've ever done."

"And now you've come back to claim your lost baggage."

Beatrice pouted at her suggestion. "Sydney, be serious for a change. I knew I wasn't ready."

"I would have waited if you'd have asked," Sydney replied with a shrug.

"I didn't know if I would ever be ready. Now I can't wait to show you off to the world if you'll let me. Assuming that's why you're here, of course. You haven't come from…?"

"Scotland," Sydney confirmed.

"…Scotland, to thank me for the book."

"I did actually."

"Oh." Beatrice's gaze lowered.

Of course it was too good to be true; too much to hope for.

"I wanted to give my thanks in person. It's the only way I could convey my appreciation the way I need to."

"Oh?" Beatrice replied, her tone a little more upbeat and hopeful than before.

Did this mean…?

Her gaze returned to meet Sydney's, just as she took a step towards her, leaning forward until there was only a millimetre between them. Sydney's parted lips lingered a moment in front of her own, as her eyes bored into Beatrice's with a longing. Beatrice gasped in a breath, her heart hammering with anticipation, urging Sydney's lips to meet her own. Unable to wait any longer, she pressed hers to Sydney's and instantly received a warm, welcoming response as the woman's arms swallowed her up, pulling her closer to her as she kissed her more deeply.

Remembering they were in a public space, Beatrice pulled back slowly to take Sydney's hand instead. She wasn't quite ready for an audience.

"I thought your brand couldn't withstand a coming out?" Sydney teased, running her tongue over her lips.

"I realised I didn't care anymore. I deserved something for me. Yes, I have a big house and fancy cars. They're only things. I'd miss them if I didn't have them, but I can live without them. What I lose to have those things is myself, and I can't live anymore without living as me. I feel so much better for it — for now anyway."

"You wrote your own narrative. The truth set you free. That always feels good."

"And I'm looking outwards from now on, not inwards, and I see you, Sydney MacKenzie, right in my eye line, where you've always been!"

Sydney lifted Beatrice's hand to her lips and kissed it before turning her attention to her fingers.

"If you ever click these at me again," she teased, "I'm going to break them."

"Oh no. I have a better use for them now, Sydney, and they are no use to you broken, trust me on that."

Sydney's eyes glimmered as her lips widened. "I do."

"If my career falters, I have enough money to live comfortably for the rest of my life. What do I need with more money when I have no one to share it with? Anyway, Ali says the phone hasn't stopped ringing; everyone in Hollywood wants me."

"They can get in line. You're mine now," Sydney smirked, squeezing Beatrice's hand. "Alison introduced me to an agent."

"She didn't tell me."

"I asked her not to. I thought we were having a clean break." Sydney narrowed her eyes. "Though apparently not clean enough to stop you from sending her a copy of my book."

"Shall we move inside?" Beatrice suggested to change the subject. "It's chillier here than in New York."

Leading the way into the entrance of the VIP lounge, they found a sofa just inside the automatic door which negated the need to go back through security. Beatrice found herself still under Sydney's scrutinising glare as they sat. She turned away from it as she answered the question there was no getting away from.

"I didn't think you'd mind if I sent it to Ali, and it's not as though I could ask you. Anyway, it deserves to be read," Beatrice replied. She wasn't going to apologise for it. A change of subject was the best solution in situations like this. "I find myself in need of a PA yet again. You don't know a good one, do you? I had this rather lovely one, but when I broke her heart she ran home to Scotland. That's what she does when she's been hurt."

She allowed her gaze to fall back to Sydney's eyes, which had softened.

"Now I'm here beside you," Sydney said, clasping their hands together. "*You* are my home, Beatrice, and I don't intend on letting you out of my sight again. If you're amenable to that, of course."

"I don't think there is anything I've been more amenable to. I can't promise we'll stay in the same place for long. We could be living in hotels, abroad for months at a time, or in a caravan in Wales, but I'd take a rabbit hutch, a chicken coop… even a horse box, as long as you're in it," Beatrice replied with a wink.

"Sounds perfect," Sydney said, kissing the back of Beatrice's hand.

"Speaking of which… where is the rabbit hutch?"

Sydney scowled. "If it wasn't for that rabbit hutch, we would never have met. I flew down. I wanted to be here to greet you. Gertie may have perked up, just not enough to beat a plane. If we're doing this, whatever this is, then I'm paying you back for Gertie's repair."

Beatrice opened her mouth to object, but Sydney beat her to it.

"No, no!" she said kindly. "When it was a bonus from

employer to employee, I could take it. If we're going to be something more, that changes things. I'm a famous writer now thanks to *our* book, and I can afford to pay you back. I can't believe how much they paid for your book advance. My percentage alone blew my mind."

"I don't mean this to sound like a brag, Sydney, but I'm not just anyone," Beatrice said. "That's the going rate for someone like me, and I will of course accept your payment if those are the terms of a relationship."

"You know people will think I didn't co-author your autobiography and that you put my name on it to help give me a leg up."

"Sydney, if I've learnt anything, and I have, it seems from my own child, it's that we can't live our lives worried about what others think."

"Wise words."

"People who want to hate will hate. It doesn't matter what you do. You and I, and those important to us, know your achievement. It was actually Alex who made me realise I couldn't hide anymore; that it wasn't worth hiding at the cost of being without you. He seems quite keen on the idea of us being together."

"I had an inkling he knew about it. Maybe neither of us was as subtle as we'd hoped we'd been."

"He saw us... that night. Only briefly, when we... you know..." Beatrice stuttered, then held her breath as Sydney leaned closer to her, placing her lips beside Beatrice's ear.

"Oh, I remember. It's all I've thought about for three months."

Beatrice gasped in a breath at her confession. Her heart

was racing, yet her lungs were free, if only she could remember how to use them. Was she cured already, or were the beta blockers still in effect?

"He also overheard you and Peter talking," she said when she regained her breath. "He knows everything." Her lips twitched into a smile as she spoke. Despite withholding the truth about his father, she was relieved Alex knew.

Sydney nodded and leaned back against the sofa. "He told me when he left."

Of course he did; the two of them were as thick as thieves. She could see they were going to outnumber her in the future.

"I hear there may be an invitation to an awards ceremony in the States?" Sydney said.

Beatrice arched a brow. "You want to be my plus one? Are you ready for the heat?"

"More than ready," Sydney answered with a firm nod.

One side of Beatrice's mouth curled up in delight as Sydney squeezed her hand. "Me too."

"I adore the heat. In fact, I recall a sizzling summer in which I wore a bikini a little more often than I should have."

"Oh." Beatrice's lips stretched wider. "I remember, Sydney. That's all *I've* thought about for the past three months."

A black Mercedes Sprinter with the airport's logo emblazoned on the side pulled up outside, catching Beatrice's attention. A middle-aged man in a chauffeurs suit and hat popped his head into the reception area a minute later.

"When you're ready, Miss Russell."

"Thank you," she called after him as he returned to the vehicle. Beatrice stood and slid her handbag on to her shoulder. She looked down at the younger woman. "I assume you'd like a ride, Sydney?"

"As long as the ride goes directly to your bedroom."

"Oh," Beatrice chortled. "Smooth, Sydney; smooth."

Sydney flicked an eyebrow up as she stood. "I thought so."

"Do you not have any more luggage than that rucksack?"

Sydney shrugged. "I kinda left in a hurry."

"I'm sure I have a bikini you can borrow."

"In this weather! My nipples will fall off."

"I'll find something warm to cover them with, don't you worry," Beatrice replied, moistening her lips with the tip of her tongue.

Sydney let out a soft whimper and followed Beatrice to the Mercedes.

"Is Jonathon not with you?"

"He flew his family out to the States for Christmas. I couldn't deny him a holiday; he'd earned it with all the PR events I've been to since the summer."

Beatrice headed down to the rear bench seat rather than taking an individual seat. It was this type of airport vehicle that had spurred her on to buy her own Mercedes Sprinter. They were practical and luxurious.

Sydney sat beside her as she had hoped.

"I must thank you for looking out for Alex when I was too focussed on myself," Beatrice said as they pulled away from the airport terminal. "You sensed he needed help when I didn't."

"We can't all give help to those we love. Even if we want to, sometimes we don't know how. I've been there with Sam. I recognised it, and I did better next time I saw someone in need of help."

Beatrice nodded. It was good of Sydney to let her off so lightly. If she hadn't been so inept at motherhood, Sydney wouldn't have been put in the position where she'd needed to help Alex.

"Is Alex still 'he' or…?"

"For now. He said I'd be the first to know if or when that changes. So get in line."

Sydney smirked. "I'm happy to. Where is he?"

"Staying with Anthony in New York. His dad's place doesn't hold the same appeal it once did."

"Good. I don't want Alex around that kind of toxicity."

Beatrice gazed at Sydney in wonder. She hadn't appreciated how much she cared for him.

"I mean… you don't?"

"It's okay," Beatrice reassured her, placing her hand over Sydney's and leaving it there. "I love that you care for my child."

Sydney's blushing smile told her the message was received.

"He'll be back for New Year," Beatrice continued, stifling a yawn with her free hand. "It gives me time to sleep off this jet lag and—"

"I don't think you'll be doing much sleeping for the next few days," Sydney interrupted.

"— and gives us," Beatrice firmly regained control of

her sentence, "enough time to head to Scotland and be back for a cosy Christmas, just the three of us."

"Three of us? Scotland?"

"You left something behind, didn't you? A chunk of metal."

"I knew you loved Gertie!" Sydney crowed.

"What? That wheelie bin of yours?" Beatrice laughed.

Sydney tucked a leg under her and turned to face Beatrice. "Shut your mouth, or I'll shut it for you."

"I do wish you would."

"Are we okay to…?" Sydney nodded to the front of the car even as the dividing screen went up.

"These drivers wouldn't have a job if they weren't discreet."

"Why didn't you commission one of these to bring you home from Biggin Hill instead of ordering me to collect you?"

"I wanted to see if you could follow some basic instructions," Beatrice answered archly.

"Oh, so you admit it was a test?"

"Mm-hmm. You were late, if I recall."

"No. You were early," Sydney replied firmly.

"Be that as it may, I'm wondering if you're still able to follow basic instructions."

Sydney flashed her a questioning look.

"I'm waiting for you to shut my mouth, Sydney. Eagerly waiting."

"Oh. Of course, how remiss of me. Let me fix my mistake."

Beatrice's lips tingled with anticipation.

CHAPTER 38

*a*s they made their way up the long driveway to Highwood House in the darkness, Sydney could sense their exact position from the bumps and turns in the road. Had it become so familiar over the weeks she'd spent there? She'd driven along it enough times.

Beatrice was tucked tightly beside her, her head resting against Sydney's shoulder and her mouth open. In the dim interior light, she could see a small dribble patch had soaked into her top and she knew then that she only felt love for the woman. It was too early to say it aloud; she didn't want to scare her away when she'd only just fallen into her arms.

The gearbox dropped a gear, indicating they were reaching the top of the hill. It was time to wake Beatrice. Leaning down she kissed the top of her head, taking in a lungful of her scent as she did.

Beatrice stirred. "Where are we?"

"Highwood... home."

"Did we?"

"You fell asleep."

"Oh, I'm sorry."

"It's fine. I'm not sure I wanted our first time to be in the back of a rental anyway."

"Good point. Do you mind if we save ourselves a little longer? I'm exhausted, and as much as I want to devour you, I think I'll fall asleep again. I want to be fully conscious when I finally get my hands on you."

She'd waited for months; one night longer was fine to wait to be devoured by Beatrice Russell.

"I'm more than up for a cuddle if you are," she offered.

"I'm going to fall into the shower first," Beatrice answered through a yawn.

Feeling a little hot at the thought, Sydney refrained from putting her coat on as she stepped out into the freezing Highwood air.

"Can I tempt you with a back scrub? Like old times?"

"You can do one better and join me."

"I won't turn down an offer like that," Sydney smirked, thinking all her Christmases had come at once.

Sydney took the key and let the chauffeur into the house so he could begin unloading all the cases. Beatrice followed slowly behind, her feet dragging on the gravel. She really did look exhausted, yet still incredibly hot. Knowing she could be the one to tuck her up in bed shortly was sending celebratory streamers to every extremity of Sydney's mind.

The entrance hall was exquisitely decorated for Christmas. A tree stood beside the staircase, drowning under the weight of haphazardly placed decorations which altogether created a remarkably stylish arrangement. Sometimes even imperfection created perfection at the right distance. The tip extended beyond the first landing, where it strained to hold a gold star. The illusive Mrs Clarkson must have been in. Sydney was looking forward to finally meeting her.

Analysing the cases in the entrance hall, Beatrice picked one up and then said, "Would you mind bringing the rest?" She closed her eyes the second she'd finished her sentence. "I'm sorry, Sydney. I'm already giving you orders. This is going to take some getting used to."

"It's fine, go up. I'll sort these. I'm not the one that's flown halfway around the world over the last few days or experienced an emotional breakthrough."

Beatrice squinted at her and then made her way up the stairs. "Don't forget to join me, will you?"

"I won't." There was no fear of that happening. It wasn't every day you received an invitation to join Beatrice Russell in the shower... naked, alone, with soap.

Sydney blew out a breath. At this rate, she was going to come before she made it as far as the shower.

The shower was running by the time she brought up the last of the cases and her own small rucksack. She'd packed enough clean underwear for a few days but would need to return to Scotland to collect the rest of her belongings — and Gertie. Planning hadn't been at the forefront of her mind when she left.

If there was an award for quickest removal of clothes, she would have won it. Standing naked in Beatrice's bedroom was strange yet arousing, not that Sydney needed any more encouragement in that department. It was clear that all Beatrice wanted to do this evening was cuddle.

Condensation covered the glass of the enormous shower; a Beatrice-shaped shadow moved behind it. The underfloor heating warmed Sydney's feet, but it didn't take the anxious chill off her body. She'd never been so nervous entering a bathroom. Every hair was standing on end.

It's now or never.

Shuffling her feet she made it to the screen and forced herself around it. Beatrice's bare butt enticed her further; she wanted to reach out and touch it, but she refrained. The invitation was for washing Beatrice's back only.

Finally finding her voice, she called out, "Hey,"

"Hey yourself." Beatrice reached back with a soapy sponge. "Would you?"

It took her a moment to respond. Her head was rushing with blood, her senses overwhelmed.

"Sydney," Beatrice chided pleasantly, "don't keep me waiting."

"Sorry."

She stepped forward and retrieved it, her hand brushing Beatrice's butt as she did, sending ripples of excitement through every cell of her body. This was going to be one of the hardest tasks she'd ever performed.

Wash back, don't touch. How hard can it be?

She brushed the soapy sponge over Beatrice's shoulders, being careful not to go beyond the invisible line she'd drawn across Beatrice's lower back. She tried not to even look down there with all that white foam running over it.

Be professional, you can do this.

They'd gone beyond the professional now, though. They were both naked in the shower. The mask she'd used to control herself around Beatrice when they were working together hadn't simply slipped; it was being washed down the drain at that very moment.

Rubbing the sponge over every inch of Beatrice's back — several times for good measure — she reached up to wipe away the soap with her hand and then placed a kiss on her shoulder. That was harmless, right? A simple display of affection, no funny business.

Beatrice groaned as she arched into the touch.

"Sorry," Sydney said. "I couldn't resist."

"It was a good groan."

"Ah, perhaps not so tired after all?" she suggested.

"Perhaps not…"

Taking this as the invitation she required, she stepped closer, pressing firmer kisses over Beatrice's shoulders. Beatrice pulled her wet hair to one side. Sydney eyed her bare neck and moved her hungry lips towards it, causing Beatrice's body to shiver and her head to drop to one side.

Dropping the sponge to the floor, Sydney grasped Beatrice's hips. Her hands knew exactly where they wanted to be and twitched nervously with anticipation.

Beatrice let out a whisper of encouragement. "Touch me, Sydney. Like you did that night; like you wanted to."

With that request, the throbbing between her legs took control of her body. Her hands reached for Beatrice's breasts, cupping and caressing them, causing her to writhe with pleasure. As Beatrice's nipples slipped between Sydney's fingers, she gave them a little squeeze. Beatrice let out a stifled whimper of delight and cupped her hands over Sydney's, encouraging her to squeeze harder than she'd dared to.

The woman was intoxicating.

Placing a palm against the tiles, Beatrice pushed her butt back into Sydney's pelvis, making them both moan.

Leaving one hand to stroke Beatrice's breast, Sydney let the other snake down her belly until it reached a soft mound of hair. She let her fingers play there for a moment, wanting to keep Beatrice waiting a little longer.

Too impatient to linger, she trailed them further down, taking a deep breath to control her galloping heart as her fingers found what they'd been waiting too long for. Warm water trickled over them as they mingled with the wetness of Beatrice, exploring every part of her they could reach. She felt incredible as she finally slid two fingers inside her. Soft, warm, and wet — so very wet.

Beatrice let out a sensual moan as her head fell back onto Sydney's shoulder. Her exposed neck begged her to devour it. She was more than happy to oblige and readily kissed every inch of it as her lover continued to writhe under her touch.

She could sense Beatrice was close; she didn't want to miss a second of it. "Turn around," Sydney demanded. "I want to see your face."

Beatrice obeyed, her hand instantly reaching for Sydney's breast, squeezing it. Her other hand made its way to exactly where Sydney needed it to be.

Their fingers worked in rhythm, the palms of their hands rubbing just the right spot.

"Oh, Bea," Sydney groaned into Beatrice's mouth as

they kissed passionately, never taking their eyes off each other.

"Sydney," Beatrice cried.

Her kiss slowed against Sydney's mouth until her lips came to a stop and a soft, contented moan escaped them. Sydney held her until her panting slowed and Beatrice's fingers re-found their rhythm inside her.

Sydney knew she didn't have long. Even though she was doing everything she could to hold back the inevitable, trying to keep the moment alive forever as she stared into the unwavering, sultry eyes of Beatrice. She could feel the tip of Beatrice's eager tongue licking her parted lips, throwing petrol on the fire burning inside her. She couldn't remember a time when her body was so impassioned. With Beatrice inside her — the thought alone of her being there — she tumbled over the edge into a twitching mess.

Beatrice wrapped an arm around her, holding their warm, wet bodies together as Sydney's quivering slowed and she let out a light whimper of satisfaction. Beatrice silenced her with a kiss.

They washed off under the warm spray, their hands wandering occasionally to explore each other's bodies. They shared a soft, tender kiss that could have easily led to round two were they both not spent.

It was everything Sydney had dreamed of — quite literally.

Beatrice joined her in the bedroom, drying herself on her towel and making no effort to cover any part of her. Sydney watched from the side of the bed where she sat in only a pair of knickers. She bit her lips in to contain her grin; this was a sight she could get used to.

"Are you hungry?" Beatrice asked, returning her towel to the bathroom.

"Is that an invitation? You're insatiable, woman."

Her smirking face appeared around the bathroom door. "No! There should have been a food delivery this morning. Go and hunt something out for us if you like."

Sydney grabbed a gown from the back of the door, inhaling the scent of the washing powder that always made her think of Beatrice. Treading the familiar path down the wooden staircase, passing the spot where she would forever see Beatrice posing in her red dress, she made her way through to the kitchen. The first thing she wanted to do, despite the freezing temperature outside, was open the patio door.

She inhaled the Highwood air with its light pine scent coming off the wood at the top of the hill. It was good to be back home, if this was to be home. They still needed to have that conversation.

Beatrice was on the sofa when she returned with a tray of snacks, the highlight being the cream cheese on crackers with a sprinkle of dill. Confirmed to be Beatrice's favourite as she reached for one before Sydney placed the tray on the table.

"Should we sort out a few domestic logistics before we get too settled?" Sydney asked tentatively.

"We should," Beatrice said, crossing her legs.

Her slip rode up high enough that Sydney could see she wasn't wearing any underwear. It took every ounce of restraint not to dive back in.

"I don't like to assume I'm moving in already."

"Why? I want you to. Three months without you almost killed me, Sydney, quite literally when I had a panic attack in the air."

"Oh, shit. Really?" Sydney asked, placing a glass of water in front of Beatrice. "You missed me that much?"

Although she pitied Beatrice for having experienced that, she couldn't help taking it as a massive compliment.

"It appears so. If you want a room of your own, you could take the room next to mine," Beatrice replied. "I don't know why you didn't take it before."

"If I remember rightly, you suggested I took one on the top floor... in the servants' quarters," Sydney snarked.

"I don't recall that," Beatrice replied as she stuffed the rest of a cracker into her grinning mouth.

"Convenient. Anyway, I liked being above you. You were close by when you couldn't be close by. And when you were irritating me, it was easy to imagine reaching through the floor and suffocating you with a pillow."

Beatrice laughed. "Was I really that bad?"

"You were all good. Beneath that exterior, this is who you were. You just took a little warming up to melt away all that ice."

"Well, I thank you for warming me up. Don't ever stop, will you, Sydney?"

Sydney slipped herself next to Beatrice and stroked her leg, letting her fingers trail up and then under her slip.

"To keep you warm, I'll need to be close by. Really close by. At all times."

"I'll clear you some space in the dressing room then," Beatrice replied with a twinkle in her eye.

Sydney woke the next morning thinking she was in one of those dreams again. It couldn't be reality, could it? Beatrice was lying beside her, partially clad, with one breast hanging out of her slip. This time they were both under the duvet.

She smiled as her thoughts drifted back to their shower, when she had finally connected with Beatrice in the way she'd desired for so long. It was tempting to poke her to check that she was real. A light touch on that soft, warm breast that was calling to her would do no harm.

"Sydney," Beatrice murmured. "Are you groping my boob whilst I'm sleeping?"

"No," Sydney was quick to deny. "I was simply checking you were real."

"I was the last time I checked. What time is it?"

"Ten."

"Why would you think I wasn't real?" Beatrice asked, shuffling herself closer.

"I had a dream. That night when I sat here and massaged your leg."

"Oh, I remember that massage. I didn't want you to stop."

"I didn't want to stop either."

Their eyes simmered at each other.

"In my dream, you were in the dressing room, in a stunning red dress."

"Aren't all red dresses stunning?" Beatrice asked.

"Yes, but this one was particularly stunning, as were

you when I unzipped it and you were wearing nothing underneath."

"Go on."

"I noticed you didn't have a cast on, and then I woke up before I'd even managed to taste you."

"Then what did you do?" Beatrice asked, attractive creases forming around her mouth.

"Erm." Sydney's cheeks flushed as she lost eye contact with Beatrice.

"You didn't! Over your employer? Oh, Sydney. I'm sure that would have been grounds for dismissal."

"And what about every time I ogled this butt?" Sydney asked, reaching around for a handful, pulling Beatrice that little bit closer.

"Well, that's different. I was ogling too."

Sydney smirked and shuffled herself forward, placing a kiss on Beatrice's cheekbones. "That… I've been dying to do that since we met."

"Really?" Beatrice's eyebrows lifted. "The day we met."

"Well, no," Sydney admitted. "I wanted to slap them then and for a short time after."

"It's good to know your self-restraint kicks in with slapping, but not pleasuring yourself whilst thinking about an employer."

Beatrice yawned and stretched.

Sydney ran her fingers along the inside of her outstretched arm, over her armpit and around her breast. "Should I fetch us some coffee?"

"Fuck the coffee. Fuck me instead."

"I thought you'd never ask."

349

"I'm not asking. It's an order, Sydney."

Sydney climbed on top of her, straddling her. Leaning over, she placed another kiss on each of her cheekbones, sliding her fingers over the creases that surfaced at the sides of Beatrice's mouth as she smiled.

"You know how I love to follow your orders," she said. "I'm never going to stop fucking you."

"Very good."

Sydney quivered, not only at her words but at the fact Beatrice chose her over her morning coffee. She was going to thank her for it — very, very slowly.

CHAPTER 39

Sydney slid the key card into the door of the £7000 per night suite in the Balmoral Hotel. Beatrice's luggage was already waiting for them in the hallway. All four brand-new Gucci suitcases were lined up next to each other. Dropping her old, shabby North Face rucksack beside them, she smiled at the metaphor for their relationship. In this instance Beatrice really was Gucci. She'd been announced as ambassador for the brand earlier that week.

Beatrice swept past her, dropping her gloves onto the hall table as she passed.

"Wow, this is something," Sydney said, following Beatrice through a spacious bedroom and into the sitting room beyond.

Beatrice didn't give it a second look. Like a moth to a light, she headed for the roaring fire in the hearth. "Get used to it."

"More than happy to. Did you need a nap before we go out?"

"Sydney, I'm fifty-one, not two, and I don't need a nap after the shortest flight I've ever taken."

"We'll go straight out then?"

Beatrice swivelled on her heel to frown at Sydney. "Can't we at least order coffee and sit down first?"

Sydney smirked as she tapped the iPad on the desk, putting their room service order through. "Would you like some pastries?"

"I won't say no," Beatrice replied, collapsing onto a sofa. "Are those today's newspapers? Can you pass them please?"

"Which one?"

"All of them."

Sydney placed them on the table in front of Beatrice and watched as she rifled through them.

"Looking for something?"

"Yes, this. Though I can't believe it's only worthy of page three." Beatrice folded the newspaper back and passed it to Sydney before turning her attention to the other newspapers. "This one has a snippet on page one."

Sydney's mouth opened as she saw Peter's face staring back at her next to the words 'Sex Pest'.

"Shit, Bea. How did the press pick up on this? Did you have something to do with it? You said you have a clause."

"I do."

"So, how?"

Beatrice shrugged. "We'll never know, will we?"

Sydney's hands went straight to her hips. "Beatrice."

"Okay. Alex came to my dressing room after the show to congratulate me and to press the point I'd made about standing up and being counted. He didn't think it was right that his father was getting away with what he did, and to be honest, although I initially agreed to the amendment, it's been eating away at me. With Alex to think of, I respected it. It's not a great look to have a sex pest for a dad."

"That kid of yours is really something."

"He is, and with his permission I had someone give an anonymous tip to the press, just enough to make them start sniffing around. You know what they're like once they get a whiff of a sex scandal. Whatever they did worked as some of the women have agreed to talk to the police."

"If he traces it back to you, though?"

"The clause only extends as far as me, and technically it wasn't me that tipped them off. Even if he was to link it back to me, is the truth not worth speaking? The worst he can do is sue me for breach of contract, and with any luck, those women will take him for every penny he took from me. It will be good to know it's going somewhere worthwhile and give those women some recompense."

Sydney took a seat beside Beatrice and let out a puff of air.

"Are you okay?" Beatrice asked, placing a hand on her leg.

"Yeah, it's a lot to take in. But I'm proud of you."

"The truth needed telling — it always needs telling."

Sydney placed her hand over Beatrice's. "Yeah, it does."

"I've come under pressure to reveal the names of those who acted inappropriately toward me when I was younger."

"Will you?"

Beatrice nodded. "Once the heat has died down around Peter, I will."

With coffee and pastries served and consumed, Sydney rang down to reception to summon the car they had ordered to take them to her mum's house.

"We have a few minutes to freshen up. Then it's time for you to meet Mum."

As Sydney emerged from the bathroom, she met Beatrice in the hallway, where she was zipping up a small holdall.

"We need to take this."

"What is it?" Sydney enquired. "You didn't buy a gift for her, did you? She'd hate the fuss."

Beatrice's face dropped. "No, I didn't. Should I have? Oh, I never thought. We can pick something up on the way."

Sydney put her hands on Beatrice's shoulders. "Didn't you hear me? I said she'd hate it if you did."

Beatrice nodded. "Okay."

"Are you all right? You're not nervous about meeting my mum, are you?"

"Of course I am."

"Why?"

"What if she doesn't approve?"

"We're a little past needing parental approval, Bea. You certainly are. Anyway, I told you Mum was fine with it, more than fine with it. She's elated. She knows you make me happy, and that's all she can ask of anyone."

Beatrice let out a breath. "Okay."

"Shall we go then?"

"Yes, could you bring the bag?"

Sydney strained as she lifted it. "Crikey. It's a dead weight. Are you going to tell me what's in it?"

"Just something I need to deal with."

Sydney rolled her eyes. She couldn't even recall there being a holdall amongst the luggage. Beatrice must have packed it inside one of her suitcases.

An hour later they drove into the small fishing town to an overture of seagulls. Sydney was beginning to feel a little nervous herself. What if her mum didn't like Beatrice? She was a very down-to-earth woman and might not appreciate the stiff nature of her daughter's girlfriend.

"Thank you," Beatrice said, tipping the driver. "We'll make our own way back."

"As you wish, ma'am."

Sydney wondered why no one ever called her 'ma'am'. Did you have to have a certain elegance about you to be called it? If so, she wouldn't hold her breath waiting.

"Be yourself," Sydney said, taking Beatrice's hand, straining with the heavy holdall in the other. "Scrap that. Try being a more relaxed version of yourself — if that's possible."

"Sydney," Beatrice growled.

Taking the hint to shut up, she knocked on the door. Although she had a key, it didn't feel appropriate to let herself in and catch her mum unawares. It wasn't every day you hosted an international film star in your tiny cottage.

Rhona opened the door in a flash, pulling Sydney into her. "Good to see you, love."

"Hi, Mum. This is Beatrice."

Beatrice offered her hand. Rhona ignored it and instead pulled her into a hug as well. Sydney stifled a laugh as Beatrice blinked. She should have warned her that her mum was a hugger.

"Mrs MacKenzie."

"Oh, we'll have none of that! It's Rhona. Come on in, both of you."

They stood like compacted sardines in the small hallway as they tried to remove their coats. Sydney was relieved to see her mum had tidied and cleaned before their arrival. The hallway smelled fresh; she hoped the rest of the house was the same.

"Should we go for a walk?" Beatrice suggested. "I could use the exercise after the flight and drive here."

"Okay." Sydney replied, sensing she was uncomfortable with the lack of space. There were cupboards at Highwood House that were bigger than the hallway, and bathrooms bigger than the entire cottage.

"I'd like to see the harbour. Bring the bag, Sydney." Beatrice backed herself out the way she'd come and waited on the pavement.

"Is she always like this?" Rhona asked once Beatrice was out of earshot.

Sydney grinned. "Not always. Just most of the time."

On reflection, Beatrice had been a bit off since they'd arrived that morning. Was it a case of nerves over meeting her mum? The previous night she'd been all smiles and giggles after they'd made love for the second time. Sydney preferred the softer, loving, relaxed version of her girlfriend, though she could more than cope with the bossy one too. Bossy Beatrice was a turn-on.

They joined Beatrice outside and walked down the hill to the harbour. The air was clear, allowing them to see for miles out to sea. Your eyes were best fixed on that as the small town itself wasn't much to look at. It's drab architecture and empty streets made it feel like something from dystopian film. When met with a backdrop of grey skies and rain it was frankly depressing. The cheap Christmas lights certainly didn't add anything to the view, especially when they were turned off.

On her last visit, Sydney had calculated that the whole town would easily fit within the boundaries of Beatrice's estate. It was best to keep that to herself; she didn't want to overwhelm her mum with exactly how rich her girlfriend was. It was difficult enough trying to convince her to take a sizeable portion of the payment she'd been given for her contribution to Beatrice's book.

The new contract for her role as co-author said 25 percent of royalties. It wasn't until a six-figure sum arrived in her bank account that she realised it meant 25 percent of the disgustingly large advance Beatrice had received. She'd phoned Alison immediately to raise what she thought must have been a grave error. It wasn't.

It turned out to be a worthwhile conversation to have. Alison asked what her plans were for the future. At the time, with Beatrice on the other side of the world, they had included drowning herself in a vat of wine and consuming a fraction more popcorn than the average human could take. Thankfully she managed to construct a sentence which included the words 'I want to write'.

Alison asked if she could send her book on to a few people and put the feelers out. Sydney was flabbergasted to hear that she even had a copy of her book. Four weeks later she received a text from Alison with a number to call. It happened to be the number of one of the top agents in one of the top agencies in London.

James sobbed, of course, when Sydney called to put in her notice with his agency. So much so he had to hang up and call her back. He blamed himself for pushing her into the clutches of Beatrice in the first place. She would miss her job, but she was going to enjoy being a full-time writer so much more.

As they reached the harbour, Sydney naturally guided them to the spot she'd stood in only a week before, a time when the world was somewhat bleak.

Beatrice lifted her sunglasses on top of her head, causing her blonde waves to bounce attractively around her face. "Open the bag please, Sydney."

She set it down and opened the zip to find two rectangular boxes. Opening one, she extracted a bag of light grey ash.

Sydney grimaced. "Oh… Bea."

"I don't want them in the house, and the harsh North Sea is the best place to dispose of them as far as I'm concerned. I, erm… I hoped you might do it for me. I can't give them the satisfaction of doing the act myself. I also wondered if scattering something may help you both." Beatrice flicked her hand dismissively. "You don't have to. Sorry… it's probably a thoughtless idea."

Rhona flattened her lips as she reached out and hugged her. The wide-eyed look on Beatrice's face told Sydney the reaction was far from what she'd expected.

Pulling back, Rhona wiped her nose with a fistful of

tissues she pulled from her coat pocket. "I read your autobiography, Beatrice, and I'm sorry for what your parents put you through. I can't even imagine what they were thinking to treat their own flesh and blood in that way." Rhona rested her hand on Beatrice's arm. "They didn't deserve you, and it's not a thoughtless idea. You need help and we're here for you. Aren't we love?"

Sydney nodded and looked to Beatrice, only to find her blurry. Blinking away the moisture in her eyes, she asked, "Are you sure?"

A firm nod was all she received. If Beatrice and her mum were happy, then she was too. It may bring some closure, if only symbolically, and she appreciated the intent behind Beatrice's request. She of all people knew what it meant to her to have her parents out of her life once and for all. If she couldn't bring herself to scatter them herself, they would haunt her to her dying day if someone else didn't do it for her.

Sydney passed the bag of ash to her mum, then wiped her eyes before taking the bag from the second box.

"Do you want to know who's who?" she asked.

"No. Don't care," Beatrice sniffed, taking a giant step back.

Sydney and Rhona opened the bags and leaned over the railings.

"Ready?" Sydney asked her mum.

Rhona nodded, and together they shook the ashes over the harbour. The wind swept them up and carried them out over the sea. Turning to check on Beatrice, Sydney noticed a glistening in her eye. It was more likely a tear shed for everything she'd lost because of her parents rather than from the actual loss of them.

Beatrice wiped it quickly with her glove and dropped her sunglasses back down.

"It's eye-wateringly chilly today," she said, by way of explanation.

"Are you sure you won't join us next week, Rhona?" Beatrice asked as she watched Sydney put the last bag into Gertie. "I can send a car or arrange a flight."

"No, I'm happy stopping here, thank you. You two lovebirds have a lovely first Christmas together. Now go and enjoy Edinburgh."

Beatrice instigated the hug with Rhona this time. "We will. It was lovely to meet you."

"And you. Look after my girl for me. She's all I have."

"You can rest assured I will."

"And thank you for making all her dreams come true with your book."

Beatrice smiled as she pulled away from Rhona. "She was more than up to the job and earned every success that will come from it too."

Turning to Sydney, Rhona opened her arms wide to receive her daughter.

"I know you don't want to move from here," Sydney said, giving her a squeeze, "but I'm still sending you the money I would have given you. No arguments."

"Thanks, love. You've always looked after me."

She wouldn't need to if she'd left the wheelhouse five

minutes earlier and insisted her dad come inside. She pushed the thought away. There was no changing the past, only living with it.

"I gave Gertie a clean inside for you and washed all the bedding. I didn't make the bed up; I didn't think you'd be needing it." Rhonda blushed a little.

"Thanks, Mum. I'm sure she appreciated her bath."

"Your uncle looked her over. Said Sam had done a superb job. I'm glad you two are back in touch. I always liked Sam."

"I know. I am too."

After a final hug, Sydney and Beatrice made their way back to Edinburgh, Beatrice's legs covered in a blanket. Sydney tried to reassure her that she would get used to Gertie's inadequate heating. Freezing her passenger's butts off in winter was just another part of her charm.

"I've missed you, old girl," she said as she clambered into the driver's seat.

Beatrice scoffed good-naturedly. "Sydney, you two have been apart a week. If you're planning on accompanying me on my travels as you make your millions as a successful writer, you are going to be apart longer than a week. Months at a time even."

"I know." She couldn't bear the thought of Gertie abandoned behind the garage at Highwood, rotting away, though it was more bearable than being away from Beatrice for more than five minutes. A pang of guilt hit her. Had she just chosen between Gertie and Beatrice?

Beatrice's hand rubbed her leg. "I'm sure Sam will babysit for you."

That brightened her mood; Sam would be up for that.

He'd already messaged to congratulate her on her fortuitous relationship and wish them both all the happiness this life could summon.

"The sea air will do her no good, though," she mused. "She might rust."

"Then we'll fix her."

Sydney nodded, forgetting that she was now considered wealthy. It was going to be odd not worrying about all the problems that she might once have had. They were now all fixable in an instant, with the tap of a card.

Back at the hotel, their private butler laid out afternoon tea in their sitting room.

"Would you take a photograph of us, please?" Sydney asked, passing her phone to him.

"Of course, ma'am."

Her initial excitement at being called 'ma'am' fell flat — it totally didn't suit her.

Beatrice sat beside her, and they posed in front of the extensive spread of goodies. The butler passed the phone back to her and made his exit.

Sydney flicked through the photographs he'd taken, finding one where they were both looking the right way with their eyes open. She hated to admit it, but they did make for a cute couple. It was still unbelievable to think of them as a *couple*.

"I thought we could send this photo to Alex," Sydney said, showing Beatrice the phone. "I assume you haven't told him yet."

"No. I was going to earlier, but I wasn't sure what to say."

"He'll be overjoyed. He told me he wanted me to stick around forever."

"Really?"

"Mm, he knew you were on to a good thing, even if you didn't."

"Oh, I knew all right," Beatrice sighed. "I just couldn't deal with it."

"Shall I message him?" Sydney asked, eager to be the one to tell him.

"If you like."

"How about, 'I banged your mum last night — twice'?"

Beatrice nearly choked on a mouthful of smoked salmon sandwich.

"No? Okay, how about I send the photo?"

"Good idea."

A message came straight back.

Does this mean?

Sure does.

K

Sydney stared at the phone, waiting for more. Had he mistyped?

"What does a K mean?" she asked, baffled.

"That means 'okay'. It's youth speak."

"That wasn't the level of enthusiasm I was hoping for."

Beatrice smiled knowingly. "Welcome to parenthood."

CHAPTER 40

"Who's up next?" the pre-ceremony presenter asked from the studio.

"Oh, it's the one we've all been waiting for! It's Beatrice Russell, and doesn't she look fabulous, wearing a strapless, red Gucci dress with a risqué split leg? She's recently become ambassador for the brand, so that comes as no surprise. And here comes her guest, is it... yes, they're holding hands! This must be her girlfriend, Sydney MacKenzie, who she publicly came out for. Also her former PA, I understand," he added with a little wink, "although her name is all over the autobiography Russell released before Christmas, so she was doing a little more than her job description, in more ways than one, it seems.

"They're coming along the red carpet now. Wow, the cameras are going wild for them. Sydney's looking elegant in a white suit. It looks like a Chanel to me. We're going to go live now to Hayley. What's happening down there?"

"Thanks, Tom... I'm here with Beatrice Russell and her girlfriend, Sydney MacKenzie. You're both looking gorgeous this evening, ladies. I adore your hair, Beatrice," Hayley said, gesturing toward her messy bun.

"Thank you," Beatrice replied, smiling so hard her cheekbones were on the fringes of popping out of her skin.

"You're in Gucci, I see. Hardly a surprise when you're brand ambassador. Congratulations."

"I've always been a huge supporter of the brand, so I'm deeply honoured," Beatrice replied, pressing her hand to her chest.

"You're up for Best Actress for a drama tonight. Your last nomination was for *Nancy*. Viewers will no doubt be wondering if the role of Nancy helped you discover your real identity."

"I've always known who I am. Nancy helped me come to terms with it, and this one here" — Beatrice kissed Sydney's cheek, taking the crowd by surprise and sending them into a frenzy of cheers — "has helped me become who I am. It only took fifty-one years."

"You seem to have made the hashtag #OutAndProud trend again. I believe we're up to fifteen celebrities that have come out using the hashtag so far."

"I have, and isn't it wonderful?" Beatrice said, using her sexiest husky voice and narrowing her eyes alluringly at the camera.

One of them was her previous co-star who had disguised his boyfriend as his PA. She'd even received a text a week ago heaping thanks upon her. The exact expression read, *If Beatrice Russell can show herself, then I bloody well can too!*

Hayley turned to her plus-one. "Sydney, how are you feeling about tonight?"

"Nervous, excited." She turned to look at Beatrice, her face melting in front of the world. "Proud."

Beatrice grinned and leaned in for another kiss. The red carpet lit up again with support.

"Well you make a lovely couple."

"Thank you," Beatrice replied, flashing the presenter another smile.

A steward led them further down the gauntlet for more photographs. Sydney was held back by a steward as Beatrice was ushered in front of the cameras by herself. Lights flashed as the crowd of photographers shouted her name, all hoping to get the money shot. She gave them their moment, resting her hand on her hip and ensuring she smiled in all directions before extending her hand to Sydney, impatient to have her back by her side. As Sydney reached her, she pulled her close and placed a kiss on her cheek.

Leading them inside, the steward directed them to another usher, who took them to their seats in the enormous ballroom. They joined three other couples; two were the film's director and producer and their 'wives'. When would she be able to say directors and their husbands more frequently, Beatrice wondered. The other couple were the film's costume designer and her husband.

Sydney leaned into her and whispered words of disappointment at not sharing a table with 'proper celebrities'. Beatrice was quietly relieved they weren't, after watching Sydney's legs wobble when Anne Hathaway passed them on the way to their table. She wouldn't have batted an eyelid at 99 percent of the celebrities in the enormous ballroom a few months ago.

Now that she was no longer working for the rich and famous, Sydney forwent all her rules of knowing who's who.

Since Christmas, she'd been consuming Beatrice's back catalogue of films and those of many other actresses she admired. Beatrice was forced to step in at one point and enforce a total ban on *The Devil Wears Prada* when she'd come down late one night to find Sydney watching it for the third time that week — that she knew of. An entire world had opened to her girlfriend, and she was embracing every part of it.

After a three hour wait it was time for Beatrice to find out if she was the winner of the award for Best Actress. A camera was directed at her and three other women in the room, all of whom she would be more than happy to lose to. Secretly, of course, she wanted this win. Although demand for her had never been so high since coming out, she needed this award to shore up her position on the world stage. Brief clips of their performances were played on the enormous screens on either side of the stage. Sydney grasped her hand under the table whilst they watched.

Beatrice had been practising her losing face in the mirror over the last week; perfecting it was vital. A lot of judgement came from whether you pulled it off or not. It was best to assume you'd lost before it was announced, all whilst trying to smile tentatively at the camera.

Time stood so still she hadn't realised they were at the point of calling out names until she heard, "Beatrice Russell," boom from the microphone.

The entire audience were on their feet before Beatrice

managed to clamber onto her own. She kissed Sydney and then hugged her director and producer; it was a win for all of them.

The applauding was deafening as she made her way gingerly up to the stage to accept the award, praying all the while that she didn't fall over or lose a shoe.

"Wow, I didn't expect to win this one." Beatrice smiled at the heavy, gold-plated statue in her trembling hand whilst she regained her breath and allowed the audience to settle down. "Not after recent events anyway. They literally had an excuse to not give it to me, and yet here I am, an openly bisexual woman with an award for best actress. Maybe we are improving as a society." She flicked her hand down in front of her, narrowly missing the microphone. "I jest of course. It's because I now fall into a fetish category…" She was relieved to see most of the room roar with laughter, though she noticed a few sullen faces in the crowd and pointed at them. "Oh, I can see a lot of men looking uncomfortable."

After trying to shove a lengthy list of thank-yous into thirty seconds, including the director and producer at her table, she moved on to her dedication.

"I dedicate this award to my girlfriend" — Beatrice took in a breath and pushed it out through pursed lips — "who has shown me the purest love, given me immeasurable support, and encouraged me to stand up and be counted. I love you, Sydney." She blew a kiss to Sydney from the lectern and watched as her girlfriend covered her mouth with her hand. After months of feeling it, to finally say it in front of the world gave her an unbelievable sense of satisfaction. "I can only hope we continue to see more people like me, standing up here in the future. That's not a suggestion; it's an order. Hashtag #OutAndProud!"

Taking one last glance at Sydney to find her mopping tears with a tissue she left the stage to resounding applause.

An hour later, she was standing outside the ladies' toilet of the *Vanity Fair* afterparty, waiting for Sydney, who insisted she couldn't go alone. After Beatrice had smiled at various faces she recognised, and a couple she'd like to slap, Sydney finally emerged from the restroom with her hand covering her mouth. She spat out a giggle as she joined her girlfriend.

"Oh my God, Bea, I just peed next to Meryl Streep! I mean, I didn't know at the time. We came out of the toilet at the same time, and then I washed my hands next to her. She even smiled at me in the mirror. Then we reached for a paper towel at the same time, and she let me go first." Sydney finally stopped for a breath.

Beatrice laughed as Sydney's knees gave way a little.

"*You saw it in the mirror*? You should have sent up an *SOS*, I would have come in and picked your jaw up off the floor."

"Do you think she knew who I was?" Sydney asked, looking back over her shoulder.

"I'm sure." She wasn't at all, but she wasn't about to rain on her parade. "You'll have to get used to that."

"I will never get used to urinating next to Miranda Priestly!"

Beatrice pictured that for a moment and smiled.

"Do you think she's here with Anne Hathaway?"

"Sydney, Miranda Priestly and Andy Sachs are not a real-life couple. We aren't living inside *The Devil Wears Prada* movie."

"Oh, yeah." Sydney shot her a goofy grin, and then her face fell flat as reality kicked in.

Beatrice's amusement at her obsessed girlfriend washed from her face a moment later as a woman approached her with a Ken doll on her arm.

"Beatrice."

"Sarah, how are you?"

Sarah leaned forward to air-kiss her cheek. Was there anything more fake? Friends hugged; mortal enemies air kissed in Beatrice's book.

"Well. And you?" Not waiting for an answer Sarah continued, "Congratulations on the award."

"Thank you. Nancy was more deserving of it, though, don't you think?"

Sarah responded with an awkward facial twitch.

"I hope there are no hard feelings about Peter, now that…" Sarah made a light gesture towards Sydney.

"Oh, you're suggesting that now I'm in a relationship with a woman, it was okay for you to sleep with my husband?" Beatrice said. "Like your actions couldn't have possibly caused me any pain."

"Well, erm…"

"As you can see, I'm much better off without him," Beatrice said, slipping her arm around Sydney's waist and guiding her away from Sarah. Stopping beside her, she added, "You would have been too. I shudder to think of the nightmares it must give you."

As they walked away, Beatrice called back over her shoulder, "Especially given recent events."

"Nicely done," Sydney said, after they'd walked a little further away.

"Thank you. I can't believe I ever had a crush on that woman."

"Did you see that necklace she was wearing? Do you think it was real diamonds?"

"Yes. Sarah always was about the *money, money, money.*"

Sydney stopped a waiter as they re-entered the afterparty, relieving him of two glasses of champagne.

"*Does your mother know...*we're here?" Beatrice said. "We should visit her when we return to the UK."

Sydney frowned and passed her a glass. "Are you humouring me with ABBA song titles?"

"Damn, I was hoping to work *Mamma Mia* in there somewhere before you noticed."

Sydney feigned disgust as she teased her award-winning girlfriend. "You wait until I get you back to our hotel suite."

"Oh yeah, and what could you possibly do to me that I won't enjoy?" Beatrice asked, slipping her arm inside Sydney's jacket and pulling her closer.

"I could make you wait. I know how you hate to be kept waiting. I could tie your hands up and make you watch as I touch myself and only myself."

"Ha! You think you could resist me? Look at me in this red dress. You can't resist that; we both know it."

Sydney twisted her lips in defeat.

"I think most of the people in this room couldn't resist

you in that red dress," she observed. "They can't take their eyes off you. I feel like the luckiest woman in the room."

"You are the luckiest woman in the room."

"Modest, Bea."

Realising she needed to clarify as Sydney couldn't recognise a compliment if it slapped her in the face, she added, "You're the luckiest woman in the room because you get to be you."

"Ah, I see your meaning now. So, are we going to discuss your speech at all?"

"No, I don't think so. From what I recall it was… *go me, boo hiss to the haters*," Beatrice replied, taking a sip of champagne.

"And an 'I love you' to me."

"Ah, that." There was no avoiding a little interrogation. She'd hoped her first declaration of love for Sydney would slip by unnoticed, despite her saying it in front of eight hundred people and those watching at home.

"It was nothing," she attempted.

Sydney rounded on her. "It was everything."

Beatrice bit her lips in to contain her smile as she gazed into Sydney's eyes.

"And I happen to love you, too, Beatrice Russell."

Beatrice could have drowned in the adrenaline that surged through her. Instead, she focused it on grasping Sydney around the waist and planting a kiss on her lips.

"Very good," she whispered into Sydney's mouth. "*Lay all your love on me.*"

Sydney groaned.

EPILOGUE

"*M*um, Syd, Ali's just buzzed the gate." Alex rushed into the bedroom and peered through the window. "There's more cars behind her too."

Sydney crossed the bedroom from the dressing room to join him by the window, where she spied three cars emerging from the wood.

"Bang on time," Beatrice said, tapping her watch as she stood up from her dressing table.

"You did threaten everyone that if they weren't on time, y— "

Beatrice silenced her with a kiss. "Yes, thank you, Sydney. I recall. So, how do I look?" She stepped back and twirled in her ivory, V-neck knee-length dress. Her blonde waves perched on her shoulders as she came to a stop.

"Hot, and like you're going to a wedding." Sydney laughed.

"Ha!"

"And me?" Sydney asked with her hands on her hips

in her trusty white Chanel suit. "I know you said I should buy something new, but I really like this. It fits well."

"As long as you don't spend the evening thinking about how you were wearing it the night you urinated next to Meryl St— "

This time it was Sydney's turn to silence Beatrice with a kiss, trying not to smudge her bright red lipstick in the process. "As if I would."

"Eww! Get a room, you two." Alex sniffed in disgust.

"We have one; we're in it," Beatrice replied.

"Oh yeah. I'll see you downstairs."

"Is Mum ready?" Sydney called after him.

"Yeah, she went down a few minutes ago."

"Shall we welcome our guests?" Sydney asked as she held out an arm to Beatrice who hooked herself through it.

"We shall."

A waiter offered them a glass of champagne before their feet even hit the wood flooring of the entrance hall. Beatrice headed for the door to welcome Alison as Sydney stopped to check on her pile of books on the table.

She stroked the cover of one of the hardbacks, allowing her finger to trace over the clear raised title *Overboard*, which sat prominently against the matte laminate. It was still unbelievable. Her very own book, in print. Author; not co-author. Her story.

Rhona sidled up beside her daughter and hooked a loose strand of her long hair behind her ear. "You look so beautiful. He would have been so proud of everything you've achieved."

"This book would never have been written if he hadn't have left us."

"It's also part of the future that we're looking to now."

"I know." Sydney sniffed away any emotion trying to surface and was grateful for the distraction of Beatrice and Alison approaching.

"Rhona, this is my dear friend and agent, Alison," Beatrice said. "Alison, this is Rhona, Sydney's mother."

They shook hands.

"Ah, I see Anthony has arrived. Excuse us." Beatrice held her hand out to Sydney as Alex skidded past them.

"Freddie!" Alex's face lit up at the arrival of his friend. He grabbed his arm and immediately whisked him away to the stairs. "Just going to show him my room, Mum."

"Don't be long. Anthony, Diane, so good to see you." Beatrice hugged them both. "Those two seem close."

"All we hear these days is 'Alex this, Alex that'." Diane smiled. "Our eldest sends her love and congratulations, Sydney. She's sorry she couldn't join us. A group of friends decided to go travelling for the summer."

"Tell her I'm sorry she couldn't be here and that I hope she's behaving herself."

Diane laughed. "I think she's learnt most of her lessons."

"Several times over," Anthony added.

Sydney left Beatrice to discuss Alex's burgeoning skills as a chef as Rosie and Greg made their way through the front door, followed by James and Sam.

"Syd! Congratulations!" Rosie said, pulling her into a hug.

It took a minute before any of the others greeted her. All eyes were on Highwood and jaws on the floor.

"Hello," Sydney said, waving her hands at them.

"I'm so happy for you," James said, finally noticing her and picking her up in a bear hug.

"Really?"

"Really?" He placed her back down. "I'm gutted of course to lose you, but our Syd has gone up in the world, and I can't be sad about that. Will sends his love and was still moping that he couldn't make it as I left."

"I'm sorry he couldn't be here too," Sydney said, stepping towards Sam for a hug. "Sam, so glad you could make it."

"I wouldn't miss this for the world, Sydy. Especially now that we're co-parenting."

"You do know Gertie is way older than both of you," James said, pointing his fingers at the two of them.

Sydney and Sam turned to him and said at the same time, "Shush, James."

Beatrice slipped a hand into Sydney's and whispered softly in her ear, "It's time, my love."

"Bea, you've met Sam and Rosie, of course, and this is Greg, Rosie's husband."

Greg stepped forward and shook the hand that was offered to him. "Er... hi... nice to meet you."

"Lucky man," Beatrice said. "Rosie works wonders with her hands."

"Don't I know it," Greg replied with a lift of his eyebrows and a wink at his wife that made her blush.

"And this is James."

"James." Beatrice turned to face him and took his hand. "I believe I have you to thank for throwing this fabulous woman into my hands."

"You do, and well caught. You've taken my best PA."

"And wasn't she the best? I give you my thanks and apologies. Now, if you don't mind, I need to steal her away." Beatrice patted his hand and then let it go, slipping hers back into Sydney's as she led her to the stairs.

Sydney watched as Beatrice took another glass of champagne from a waiter and then climbed a couple of steps. She smiled as the woman she'd grown to love — even more deeply than when she last stood on that spot — gazed down at her and winked. Beatrice's red nails tapped on the glass, and all eyes in the room turned to her.

"Thank you all for joining us for a little get-together to celebrate Sydney and her incredible book," she announced. "We wanted something more intimate for friends and family after the official book launch yesterday, which was…" She turned to Sydney.

"Overwhelming, exhausting, unbelievable," Sydney supplied.

She felt her face flush as light clapping filled the hallway.

"So do make sure you all take a copy home. I've made sure she signed them all."

"Devalued them all." Sydney grinned, creating a light chuckle around the entrance hall.

"We also have another reason to bring everyone together this afternoon. It's been just over a year since this remarkable woman walked into my life and shook it up a little."

"A lot," Sydney corrected her.

Beatrice squinted back at her. "I knew early on that I never wanted to be apart from her, but as the story goes —

and she tells it so well to anyone who cares to listen — I did let her go."

A resounding *boo* filled the air.

"Yes, thank you. As the story also goes, I came to my senses." She winked at Alex and received one right back. "And now I am never letting her go again. So much so that two months ago, I asked Sydney if she would marry me."

Sydney stepped up beside Beatrice to gasps around the room. "And I said yes."

"So yes, we are here to celebrate a book launch, but... we'd also like you to bear witness to our marriage."

Alex opened the door of the drawing room to reveal it laid out in readiness for a wedding ceremony.

"Please don't let this overshadow the remarkable achievements of this exceptionally talented writer, whom I'm immensely proud of, and whom I'm about to make my wife," Beatrice instructed the crowd. "If you'd like to make your way in, we are already a few minutes behind. Be sure to stock up on champagne on the way. We'll no doubt take all your questions after."

Sydney looked to her friends for their reactions as Alex and Rhona ushered them into the drawing room. Rosie blew her a kiss, and James was already wiping away a tear. Sam shot her a wink and a smile.

A tall, thin lady approached the brides and took each of their hands. "Oh, I'm so nervous! And so excited too."

"You'll be fine, Mrs C," Sydney said, lightly patting the woman's trembling, wrinkled hand. "I've heard you practising, and you play beautifully."

"When you're ready, Mrs Clarkson."

The woman squeezed their hands, took a deep breath, and headed off to the piano.

"I do wish you wouldn't call her that," Beatrice whispered.

"What? Mrs C? She likes it. She said it made her feel young."

Beatrice scoffed. "I just like to keep things professional with the staff."

It was Sydney's turn to scoff. "Seriously! Might I remind you that you are about to marry the hired help?"

As Beatrice opened her mouth to reply, Rhona and Alex assembled beside them.

"They are ready for you both. Shall we go first?" Rhona asked, holding her arm out to Sydney.

Sydney flashed a wink at Beatrice. "See you in there. Hit it, Mrs C."

Mrs Clarkson's fingers hit the keys and Wagner's bridal chorus rang out through Highwood House.

As she and her mum walked away, she could hear Alex behind them, telling his mum how proud he was of her. Sydney fought back tears; she couldn't cry before they'd even started.

She was greeted by smiles as she and her mum ambled down the aisle. As they reached the two registrars in front of the Victorian fireplace, a quick check over her shoulder confirmed Beatrice was right behind her. The beaming faces of those dearest to her gave her every confidence that she had their support.

A flutter of excitement fizzed in Sydney's abdomen as the time to exchange vows arrived. She met Beatrice's glistening, impassioned eyes with equal tenderness as her fiancée placed a gold band onto her finger and her bewitching mouth opened to speak. They had agreed to write their own vows, and although she was desperate to hear what she had to say, she was equally desperate to get to the part when she could kiss those ravishing lips.

"Sydney, the moment I met you and you bought me a black coffee because they didn't have cream, I *thought* you could be extraordinary. When I thought you'd skipped out on me one evening, only to find you close by the next morning... I *knew* you were extraordinary. Sometimes it's the simplest, smallest gestures in life that have the biggest impact, and every day you continue to surprise me with another way in which I can love you.

"I've been through a lot in my short years." Beatrice squinted at their guests as they sniggered, then smiled with them. Returning her focus to Sydney, she continued. "Some good, some bad, and yet I wouldn't change a moment of it as it led me to this moment, standing here with you as we take the first step on what I hope will be a very long and happy journey together."

Sydney took a deep breath and wiped a tear that threatened to fall down her cheek any moment. It was her turn.

"Beatrice, I knew you were going to be trouble before I even met you. The first time we spoke was when you phoned me in the middle of the night whilst *clearly* having a full grasp of time zones. Even after we met, you would text me tasks in the early hours of the morning and then call me to make sure I received them if I didn't acknowledge you — *because I was asleep*. And that time when you threw a tantrum at spending one evening without me…" Sydney winked, "let's not even go there."

Beatrice pursed her lips and pulled them to one side as she narrowed her eyes.

"I, too, wouldn't change a second of it, because I passed all these tests and challenges, and ultimately, I won the biggest prize. You. And every infuriating moment with you just made me love you more."

Sydney's breath caught in her chest as the softest whisper of 'very good' escaped Beatrice's lips. Paired with the smouldering look in her eye, her intent wasn't to congratulate her on her words but to tease her. Beatrice knew by now what those words did to her, and she used them at all sorts of inopportune moments to make Sydney weak at the knees, challenging her not to react when react was all she could do.

After the ceremony, Alison was first to approach them in the entrance hall. The three women took a glass of champagne from a waiter and chinked glasses.

"Another secret. Really?"

"Ali… I," Beatrice said, flustered.

"I'm pulling your leg, Bea." Alison chuckled at her discomfort. "You have Sydney now; I see that, and I couldn't be happier for you. Just don't forget me. I'm always at the end of the phone."

"I know. We speak every day."

"You know that's not what I mean."

Beatrice nodded and stepped forward to hug her.

"Okay, well, I'm going to leave you two to finish this… whatever it is, and check on my friends," Sydney said, placing a kiss on her wife's cheek to find Alex snapping a photograph on his phone.

Rosie was already fidgeting on the spot as Sydney approached her.

"How did she propose then?" Rosie asked as she pulled back from a congratulatory hug. "Did she get down on one knee? She wouldn't have managed that this time last year."

Sydney laughed at the thought of Beatrice being stuck on one knee in a pink cast, cursing as she tried to get up.

"No… we were in bed actually."

"Oh." Rosie covered a grin with her hand.

"I think it kind of slipped out accidentally, when we were erm… she, erm…" Sydney felt her cheeks blush. They really should have created a cover story; people were bound to ask how it happened and expect some tale of romance. "I held her to it."

Rosie's eyes creased as she sniggered behind her hand. "To think you never even wanted to come here and now it's your forever home. Well done, Gertie."

"I sometimes think she was keeping her shit together all those years until we got to your wedding."

"Me too," Rosie agreed before taking a swig of champagne.

James approached with his arms wide open.

"James, don't cry," Sydney said, squeezing him. "We don't have enough tissues in the house."

"Sorry." He turned away and fanned himself. "I just love weddings."

"If you and Will ever decide to get wed, the drawing room is fully licensed for weddings. It took some doing at short notice, too, I can tell you."

"I'll think about it," James replied with a sly grin and a twinkle in his eye.

"He wouldn't be able to make it through his own ceremony," Sam put in as he appeared at Sydney's side and pulled her into a hug. "Congrats, Sydy. That was a lovely surprise."

"No official photographer?" Greg asked. "You could make a fortune selling the photos."

"Alex is doing a superb job with a mobile phone. Privacy is what we value, not money."

Greg scoffed. "Privacy. We all saw Beatrice on that stage six months ago declaring her love to the world."

"Since then we've become a rather hot topic, and not just because of our relationship."

James's gaze swept around the room as he leaned towards Sydney and whispered, "What is the latest on Peter?"

"He's due to be sentenced next week."

"What does assaulting ten women get you these days?" Greg asked, with less subtlety than James.

"Elected as prime minister?" Sam suggested to everyone's amusement.

Two hours later Sydney flopped onto a stair, breathless from dancing. Resting her elbows on the step above her, she smiled at Beatrice and Alex dancing to the music piped through the house's sound system. Highwood made for a great party house, and with its pulse beating, it was a stark contrast to the first time she'd walked through the front door.

Beatrice joined her, leaving Freddie to take over with Alex.

"What are you thinking?" she asked as she eased onto the stair.

"What a different house this is to the one I walked into a year ago."

"I can't imagine where I'd be now if you hadn't come into my life that day."

"America probably."

"I don't mean geographically, Sydney," Beatrice said, knocking shoulders with her wife.

"I know you don't," Sydney replied with a cheeky grin.

"You've changed me, and every bit for the better. You helped Alex, and our relationship." Beatrice nodded towards Sam as he danced with Rhona. "You've even fixed your own with Sam."

"Don't forget Gertie."

Beatrice rolled her eyes. "How could I?"

Sydney leaned against Beatrice and dropped her head onto her shoulder. "Would it be rude to throw everyone out now? As much as I love to see Highwood alive, I want you all to myself again."

"I'm sure we can arrange that."

With books handed out, hugs exchanged, and tears mopped, they said farewell to their guests.

"We'll see you in a few days with Gertie, Sam," Sydney said as the old friends parted.

Rosie frowned. "I thought you were off to the States?"

"We are, next week, but I've persuaded Beatrice to slum it in Gertie for a few days as a sort of honeymoon. We're going to roll around the countryside, see where it takes us. Find some cute villages, visit the odd ruined abbey or castle, and then end at the harbour."

"I'll look after her for you, don't you worry," Sam said as he opened his car door.

"Regular baths," Sydney reminded him.

"I know, and I'll burp her after meals."

Sydney pointed a finger at him. "Don't let her see the table you made out of her old engine."

He laughed. "I promise."

"Thanks, Sam."

With the last car waved off, Sydney wrapped her arms around her wife's waist and let out a long, happy sigh.

"Come on, let's go to bed," Beatrice said, placing a kiss on her forehead. "I'm exhausted and I've been waiting for my final course all day."

Sydney took her by the hand and led her across the threshold. "Help yourself. It's an all-you-can-eat buffet."

"Very good."

THE END

Please consider leaving me a review on Amazon, BookBub or Goodreads. Even a simple rating makes a huge impact for authors.

Keep turning for a free book!

REVIEWS

If you enjoyed this book please consider leaving me a review on Amazon, BookBub or Goodreads. Just a rating or a line is fine. They really make a huge impact for authors.

AMAZON REVIEW LINK

JOIN MY READERS CLUB

If you'd like to hear about my new releases, sign up to my
newsletter and receive a FREE sapphic romance,
The Third Act...

*At the suggestion of her daughter, Amy, widowed Fiona attends
an art course at the local college where she meets the confident,
inspirational teacher, Raye.*
*Raye awakens feelings long suppressed, but as Fiona rediscovers
her sexuality, fear grows over how Amy will react.*
*Can Fiona find the courage to follow her heart, or will she be
destined to spend her third act alone?*

5 - Absolutely loved this book! Great story line, well developed
characters and beautifully crafted. It is really refreshing to see
the older lesbian represented for a change!*

www.emilybanting.co.uk/freebook

ALSO BY

THE NUNSWICK ABBEY SERIES

4.5* Rated Series

LOST IN LOVE

A heart-warming, quintessentially English village novel, centred on the ruins of Nunswick Abbey...

Historical tour guide Anna Walker is determined to make a good impression on her new bosses, but juggling a full-time job with caring for her ailing father is putting her own health – and potentially his – at risk.

When she meets Dr Katherine Atkinson, a charming yet intimidating new arrival to the village, Anna is infuriated by the doctor's attempts to convince her that her father needs professional, full-time care. She's even more frustrated by her growing attraction to the classy, wealthy doctor.

Anna's determination to prove she can cope forces Katherine to divulge a painful event from her past that still haunts her, hopeful it will make Anna see sense before it's too late.

With Katherine's heart lost to the past and Anna's overwhelmed in the present, can the two women help each other overcome their struggles and move forward? Will a curtain-twitching busy body curtail any blossoming attraction before it even has a chance to bloom?

Anna and Katherine's story continues in book two, Trust in Truth, and book three, Forgive not Forget.

PRAISE FOR THE SERIES

This is one of the best books I've read in a very long time. I laughed out loud, cried, and even became indignant at one point. I love a good age-gap slow burn and this checked all the boxes!! Well done!!

LOVED this quintessential English romance novel!! Beautifully written, the plot is tight and the main characters - and those around them - precisely drawn. It gripped me from the very first page and I finished it less than 24 hours!

I do not think there is a heart string left that this author didn't strum. I am a mess of happy and sad and just all out of sorts hahaha. Superb writing. Everything the characters feel, you are going to feel so maybe a few tissues, a pint of ice cream and a hug from a friend should be added to your list of things you'll need after enjoying this book.

I rated this book 5 stars because it's absolutely breathtaking, the atmosphere of the quaint little village with the ruins of an abbey is such a beautiful picture and reminds me of a town near to where I grew up. It's so hard to find sapphic books in general and it's even harder to find one as good as this! I'm in love with Katherine and Anna's relationship and I'm so excited to continue the series. Also this was such a fun book to read that I read it in 1 day and I'm usually a slow reader.

PURCHASE HERE

Printed in the USA
CPSIA information can be obtained
at www.ICGtesting.com
LVHW041357281123
765135LV00071B/1136